TA SAADUM

The Collapse

By Matthew Merten

PublishAmerica
Baltimore

ISBN: 1-4241-1767-4
PUBLISHED BY PUBLISHAMERICA, LLLP
www.publishamerica.com
Baltimore

Printed in the United States of America

Dedication

Rebecca and I dedicate this novel to all the underdogs out there who just want to do the right thing.

Acknowledgements

Thanks to Rebecca Merten, Patsy Wurl and Michelle Flowers for all their help with correcting my errors in American English.

Thanks to Massimo for unwittingly giving me the final piece of the puzzle: the EX-1.

Poor Old Lu, your CD *The Waiting Room* is a superior accomplishment. I listened to nothing else while I wrote this novel.

Steph and Morgan, I miss you. I hope you like your namesake characters in this book.

Table of Contents

Overpopulated? What do you mean by that?
The world is not overpopulated, you clone.
The world is mismanaged.

—Theodore Newgent
areyoulistening.com October 2005

CHAPTER ONE

There Were Two Thoughts

There were two thoughts on Stephenie's mind now the bullets began to shred the copse of trees in which she hid. The first thought, and the most relevant thought, was remembering how to load the rifle she held in her hands. Five minutes before the bullets began to fly, Stephenie had been given the rifle by a man known only as Rick. Rick had also given her a fanny pack stuffed with shells and brief instructions on how to load the shells into the rifle.

This *Rick* character frightened Stephenie. All it took was one look into his eyes to send shivers up and down her spine. As with everyone else Stephenie had met in the last six months, Rick constantly wore a look of weariness on his face. Like everyone else, Rick seemed to have lost his ability to smile. However, unlike everyone else, there wasn't the slightest glimmer of life in Rick's eyes. It was as if his soul had become a vacuum into which all light was drawn and completely extinguished. *I suppose war can do that to people*, Stephenie thought to herself just after looking into Rick's eyes for the first time. *Wars.* These were wars, uncivil wars; and Stephenie had wanted no part in them from their beginning.

For Stephenie the beginning of the wars had come months before the first weapon discharged. It was this fact that led to the second thought on her mind. She had seen the whole thing coming, the Collapse as well as the wars, and hadn't been able to do a thing about it.

On the other hand, had I?

Now the trees around her exploded with a variety of projectiles fired from an unseen enemy. The noise was tremendous enough to shake the muddy dirt at Stephenie's feet.

What kind of weapons are they using? Stephenie thought, *those aren't guns.*

Fragments of former tree limbs and tree trunks rained down upon her as she dropped her rifle in an attempt to cover her neck and face with her hands. For protection she curled her body at the base of a tree trunk and pulled her jacket over her shoulders to cover her face. Someone near her began to cry out in pain. Stephenie's immediate internal response was to locate the source of the crying voice and administer whatever medical attention she could. For the last four months, this is exactly what she had done: treat the sick and injured to lessen their pain. Stephenie had helped many people survive their wounds. She had watched exponentially more die despite her attempts to hold off death. For four months, she had but one role: to attend to the wounded and dying. It was a role accepted as valuable by all sides of the wars. For months, she had wandered the farmland unhindered by any form of aggression. Pickets and warriors saw the red cross on her white ball cap and left her alone. It was like an unwritten code: leave the medical people alone.

Nevertheless, earlier that very morning Rick had violated that unwritten code. At gunpoint, he took the meager collection of first aid supplies from Stephenie, threw a rifle at her and ordered her to fight. Rick had given strict orders that no longer could his clan support the injured or wounded.

"If ya can't walk," he addressed his clan, "then ya ain't comin' with us. We don't need no nurses." Clearly, those who could not pillage or fight on their own were abandoned to fend for themselves. This new command from Rick brought forth yet one more phase of an ever-declining social disorder that Stephenie had witnessed.

Who would have known that we would fall so far so fast?

I'm telling you, are you listening? This country *is* going to self-destruct. There are thousands of dooms-dayers out there telling you it will come with an attack from outside our borders. Horse feathers! The attack will be subtle and ease its way into our society. One morning we'll all wake up to find that all our precious systems are worthless. The dollar will be worthless. The government will be worthless. Our possessions will be worthless. And yes, even our computers and the dear Internet will be worthless. Do I know *how* the attack will take place? No. However, I do know this: when it happens, and it *will* happen, our fall as a nation will be swift and severe.

Theodore Newgent
areyoulistening.com April 1996

A week after the Collapse, the standard of living had disappeared. Physical comfort had ceased as a priority a week after that. Replacing it was the need to scavenge for simple daily nourishment. People began to group together into clans. Food became the valued commodity and collecting the food, the main occupation. Many people starved to death as the food supplies became scarce. Survivors became experts at deciphering which can of beans was edible and which had spoiled without having to open the can. Eventually even a spoiled can of beans was stashed as a final reserve to stave off possible starvation. A few weeks later it seemed that the scavenging for a can of beans became just as important as having enough ammunition and weapons to protect what little food stores were collected. And just this morning the worth of one human life became less valuable than a spoiled can of beans.

Rick said so. He's the leader, he's insane and what he says goes.

The volley of projectiles from the unseen enemy continued to shatter the silence of the cold December morning air. Stephenie curled into a semi-fetal position, poised against her protective tree trunk and remained motionless throughout the barrage. She felt the body of another human trip upon her back and fall to the muddied earth beside her. She pulled aside her jacket to peer into the face of Rick. He was shouting something but for the noise of the mortars crashing around the thicket could not be heard. Rick grabbed Stephenie by the lapels of her jacket and began to shake her violently as he continued his screaming tirade. Just as he threw her against the tree trunk, the mortars ceased and Stephenie heard him yell, "Where's your rifle?" Scrambling on his hands and knees to where Stephenie's rifle had fallen, Rick hovered above the weapon in a crouched position. He then sniffed the air, took in a 360 degree view, cleared his throat, spat on the ground and began to yell again.

"The mortars were just their way of announcin' for an all-out ground assault," Rick stood erect and yelled to no one in particular. His voice carried through the cold air, now strangely silent. It became apparent that he was addressing the entire clan when he continued yelling. "Stay in the trees. No matter what, don't leave the trees. Don't run inta the fields. If you get surrounded and hafta run, run to the food stores. Protect the food. They'll be comin' for us any time now, so y'all keep your eyes open and heads down. Shoot only if you've gotta clean shot."

Rick hefted Stephenie's rifle and inspected it. "There ain't no bullets in this unit," he spat. He then walked toward her without warning and kicked her in the leg. Stephenie returned to her fetal position, braced for another blow that never came. Instead, Rick stood over her, gently leaned the rifle against her quivering body and spoke sternly, but kindly. It gave Stephenie the creeps.

"I gave you a chance at survivin' this morning by givin' you this rifle. I gave you life by givin' you somma my ammo. Now, if you don't defend the food, you ain't gonna eat. Capeesh?"

"Uh, yeah." It was all Stephenie could muster to say. She was still waiting for another kick to her body from the figure hovering above her.

"Good. Now load the weapon like I showdya and get ready ta defend our food." Rick stopped talking and the copse of trees was silent again except for the fading sounds of Rick's footsteps as he crunched his way through the withered winter underbrush.

Rick's message had taken root in Stephenie's mind, although her heart was far from agreeing with it. Stephenie watched her shaking hands fumbling for the opening to the fanny pack containing the bullets for her rifle. Her fingers were aching from the cold air and the lack of gloves; they protested every movement and the pain would have driven her to tears if she'd had the capacity to cry. Her crying had ceased months before.

On many levels, it was nearly impossible for Stephenie to obey the command of Rick to load her weapon and defend the food. One reason was that she didn't want to kill anyone, even if it meant saving her own life. She had managed to survive the wars up to this point without killing another human purely by playing the role of a self-proclaimed nurse.

Some nurse I am, she thought.

If she had any sense of humor left in her soul, she would have laughed at that thought. Before the Collapse, she couldn't stand the sight of blood and would nearly pass out at the unveiling of a hypodermic needle. The Collapse and the wars had changed all that. At the first sign of mass premeditated aggression, Stephenie had been in a position to pose as a nurse, with supposed nursing experience prior to the war. In that particular situation, no one could tell the difference between a real nurse and a person faking being a nurse, so Stephenie became one. She figured it would be easier to aid people in their suffering than it would be to kill them.

Another reason that she couldn't obey Rick's order was that her fingers weren't altogether functioning properly. She was frightened and overwhelmed by the coming onslaught. She was hungry. She was tired beyond explanation and she was cold. It was December in the old Midwest. At least, she thought it was December. Stephenie couldn't quite remember what month it was. She had been diligently marking the days off on a pocket calendar that she had kept ever since the Collapse. Even as her aching, shaking fingers reached into the fanny pack for a bullet, she wanted to check that calendar to see what day and month it was. However, the calendar was in her medicine pack and Rick had taken the calendar from her when he confiscated her belongings that morning.

Rick wanted her to load her rifle with bullets. She couldn't feel the bullets with her fingers, so she had to reposition herself to peer inside the fanny pack. After several frustrating attempts, she succeeded only in spilling most of her precious bullets out of the fanny pack and onto the semi-frozen mud at her feet. Eventually she managed to pick up a bullet and slide it into the loading chamber of her rifle, just as instructed that morning. She held the rifle in both hands and began to ponder if there was a more efficient method for loading it, considering her current circumstances.

It was in this moment of pondering that the second thought on her mind came back into prominence once again. The second thought had a tendency to haunt her. Not so long ago she had held a different device in her hands and had speculated its precise purpose. That device was not, in any way, shape, or form like the rifle that she now held. No, that device was far more deadly. Not realizing it at the time, Stephenie had held in her hand one of the many similar objects that would lead to the Collapse. The agony of this second thought was that its origins took root two days prior to the Collapse. Stephenie had spent the last four months attempting to forget this second thought but it would not leave her alone. Doubt would creep in and pose the question: *Did I really do everything I could to prevent the Collapse?*

At the eleventh hour, Stephenie and her brother Morgan had discovered the function, and therefore the purpose, of the deadly device. In an attempt to uncover the source of the device and possibly prevent the Collapse itself, Stephenie became separated from Morgan and unavoidably detained. She ran out of time to prevent the Collapse and made a valiant attempt to rejoin her brother. As far as she could tell, only she and Morgan knew why the Collapse had occurred. On a few occasions after the Collapse, Stephenie had communicated to other people of how she discovered the device and its purpose, only to face apathetic or violent responses. What good is it to instruct a drowning sailor why his ship sank?

By the second month post-Collapse, it became apparent that no one cared why it had happened, because nothing mattered beyond staying alive. If a person made it past the second month, he or she was lucky, tough, insane or cold-blooded. Most survivors were a little of all those things, as was evident in the fact that no one smiled anymore. Recently Stephenie had come upon a stack of catalogues in a house she had been using as a makeshift hospital. Most of the people in the magazine photographs were smiling. The smiles from the people staring back at her from the catalogues made Stephenie feel....uneasy. It gave her the same uneasiness that she used to get when looking at old black and white photographs from the days of her great-grandparents. In those pre-1920's photos, no one smiled, and as a child, she wondered why. She was relieved when her grandmother explained that the people had to stand perfectly still or the photo would blur. Grandma said that smiling would mess up a photograph back then.

So why had the recent catalogue episode made Stephenie so uneasy? Because she hadn't seen anyone around her smile for such a long time that it seemed foreign. The survivors of the Collapse were all weary. They all lived in constant fear of starvation, violence, and death. The faces of the war-torn were now the norm. While paging through the catalogues she discovered in the makeshift hospital, Stephenie found herself gazing into a mirror for the first time in weeks. The mirror hung on the wall of the bedroom with the magazines. In her reflection she saw this same look of fatigue, and fear that she saw on the faces of the Collapse survivors. After looking in both directions to ensure that no one was watching, she attempted to smile into the mirror just to see what such a thing looked like. The results of her experiment left her feeling foolish. The smile had been forced and looked as such.

Suddenly her brain jumped from memory land. There was the sound of movement in the tangled brush and fallen tree branches thirty paces to Stephenie's left side. Someone or some thing was heading directly toward her. It was impossible to see what it was. She crawled to her right in order to put the tree trunk between her and the advancing thing. Only after she did this did she realize that now she was an open target to the unseen enemy that, according to Rick, would be arriving at any moment. Indecision pressed upon the former nurse as she frantically took turns looking in the direction of the approaching noise before her and the unseen enemy behind her. Eventually the noisemaker broke through a tangled mess of natural rubbish at the base of several trees that were twenty paces away from Stephenie, and took the form of a human dressed head to toe in a muddy camouflage suit. He carried no weapon that Stephenie could see. The identity of this newcomer was a mystery to her. She could tell it was a man by the way it walked, but the hood of the camouflage suit and a pair of dark sunglasses it wore had masked all distinguishing facial features. The figure looked directly at Stephenie as it continued in her direction. She pointed her rifle at the approaching man and was preparing to speak some form of challenge when he spoke first, "Hey, Steph, you got some aspirin?"

She recognized the voice of this man and immediately lowered her rifle. His name was Jim, Jim Doty. She and Jim had met two weeks before in that same makeshift farmhouse hospital not more than ten miles from where they now hid in the copse of trees.

Had it been two weeks? Stephenie wasn't certain.

Regardless of the time spent, those days with Jim had been the best days Stephenie had experienced since the Collapse. Jim was a silent but kind man who knew his way around the farm country. He had shown Stephenie on several occasions in the last two weeks that he was a man she could trust and that he was courageous. Jim had labored alongside Stephenie and proved himself resourceful in acquiring food. Most important to Stephenie, Jim had promised to help her get to Stewardson.

Stephenie had heard of a good clan in that area. She wanted to be part of that clan and convinced Jim to go there with her. The two had set out into the war-torn farm country to find this good clan near Stewardson. For two weeks, Jim and Stephenie had waded through drainage trenches and pushed through dried cornfields, as they wanted to be invisible to other humans. At this point in the *food wars*, a person just didn't have the time to learn whom to trust and whom not to trust. Some violent people had plagued the farm country in the last few months, and it was better to avoid any contact with humans than to risk being killed. In two weeks of carefully traversing the farm country, Jim and Stephenie had made it nearly to Stewardson without encountering another human. Then this morning Jim had noticed smoke rising from a copse of trees directly in their path and had decided to skirt around it to the west. Inadvertently, Jim had led himself and Stephenie away from an abandoned campfire and directly into the front line of a raiding clan that had been preparing for a reprisal attack of yet another clan from which they had just stolen food. Unfortunately for both Jim and Stephenie, this raiding clan, the clan controlled by Rick, captured them. Rick gave Jim and Stephenie the option of fighting for his clan or having their throats slit. It wasn't much of a choice. Rick took Stephenie's medical supplies, gave her some shells and a rifle, and then ordered her to take a defensive position just on the outer edge of the tree line. Jim was on the west side of the food stores and Stephenie placed on the south. Now, after the bullets and the mortars had ceased, Jim had returned to Stephenie's position.

Jim kneeled down on the mud and dead grass next to her and breathed a heavy sigh.

"I got a headache," he said as he labored to breathe. There was something oddly mechanical about his movements and he seemed to be experiencing difficulty in speaking, for his words were slurring. "And it hurts bad to move my neck," he added.

Stephenie turned to look in the direction of the *unseen enemy* Rick had warned her about, laid her gun down and slowly crawled across the mud to Jim. Before she could get close enough to touch him, she noticed something odd about the jacket hood that covered the back of Jim's head. A severed limb of a tree branch about two inches in diameter protruded from a hole torn in the hood. Blood was slowly dripping off the ten-inch protrusion, forming a splatter pattern on the back of Jim's camouflage suit. In the latest mortar assault a fragment of tree debris struck Jim in the back of his head. It was apparent to Stephenie that Jim was dying.

"You got that aspirin coming there, Steph?" Jim asked as if nothing was the matter.

"Yeah sure," she replied as she slowly backed away from the dying man in front of her. She was putting her best effort forth to keep from showing her fear. "I'll, uh, get it from my bag, yeah."

"Good, cause I got one heck of a headache and it's getting hard to see."

"Let me get my bag," Stephenie said as she ungracefully scooted backward on her hands and posterior in an attempt to put some distance between her and Jim.

What Stephenie didn't realize was that one of the *unseen enemy* had slowly crept upon the position she was supposed to be guarding. The enemy was crawling on his belly in the mud and dead grass a mere fifty feet from her. As she was scooting away from the dying Jim, Stephenie was scooting toward the living enemy and his rifle, which would discharge the bullet that would travel through her back, through her heart and cause her to die. The body of Stephenie, the imposter nurse, fell backward into the mud and remained motionless. The shooter arose from his hiding spot and ran in a zigzag pattern toward the spot where he had made the kill. Bullets from other positions in the copse of trees zipped and whizzed around him, but he made it safely to Stephenie's former defensive position by the tree trunk and dove for cover. Upon impact with the ground, the shooter surveyed his immediate environment. To his left was the body of a human lying face down in the mud. It wore a blood-spattered camouflage suit. There was a piece of wood sticking out of the back of the victim's head and its body was shaking in spastic motion.

"Hey, Hand," the shooter spoke quietly to the dying body of Jim Doty, "How'd you get the lobotomy?" The shooter then noticed something at his feet. It was an old hunting rifle so filthy with mud that it was difficult to see. Keeping an eye on the body in the camouflage suit, he grabbed the rifle and quickly inspected it. It had one round in its chamber. *Only one round?* There was a trail of unfired shells scattered on the ground, that led to the person he had most recently shot. *A clean shot*, the shooter thought to himself as he looked at the silent, motionless body. The body lay in the prone position with its face turned toward the shooter. He noticed it was a woman. *Wait, she looks familiar.* The shooter crawled to where his latest victim lay in the mud and pulled her jacket hood away from her face.

"Stephenie?" The shooter nearly choked upon that one word.

CHAPTER TWO

Jim and Dale

They'd been hunting for days and hadn't seen much more than birds, thousands of birds, and not one of those birds was worth wasting ammunition on. Jim had to make Dale aware of the fact that the birds just didn't have enough meat on them to justify expending a single bullet in their general direction. Dale was a little slow in the understanding department at times, so Jim told him that under no circumstances was he to shoot at any bird. Even though Dale agreed not to *shoot* birds, it didn't stop him from talking about them.

"There's a blasted jay right over there," Dale said, pointing to a tree limb about thirty feet away from where the two hid. Jim tried to ignore Dale. Four hours earlier, they had come upon an abandoned combine on the edge of a fallow field. The windows of the combine were intact, so the two climbed into the cab in order to get out of the chill of the constant morning wind. The windows, although smudged with a thin layer of dust, offered a relatively unhindered view of any animals or humans that might be approaching from 360 degrees. Dale was perched in the driver's seat; Jim was balled up in a tight space in the back of the combine's cab. Dale scanned the immediate area in all directions for movement of any kind as he continued speaking, "If I had my pitching arm like I did when I was a kid, why, I'd bean him with a rock and we'd be eating that jaybird right now."

"You ever eat a jay?" Jim asked from his crouched position next to Dale.

"Nope, can't say as I have. Have you?"

"Yeah."

"You did not!"

"Did too, back in '80. Shot a jay when I was out hunting with Bobby Jensen. Remember Bobby?"

"Man alive, I know him. He's the one with the crooked teeth."

"Yeah, that's him, Bobby Jensen" Jim said as he attempted to stand in order to stretch out his legs and lower back. "Mind taking over for a bit? My back's buggin' me and I need to stretch out."

"Sure," Dale said as he awkwardly stood and began shuffling his body to the back of the cab to make room for Jim in the driver's seat. The two bumped heads during the exchange and both let out a curse as they rubbed out the temporary pain of the physical collision. Once the change of positions inside the combine cab was complete, Dale spoke up again. "So, what was it like?"

"What was what like?"

"The blue jay! How'd it taste?"

"Like crap. You don't ever want to eat one, so don't waste your time on them."

The cab became silent long enough for Dale to get nervous about it. Dale wasn't so happy with silence. Back before the Collapse, Dale was one of those folks that always had to have a radio, or TV, or some kind of electronic noise-making device going in the background, no matter what he was doing or who was with him. If Dale didn't have a source of noise where he was, he tended to make noise himself.

"That retard just won't shut up," was a phrase often heard in Dale's wake. Dale was what the locals called *slow*. He never quite finished high school and his parents were too dysfunctional to take him to a specialist for help.

These personality quirks made Dale a worthless partner to take on a hunting trip. He was always filling the silence with noise of one form or another. On more than five separate occasions when Dale was a boy, he blew someone else's hunting experience with an untimely sneeze, comment or bodily noise. Worse yet was when Dale started humming. He'd hum the same ten to twenty notes repeatedly. There was no melody to the tune Dale hummed and every note was off-key. It was an annoying habit to all but Dale.

The word spread among the local boys about these quirks and Dale no longer was invited on the hunting trips. In an area of the country where just about every boy grew up with a hunting rifle in his hands, this social isolation was harsh on Dale. Jim had known Dale since they were children and had been a witness to one of those five blown hunts. Since that time Jim had spent fifteen successful years dodging Dale's requests for another chance to *get one of them ten-pointers* out on his uncle's farm near Cowden. Back before the wars, the odds of Jim relenting to Dale's hunting requests were about as slim as those of finding an honest congressman. Now, after the Collapse, things were different. As much as Dale's constant jabbering frustrated him, Jim found in Dale a person he could trust. Trust was a rare commodity in the post-Collapse world.

> Tell me honestly, do you know your neighbor? Do you talk with the people who live near you? Do you know anything about them? Have you ever had them over to your house to eat dinner? If you answer in the negative, you are in the majority in this country. We don't know our own neighbors. I can remember when houses were built with a front porch. Now we build houses with only back porches. We're hiding from each other. Why is this? Maybe we're all just lazy. Maybe it's because we're just a bunch of selfish weasels, afraid of having someone take up an hour or two of our precious time. It seems that time has become our most precious commodity. Could you trust your neighbor with an hour of your time? Could it be that we don't trust ourselves? Maybe, maybe not. One day in the future the most precious commodity will be food, followed in a close second place by

the trust between two human beings. At that point in our country's history, time will be meaningless.

Theodore Newgent
areyoulistening.com March 1998

"Man alive," Dale whistled from the back of the cab, "you stink. I can smell you from way back here."

"We all stink" Jim said. A few more seconds of silence passed before Dale was back to talking.

"I never thought I'd see this part of the state without critters. It seems like the whole place is hunted-down. Did you ever see so many deer carcasses like we have? Where'd all these yokels come from anyway? Man alive, they cut down a doe and take only the hindquarters. Leave the rest for the birds. Remember the flies we got back in….what month was that?"

"I think it was October," Jim answered. As much as it irked him to do so, Jim just couldn't help but join his babbling friend in conversation. The very things that Dale was discussing had been pressing on Jim's mind as well.

"Yeah, it probably was. I don't rightly know what day it is today, or what month it is. Anyway, first came all the city folks hunting down the critters, then the rotting critter corpses and then the swarms of flies. Now we can't find a single four-legger and I'm hungry enough to eat one of them rottin' animals."

It *did* seem as though all the wildlife had suddenly vanished. In the past, a person couldn't have driven through this area on one of the farm roads for more than a mile without seeing a deer, a pheasant, an elk, a rabbit, a raccoon or even one of those cursed opossums. Even when the corn and soybeans were at their peak, and the fields provided excellent camouflage for the four-legged animals, a hunter could always find an edible critter. Jim, raised in the area, had learned how to kill and dress just about every animal there was. He had learned the value of a hard day of work, even if spent with a rifle propped between your legs while freezing your butt off in a tree stand. He had learned patience, knowing that even if you didn't get a buck this year that there was always an opportunity the next year. The laws of the land kept the hunting to a controlled level in order to preserve the next year's reserve. However, the known world had changed in the last five months. The laws that protected the wildlife from over-hunting and had kept it in abundance for decades had ceased to exist.

"Jim," Dale said, somewhat hesitantly. "I wanna thank you for lettin' me tag along and all that."

"You would've done the same for me," Jim replied without emotion as he continued to gaze out the dirt-smeared windows of the combine cab.

"How do you know that? Or are you just sayin' that to get me to finally shut my yap?"

With that last comment Jim turned around to peer at Dale, who looked about as miserable as a person could, all balled up in the space behind the combine driver's seat. Jim waited until Dale's eyes met his before he spoke.

"Dale, you took care of my family when they got sick. That's the best thing anyone has done for me since this whole thing started. I owe you. You owe me nothing."

"I'm sorry about all that, Jim, I really am, I mean, you were away up in Champaign, and I tried…"

Dale broke eye contact with Jim and for a moment looked like he was going to cry. *I haven't seen anyone cry for the longest time*, Jim thought.

"Dale, you got to get it into your head that they were going to die anyway. The flu just about wiped out half the population by the time I got home. There was nothing more you could have done about it." Jim looked away for a moment, and then returned his gaze back to Dale. "You did more for me and mine than anyone could have. I owe you, you don't owe me."

Suddenly Dale's body tensed and his head turned to look out the back window of the cab. Jim noticed this movement and attempted to follow Dale's gaze. At the edge of the open field was an object that hadn't been there earlier. It was about the length of a football field away and was moving in a random pattern.

"I can't see what it is," Dale whispered a curse as he made a vain attempt to spit on the window and wash it off with the sleeve of his jacket. "The darn window is too dirty on the outside."

"It looks like it's moving," Jim shifted his position on the driver's seat and reached for the cab door. "I'll take a look-see from the door. If it's what I think it is, get yourself ready to run."

"What do you think it is?"

"A dog."

"A dog? Why do we gotta run if it's a dog?"

"Because," Jim had the cab door cracked open and was peering intently through the crack in the direction of the moving object, "Molly, from the Crossroads Enclave told me there's a clan out here using dogs."

"Oh," Dale scrunched his face in confusion. Seconds of silence later, his facial expression shifted from confusion to recognition. "Oh, I get it. One of *them* clans. What clans are you talking about?"

"I'll tell you later," Jim now had the cab door open entirely and slowly stepped outside onto the combine's chassis. No more than five seconds later Jim was lunging into the cab to retrieve his rifle from its resting spot on the dashboard. "It's a dog!"

The two men made as swift an exit from the cab of the combine as they could before dashing into the high brush bordering the fallow field. In order to get to this hiding place safely, they had to run at an angle through the field for a good hundred feet to keep the combine in between the dog and themselves. By the time Jim dove to the ground, Dale was short of breath and attempting to suppress the cough he had been battling for the last two weeks. Jim pulled a rag out of his jacket pocket and gave it to Dale. Dale immediately stuck the rag into his mouth and gritted his teeth together as a way to silence his coming coughing fit. What little noise was emitted from Dale's lingering flu symptom would be inaudible to human ears, but not to a dog. Jim propped himself up on his elbows, then slowly raised his upper torso to peer through the bushes in which his companion and he hid. He saw the dog. It was sniffing the combine. Jim swore under his breath.

"Whadizzit?" Dale whispered between gritted teeth.

"A hound."

"Izzat bad?" Dale asked. Jim nodded and reached his hand out to Dale.

"Give me your gun; yours has a better aim."

"Y'gonna shoot d'dog?" Dale asked as he handed his rifle to Jim.

"Yeah, if I see someone following it."

"What if it doesn't come this way?" Dale now had his cough rag out of his mouth; the coughing fit had run its course.

"Oh, it'll come, I guarantee it. Don't worry; I'm only shooting the dog if I see humans following it."

"What's it doing now?" Dale looked up toward Jim who was poised in a crouch, his head just above the level of the bushes surrounding them.

"It's circling around the combine, probably smells your urine."

"My what?"

"Your pee," Jim looked back at Dale in amazement and with just a little impatience. "When you peed out the side window this morning."

"Oh, shoot, sorry about all that, Jim," Dale said with a tinge of remorse in his voice.

"It's nothing to be sorry about. It's a good thing. Buys us a little decision making time."

"Oh," Dale suddenly brightened and then just as quickly returned to an expression of concern. "Man alive, he's barkin', I hear him."

Jim swore and stood erect. Raising the rifle to his shoulder, Jim calmly said, "Dale stand up and start running away from the field."

"You want me to run?"

"Get up," Jim now let his impatience show, "and run! I'll be right behind you. Just run, now."

Dale grabbed Jim's rifle and began running away from Jim. Dale heard a single rifle shot resound sharply behind him. Then he heard a person running behind him and took a moment to peer over his shoulder. It was Jim and he was pointing to his left, across an old one-lane farm road and toward a field of dried corn stalks. Just as Dale reached the edge of the cornfield, a shot echoed from the direction he and Jim had just come. Dale collapsed into the dried corn stalks and didn't get up. Jim pivoted and began running a zigzag pattern toward Dale's motionless body. He found it in a large drainage ditch, lying face down in four inches of standing water. Jim rolled Dale's small frame to his side and leaned forward to feel for any sign of breath. Just as he got close enough, Dale vomited up muddy water and began to cough. There was blood in the vomited liquid. Jim swore and began to inspect Dale's body for the entrance wound. He found the bullet had entered Dale's upper left side but hadn't exited. Jim scrambled his brain trying to remember anything about anatomy that would tell him how severe the damage from the bullet might be in that particular region in the human body. Dale still had his cough rag in his hand. Jim pulled it away and attempted to stuff it under Dale's jacket and layers of shirts as a bandage for the bullet hole. Once the rag was in place, Dale pulled his hand out from under his friend's clothing, only to find it completely coated with fresh blood. He felt panic coming over him, and would have let it take him if it hadn't been for the shouting of human voices nearby. With a quick look above the edge of the drainage ditch Jim saw the owners of the hound closing in on him and Dale. There were at least eight humans in hunting gear pacing through the brush area he had just left. The hunters maneuvered in a non-predictable manner, like something out of a war movie he had once seen. *These guys know what they're doing*, Jim thought.

Dale began to moan and move his arms. Jim scrambled to Dale's body and performed a fireman's carry wrestling maneuver to get Dale upon his shoulders. He was surprised at how easy it was to heft his companion. *Maybe it's adrenalin.* Jim crouched down and retrieved Dale's rifle, leaving his own behind. Dale had a slight frame, so it was easy to lift him; but carrying him while he was struggling to breathe, struggling to move within his unconsciousness was a different matter. As Jim maneuvered down the drainage ditch in a ninety-degree direction from where the hunters were approaching, it took all his will to keep from stumbling. He had seen a culvert in the drainage ditch up the farming road a few hundred feet. The culvert told him there was a dirt road of some sort that started at the farming road and led into the cornfields. He needed to get to that dirt road. He wanted nothing to do with the hunters because they had arrived with a dog.

Four weeks before, while he was trying to locate his family, Jim Doty stumbled into the Crossroads Enclave by accident. He then snuck into the Service Center where a woman named Molly caught him trying to steal some food. Molly hooked Jim up with Dale and helped them escape.

She informed Jim that several clans in the areas outside the Crossroads Enclave were using dogs to hunt humans. The logic was that any human found outside the clans could survive only by having ammo and weapons. Any human, like Jim or Dale, who had survived without being part of a clan would also have food, or know of a source of food. The two most valuable commodities in the current unrest were food and ammunition. Molly also told him that if one of these groups caught him, he would be tortured until he confessed where his food stores were and then killed after finding the food.

Jim was alone in life. His wife and two children died from the flu that had swept the region. His other family members had disappeared and he had no way of finding them. Jim Doty had become disgusted with humanity since the Collapse. Everywhere he went, he found people were either cowardly or superstitious, and both types were capable of murder to gain a crumb of bread. After hearing from Molly that his family was dead, Jim wanted nothing to do with staying at the Crossroads Enclave and planned to return to the countryside. Instead of turning him in, Molly pleaded with Jim to take someone with him.

"I've been out there without a clan," she told him, "you need two sets of eyes. Take someone with you. I can't go; I have my kids here. Grab Dale and take him with you. I know he's slow and all that, but you aren't going to find a better companion. That man worships you, Jim."

Molly ensured Jim had two rifles, a good supply of ammo and a few extra cans of sardines. Less than an hour later Dale met Jim in an abandoned fast food restaurant and the two set out into the farm country.

Now Jim was carrying a wounded Dale on his back. As he reached the culvert, he hoped it would lead him to a dirt road and his route for escape from the hunters. The dirt road was there, just as he had hoped. Jim turned for a moment to peer above the drainage ditch to see where the hunters were. They were nowhere in sight. Jim stumbled up the side of the drainage ditch and onto the dirt road. To his advantage, the dirt road made a bend after a few hundred yards and disappeared into a cornfield. Jim followed the road as fast as his legs and lungs would allow until he had passed the bend where he, too, would disappear from the view of the farming road. He prayed that the hunters didn't have another hound.

Once out of view, Jim pushed his way into the cornfield and lay Dale down on a bed of flattened dried stalks. After a few minutes of rest, Jim decided to explore his environment. He that he couldn't stay where he was. He had to find shelter for the night and some way to get help for Dale.

Dale didn't look very good. His breathing was coming in short and rapid rasps. Every so often he would come into what seemed full consciousness and mumble some words about "not having enough cash to pay for it." These mumblings frightened Jim into action. He returned alone to the dirt road and continued following it until it reached a farmhouse surrounded on all sides by fields of dead corn stalks. There he waited, hidden in the cornrows, casing the place. It was difficult for Jim to determine if there were humans in the house. He saw no forms of light through any of the windows, but eventually noticed a stream of smoke leaving a chimney on the opposite side of the structure. There was movement inside the farmhouse, at least four people, one a woman who seemed to be the most active. She came outside the farmhouse and retrieved an armload of wood from a stack leaning against the side of the house, then disappeared inside again.

She didn't even look around, Jim thought, *must not be afraid. I wonder why?*

Taking a chance, Jim stepped out of his hiding spot in the corn and ran to the side of the house near the woodpile. Climbing up on the woodpile, he was able to look into a window by carefully rubbing off a layer of dust from the glass pane and cupping his hands over his forehead. After a few moments of letting his eyes adjust to the darkness in the room, Jim was able to decipher why there seemed to be no concern at this house for guards or guns: it was a makeshift hospital.

One of the odd things about the Collapse and its aftermath was that doctors and nurses had become indispensable. There was no need for a medic to carry a weapon, because medicine and the treatment of the sick had become a sacred occupation. Jim had heard stories about members of warring factions sharing a bed in an overcrowded first aid station. He had heard stories about makeshift hospitals becoming a neutral territory, a sanctuary…a place for his friend Dale.

Jim jogged back to the hiding spot where he had left Dale, hefted the unconscious man onto his shoulders once again and carried him to the farmhouse. Intentionally, Jim left his rifle on the blood-soaked cornstalks where Dale had lain. As he approached the farmhouse, Jim began to call out in a loud voice that he had no weapon, that he had an injured man with him and that he was seeking medical aid. He ascended the steps to the front door just as the door opened a crack and a male voice said, "You got any food?"

"No," Jim lied. He had a can of sardines in his jacket pocket.

"Can't let you in unless you got some food." The voice said as the door began to shut. Jim threw his body against the door, careful not to hurt Dale. The door made contact with the owner of the male voice on the other side. Jim's momentum carried him into the farmhouse where he met the woman he had seen outside. She was walking down a hallway from another room as Jim, carrying an unconscious Dale on his shoulders, came barging in.

"What's going on here?" She demanded.

"I got a sick man here," Jim said once he regained his footing. The woman stood with her arms folded and a scowl on her face. She looked behind Jim to a man that was sitting on the floor by the now fully open front door. The man had one arm in a sling and held a bloody nose with the other hand. He was sitting with his legs crossed, rocking back and forth in obvious pain and was trying his utmost not to cry out in agony from the recent blow to his face.

"Carter? What's going on?" She asked the bloody-nosed man.

"He wouldn't let me in," Jim interrupted, "unless I gave him some food. So I kicked the door in on him."

"Carter, get your butt in the back room right now," she scolded the man on the floor, who silently conceded defeat and left the entryway of the farmhouse for another room. "Now, you," she said to Jim, "bring your friend into the room over there and lay him on the table." The "room over there" was the former farmhouse kitchen. Once Dale was on the kitchen table, the woman entered the room with another man following close beside her. The man was carrying a bucket of steaming hot water, which he placed inside the kitchen sink before leaving the room. The woman asked Jim a few quick questions about what had happened to his friend, then began removing Dale's clothing while performing a few elementary physical checks upon him. Nothing that the woman did to Dale looked more complicated than anything someone with a two-hour first aid course could have done. In less than two minutes from the time she started her examination of Dale, the woman turned to Jim and announced that his friend was going to die. She turned her back on Jim, placed her hands in the bucket of hot water and began washing Dale's blood from them.

"That's it?" Jim asked defensively. He approached the body of his dying friend, gripped the nearest hand and continued talking. "You do a few quick checks, and, and…"

The woman turned to face Jim and matter-of-factly said, "Yes." She didn't turn her back to Jim this time. She looked at him with a face that was expressionless.

Jim looked away from the woman toward Dale and silently swore. Without looking up again, Jim asked the woman, "Can I stay here with him until it's over?"

"Yes," she replied as she turned back to the task of washing her hands and forearms. "But if we get another bleeder, your friend will have to take a place on the floor. We'll need the table. You understand that?"

"Jim," Jim said.

"What?" the woman asked as she grabbed a stained towel from the counter top next to the sink.

"My name is Jim. This here is Dale. He's a good man. Was a good man. And, yeah, I get the drift about the table."

"Stephenie," the woman replied.

"Yeah," Jim replied as he took his eyes off Dale and looked at the woman. "Oh, and this is for you, uh, Stephenie." Jim pulled out the can of sardines from his jacket pocket and laid it on the table next to Dale's feet.

"Thanks, Jim," the woman said. "You're a good man too," she said as she left the kitchen without taking the sardines.

Dale died that afternoon as the darkness descended upon the farmhouse. It was an ugly death. Coughing, spasms, moaning and bleeding, Dale finally shook one last time and then lay still. Jim had watched it all while holding Dale's hand. Someone, Jim couldn't recall who, had brought him a stool to sit upon as he waited for his friend to die. Several times throughout the ordeal, other people in the farmhouse had come into the kitchen to perform some form of task or retrieve some needed object, but no one spoke and no one looked at the kitchen table. Once Dale was gone, Jim let go of his hand and stood from his stool. Just as he stood, Jim heard the voice of Stephenie speaking.

"Do you want to bury him, or do you want us to take care of the body?" She was standing in one of the kitchen doorways, leaning up against the jamb with her arms folded across her chest. Jim noticed for the first time that if it weren't for the weariness this woman wore on her face, she'd be quite attractive. It made him wonder how his own reflection appeared to others; it had been weeks since he'd seen a mirror.

"What will you do?" Jim asked.

"Well, since we're where we are, we burn dead bodies along with a pile of corn stalks." There was no hesitancy or emotion to her voice when she said this.

"Yeah, go ahead. It's the best thing to do anyway."

"Good," she said plainly. Stephenie then nodded to the sardine can still sitting on the table between Dale's feet. "You don't owe me a thing. But I'll *share* that can with you, if you don't mind."

"Sure," Jim said as he picked up the sardine can. "Anywhere but right here."

Stephenie silently nodded and motioned for Jim to follow her down a hallway to another room. Jim heard hushed voices coming from the direction he and Stephenie were approaching, as if a muted discussion was taking place. The moment Stephenie entered this room, all talking ceased and the room became silent except for the crackling of the logs in the fireplace.

This room was wall to wall with beds of every conceivable nature. Some of the beds came complete with mattress, frame, sheets, and blankets. Others were sparse, consisting of couch cushions covered with scratchy wool blankets. Jim had viewed this room earlier that day when he had peered into the house from his perch on the woodpile. Every bed had at least one man lying upon it. Before the Collapse, it was a living room or family room for its occupants. Now it was a crowded recovery room of a makeshift hospital. There were other rooms in the house, larger rooms, that could be used. However, this one had a fireplace, and this is why everyone crowded into it.

Stephenie motioned for Jim to wait outside the recovery room while she maneuvered through the maze of beds to the fireplace. From the fireplace mantle, she retrieved two candles and used a twig from the fire to light them. Ensuring the candles lit, Stephenie carried both candles back to where Jim stood. No one in the room had talked or moved a muscle the entire time Stephenie had been in their presence. All eye contact was avoided. It was as if these people were afraid of her. Something was dreadfully wrong with these men and it gave Jim an uneasy feeling. Stephenie's eyes met Jim's as she gave him one of the candles. She motioned with her head for Jim to follow her down yet another hallway, away from the recovery room. It was on this occasion, after Stephenie led Jim down a hallway to an empty bedroom, that he would form a friendship for the last time in his life.

There was no furniture in the room down the hall. All beds and chairs from the entire house had been moved into the living room to take advantage of the warmth of the fireplace. The bedroom would have been completely empty but for a mirror that leaned against one wall and a stack of magazines near its base. Jim and Stephenie sat on the floor in the center of the room with the candles between them. Using nothing more than their fingers, they shared the tin of sardines Jim brought. They ate in silence until the can of sardines was empty, with the exception of a small amount of oil and sardine flakes. Jim turned the can toward the candlelight and waited for the oil to seep into one corner of the tin. Stephenie reached for a hidden object from within her jacket pocket. It was a plastic bag with a zip lock seal. Opening the bag, she pulled out what looked to Jim like a dried kitchen sponge.

"Here," Stephenie said, motioning for the can. Jim carefully gave it to her and watched in puzzlement as she stuck one edge of her sponge into the collected oil of the sardine can. A moment later, she gave Jim the sponge and said, "Its bread. Go ahead and take a bite."

"Bread?" Jim asked with a distrusting expression. "How old is it?"

"About three weeks."

"You make it?"

"No," Stephenie replied without expression. "A patient of mine made it."

Jim took a bite from the bread and gave it back to Stephenie. She repeated the dipping process in the sardine can until clean, then tore off the oil-soaked area of the bread and ate it. Returning the bread into the zip lock bag and then back into her jacket pocket, she maneuvered the can closer to the candles to observe it better.

"I used to throw things like this into the garbage without a thought otherwise," she began, "but now I think about it before chucking anything. In this can I see a storage container, or a sharp edge for cutting." Jim remained silent but kept his eyes upon Stephenie's face. "Anything that's lightweight and has more than one use, I usually keep."

"You have any family before all this happened?" Jim finally spoke.

The abrupt way that Jim changed the topic caused Stephenie to shoot a quick glance at him. Jim continued to stare into her face with all his might as if trying to see something that was faintly visible.

"Yeah," Stephenie replied in a whisper. "I had a brother. My parents died a couple years ago. No husband or kids." She didn't show a bit of emotion as she said this, nor did she offer any explanation about her brother. She returned her concentration to the empty sardine can.

"I was in Champaign," Jim broke the silence. "It took me two months to get here. The man in the kitchen, Dale, he tried to save the lives of my wife and kids but the flu took them. I've been with Dale for a while since then."

The room fell silent as the two occupants continued to stare at each other. Stephenie put the sardine can on the floor and used the motion to break eye contact with Jim. "You don't have a clan?" She asked him as she stared at the can on the floor.

"No, but I've been to the Crossroads Enclave."

"You were there too?"

"Yes," Jim replied as he closed his eyes. It was as if he was trying to repress a memory and it was hurting him. "How about you?"

"I was a prisoner there. My friend and I escaped. We couldn't stay there so we had to come out here." Once again, Stephenie had mentioned another person in her life, yet failed to explain why they weren't with her. Jim Doty noticed this but didn't press the issue.

"Me and Dale were on our own for a while until this morning when the hunters caught us."

"Did they have dogs?" Stephenie once again looked at Jim's face.

"Yeah. I shot one of their dogs and they shot Dale."

"Most people don't get away from those kind of hunters. There are some insane folks out there. I've been hearing some bad news about the hunters that use dogs. You must know your way around this area."

"I was born and raised around here," Jim said. "I used to hunt a lot around here, too."

"How's the hunting now?" Stephenie said with more than just a little sarcasm in her voice.

"Yeah," Jim answered, "it seems that humans are the only thing out in the fields."

"So, what are you going to do now, Jim?"

"I don't know." Now it was Jim's turn to look at the sardine can on the floor between them.

"I noticed that you don't have a weapon with you," Stephenie said as she leaned forward a little.

"I left my weapons in a field about a quarter mile from here. I cased your place for a while before I brought Dale here. I didn't see any guard or picket on duty; didn't see any weapons at all. I figured since this place was a medical concern, there would be no need for a weapon."

"Come with me, Jim," Stephenie blurted with sudden emotion. She was now leaning forward, reaching out and touching Jim on the shoulder gently.

"What?" Jim said as he tensed slightly upon her touch.

"I've just about run out of medical supplies here in the cornfields. I need to get supplies, Jim." Stephenie had an insane look into her eyes. "I've been low on supplies for weeks. I've got to get out of here."

"What about all these other men here?" Jim asked. "Why don't they go get supplies? Why don't *they* go with you?"

"I don't trust them." Stephenie replied without hesitation.

"How do you know that you can trust me?" Jim said as he looked into her eyes.

"You were willing to give me your food, even though I couldn't save your friend. These *men*," Stephenie waved her hand toward the bedroom door, "These men have given up on life. Most of them aren't even sick. Only one or two help me out around here. You wouldn't think that there would be laziness from anyone in times like these. But most of these men are lazy and I can't seem to get rid of them. I don't trust them. Come with me. Take me out of this place."

Jim reached up his hand and placed it upon Stephenie's hand that was still on his shoulder.

"Where would we go?"

"There was this man, a guy named Pat, or something like that. He and a group of other people, all on horseback, came through here about ten days ago. He said they were looking for family members. I guess these relatives of his used to live in this house before the Collapse. I told him that I found the house empty and didn't know of the whereabouts of the former occupants. Pat said he came from the *Sturtson* area. He said there's a Christian clan going there. He gave me food and some medical supplies. Jim, that's the kind of folks I want to be around, you know? These are the kinds of people that go looking for family, people that give what little they have in short-handed times like these. They were the kindest folks I've met since the Collapse. Let's go to *Sturtson*."

As her last word hung in the still air of the empty bedroom, Stephenie was nearly face to face with Jim. He could smell her unwashed hair, her unwashed clothes and her unwashed body. He felt the warmth of her exhaled breath on his face and neck. It smelled like sardines. He began to wonder if she sensed these very same things about him. God knew he hadn't spent much time caring for his hygiene in the last four months. Such things didn't matter when facing starvation. The look in her eyes still reflected a sense of insanity. The woman before him had seemed so in control, almost professional, just moments before, and now was wild-eyed and pleading. Jim figured he had only one choice in the matter.

"Yes, let's go to Sturtson." Jim said. Stephenie moved forward and hugged Jim around his neck until she was sitting in his lap.

"Thank you, thank you," she kept repeating into his ear as she began rocking back and forth. Eventually her motion stopped altogether, until she lay limply against Jim's chest. Jim's back began to ache and he was about to say something about it to Stephenie, when it dawned on him that she was asleep. Jim laid her down gently on the floor. He retrieved a blanket from the living room area, draped it over her sleeping body, blew out the candles and then snuggled down next to her to keep her warm. Stephenie had found someone that she could trust and so had he.

CHAPTER THREE

The Crossroads Enclave: Fleeing Security

Sam Morton was officially happy for the first time in his young life. He awoke from a deep sleep on this particular October morning with a grin on his face. He couldn't wait to face the day ahead. As Sam threw off his blankets and sat up on the edge of his bed, he felt the chill of the morning invade every exposed part of his body. He didn't mind the shiver that took control of his entire nervous system and made him shake spastically for a couple of seconds. *Why do I feel so good?* Sam thought. Looking across the dimness of the room, he spied some clothes draped across the back of a chair. *Maybe it's the uniform?*

In the bed next to Sam's was a prone figure under a covering of several blankets. The body beneath the blankets belonged to Tim Slater, Sam's roommate. Tim and Sam shared a room in Housing Unit #6. Housing Unit #6 had been a hotel prior to the Collapse. When the Crossroads Enclave established its boundaries, the Council decided to utilize the hotel to house a large majority of its Security Force personnel. Sam's original room was on the third floor with a man named Erich. When Erich died from the *Influenza*, Sam was reassigned by the SFers to a room on the second floor with Tim Slater.

Tim Slater was a good-old boy most of the time, but experience had taught Sam to avoid Tim the first hour after he awoke. Tim could be particularly mean spirited in the morning. It was for this reason that Sam trained his internal clock to wake him at least thirty minutes before the Housing Unit #6 morning alarm sounded and tore Tim Slater from his slumber. It was the only feasible way to avoid his grouchy roommate in the morning. The only downside to getting up ahead of the general alarm was that there would be no electricity, and therefore, no lighting in the room. As a general policy, the Council ensured its citizens had electricity available to their housing units between six-thirty and seven o'clock each morning. Sam therefore had to grope around in the darkness to get dressed and out the door. To do this task without waking Tim had become a challenge that Sam was willing to adapt to in order to avoid his roommate's wrath. In order to attain success in the endeavor, Sam had to plan the night before by staging his clothes in the order donned the next morning. It also meant that he had to take a shower during the allotted evenings instead of mornings. It was worth it to Sam to endure these inconveniences. For the first time in his young life, he was waking up in the morning with a good attitude. He wanted to avoid anything that might put a dent in his happiness. That included a crabby roommate.

Sam arose from his bed and donned his uniform. As uniforms go, Sam's wasn't much to look at. Grab any pair of pants, any type of shoes and socks, and put them on; those things didn't matter. What mattered was the long-sleeved, brown shirt. That brown shirt made all the difference in the world. It was the shirt worn by every member of the Security Force, the Crossroad Enclave's peace officers and law enforcement entity. Stenciled above the front right pocket of the shirt were the letters, *SF,* standing for *Security Force.*

Officially, the long-sleeved brown shirt was the first choice of the Crossroads Enclave Council as the official Security Force personnel uniform. The Council, as well as the SF officers, unilaterally held the position that the brown shirt was *specifically designed* as the uniform of the Enclave peace officers. Unofficially though, a second explanation had filtered through the SF ranks. This alternative story dictated that, at the time of the Collapse, the Enclave Equipment Center, when it was still a

Menards store, had accidentally ordered four thousand of these brown shirts and never had the opportunity to send them back to their distribution center. This unofficial story reasoned that when the Enclave Council took control of the Service Center and the Equipment Center, the brown shirts were in an abundance that justified their use by the largest organization of human resources in the Enclave: the Security Force. Regardless of the reason for the choice of the brown shirt, the Enclave Council directed every single one of the shirts to have "SF" stenciled above the right front pocket and that no one but a qualified Security Force member could wear such a shirt.

Anyone who wanted to become part of the SF had to be at least sixteen years of age and pass the three-week SF Basic Training. When a new recruit had completed his Basic Training, he received two SF shirts and immediately stenciled his last name above the left breast pocket. Sam often reflected on the day he stenciled his last name, MORTON on his first two SF shirts. It was on that day his happiness began.

> I can remember the day I became an Eagle Scout. I walked home from the ceremony feeling proud of my accomplishment. Before I got home, a gang of low-life scum surrounded me, pushed me to the ground, kicked me and called me a *fag*. Three years later, I'm in 'Nam surrounded by a group of Vietnamese who pushed me to the ground and began kicking me. They called me a *dog*. After a brave group of Marines came in and rescued my POW butt, I got sent home in my freshly ironed uniform only to be called a *baby killer* by a gang of ignorants. America has a love-hate relationship with the uniform worn by authority. It doesn't matter whether the uniform is worn by a Boy Scout, a policeman, a fireman or a soldier; the moment you put on one of those authority-based uniforms you evoke passionate responses from those around you. I've kept the uniform I wore when I was discharged from the Marines in 1973. It may sound strange to some, but every so often when I get to feeling old, I put that uniform on and stand in front of the

mirror. Soon I feel young again. I feel proud of myself. I feel like nothing is impossible. I take off the uniform, put it back into storage and go on with my life.

Theodore Newgent
areyoulistening.com September 1998

After donning his uniform, Sam groped around on the nightstand next to his bed and found his flashlight. He cupped his hands around the flashlight's beam and clicked it on. With a subdued light source as his guide, Sam silently slipped from the room, leaving his sleeping roommate behind. Once he was outside the door and in the hallway, Sam Morton used the flashlight with impunity as he strode confidently past the silent rooms of his fellow citizens toward the stairwell. As per his usual routine, Sam made his way to the housing unit entrance to chat with the night guard. For reasons of security, the entrances of each housing unit remained well lit throughout the night. Sam appreciated the fact that his morning conversation with the night guards had the advantage of full lighting. It made reading body language part of the ritual. The purpose of this visit went beyond the mere social aspect of conversation. For Sam it was a morale booster because he knew the night guard would be a SFer like himself, and therefore an instant comrade. *Maybe it's not just the uniform*, Sam thought as his flashlight guided him down the dark first floor hallway toward the housing unit entrance, *maybe it's my role as one of the SFers that makes me so happy?*

On this particular morning, Sam met with a pleasant surprise as he approached the housing unit entrance. The night guard wasn't one of the three young men that normally held the post; this time the night guard was female, and attractive at that. She was on the business side of the entrance counter and lounging in a comfortable over-sized office chair. She propped her feet upon a hidden horizontal surface on the other side of the counter and a blanket draped over the entire length of her body. As Sam approached the woman, he noticed that she had beautiful dark hair that flowed over her blanketed shoulders. She also had beautiful eyes. *At least her eyes are open and she isn't sleeping on the job*, he thought, attempting to break the reverie of the moment and return to a more professional line of thought.

"Hey, what's up?" Sam asked in a voice just a little louder than he meant to use.

"Not much," the woman said as she kicked off the blanket, stood from the chair and stretched with a yawn. She even yawned with poetic motion. *What's her name?* Before Sam could read the stenciling above her pocket, the woman reached for an object on her side of the counter and held it up for him to see. The object was a wind-up alarm clock.

"Geeez, you're up awful early," she spoke in a playful, singsong voice as she waved the clock in Sam's face. Sam looked shyly toward the carpeted floor and grinned sheepishly.

"Yeah," Sam returned his gaze toward the woman on the other side of the waving alarm clock, "some folks say I'll be early to my own funeral."

The alarm clock stopped its waving as the young lady gave Sam a sideways glance accompanied by an uncertain smile. She put the clock back on her side of the counter, leaned forward and read Sam's stencil, "You're cute. Morton, huh?"

"Sam," he replied.

"Well, Sam Morton," she said as she looked down at her chest and grasped her brown shirt on both sides of her stenciled name, "I'm a Niemerg. Trista Niemerg." Her approach was confusing to Sam. *Is she being overly friendly or intentionally seductive or both?* Before Sam could reach a conclusion, Trista tilted her head again and said in a straightforward manner, "You're cute, Sam. I like cute. You work day shift?"

"Uh, yeah," he replied unsteadily. Sam was clearly staggered by this girl and this conversation. His eyes kept playing ping-pong between her face and the word NIEMERG above her left breast. It astounded him how her body defied the normally male-oriented shape of the brown SF shirt she wore.

"Too bad," she said with an exaggerated sadness to her voice as she slowly shook her head, "I sure could use someone like you to keep me company on these cold and lonely night shifts."

"I get off at nineteen hundred," Sam spoke with hope and enthusiasm before his brain had time to think about it.

"I go on shift at nineteen hundred," Trista said in a disappointed manner.

"I can…I can get up earlier in the morning?" Sam now sounded like a five year-old on Christmas Eve.

"How early?" Trista spoke in a serious tone. She knew she had Sam's number and wasn't about to let it go.

"Um," Sam now looked at the ceiling in rapt thought as his mind began to process how early he could get to sleep at night, how much sleep he actually needed to function at his job and how much time he wanted to spend with this whirlwind of a woman. "Look, I'm getting up now using an internal clock. I don't know if I can wake myself up any earlier."

"Well," Trista said with a sly smile, "I'll just have the roving watch wake you up."

A confused look drew across Sam's face. "I didn't know there were two SFers on shift here at night."

"There aren't, Mr. Morton."

"Well, then how are you…oh, I get it. *You'll* wake me up."

"Yeah, and you are living in…" Trista scanned a clipboard she had pulled from a hidden recess on her side of the counter, "room 234, right?"

"234, yes, but I have a roommate who doesn't like being woke up early for any reason. If you knock at the door, it'll wake him up and I'll never hear the end of it."

"Problem solved," Trista spoke in her singsong voice as she reached in her SF shirt pocket, pulled out a brass colored key and waved it in the air. "I've got a master key to all the rooms. No need to knock. I'll just waltz right in and wake you up, say, around four?"

"Miss Niemerg," Sam said as he shook his head, "you are either mad or you are a genius."

"Maybe I'm a little of both."

Sam laughed at Trista's comment and then became serious when a troubling thought crossed his mind. He leaned against the counter that separated him from Trista and took a chance to voice his thought. "Can I ask how old you are?"

"Sure," Trista held her palms up and shrugged her shoulders.

"Well?" Sam asked slowly in anticipation of her answer.

"Well what?"

"Aren't you going to tell me how old you are?"

"I'm waiting for you to ask me. You asked if you could ask me how old I am, and now I'm waiting for you to ask me."

"Oh, man," Sam rubbed his forehead and smiled. He suddenly realized that she was about to play a major head game with him, and he wondered if it would be worth the energy to endure it. "Okay, Miss Niemerg, how old are you?"

"I'm not going to tell you until I know you better."

"Oh, come on," Sam stepped back from the counter and crossed his arms in front of his chest. "You said you'd tell me how old you are."

"No, I did not," Trista said plainly. The smile vanished from her face as she put the master key back in her pocket. "I gave you permission to ask how old I am. I didn't promise to tell you."

"Right," Sam closed his eyes and nodded his head, a grin fighting a grimace for control of his face. The legalistic path the conversation was taking gave Sam a headache. To gather his thoughts he decided to focus on something other than the distractingly beautiful face of Trista. It was then he noticed the clock on the wall behind her and realized he was already late for a previous engagement.

"Oh, shoot, I gotta go," Sam said as he turned and pushed his way through the glass doors of Housing Unit #6. "Wake me in the morning."

"Wait," Trista yelled as she leaned over the counter to watch the disappearing form of Sam Morton, but it was too late, he was gone. "Huh," she muttered aloud as she sat down in her office chair, "*that* was weird."

Young Sam Morton strode across the Service Center parking lot at a pace just under a jog. He had promised to meet the Food Distribution Supervisor, Tom Craven, at the main warehouse at five o'clock and it was five minutes past that already. Sam was hoping to convince Tom to reassign him to permanent duty as Service Center security, an assignment that had recently been elevated in importance among the SF ranks. Sam figured if transferred into an assignment with a high profile, it would help him in his chances to become an officer. Yesterday he had arranged a breakfast meeting with Tom Craven in order to put his name in the forefront.

Sam reached the back entrance of the warehouse where a fellow SFer waved at him as he approached a makeshift booth near the security doors. Sam motioned for the security guard to open the sliding Plexiglas window of the booth.

"Hey," Sam asked the SFer, "Have you seen Craven?"

"Yeah, he went inside, oh, about fifteen minutes ago."

"Did he come back out?"

"Naw, must still be in there."

"Okay," Sam nodded as he walked toward the doors of the warehouse rear entrance, "If Craven comes back out this way, tell him Morton is inside looking for him."

"Will do," the SFer replied as he shut the sliding window.

I sure miss cell phones, Sam thought. *If we had cell phones, Craven and I would be able to find each other within the next minute.* As it was, the chances of Sam finding Tom Craven in the Service Center warehouse were slim at best. He decided to make for the center aisle and walk straight down the length of the building, peering quickly down the side aisles as he went. The place was huge and filled from floor to ceiling with massive shelving units. It was at this location that all the foodstuffs used to feed the five thousand citizens of the Crossroads Enclave were stored. The thought crossed his mind to yell out Tom's name in hopes of locating him, but Sam knew that would be a lost cause. All the storage structures around him would muffle his voice. As Sam walked through the maze of huge shelving units that filled the Service Center warehouse, he kept his eyes open for any sign of Tom Craven. Every time he passed by an open aisle, he shot a glance both to the left and the right in a simple process of elimination. Sam located a dozen or so people in the aisles, but none of them were Tom Craven. There were usually fifty or more citizens pulling items off the shelves at this time of the morning in preparation for the lunch meals. No one paid Sam attention in his semi-frantic search for Tom Craven, until he neared the last available aisle to search. Just as he rounded the corner at the far end of aisle #67 to check Tom Craven's backroom alcove office, Sam came face to face with a woman in dirty grey overalls. Much to his dismay, the woman was Molly Niebrugge.

"Can I help you find something?" she spoke assertively, as if Sam had violated her personal workspace.

"I'm, um, looking for Tom Craven," Sam stammered. He felt taken aback by the aggressive way Molly held her hands on her hips and refused to let him pass.

"Craven?" Molly pointed in the direction Sam had just come, "He left here five minutes ago, mumbling something about wishing he had a cell phone."

"Cell phone?" Sam felt like laughing at the irony, yet held his facial expression in check for fear of what this woman might do to him if he so much as smirked. Every SFer knew the legend of Molly Niebrugge and feared her for it. She folded her arms in front of her chest and took a step toward Sam, glaring at him as if she wanted nothing more than to tear his head off. Sam Morton fully understood the volumes of anger her body language was speaking, although he knew not why she acted this way. "Well, okay," Sam took a step backward and attempted to stick his hands inside his pants pockets, "Guess I'll look for Tom elsewhere."

"Sure," the woman replied with a nod of her head, yet remained motionless otherwise.

"Yeah." Sam turned and walked in the direction he had come, wondering intently if Molly would have him demoted a few ranks. The legends said she would.

The woman in the dirty grey overalls remained motionless for another ten seconds. *Keep going, Junior, just keep on walking away,* she thought as she watched Morton disappear in the maze of warehouse shelving units. Once she was certain that Morton would not be returning, Molly felt a surge of relief flood through her and she nearly collapsed. She had to grab the nearest shelf to keep from fainting.

"Man, that was a close call."

"What the heck is going on here?" a male voice whispered from under a shelf on the opposite side of the aisle. The woman stood erect again, walked across the aisle to the source of the male voice and acted as if she was straightening a stack of burlap bags on the floor level.

"Do you know where you are?" Molly asked the stack of burlap bags.

"This is Effingham, right?" The man's voice came from somewhere just behind the burlap bags. "I mean, this is the Wal-Mart store in Effingham, right?"

"Not any more," the woman spoke with a clear tone of sadness. "It's no longer Effingham, at least not this area. We call this the Crossroads Enclave now, and this building is the Service Center. I don't know how you got into the Enclave undetected, or how you got into this building, but you and I are in big trouble. That's why I pushed you behind the stack of bags when I heard the SFer coming. Those SF folks are crazy."

"What the heck is an 'Esseffer'?" The male voice spat in confusion, and then demanded, "What's going on here?"

"Look, it's not safe here anymore, the SFer might come back," Molly spoke quickly as she glanced back at where Morton had disappeared. Pushing the stack of burlap bags aside and peering at the haggard face of the man hiding behind them, she motioned with her thumb and said, "Grab some of these bags and follow me, I know a place where we can talk."

If anyone had been watching the far end of aisle #67 from a distance at that moment, they would have seen nothing more than two Enclave citizens carrying a few-hundred burlap bags to another area of the Service Center warehouse. Just as Molly had hoped, no one had been watching. The two bag carriers disappeared into a recess that was located in a wall partially hidden behind a pile of broken shelving parts. The woman motioned for the man to enter the six-foot-by-six-foot recess and used the burlap bags as camouflage to hide the entrance. Once the bags were securely in place, Molly turned to face the man she had just met under unusual and stressful circumstances. He had lowered himself to the floor, his legs outstretched before him with his back to one wall. His clothes were beyond filthy, his hair unwashed and his face covered by the dirtiest facial hair she had seen since the Collapse. He looked worse than any homeless person she had seen in any big city prior to the Collapse. Yet, there was still a sense of sanity in his eyes that she felt she could trust. Hoping her intuition was correct, she crouched down on her knees in front of the man, stuck out her hand, and introduced herself.

"My name is Molly. Molly Niebrugge."

"Jim Doty," the man said cautiously, returning her handshake.

"Jim Doty?" Molly suddenly let go of his hand and nearly fell backwards, a look of complete surprise sprayed across her face. "Did you have a farm out on 700th?"

"Uh, yeah," Jim leaned forward with a puzzled look on his face, "Do I know you? Have we met before?"

"No, we haven't met, but do you know a man named Dale? Dale Koester?"

"Dale? Dale, I-can't-stop-talking-and-making-noises-Dale?" Jim's eyes flashed a sense of recognition to match the sarcasm in his voice. "Dumb Dale, kinda slow in the mental facilities department. Is that the Dale you're talking about?"

"Um," Molly suddenly seemed embarrassed by what Jim had said about Dale and looked at the floor for a few seconds before returning her gaze upon Jim. "Jim, Dale's been waiting for you to show up here for over a month now, ever since he brought your family in…"

"My family is here?" Jim asked while attempting to stand. Without looking up at Jim, Molly reached out, grabbed Jim by his arm and attempted to pull him back down to the floor. Jim resisted and remained in a crouch, like a runner waiting for the shot from the starter's pistol. Molly held firmly onto the sleeve of Jim's grimy jacket and shook her head as if to say, *No, don't go, it's no use leaving.*

"Where have you been, Jim?"

"What do you mean by that?" He replied in a defensive manner.

"Where have you been since the Collapse?" Molly asked sadly.

"The Collapse?" Jim asked with a confused look.

"That's what we call this whole thing, the Collapse. I've heard that the term came from some ham radio operator in Montana. The story goes that he used that word to describe what happened to the entire country just before he signed off for the last time."

"The entire country is like this?"

"It seems so, Jim," Molly paused for a moment, shook her head, and then asked, "Where have you been, Jim?"

"I've been trying to find my family. For months now. I was in Champaign when the lights went out. I've been making my way back since then. Man, it's crazy out there. Everyone's got a gun and you can't trust a single one of them. Everyone's forming into clans and they won't feed you unless you join their clan."

"I've heard about that from a couple of recent arrivals here at the Enclave," Molly interrupted. "Did you get caught by any of these clans?"

"Fortunately, no. That's why it took me so long to get here. I spent most of the time hiding from people. A couple of days ago I finally made it to the farm, but the place was trashed. My family was gone; the minivan was gone, too. I figured they made it into town."

Molly released her grip on Jim's arm and breathed a heavy sigh. Her mind was attempting to fathom a world so dangerous that it took a healthy man three months to travel just over sixty miles. It was a crazy world since the Collapse. She realized that she was seconds away from telling a man that his purpose for living, to be with his wife and children, was gone. How do you tell a man such a thing? Before she could open her mouth to break the tragic news, Jim broke the silence.

"So where is my family, Molly?"

"They're dead, Jim," Molly said softly.

"They're what?"

"Dead. Tammy and the kids. They all died."

"How do you know this?" Jim spoke with the disbelief of a man crushed by a tidal wave of mourning.

"Dale told me all about it, Jim," Molly spoke calmly as Jim slowly lowered himself to the floor. Molly finally looked at Jim, bit her lip and continued speaking slowly. "I met Dale at Indoctrination. It's like a boot camp they make you go through here at the Enclave. Dale's a good man, Jim. I trust what he says."

"How...how does Dale know about my wife, my family...?" Jim's voice broke as he closed his eyes, covered his mouth with his hands and spoke through his fingers.

"He tried to save their lives, Jim. It was the *Influenza*. It was a disease that took-out half of the Enclave. It took-out Dale's parents. It took-out your family. He went to your house at the farm and found them all sick. He put them all in your minivan and drove it into the Enclave. They weren't going to let him in. Dale wouldn't take no for an answer. I don't know if it was because he's not so smart or because he's brave, but the word is he faced down a handful of very angry Security Force guards armed with Uzis. Dale made sure that your family made it to the medical clinic before the bastards beat him up. Despite all that, Jim, your family all died from the Influenza."

Jim closed his eyes, dropped his hands to his lap and leaned backward until his shoulders encountered the wall behind him. Molly sensed that Jim had just gotten the spiritual wind knocked out of him and would need some time to recover. It began to dawn on her that this man had spent the last three months surviving against insurmountable odds, only to discover he was too late. For several minutes neither he nor Molly spoke. Occasionally a noise from outside the alcove would filter in and cause Molly to peer over the pile of burlap bags. She was obviously doing something wrong by talking with Jim and did not want to get caught. Jim snapped out of his haze enough to whisper a few four-letter words. Molly took the opportunity to open the dialogue again.

"Jim, how did you get into the Enclave undetected?"

"What do you mean when you say 'the Enclave'?" Jim asked impatiently.

"The razor wire fences and the barricades," Molly whispered as she waved her arm in all directions, "they mark the Enclave boundaries. There are only three entrances into this place. Each guarded by armed Security Force thugs. No one has been able to get inside the Enclave without being shuffled into the detention area and then going through Indoctrination." Molly paused to study Jim's face for any signs of recognition, but there were none. "You don't have a clue what I'm talking about, do you?"

"No, not at all." Jim said as he shook his head and continued speaking. "It took me three days to walk from my farm to Effingham. I had to skirt around the farms and the highways. I didn't want to be seen. I walked through the woods on the northeast side of town. It was dark by the time I got to the last hill. There was this gap in the tree line. It looked like all the trees had been cut down and cleared out, like someone was going to build a road up there or something. I waited for a while to make sure no one was around and then decided to cross the gap to the other side. That's when

I ran into some barbed wire, or something like it," he stuck his fingers into several cuts in the fabric of his dirty jacket.

"That's the razor wire," Molly nodded. "They put up about twenty miles of the stuff around the borders of the Enclave."

"Well," Jim continued, "I didn't know why it was there, so I decided to grab a broken tree branch and beat it to the ground. That's how I got in."

"You made a hole in the border?" Molly gasped as her eyebrows arched in disbelief and fear.

"Yeah," Jim said defensively, "How else was I supposed to get around that crap? It went on for hundreds of yards in either direction and I didn't feel like walking around all night looking for the end of it and…"

"Jim," Molly interrupted, "that's not what I'm talking about. They send SFers twice a day to inspect the borders. If they find a gap in it they'll know someone got in undetected. They'll find you, Jim. You'll disappear. I've seen it happen. You've got to get out of the Enclave as soon as possible."

"You're serious," Jim said incredulously.

"Dead serious," Molly nodded, "The only way for you to get out of this alive is to sneak back outside the Enclave border and try to get back in at one of the check points, or sneak back out and just keep going away from the Enclave. Either way, the sooner you get out of here, the better your chances of survival."

"Well, I don't want to stay here," Jim spoke sarcastically as he waved his hand in the air, "This place is like a concentration camp. If I leave here, I'll be leaving here for good."

"Okay," Molly seemed to hesitate as she bit her lip and looked toward the ceiling.

"Well, I'm glad you approve," Jim said as he stood up and began pulling down the stacks of burlap bags.

"Wait, wait, wait," Molly said as she jumped to her feet and positioned herself between Jim and the burlap bags. She pressed her hands against his chest to keep him from leaving the hidden alcove, "I'm trying to think, just give me a minute."

"A minute for what?" Jim asked impatiently. "You just said that I've got to leave here, ASAP."

"I've got it," Molly spoke with a rapid intensity that couldn't be ignored, "stay here. Stay right here. I'll be back in the next fifteen minutes."

"Look, if I've got to get back over that razor wire before it gets light outside, I better do it now."

"Jim, just wait." Molly commanded. The assertive Molly was back and would stand her ground. "I'm going to get Dale."

"Dale?" Jim asked in disbelief. "Why him?"

"Jim, trust me on this one. Dale worships the ground you walk on. All he's done since I met him is talk about how kind you were to him and how much he respects you."

"Kind?" Jim was baffled. He scrunched his face up in a look of confusion as he continued, "I treated Dale like crap, just like everyone else. How could he respect me?"

"I don't know, Jim," Molly whispered as she peered over the stacks of burlap bags, "but you can't go out there alone and survive. Trust me. I know. I saw some…" Molly turned to face Jim as her voice drifted off. She looked to the floor as she continued. "Before I came to the Enclave I witnessed some very bad things, horrible things, Jim. Yes, this place sucks. I hate it here. I hate the Security Force. I hate the fear I constantly live under. But I've got two kids, Jim, and this pit is a heck of a lot safer for the three of us than the outside."

By the time Molly finished her dialogue, she was looking Jim straight in the eyes. The look in her eyes brought Jim's mind all the way back to his childhood. He had seen that look before when he was five years old. He had seen it in his father's eyes the day his father caught five-year-old Jim playing with his dad's handgun. "Jimmy," his dad had said in a frightened tone of voice, "put the gun down. Son, I'm not mad at you. Just put the gun on the floor." Now Jim was seeing that same look in the eyes of Molly Niebrugge. He knew she was speaking the truth.

"Okay," Jim nodded as he sat down on the floor of the alcove again, "Go get Dale."

"Thank you," Molly said as she breathed a sigh of relief. She turned toward the alcove entrance and began to push the stack of burlap bags aside before turning back to Jim again. "One other thing I've got to tell you before I get Dale. I'm going to tell you something that I don't think Dale needs to know about. He tends to obsess over certain things."

"That's for sure," Jim said without humor.

"Yeah, well, here it is" Molly said slowly as she closed her eyes, folded her arms in front of her chest and took a deep breath. "While you are outside the Enclave, if you see a group of men hunting with dogs, run. Shoot the dogs first and run. Or, just run as fast as you can. Just get as far away from the dogs as you can."

"Can I ask why?" Jim asked with a cautious voice, as if afraid of what the answer might be.

"These men are evil, Jim. They use the dogs to hunt humans. These men capture the humans. They torture the humans. Then they kill the humans. Then they feed the human bodies to their dogs."

"Why would they…" Jim stopped in mid-sentence and answered his own question with one word, "food."

"Yes, for food. They figure that anyone still wandering outside a clan must have a hidden stash of food somewhere."

"I'll keep it in mind, thanks, Molly," Jim said.

"Good. I'll be back as soon as I can," Molly said over her shoulder as she disappeared from the alcove.

Molly knew exactly where to find Dale, and fortunately, it was nearby. The Enclave had created a holding pen for all livestock in the open fields just north of the Service Center. Molly knew that Dale suffered from insomnia since he came to the Enclave. Often he would wander among the animals in the holding pen during the early morning hours. Molly spied Dale sitting upon the highest platform of a makeshift truck-loading ramp on the holding pen perimeter. He had his back to her as she approached him.

"Having trouble sleeping?" Molly asked as calmly as she could, considering the bomb that she was about to drop on the unsuspecting Dale.

"Hi Molly," Dale said with a smile as he spun himself around to face her. "You come to see the cows?"

"No," Molly shook her head in amazement that this man had survived as long as he had. "No, Dale, I came to see you. I have a question for you. Would you like to see Jim Doty again?"

"Shoot, yes ma'am!" Dale nodded his head in an exaggerated manner.

"Would you like to go on a hunting trip with Jim Doty outside the Enclave?"

"Oh, man alive, yes," Dale blurted as he pounded the palms of his hands on the plywood of the loading ramp. "We hunted all the time when we was kids. Jim Doty was the best hunter around, even better than Bobby Jensen."

"Yeah, yeah," Molly interrupted assertively. She had heard the same story from Dale dozens of times and wanted to get to the point of the conversation. "Well, I ran into Jim this morning and he needs your help."

"Jim is here?" Dale had shot to his feet and was holding his hands in front of his face as if looking through an imaginary pair of binoculars. "Where is he? I think I see him over there. Is that him over there?"

"Dale, Dale!" Molly nearly shouted to get Dale's attention. Dale went immediately into a pout and shoved his hands in his front pants pockets. The abruptness of the change almost made Molly burst into laughter. "Look, Dale," Molly continued, "Jim's in trouble. He needs your help. He's in the Enclave right now. He's hiding because the SFers are looking for him."

"Oh, no," Dale whined.

"Yeah, it's serious, Dale. He knows how to get out of the Enclave, Dale. Jim knows a way out, but he needs your help to get out."

"He knows a way out?" Dale asked in awe.

"Yes. He said that he wants to get out and hunt with you, just like you two did when you were kids."

"He does?" Dale seemed surprised at this news, even though he had been preaching those same words to anyone who would listen for the last two months.

"Do you want to go with him?" Molly asked as if she didn't know how Dale would respond.

"Man alive, yes!" Dale whispered as he took a step forward until his nose was a mere inch away from Molly's nose. Molly went cross-eyed and had to slowly back away from Dale.

"Good. Now Dale," Molly pointed toward a group of buildings on the northwest edge of the Enclave, "you know that one building over there that used to be a fast food restaurant?"

"Uh, no," Dale answered unhappily.

"Sure you do, Dale, it's the one where the shelving unit fell down that one day. Remember? The day I cut my hand?" Molly said holding her hand palm up to Dale to reveal a pink three-inch scar.

"Oh, sure. I know that building. It's the place you cut your hand."

"Good. Now, Dale, I want you to go over there now and wait for Jim to come, okay?"

"Right now?" Dale asked as if unsure of himself.

"Yes, right now." Molly said confidently, nodding her head and smiling.

"By myself?" Dale now seemed frightened.

"Yes. Dale, if you want to go hunting with Jim, you need to sneak into that building and wait for Jim to show up. Right now."

Dale looked in the general direction of the building in question and made a few noises with his tongue and teeth. It seemed to Molly that Dale was either concentrating deeply or trying not to think at all. Suddenly Dale turned his back to Molly and yelled at the milling animals in the holding pen, "Bye cows! I gotta go." Then he walked past Molly, humming the same twelve off-key notes repeatedly and acting as if she wasn't there. For the first time in several long months, Molly watched a human walk with a bounce of happiness in his step.

CHAPTER FOUR

The Crossroads Enclave: A Chance Meeting

Just after she had carefully placed the Styrofoam boxes into the top pouch of her body pack, Stephenie heard a rattling noise echoing from the direction of the front doors. The thought crossed her mind to race over to the storage room and flip off the light switch.

But once the lights were out, where would I hide?

The storage room consisted of an eight-foot-by-forty-foot floor with one aisle down the middle and shelves on both sides. She had found the side door of the storage room unlocked when she entered it, but there was no way to lock that door from the inside. Whoever was testing the front doors of the small building would most likely attempt all the other doors as well, and that meant they'd find the storage room door unlocked.

God, please let it not be one of those Security Force scum.

Seconds later Stephenie heard the metal-to-metal sound of yet another set of doors being tested, these being on the main side of the building closest to the storage room. She looked at her body pack and noticed the blatant word *Morphine* printed on the topmost Styrofoam box inside. She couldn't hide the body pack. It was too large to stuff onto a shelf, what with it being crammed full of first aid supplies. Stephenie reached up above her head, pulled a few rolls of gauze from a shelf and placed them upon the boxes of morphine inside her body pack. Just then, the door to the storage room opened and a lone figure stood in the doorway.

Stephenie, who had intentionally positioned her back to the door, slowly turned around and did her best not to look guilty. The intruder was a woman. She did not wear the SFer uniform. At least, it didn't look like a SFer uniform. It was difficult to tell, because she was covered from head to toe in white powder. The intruder was pressing a bloody rag against one hand with her other hand. She didn't look threatening.

"Well," Stephenie exclaimed as she approached the bleeding woman, "what in the world did you do to your hand?"

"Are you with the clinic?" the woman asked, taking a sudden, cautious step back as Stephenie walked toward her. Stephenie stopped two paces from the woman and looked into her eyes.

"Yes," Stephenie replied, lying, "I'm with the clinic. I came over here to get more supplies."

"Over here?" the woman asked with a quizzical look on her face. "Isn't this the Southwest Clinic?"

"No, this is a medical supply storage room for that clinic. The Southwest Clinic is the next building over. You know, the old Taco Bell."

"Huh," the woman said, breaking eye contact with Stephenie and staring at the floor as if looking for her thoughts. "Darned if I can ever figure this place out."

"That makes two of us." Stephenie said with just enough bitterness to catch the attention of the woman with the bleeding hand. She looked back at Stephenie with a concerned face, as if uncertain whether the woman before her was angry with her or the Enclave as a whole.

"Well, should I go there to get this taken care of?" she said as she held up her two hands and the blood-soaked rag.

"Uh, no," Stephenie said rapidly, as she swerved around the woman and shut the storeroom door. In seconds, she pulled two five-gallon buckets of disinfectant from a floor level shelf and pointed for the woman to sit on one of them. "Take a seat and I'll have a look at you."

The woman reluctantly did as instructed. She waited for Stephenie to sit in front of her before she held out her bleeding hand. Stephenie unwrapped the bloodied rag and slowly pushed on either side of the wound. After a cursory inspection, Stephenie pushed the bloody rag back in place and began attempting to clean the immediate area around the wound.

"What is this powder?" Stephenie asked, in reference to the white substance that covered the woman's clothing and most of her exposed skin.

"Baking soda." The woman said.

"Baking soda?"

"Don't ask."

"Looks like I'll have to stitch it up for you," Stephenie said plainly, in the same way as she might have said, "The sky is blue" or "water is wet." The woman across from her didn't have the same perspective.

"You're going to be able to shoot me up with some kind of pain killer before you do that, right?"

"Oh, yeah," Stephenie said nonchalantly, as she stood from her bucket and began scanning the shelves. "Look what we have here. I've got just the ticket." She brought down a cardboard box full of syringes with safety caps on the needles. "These make life a lot easier. They've got just enough juice in them to numb your entire hand. Let me get you fresh gauze for the wound. I'll need you to hold it in place while I apply the pain killers."

"Molly," the woman said unexpectedly.

"What?" Stephenie asked as she stood and began to survey the shelves for the gauze that she would need. Suddenly she seemed nervous.

"My name is Molly," the woman said as she eyed Stephenie cautiously.

"Oh, yes," Stephenie looked back at Molly briefly, as if irritated by something. "They call me Stephenie."

Stephenie's irritation stemmed from the fact that she had already pilfered the last of the storeroom gauze. Two plastic bags of gauze now sat atop the boxes of morphine in her body pack, in clear view of Molly's eyesight. She had no choice; she needed the gauze to stitch Molly's wound, so she stepped over to the body pack and pulled out one of the plastic wrapped packages of gauze. In doing so, she exposed a box of morphine. Molly noticed, yet she said nothing. Stephenie tore into the gauze bag, pulled out a roll and began unrolling it into a wad. From her breast pocket, she extracted a pair of scissors, which she used to cut the gauze. Instructing Molly to press the gauze tightly to her wound, Stephenie withdrew a hermetically sealed alcohol swab from the same breast pocket, lightly scrubbed a patch of skin, and then quickly injected the painkiller from the syringe into two sites near the wound. Having done this, she reached into a side pocket of her body pack and extracted a small plastic box. From this box, Stephenie withdrew a small pair of forceps and a handful of sutures.

"Are those metal?" Molly asked.

"What, these sutures? No, they're plastic."

"Plastic?"

"Yes," Stephenie said with a slight bit of aggravation as she attempted to rig up the first suture to the forceps. Her mind raced to say something that sounded medical in nature, to keep up her ruse. The only thing she could conjure was some engineering terms from the recesses of her brain. "These sutures are made of an organic composite that ranges somewhere in between latex and lexan without the negative side effects of either." She hoped she hadn't contradicted herself in her lie. She had no idea what materials were used in the making of the sutures. In reality, Stephenie had no formal medical training.

"Sounds medical enough," Molly shook her head as if just recovering from some kind of dizziness. "What the heck do I care, so long as I get my hand taken care of, right?"

Stephenie stopped loading the suture pliers for a moment and looked into Molly's face as if trying to read it.

"Right," was all she said.

Once both women were certain the hand was numb, Stephenie applied the sutures as well as she could manage and dressed the wound with a new gauze bandage. Stephenie gave Molly the leftover roll of gauze, a handful of pills to manage the pain and instructions on how to care for the wound until it healed. Molly stood from her bucket and began to walk to the storeroom door. Just as she was about to open the door, she turned and looked at Stephenie, who was standing near her body pack pretending to read off a wish list of medical supplies from a black book in her hand.

"You're leaving, aren't you?" she asked Stephenie.

"Yes, in a minute, I've got to get this stuff over to the Clinic."

"No," Molly said as she leaned her back on the storeroom door and folded her arms across her chest. "You're leaving the Enclave altogether. You're going back out there into the wilderness. Aren't you?"

Stephenie silently retreated to one of the five-gallon buckets and sat down with a sigh. It was as if Molly's words had knocked the wind out of her.

"Was I *that* obvious?" Stephenie asked, looking up with despairing eyes.

"No, not really," Molly shook her head, unfolded her arms and returned to her previous spot on her bucket, once again facing Stephenie. "I studied psychology in college. I've got a gift. That's all."

"What gave me away?" Stephenie asked after an elongated pause.

"Well, for one, the pack over there, the one you were supposed to use to transport the supplies next door? You know that pack too well. It's your pack and you know where everything is, where the sutures were, where the pills were. That told me the things inside were meant for your use, and not the Clinic's."

"You've got a good eye for detail," Stephenie said, shaking her head in amazement.

"Oh, that's not all. You had me going on the whole suture thing; I don't know an organic suture from an inorganic one. But no formally trained nurse I have ever met ever just went about administering drugs without a few questions about allergies."

"Oh, man," Stephenie looked at the ceiling and exhaled. "I really have to work on this, don't I?"

For the first time in a long, long time, Molly felt like laughing, but something in her brain prevented it. Instead, she stuck her non-wounded hand out to Stephenie. Stephenie wasn't certain what the gesture was all about but she could only guess it was a handshake, a sign of peace. She reached out and awkwardly shook Molly's hand.

"Hello, my name is Molly Niebrugge," Molly said in a flat voice. "I am a widow, a mother of two children under the teenage years, and I am currently managing food distribution for the Enclave."

"Stephenie Plasters," Stephenie said in return. "I have an electrical engineering degree. I'm currently acting as a nurse even though I only have two months of field experience. I got stuck in this concentration camp a month ago against my will. And, yes, I'm about an hour away from sneaking out of this place."

"You have no formal nursing experience?" Molly asked.

"None."

"Why are you nursing now?"

"Because no one in this crappy world expects a medical professional to kill another human." Stephenie stood from her bucket again and began to pace the back area of the storage room. "Literally, from the moment I started acting like a nurse the whole world started giving me a wide berth. A war breaks out between two clans and I can cause a cease-fire just by leaving one camp and going to the other. I haven't had to carry a weapon since I started my journey. All I have to do is wear this," Stephenie pulled a stained white ball cap with a red cross sewn on the front from her body pack and placed it on her head, "and people leave me alone."

Stephenie had stopped her pacing and busied herself in tying down and adjusting the zippers and straps on her body pack. It dawned on Molly that Stephenie had used the word *journey* to describe her post-Collapse experiences. This *journey* concept, and the fact that Stephenie was attempting to flee the Enclave for the violent world of the wilderness, piqued Molly's interest.

"Where were you when the lights went out?" Molly asked.

"East St. Louis," Stephenie replied. "And you?"

"About fifteen miles north of here."

"Sigel?" Stephenie asked.

"Yes, exactly," Molly tilted her head in a whimsical fashion. "Do you know this area?"

"Not too well." Stephenie picked up her body pack and slid one arm through a molded-cushion shoulder strap. "Look, um…."

"Molly," Molly replied evenly.

"Yeah, Molly," Stephenie continued to speak even as she attempted to shuffle past the seated Molly, "I know you'd love to hear my story and all that. But as it is, I'm carrying my death warrant on my shoulder and unless I get outside the Enclave in the next hour, I will be dead in the next twenty-four."

"Stephenie, just out of curiosity," Molly said as she pivoted her body forty-five degrees to look over her shoulder the other forty-five, "where were you planning on crossing?"

"The northwest forested area," Stephenie paused by the door, yet seemed irritated to do so. Even so, the woman named Molly was letting her go with no strings attached. To show her appreciation before stepping through the door, Stephenie replied, "They don't have any razor wire up that way yet. My informant told me that they've been relying on the density of the trees to keep folks from passing."

"Well, you'll get as far as the road construction site and then you'll have to come back. So you might as well stay at my apartment tonight and I'll get you out tomorrow morning." Molly spoke with an authority, yet it seemed that her words didn't register with Stephenie. Stephenie shrugged her shoulders and turned to leave. Molly had just passed along privileged information about the Enclave's latest security project that only a handful of citizens knew about, and Stephenie had acted as if she hadn't heard a word of it. Realizing this, Molly rushed to the door and at Stephenie's back she added, "I'm at housing unit number four, room two-two-eight. Remember that, housing unit four, room two-two-eight."

"Okay," Stephenie said as she disappeared around the corner of the building.

The remainder of the day for Molly was hectic. Being in a managerial position for the Enclave Service Center meant that she had responsibilities beyond the understanding of the average Enclave citizen. What made her job more difficult was that she was responsible for the distribution of the most important commodity on the entire continent: food. Because of her gift of discernment, her boss had placed Molly on the fast track to manage the department, thus bypassing several other citizens who felt they should have the position. These bypassed citizens were in the process of an attempted coup when Molly prevented the upheaval with a swift public firing of the perpetrators. The recent changes and upheavals within the food distribution department had left Molly with fewer than half the workers and no less work for them to perform. Thus, Molly, by the consequences of her own decisions, temporarily left the confines of her office and worked in the field until replacements came.

Upon returning to the Service Center, Molly was immediately responsible for solving six problems at once. Only one of which could be solved without the phrase, "Look, we're *all* suffering through this transition." It was a typical managerial defense but seemed to work to squeeze out the extra 20% effort from the warehouse workers under her direction. The one problem that could immediately be resolved was summed up this way: "What do ya wanna do with this guy named Dale? He showed up with a couple shopping carts and claimed that you hired him to work in food distribution even though that's impossible because he's dumber than a rock and couldn't pull it off even with one of us holding his hand along the way?"

Molly heard this question from one of her food distribution runners who just happened to be huffing a cartload of food across the Service Center parking lot toward the south cafeterias. It was a good question. It was a question that needing immediate addressing. If forced to tell the truth on the issue of hiring Dale, Molly would have to confess that she did it entirely on personal intuition. There was no logical, pragmatic, or common sense reasoning behind her decision. Molly found Dale sitting on a folding chair just outside her office door. His body language spoke volumes about how frightened he was in this new environment and among these distrusting people inside the Service Center. His forlorn facial features brightened the moment he recognized Molly. It was then Molly remembered exactly why she had transferred him to her department. Dale was, above all things, loyal, and loyalty was the ingredient missing from Molly's work life. As for what to have Dale *do* in food distribution, the solution to this problem came the moment Molly reached for the knob of her office door and Dale said, "Man alive! You got your hand all fixed up. Let me get that door for you, Miss Molly." Until her hand healed, Molly would need Dale around to do her physical tasks. Dale Koester, one of the least likely to succeed in the Enclave, had become the indispensable personal aide to Molly Niebrugge, one of the brightest in the Enclave. In the back of Molly's memory echoed the phrase, "I will use the foolish to confound the wise." It was another church phrase she had memorized as a child and thought she'd forgotten. Yet recently these Christian phrases had taken on a life of their own in the heart of Molly Niebrugge, as if something large and powerful was trying to get her attention.

Molly was more than ready for the day to end as she and her two children made their way across the Service Center blacktop toward their housing unit. Being autumn, it was already dark at seven o'clock, which made navigating the unlit world outside difficult at best. Her son Aaron took the lead as was his usual role, his sister lagged behind with her mother, clinging to her right hand in silence.

Before the Collapse, Molly thought, *there would have been many questions on the children's minds about her injury that day and much chatter to accompany these queries.*

She knew that her son would have wanted her to remove the bandage just enough to get a glimpse of her wound, the swollen discolored scar, the sutures. Her daughter would have been squeamish and turned her head so as not to see the injury, but would have been inquisitive at how much it hurt or how it felt. That was how it might have been if the Collapse had not occurred. The memories of how things had been a few months ago filled Molly with a melancholy gloom. No one would have thought the world could change so rapidly. No one would have thought so many people would murder. No one would have guessed so many would die from starvation and disease. In addition, no one would have predicted that in order to continue living, the surviving children would have to work twelve-hour days. Molly became weary at the burden she carried for her children. She wondered if it had been such a good idea to come to the Enclave. This, in turn, made her ponder how dangerous it would have been to stay outside the Enclave in the wilderness of the farmlands. She recalled a memory from the recesses of her mind about a conversation with someone who wanted to return to the frontier. The memory was unclear, but she knew it had been recent.

If I could just rest for ten minutes, Molly complained to herself, *maybe I could think clearly again.*

Finally, the visual image of a woman named Stephenie flashed across Molly's mind. The memory filled her heart with a small amount of excitement mixed with just enough fear to shake Molly from her trance-like thought process.

She might be inside our room.

Just as her son Aaron was ascending the stairs to their second story room at Housing Unit #4, Molly called across the parking lot for him to stop as she jogged toward him. Aaron stood still on the stairway and waited for his mother and sister to catch up with him. The young man didn't question his mother when she told him that she wanted to be the first to enter their room. Aaron was too tired to care and simply shrugged his shoulders as she passed him on the stairway. Molly opened the door to their room and immediately and shut the curtains before flipping the light switch on. The pre-curfew electricity was apparently available to Housing Unit #4, because the room light came on and lit the room.

Just as Molly had thought, Stephenie was inside their room at the housing unit. It was fortunate that Molly entered first, instead of her son Aaron, because Stephenie was in a state of agitation just short of shock.

"Oh thank God it's you," Stephenie exclaimed from her hiding position between one of the beds and the nearest wall. She crumpled in a heap against the wall, bowed her head, and attempted to hide her face behind her shaking hands. "I've had a bad day," was all she could say.

Molly's two children stood in the doorway of the room, uncertain of whether it was safe to enter. Molly slowly approached the shaking woman and bent down to touch her shoulder. The woman didn't recoil at her touch, yet neither did she acknowledge the act of kindness.

"Mom," Aaron spoke apprehensively, "Is it okay to come inside?"

"Yes," Molly said, not taking her eyes off the unstable woman before her. "It's okay. It's going to be okay."

Aaron and Jenny entered the room, shut the door behind them and silently made their way to the closest bed. Crawling upon the bed, Aaron put his arm around his sister's shoulder and held her close while he waited for something to happen that would explain why this frightened woman was in his housing unit room. Nothing in his current situation seemed safe. Both he and his sister knew the presence of this strange woman, and the way their mother was reacting to her, could spell nothing but trouble for them.

"Stephenie," Molly spoke in as calming a voice as she could muster, "Uh, you look pretty shaken up." Molly noticed that Stephenie had brought her body pack full of medical supplies, now stuffed into the corner where two inner walls met.

"Yeah, I'm not doing so hot right now. I've just gotta…" Stephenie stopped short and pulled her hands away from her eyes long enough to notice there were two children in the room. She looked into Molly's face and asked, "Who are they?"

"My children, Aaron and Jenny," Molly said evenly, trying not to react to the disturbing way that Stephenie was acting.

"Oh, I'm so sorry," Stephenie said as she reached for her body pack, began to stand up and walk across the room toward the front door, "You've got kids. I guess I forgot that you told me about them. I shouldn't involve you with my troubles."

"Wait, Stephenie, it's not safe out there right now. Too many people are coming back from work details. Don't go out there."

"But I don't want to get you all killed," Stephenie said desperately as she turned the doorknob, cracked open the door and peered out. This statement sent looks of concern between Jenny and Aaron. Molly noticed this and slowly approached Stephenie.

"Stephenie," Molly spoke softly but sternly, "If you stay here for a couple more hours, I can guarantee your safe exit from the Enclave and *our* safety as well."

"Well, aren't you one of the managers around here?" Stephenie now closed the door and turned to look at Molly, who now stood a pace away from her. "Why do you want to help me escape?"

Molly had to weigh her answer carefully. The Security Force of the Crossroads Enclave had indoctrinated her children. They worked in the Service Center under the watchful eye of this power-hungry Security Force. It was commonplace for the Security Force officers to put pressure on the younger children to become SFers when they got older. It was commonplace in the Enclave for children to *turn in* their parents to the Security Force in order to secure a position as an SFer. Although Molly had worked diligently to dissuade her children from participating in the Security Force's mind games by constantly debunking each aspect of their religion when the opportunity arose, she couldn't control what entered the minds of her children in her absence. Therefore, Molly was well aware that the words she now used before them would weigh heavily on their minds and possibly affect all of their futures.

"Stephenie," Molly said as she drew in a deep breath and slowly exhaled. "I came here to the Enclave to keep my children from starving. My job here is to ensure others don't starve, as well. I'm a manager because someone realized that their bureaucracy needed some brains to make it function, not because I toe the company line. In my own way, I hate this place just as much as you do. Nevertheless, I'm placing my bets down on the idea that, no matter what happens in the next five years, my children will survive and one day learn how to laugh again. Would I return to the outside again if my children weren't with me?" With this question, Molly paused intentionally and received the desired effect when the other three people in the room turned their eyes upon her and waited for her answer. "I don't know if I'd stay or go in that case, I really don't know. I believe that *you* should have a choice, Stephenie. Earlier today, you told me that you were on a journey. I just want to help you have your journey. That's all."

Stephenie released the doorknob, let go of her grip on the body pack and let it slide to the floor. "Okay, I'll wait. I'll let you help me."

With that, Molly tucked her children into bed with the explanation that she was going to leave the room soon with Stephenie, but also with the assurance that she would return. The curfew lights went out; Molly led Stephenie from Housing Unit #4 and vanished into the darkness of the unlit Enclave. Much to Stephenie's surprise, Molly led her right into the busiest place in the Enclave, the Service Center. On several occasions, Security Force officers challenged the two women, but when the SFers recognized Molly, they lowered their weapons and allowed the two women to pass. At one point in the journey, after having been stopped twice and questioned by SFers, Stephenie questioned Molly's reasoning in coming right into the SFers' nest as a way to help her escape the Enclave. Molly's answer was short and failed to answer the question: "Because we need to get two vital things."

Eventually the pair found themselves in the well-lit Service Center, walking through aisles and aisles of floor to ceiling shelving units. Both regular citizens in work clothes and SFers in their brown shirts milled about the aisles. All seemed to have some task to perform. Stephenie muttered one word as they entered an aisle empty of people, "Incredible." Finally, the journey through the Service Center led the two women through a hallway and into Molly's office.

Molly immediately sat behind her desk and began rifling through a file folder. Stephenie attempted to shut the office door. Stephenie warned Molly not to, with the explanation, "It's less suspicious if the door is left open while we're in here." Molly seemed to find what she was looking for in the form of two pieces of paper that she laid upon her desk. "This is good," she said as she closed her eyes, cradled her injured hand in her lap and leaned back in her chair.

"You have a plan to get me outta here, right?" Stephenie said hopefully.

"Yes," Molly spoke without opening her eyes. "You see, every day we send out a couple dozen empty trucks into the outlying areas of this former town of Effingham. Citizens, non-SFers, drive the trucks. Heavily armed SFers in jeeps and ATV quads escort the trucks. We call this the Collection Unit. Their job is to systematically pick a neighborhood each day and search the abandoned houses for any food that might remain in it. It's a dangerous job because several smaller clans in the area are attempting to do the very same thing. There are firefights going on out there every day involving the Collection Units. People are injured. People are killed. People get taken prisoner. It's an ugly mess."

"Wait," Stephenie looked suspiciously out the door of Molly's office and then back at Molly, "You mean there is still food in the city? After all this time?"

"Crazy, isn't it?" Molly opened her eyes, leaned on her desk with her elbows and pointed to the pieces of paper with her good hand. "Here's what's crazier. Each night we send out a small group of teenager SFers, kids really, with night vision goggles. These SFers are our scouts. They sneak around the various buildings in town and search out where the food supplies are located. These crazy little monkeys sleep during the day and work during the night. After a few nights of information collection, these scouts come back to the Enclave and hand in their reports. These reports go to my desk and I create the assignments for the Collection Units. This little piece of paper came to my attention less than two days ago, and for some reason I couldn't get it out of my head. When I found you in my room tonight, it dawned on me how I can get you out of the Enclave. Right here," Molly said as she pointed to one of the papers on her desk, "written in ink by the hand of a stranded scout, is the request for medical attention and an Evac."

"An Evac?"

"Yeah," Molly shook her head in disbelief, "One of the scouts went to sleep in a tree one morning, fell out of the tree and broke her ankle."

"*Her* ankle?" Stephenie asked incredulously.

"Oh, yeah, you should see the crazy stuff these Enclave girls are willing to do. Anyway, she hooks up with another scout who, for some reason or other, can't help the injured SFer back to the Enclave, but was more than willing to bring back this note. The injured scout wants someone to come out to her position and rescue her."

"And I suppose this is not normal operating procedure?"

"Not only is it not normal operating procedure, it's against the rules. We do special ops for food, not for fallen comrades. That comes right from the Crossroads Enclave Council."

"I hate those…monsters," Stephenie spat her words out with an angry venom that Molly wasn't expecting.

"Wow that was blunt."

"I've got my reasons," Stephenie's hands began to shake uncontrollably again.

Molly waited for further explanation to Stephenie's response, but received none. It took a moment for Molly to regroup her thoughts back to what she had been saying. It had been a long day and her injured hand had begun to throb. She reached into her pocket, retrieved the bottle of painkillers that Stephenie had given her earlier that day and set the bottle on the desk next to the two papers. Then Molly reached into one of her desk drawers and retrieved a large bottle of what seemed to be 180-proof whiskey. This too, she set on the desk next to her papers.

"My hand is starting to throb," Molly spoke as she looked into Stephenie's eyes, "Should I take the pills, the booze, or both?"

"Where did you get that?" Stephenie asked.

"The pills? You gave me those." Molly replied blankly as she put the pills back in her pocket without ever opening the bottle.

"No, the booze. I heard that stuff was the first thing outlawed when the Council took power of this place. I haven't seen any alcohol in over two months."

"Call it a gift from my boss, Tom Craven," Molly said with a sigh, as she removed from the same desk drawer a coffee mug and a can of Coke. "He told me to save it for special occasions. Well, this is the best special occasion that has come up, so let's party." Molly opened the can of Coke, poured half of it into the coffee cup and then began adding liberal amounts of whiskey to both the can and the mug.

"Whoa, whoa," Stephenie called out as she attempted to stop Molly from putting more whiskey into the mug, "take it easy. That's a lot of booze. I haven't had any for a while. I want to get out of here tonight, you know."

"Yeah, I know, Stephenie. But you've had a bad day, bad enough to make you jump at your own shadow. And you seem to be reluctant to talk about it. I need you loosened up. We both need to be loosened up, really," Molly replied as she poured a few more drops of whiskey into each of their drinking vessels. Then she returned the bottle of whiskey to its hiding place in her desk drawer.

"Why? Why do we need to get so loosened up?"

"Because," Molly said as she handed the coffee mug to Stephenie and acted as if she was proposing a toast, "we are going to help Sarah Blankenbiller get back to her grandmother." Molly then took a sip from her Coke can and encouraged Stephenie to do the same with her mug.

"Who?" Stephenie reluctantly took a sip from her mug. After putting the mug down, she began to chew on the bend of the thumb knuckle on her left hand. Molly guessed that Stephenie had developed this quirk in early childhood as an outlet for internal turmoil.

"Sarah Blankenbiller," Molly said with a wince, as the first fire of the whiskey scorched her throat. Then she tapped her finger on the paper in front of her. "Sarah is our lost little scout, the one with the broken ankle. I know exactly where she is. I am going to grab an SFer or two, and I am going out to find her tonight."

"What makes you think you can pull this off?" Stephenie asked as she herself winced at the effects of the whiskey in her drink. "You just said it would be illegal. Won't the SFers know it's illegal?"

"Of course they will. But when they see the name of the person we are going out to rescue, they will fight each other for the opportunity to break the law of the Council."

"Okay," Stephenie took another sip and shook her head in disgust, "who is this Sarah Blanken-whozits anyway?"

"Blankenbiller. She's the seventeen-year-old granddaughter of Marion Hoelstetter."

"Massacre Marion?" Stephenie nearly choked when she said this. "You mean the meanest monster on the Council?"

"Ironic, isn't it?" Molly almost felt like smiling. "One of the people you seem to have the most hatred for right now is going to be your ticket out of here tonight. I got this note on my desk less than two days ago. Only three people know about it: the scout that brought it in, me, and my boss, Tom Craven. A toast to Tom." Molly urged Stephenie to take another drink and succeeded in her efforts.

"Wait, I don't get it," Stephenie said as she shook her head and noticed that the taste of the whiskey wasn't as potent as the first few sips. "How does this get me out of the Enclave?"

"Well, doggonit," Molly said teasingly, slapping the palm of her good hand on the desktop, "I can't do it alone. I need a couple of courageous, if not glory-seeking SFers with loaded weapons. I need a jeep and driver. I need a nurse because God only knows how hurt this poor Sarah Blankenbiller is. Why, she might need a tranquilizer from that body pack of yours, a strong tranquilizer, one that'll knock her out. While the rest of us have to huff-and-puff as we haul her butt back to the guarded jeep, you slip off into the night. I'll make a good enough effort to find you, of course, but you aren't as important as

Miss Blankenbiller, so the SFers will order me to call off the search for you."

Stephenie put her mug down on the desktop and eyed Molly suspiciously. Suddenly her body language, which had been loosening up in the last ten minutes, became tight and defensive. She folded her arms in front of her chest and looked sharply at Molly. "Then what in the heck are you getting me drunk for?" Stephenie demanded.

"Because you need to lose some weight."

"What?"

"Stephenie, you're carrying a heavy load and you've got to let go of it for a while. If you don't let it go, you won't get outta here tonight."

"I'm, uh, its just that…"

"What happened this afternoon when you tried to escape at the northwest road?" Molly asked in an almost compassionate manner. She knew that she was asking Stephenie to talk about something she had witnessed earlier that day. It was something obviously horrible, judging by the way that she had been reacting since their meeting in the housing unit room. The success of this night's mission depended heavily upon how Molly handled the fragile psyche of her partner in crime. This was why Molly used such compassion in her voice when the question came forth.

Stephenie's body immediately tensed for a few seconds and then slowly released into a more relaxed posture. "I had a partner. The monsters held us captive in the Quarantine Compound. We didn't know why. Others were allowed to leave if they survived, but not us."

"Wait a sec," Molly leaned forward and nearly toppled her Coke can, "Are you telling me that you are the famous Florence Nightingale?"

Stephenie seemed stunned. "So, Hammer wasn't lying? I really *am* a legend outside the Quarantine Compound?"

"I don't know what hammer you're talking about," Molly said as she leaned back in her chair again, "but, yeah, you're a legend. Everyone that made it out of that Quarantine Compound alive talked about you and the other guy, what did they call him? Um, Doctor something-or-other." Molly, feeling the effects of the alcohol, drifted off for a second in silent thought.

"Yes, I had a partner," Stephenie continued, "He and I found out that the Council wanted us dead. We got an advance warning. A disgruntled SFer set up an escape for us. We got out this morning. Our instructions were to go to the northwest road and attempt to cross it into the trees. There wasn't supposed to be anyone up there, but when we got near the road we found ourselves surrounded by SFers. They were guarding the road while over a hundred or so workers were clearing the brush with machetes and laying the last of the razor wire. You were right, Molly, we shouldn't have tried it. He..." Stephenie began waving her hand in the air as if to swat away an unwanted memory as her words drifted in and out with her thoughts. "...well, I tried to explain to him what you told me about waiting at your room...we looked around some more and thought we'd found an unoccupied area...he took off first across the road...well...if he'd only listened to me..."

Molly leaned forward and pushed Stephenie's mug a few inches closer toward her, then took a sip from her Coke can. As if on autopilot, Stephenie lifted her mug and took a large drink, waited a few seconds and then repeated the act.

"Give him a name," Molly urged.

"Matthew, his name was Matthew."

"He tried to cross the road and got caught?" Molly offered.

"The SFers hauled Matthew into the woods on this side of the road. I saw a couple of SFers grab some machetes from the workers and return to where they had Matthew...they must have...I couldn't see what they...the screaming went on for..."

"How did you get out of there?" Molly asked quietly.

"They made so much noise...I just scrambled through the trees back to the housing units..."

"I'm glad that you told me this, Stephenie," Molly reached across her desk and touched Stephenie's shoulder. Looking at the clock on the wall of her office, Molly said, "Shift change was a half hour ago. Good. We have to act now. Stephenie, I can get you out of here if you can promise me one thing."

"What's that?" Stephenie looked up at Molly as if suddenly waking from a dream world.

"Take all that anger at what happened today and aim it at me."

"What?"

"I've just awakened you from a deep sleep, okay?" Molly said as she took the coffee mug from Stephenie's hand and returned it, along with her own Coke can, to the drawer with the whiskey bottle. "You were sleeping in your room when I personally came and woke you up. I haven't told you why I've woken you up, okay? I've just ordered you out of your room and told you to bring your first aid gear with you. You got that?"

Stephenie seemed befuddled at this sudden turn in the conversation. Whether it was the effects of the alcohol or the events of the day, it was suddenly difficult for her to concentrate on what Molly was saying. She shook her head as if to clear it. Meanwhile Molly retrieved a small metal tin from her desk drawer. From the metal tin, she extracted a handful of small round tablets.

"Chew a couple of these," Molly said as she offered a few of the tablets to Stephenie, "They're breath mints. We've gotta mask the smell of the booze. Grab your pack and follow me. As we walk through the Service Center I want you to act angry at me, okay?"

"Sure," Stephenie said as she hefted her pack and began to follow Molly out the office door and down a hallway.

"Start now," Molly said over her shoulder as she turned the corner of the office, "start complaining to me about having to get out of your bed for no good reason."

"Right now?"

"Yes, right now."

The legend of how Sarah Blankenbiller was rescued by a handful of brave SFers, the assistant manager of food distribution and *some nurse that got lost in the darkness* began with an argument overheard by two nightshift Service Center workers who just happened to be in the area of the office hallway that night. Molly Niebrugge, it was told, was being followed by a woman nurse carrying a body pack of some kind, who seemed quite upset at being dragged out of her bed that night with no explanation of why. This argument continued loudly through the bowels of the Service Center and to the northern loading docks. There the commotion quieted in a clandestine meeting of the food distribution manager, the angry woman and six Security Force guards. In hushed tones the food distribution manager told the guards of a fallen comrade left abandoned in the wilderness, needing medical aid and transport back to the Enclave. The nurse, rumor has it, once again began raising a clamor at not wanting any part of the mission, whereupon the SFers thus ordered the nurse to not only comply, but to shut her loud mouth. At this point, the legend blurs depending on which side of the political fence you hear it. Some say that the guards on duty drew straws to see who would assist Molly and the nurse in rescuing the fallen comrade. Others say the SF guards almost drew weapons upon one another to get the assignment. Either way, the stories all agree that five people climbed into a Security Force jeep that cold October night.

On hand for this fabled mission was Molly Niebrugge, 3 valiant SFers and a nurse of unknown name. Cautiously the evacuation team drove into hostile clan territory to a designated spot near Lake Sarah and, donning night vision goggles, began searching a small stretch of waterfront for Sarah Blankenbiller.

All the legends agree that Sarah hid in a small boat she had discovered abandoned in a pile of underbrush, twenty feet from the waterfront dock of a former private property. Sarah began babbling incoherently the moment rescued. The evacuation team seemingly slipped in and out undetected. The only shot involved in the entire operation was the tranquilizer injection received by Sarah Blankenbiller at the hands of the nurse, who, after administering the shot, watched the other evacuation team members carefully carry Sarah back to the jeep. The nurse was never seen again. All tellers of this legend say that the nurse stayed behind to put her medical supplies back into her first aid pack, then, disoriented by the darkness, was kidnapped after she walked into clan territory. The three Security Force grunts, immediately promoted to the rank of Officer, were given the honor of creating a Fallen Comrade Retrieval task force. Molly Niebrugge became a special advisor to one of the Crossroads Enclave Council members. From that day forward, every lower rank Security Force member secretly feared Molly.

CHAPTER FIVE

The Crossroads Enclave: The Service Center

One sunny September afternoon, Molly Niebrugge, along with her children and approximately forty former *new arrivals*, were escorted by one Security Force guard named Smith to the exit gate of the Indoctrination Center. They all knew Smith. He had been one of their indoctrinators. They all feared Smith. For the last six weeks he had made life miserable for each of the new arrivals. Today they would be leaving Smith and the Indoctrination Center behind. The new arrivals carried plastic trash bags in their hands as they stood silently at the gate. Each plastic bag contained the personal possessions the Security Force allowed the new arrival to keep. Waiting for them at the gate was yet another SF guard; this one's shirt had MORTON stenciled on it. Molly noticed that neither Smith nor Morton carried weapons. Because the indoctrination process of the Compound had done its job, no weapons were needed. Instead of weapons, both SF guards carried hand held radios clipped to their belts. Morton unclasped his radio from his belt, held it near his mouth and spoke, "Central, Central, this is Morton."

"Go ahead, Morton," sounded a tinny female voice from his radio. "I've got a group of forty from Indoc heading your way."

"Ten-four, Morton, we'll be expecting you."

Morton clipped his radio to his belt and ordered the new arrivals to follow him through the Indoctrination Center gate. Morton escorted the group from the razor wire compound past the remains of a former gas station to a large parking lot. He ordered them to stand in a line and wait. Morton walked across the parking lot and entered a set of glass doors on the west side of a large structure. Molly knew what the structure had been before the Collapse. She had been inside that building hundreds of times in her life. She wondered what the inside of the former Wal-Mart looked like now that the Enclave Council had control of it. Removed were all former Wal-Mart marquees, leaving discolored paint and torn electrical connections as vestiges of their former locations. No longer did the building boast of being "Open 24 hours" or of any of its other former services rendered within. Instead, the enclave workers had erected one sign on the west side of the building. In giant red letters on a white background were the words, *Crossroads Enclave Service Center.*

"Servicing who?" Molly wondered aloud to herself.

"What did you say?" Her son asked her, his upturned face scrunched against the glare of the afternoon sunlight.

It was then that she noticed how much her son looked like her husband. Former husband, she reminded herself. Pain ripped through her heart and caused her body to shudder. She couldn't let herself look weak. She had to look strong for her children. Molly pushed the pain back, took a breath, hugged her son, and said, "I'll tell you later." A still small voice spoke within her again, as it had done so often in Molly's heart over the last several months. This time the voice said, "Lay your burden upon Me, Molly, because to Me your burden is easy and light." Molly shook her head and wondered if God really existed in this new and terrible world.

For ten minutes the line of former new arrivals-men, women and children-stood in the middle of the asphalt parking lot, in the heat of the late summer sun, and did not move. Hundreds of Enclave citizens were coming and going in the immediate areas around the parking lot. None of them came near the line of former new arrivals. Few of them wore the brown shirt of the Security Force. Molly, intrigued by this situation, had a mental image of Morton entering the building, gathering a few comrades to the Service Center entrance and pointing out the fools in the parking lot. She pictured them laughing and mocking the frightened party of immigrants, many carrying plastic trash bags holding their meager personal possessions. Old black-and-white photographs of Ellis Island came to her mind. She wondered if the Council would make her change her last name.

Morton eventually appeared at the entrance of the Service Center and waved for the forty new citizens to walk toward him. As the new citizens entered the Service Center for the first time, they encountered a sight they would never forget. All accustomed visual memories of the former Wal-Mart store were gone. Where the cash registers had been was now an open sea of office desks with busy citizens performing clerical tasks. The optometry area was now an office of some sort with a twenty-foot banner hung from its ceiling that read, *Work Detail Assignments*. Where once there had been a beauty salon now was a communications center filled with telephones, CBs and handheld radios. The local bank affiliate office was now a Security Force weapons center. The liquor store and the photography shop had become one room and now served as a shopping cart checkout office. The former Customer Service area had rows of folding chairs that faced the interior of the building and was now a waiting room for the new *citizens* of the Crossroads Enclave. Maybe the thing that stood out the most, even greater than all the changes, was the fact that this building was illuminated by electric lights. Not one of the new citizens had seen a functioning electric light since the Collapse. For many of the new arrivals just standing in the glow of the lights inside the Service Center building felt like being greeted by a long lost friend.

Morton escorted his group of new citizens into the waiting room and ordered them to sit in the chairs. As soon as Molly's son Aaron sat down in his folding chair he pointed toward the Service Center interior and asked his mother, "What is that?" The object he pointed to was a partition wall erected across the floor of the Service Center, separating the building's deep interior from the nearby entrance area. The wall stood eight feet tall and consisted of two-by-fours with sheets of oriented strand board hand-nailed in place. Obviously built in haste, none of the wall was painted and, in several spots, there were small gaps between the strand board sheets.

Morton had overheard Aaron's question. As if it was the most important task in the known universe, Morton walked in front of Aaron and began to address the group of new citizens.

"This young man here has asked an important question and I think it requires an immediate answer for all of you. You see that wall behind me?" Morton asked as he pointed with his thumb in its direction. "That wall was erected by order of the Council as a way to protect our food supplies. You see, on *this* side of the wall we have all the administrative functions of the Service Center. All these folks working at the desks-where the cash registers used to be-they are the folks that make sure there's always enough food coming in to cover what's consumed by the Enclave. On the *other* side of the wall is a giant warehouse and some offices that are used to carry out the food procurement activities." Morton turned his back to his captive audience, pointed to the wall, and said, "On the other side of the wall is our food stores. To the left you will see the one and only door to the storage area from this side of the wall. Do you see the Security Force officer standing by the door? Well, there are more just like her on the other side. No food ever passes through that door. The only things allowed through that door are Security Force personnel."

Morton walked twenty paces to his left and returned to front and center pushing a large chart suspended from a rolling projector screen. On the chart was a drawing of the Service Center building layout. Morton grasped a pointing stick from a clip on the side of the screen and began a rehearsed explanation of the Service Center layout.

"This is where you are right now, in this blue area," he spoke as he utilized the pointer and then looked back over his shoulder to ensure every one of the new citizens was paying close attention. Satisfied, Morton continued. "Over here is the wall, and right here is the door to the stores. Don't ever attempt to go through that door unless you are a Security Force officer. Now, the Procurement Officers interview every citizen here at the desk area. From there you will be sent elsewhere inside the Service Center, assigned a place to live and a job to do." Morton turned to face his audience and took a step toward them before raising his voice a notch higher than before. "Everyone works. Everyone. Women, men and children. In order to survive this coming winter, every citizen must pull his or her weight and earn the right to eat. The focus right now is food procurement, the gathering of food from the areas outside of the Enclave boundaries. All food collected must be turned in to the Service Center. *All* food collected. Anyone caught hoarding food will be dealt with in extreme terms, I assure you. Any questions so far?"

For several seconds no one spoke. The typewriter tapping of the Procurement Officers at their nearby desks and the sounds of the warehouse workers on the other side of the wall filled the silence. Suddenly, Morton's expression changed as he peered at one area in the waiting room and said, "Yes, what is your question?" This caused the new arrivals to turn around in search of whom Morton was talking.

A man in the back row had hand raised and was in the process of standing from his folding chair. Molly recognized the man, and a smile drew across her face. She had spent two days at the Indoctrination Center digging ditches with him. He wasn't supposed to be working with the women during the work detail. He was supposed to be with the men but he kept forgetting. In her several brief talks with this particular man, she came to the realization that he was *special*. He, being mentally challenged, saw the world through the eyes of an eight-year old boy, though his body told you he was at least thirty. Molly smiled at this moment because she knew his lack of adult understanding would challenge Morton and possibly add a few brief moments of jocularity to an otherwise serious lecture.

"Hi, my name is Dale Koester," the standing man spoke directly to Morton. His face wore a childish smile that seemed to mock the circumstances. His clothes and his hair were disheveled and there was just enough timidity in his posture to make him seem non-threatening. "I just wanna know what you mean by that one word you used."

"What word are you talking about?" Morton spoke in a direct manner, still keeping the atmosphere as heavy as he could.

"You know, the word you used, um, I think it was whoring," Dale was looking at the ceiling in intense concentration as he said this. "Yeah, that's it. You said we couldn't whore food." This brought several stifled chuckles from the assembled new citizens.

"Yes, I see," Morton seemed to be suppressing the urge to scream. He scrunched his face up in anger, which caused creases to form across his forehead. Morton was attempting to compose himself and take control of the lecture again. Before he got the chance, Dale spoke up again.

"Y'see, I know what a whore is. Man alive, Bobby Jensen told me about that a long time ago." Dale was now scratching the top of his head with one hand and had jammed the other into the pocket of his pants. "But I don't see how we could do that to food. Do you?" The waiting area erupted into full-scale laughter; even the young children, who had no understanding of what was occurring, began to join into the laughter.

"Hor-ding," Morton nearly screamed. The entire staff of Procurement Officers stopped what they were doing when Morton said this and sat staring at him from their desks. The laughter immediately died away in the waiting room and Dale stood alone with a confused look on his face. Morton took a few steps toward Dale and began to explain himself, this time in a calmer tone of voice.

"I said hoarding. That means keeping food for yourself. You can't keep food for yourself. All the food you collect you must turn in to the Service Center. You must not keep it for yourself. You must not hoard it. Do you understand now?"

"Oh, I get it now," Dale brightened and began to bounce on the tips of his feet, as if in jubilation. "If I find some food I gotta give it to this place, right?"

"Well, yes," Morton returned to his Service Center drawing and pointed to a spot marked with a large yellow star. "All food collected must be turned in to the Service Center at this point right here, in the back of the building at the loading docks. Do not bring any food to the front of the Service Center. Bring it to the back. Do you understand this?" Morton spoke this to Dale as if he were the only other person on the planet.

"Yeah, I get it. Don't bring food in here," Dale nodded and pointed toward the floor.

"Good," Morton shook his head and turned back to the drawing as Dale began to sit down.

Dale looked like he had another question to ask but a mean look from Morton put him back in his seat again.

"Okay," Morton said as he pointed to the drawing with the stick, "We are all here, on this blue spot. Next, you will go over here, to the desk area to get your paper work transferred, and then you'll go over here to get your work assignment. I've got a list of your names on my clipboard. We will process each of you in a specific order by using your last name, and yes, families can be processed together. Any questions?" The tone of voice Morton used to ask this last question made it sound as if he would kill the next person to raise a hand. The words were a statement to be understood and not a question to be answered. No one raised a hand this time, not even Dale Koester.

"Very well," Morton announced with a voice full of forced authority, "I'm now turning you over to the Procurement Officers. Wait in your chair until you hear your name called. When you hear your name called, I'll tell you what desk to go to." Morton read the first name from his list and directed that person to a specific desk. One by one, or by family unit, the new citizens shuffled to the desk area of the Service Center. The Procurement Officers interviewed them, collected basic data on each person and then typed this information onto multi-layered impact copy forms using manual typewriters. As each form was completed, the desk clerk would separate the copies by color. The yellow copies went in a folder that sat on the right hand corner of the clerk's desk and the pink copies went in the desk drawer. The white copies were tossed into a common data collection box on the left corner of each desk. These white forms were collected by a runner who took them to the Housing Office area of the Service Center, formerly the Men's and Women's restrooms. From the confines of the tiled walls of the Housing Office, the runners returned with a list of names and housing assignments.

Molly and her children were assigned housing in room number 228 in Housing Unit #4. With her housing form and trash bag of valuables in hand, Molly and her children walked to the Work Detail Assignment office. A feeling of melancholy swept over Molly as she stepped into the former optometry center. The last time that she was inside this building was to pick up a set of bifocals for her husband, Mike. Years before, Tom had begun to complain that he couldn't see up close. When children came into his life, this problem exaggerated since children have a tendency to shove objects in the faces of adults. His daughter would push a toy into his face, say "See dis Dad?" and instantaneously send Mike into a queasy world of dizziness because his eyes couldn't adjust fast enough. It made Mike nauseous. It made Mike angry. After about the tenth time that Mike yelled at his children for making his head spin, Molly dragged him into the optometry center of the local Wal-Mart to get a set of bifocals. A week later, she received a phone call that Mike's glasses were ready for pick-up. That was the day before the Collapse.

Now her husband was dead, brutally murdered. She had been raped and her children had witnessed the entire horror. These were horrible thoughts that Molly was normally able to push aside. As she walked with her children to the former optometry center, it was all she could think about. "Molly, put your burden upon My shoulders," the voice said.

How will that help? It won't change the past, Molly thought. Suddenly Molly was pulled from her deep, dark thoughts by the overly joyful voice of a young woman in an SF shirt, stenciled DETERS.

"Welcome to the Work Detail office," the SFer said in a singsong voice, as she stood from her desk and reached out to shake Molly's hand. "My name is Emily Deters, and I'll be assigning you all to work details this morning."

Molly awoke from her dark thoughts so abruptly that it caused a temporary block in her ability to speak clearly. Instead of responding in like manner to the bubbly young woman behind the desk, Molly managed only to say, "I'm finding, I mean, I'm okay," as she shook Emily's hand and then jerked her hand away, as if she had received a shock in the process.

Emily took note of this odd behavior for a moment and glanced at Molly, with her head tilted and a confused look across her face. After holding this facial expression for two seconds, Emily shrugged her shoulders and returned to her former, happy self, as if nothing had ever happened.

"Do you have your housing assignment form with you?" Emily asked as she sat down in a chair on her side of the desk and motioned for Molly and her children to do the same on the other side. Molly looked at the chair in front of her, then to her left and to her right. It was as if she was surprised to find her children standing next to her. She was here to pick up Mike's glasses…no. Then, as she reached out to pull the chair away from the table in order to sit in it, she realized she held a trash bag in her hand. She was having a difficult time processing her present after such a deep journey into the past.

"It's here in my pocket," Molly said absently, unable to meet the eyes of the bright young woman on the other side of the desk.

"Good," Emily said with a wink to little Jenny, "I need to see it in order to get you started on your work detail."

"They didn't tell me that at the last desk," Molly said as she retrieved a piece of paper from her pants pocket and began to unfold it before handing it to Emily. "So I folded it up and put it in my pocket."

"That's okay," Emily said as she went to work writing information onto a clipboard while scanning Molly's housing assignment form. "I just need to get some basic info from it."

As Emily transferred the information to the work detail form on her clipboard, Molly's daughter Jenny crawled halfway into Molly's lap and whispered something into her ear. Molly nodded and answered quietly, "You'll have to wait just a minute, Jen."

"Is there something wrong?" Emily asked cheerfully as she put down her pen and took turns peering at the faces of Jenny and Molly. Embarrassment crept across Jenny's little face as she turned red and looked at the carpeted floor.

"Well, my daughter needs to use the restroom," Molly started with the clearing of her throat, "I suppose she can wait until we're done here and I can walk her over to the restrooms." Molly had turned and pointed in the direction of the women's restroom around the corner from the former optometrist's center.

"Oh, sure, I'm just about done here," Emily said brightly, "but the restrooms inside this building are no longer in operation. They used too much water. There's a row of port-a-potties just outside the door of the

Service Center. You'll pass right by them as you walk over to your housing unit."

"Oh, sorry about that. I forgot about not having running water. Force of habit," Molly said as she gave her head a shake.

"Oh, the Enclave has running water, Mrs. Niebrugge," young Emily assured her. "It's just that too many people were coming inside the Service Center to use the restrooms. It was causing too much noise, so the Council put port-a-potties outside and tore out the toilets inside the Service Center."

"Sorry about that," Molly said. "It's my first day here."

"Don't worry, Mrs. Niebrugge, it happens all the time," Emily said sympathetically as she finished her paper work, "in fact, just this morning I reached out to turn on a light switch before the wake up call at my housing unit. I flipped the switch, nothing happened and then I remembered that the lights wouldn't come on for another five minutes."

"They have electricity at the housing units, too?" Molly's son Aaron said excitedly, as he suddenly sat up from a slumped position in his chair. "Not just here in this building?"

"Yes, the Council turns on the electricity twice each day at the housing units," Emily gleefully informed the ten-year old boy, "a half-hour in the morning and a half-hour in the evening. You'll be told all about it when you get your housing unit tour, which is where you are going to next. Of course," Emily leaned over and spoke to eight-year-old Jenny as if sharing an inside joke, "that's after you take a little stop over at the port-a-potties." Jenny leaned toward her mother and hid her face under her arm. Emily wasn't expecting such a reaction and sat up straight with a disappointed expression.

"What's her problem?" Emily muttered under her breath. Molly noticed Emily's reaction and hugged her daughter passionately, kissing the top of her head.

"Emily," Molly spoke directly toward the disappointed expression, "how long after the Collapse did you come to Effing…to the Crossroads Enclave?"

"About a week after," Emily said confidently.

86

"So, you haven't seen the carnage outside this sheltered little…" she wanted to say *concentration camp*, but said instead, "enclave?"

"Hey, Mrs. Niebrugge," Emily spoke defensively, with a slightly raised voice, "Things haven't been easy for anyone, so don't…"

"This little girl," Molly interrupted with a hiss of hatred, "has seen things that would leave a person like you babbling incoherently. Moreover, what she saw all started with a stranger, just like you, talking like a lame ass, just as you did, right into her face. Of course, you had no idea that what you were doing would result in such a response, but your reaction afterward spoke volumes about your ignorance. Now, if you'll just finish your responsibilities with our work assignments, we'll be on our way."

"Gladly!" Emily replied in disgust. She ripped a piece of paper from her clipboard and tossed it at Molly. "These are your work assignments for today. You can have the person at your housing unit tell you where to go. Now get out of here before I put you in the Quarantine Compound."

"Come with me, kids," Molly tried to sound calm as she spoke to her children, "Let's go see our new home." Molly stood from her chair and shuffled her children out the southwest doors of the Service Center. She wondered what this Quarantine Compound was all about, but she was currently in no position to ask Emily. Molly stored the thought in her memory files for another time.

The sun was bright in her eyes and Molly had to stop a moment to allow them to adjust before locating the row of ugly green latrines to her left hand side. She led Jenny into one of the latrines and talked her son Aaron into using one as well, reasoning that she didn't know when they would get another chance to use a toilet. As she waited for her children to finish, Molly took the opportunity to exercise the stress from her mind and body by inhaling deep breaths and letting them out slowly. During breath number two she tried to assure herself that she had every right to put Emily in her place. During breath number four, she tried to assure herself that the things that happened this morning were part of 'the past' and better forgotten. During breath number nine she tried to convince herself that she and her children would survive this Crossroads Enclave experience. So deep was her moment of meditation that she failed to notice the undeniable stench of the chemicals and human refuse wafting from the vents of the line of latrines. Or the hundreds of people walking back and forth around the Service Center parking lot. Or the fact that her children were out of the latrines and now were reaching up to touch her arms.

The Niebrugge family found Housing Unit #4 without much effort. Housing Unit #4 was one of a handful of low-cost motels located on the west side of the Enclave, across the now defunct highway. All families with small children abided in the motel district because of its location furthest away from the business end of the Enclave. The last thing the Council wanted was to have any children wandering around the Service Center or Equipment Warehouse. As she walked across the enclave toward the family housing units, Molly became aware of several unusual sensations in her mind caused by the circumstances of her current environment.

The Crossroads Enclave was eerily quiet considering how many thousands of people now lived within its boundaries. This absence of sound was the direct result of the lack of a single combustion engine in that area at that time of day. This silence was more profound the closer she came to the old highway. For years prior to the Collapse, this stretch of highway was the only place in town one could find a traffic jam. These traffic problems were all due to the design of the confluence of several service roads: four on ramps to the 70/57 Interstates and four main drags that ran perpendicular to the highway. On some days, the highway traffic would gridlock all the way from the Avenue of Mid America down to Temple Street. The locals felt outrage at having to spend ten minutes of their time to drive less than a mile in distance. Year after year, the gridlock problem was addressed at various levels of local, county and state representative meeting. Eventually funds were found for a major reconstruction project spanning the years between 2005 through 2007. Because the reconstruction never included a parallel back road for the Effingham locals to use in order to avoid the interstate clutter, the gridlock remained. Now, after the Collapse, Molly and her children walked leisurely across the former highway without a vehicle in sight. She wondered what all those civil committees would think about the traffic problem now. The thought almost made her smile.

One of the most peculiar things that stood out for Molly on her first day as a Crossroads Enclave citizen was the lack of eye contact with her peers. This peer group consisted of normal citizens like her, not those who wore the ugly brown shirt of the Security Force. In her first ten minutes of full citizenship, she had come into close physical contact with over one hundred citizens and not one had looked her in the eye. It reminded her of the many times in her past when she found herself walking the public streets of a major population center. People in the big cities never made eye contact. From her studies in psychology at graduate school, Molly knew that living in overpopulated areas converted direct eye contact from *normal human communication* into being a *direct threat*. She also knew that people in overpopulated areas had grown accustomed to a certain amount of social anonymity and found eye contact to be invasive.

Molly walked through the streets of her former hometown where, until two months ago, just about everyone you met made eye contact and said a quick hello to total strangers. Two months after the Collapse, not one citizen of her hometown would go so far as to look her in the eyes. Several times on her way from the Service Center to Housing Unit #4, Molly attempted to make verbal recognitions of the strangers that she passed by, but no one would acknowledge her attempts. By the time she reached the entrance to her housing unit, Molly began to wonder if it was just her perception, or if it was really happening.

Maybe its just because I'm the only one carrying a plastic trash bag, which means I'm new to the place? The clinical student inside her had to know.

She led her two children to a parking lot curb in front of the housing unit and told them to sit quietly with her for a while. When her son asked her what she was doing, she asked Aaron and his sister to join her in an experiment.

"Aaron, Jenny," she said with a hand cupped over her eyes to cut out the glare of the September sunshine, "help Mommy for a minute or two. Watch the people as they walk around. See if you notice any of them talking to each other, waving at each other, nodding to each other or saying hello. Tell me if you see anyone doing anything like that, okay?"

After ten minutes and hundreds of possible contacts, not one of the three observers saw any citizens acknowledge each other. The citizens looked at the ground, either straight ahead or in another direction when approaching one another. Contrarily, the members of the Security Force hailed one another with smiles, nods, words and the occasional waving of a hand. This fact was not lost on Aaron.

"Mom," he said from his perch on the parking lot curb next to Molly, "The SFers seem to be the only happy people around here."

> We've lost our young people. Do you know why we've lost our young people? It's because we've replaced the *family unit* with the *social unit*. We've neglected to discipline our children and have called it *building self-esteem*. Now, I'm no Christian, but that whole bit about the man being the head of the household makes more sense as each year of the failed women's lib movement passes. Break apart the one-man to one-woman marriage and what do you get? A vacuum. What gets sucked into a vacuum? Anything that will fit. Violent and anti-social behavior. Lawlessness and arrogance. What I'm talking about is how gangs are formed and prisons are filled. Someday soon, our society will collapse and into the void will rush our young. All it will take is the right person at the right time to parrot the *social unit* clichés and young people will flock in droves to join the most violent, anti-social, lawless and arrogant gang they can find. Think I'm crazy? What was the SS of Germany in the 1930's all about?
>
> Theodore Newgent
> areyoulistening.com May 1999

Molly let out a heavy sigh and dropped her gaze to the folded hands in her lap. It was obvious that she was not pleased with what her son had just said. Since arriving at the Crossroads Enclave, Molly had worked consistently to instill the thought into the minds of her children that the SFers were bad. She had taken every opportunity possible to isolate her children from the prying eyes and straining ears of the Security Force in order to explain why they were not to be trusted. Every time she knew her children had been witness to a specific incident involving the Security Force, Molly would pull them aside and explain the situation from her point of view, always stressing the point that the Security Force was controlling their lives. Now, her ten-year-old son had just commented that the Security Force members seemed to be the only happy people in the entire Crossroads Enclave. This did not make Molly happy, and Aaron could tell by her reaction to his previous observation that he had said something to disappoint his mother.

"I know that the SFers are a bunch of jerks to us," Aaron quickly said in his own defense, "but it's true about them being happy. Look at them Mom."

"I know, Aaron. It's all part of the game they play." Molly reached over and gave her son a tight hug. "Can you promise me something, Aaron?"

"What's that?" Aaron asked his mother, squinting against the sun's glare to look into her face.

"Promise me that you will never volunteer to become a Security Force officer. Can you promise me that?"

"Sure, Mom. I don't want to hurt anybody."

"Good. I love you two. We'll survive this ordeal. When it's all over we can go back home, or find a new home, and not have to deal with these Security Force people."

Molly led her children into the lobby of Housing Unit #4. Once inside, it dawned on Molly that she had been in this building once before. A college friend who was visiting during the summer two years before had stayed in this very building. Two years ago, this building was a motel, now it was a Housing Unit. Molly stood in the entrance area of the lobby, holding the hands of her children and pausing as if smelling a memory. Not much had changed inside the lobby since the Collapse. The cushioned chairs still sat in the corner by the small table, the imitation potted plants still hung from their ceiling hooks and the carpet still had a strip of duct tape stretching across the floor to cover a lifted seam. She could almost smell the perfume of the old woman behind the counter who ran the motel during the day hours. A young man wearing the long-sleeved, brown Security Force shirt leaned over the counter and asked, "Can I help you?"

"Oh, yes," Molly shook her head as if just waking from a dream, "We were assigned a room at this motel—um, Housing Unit."

"Do you have your housing assignment form with you?" the young SFer asked as Molly shuffled her children toward the lobby counter. Molly eyed the name on his front left pocket. LOUER it read. She had known a family with that last name before the Collapse and wondered what relation this young man was to them.

"I've got it right here," she said, shaking one hand free from the grasp of her daughter, dropping the trash bag from the other hand and retrieving the folded piece of paper from the back pocket of her jeans. "It says we're supposed to be in room two-two-eight"

"It sure does," Louer said as he perused the assignment form. "Okay, um, normally we have someone here to give you a walk-around of the Housing Unit, but everyone else is eating lunch. So, let me just give you this list to read." Louer pulled a clipboard from a hook on the wall behind him and laid it on the counter top so Molly could read it. "This is a standard set of rules for all the Housing Units," Louer continued as he pointed to the paper on the clipboard. "The long and short of this list is that anyone who breaks one of these rules can be expelled from the Crossroads Enclave. I'll give you a minute to look it over and then have you sign your assignment sheet."

Molly stared at the list of Housing Unit rules attached to the clipboard before her. She had gotten no further than the first rule on the list before her brain jumped into overdrive in order to keep her mouth from spewing out the anger that welled up inside her. Rule number one stated that at no time will a locking device of any kind be permitted on any door in any room of any Housing Unit. This applied to cabinets, dressers, main entrance doors, bathroom doors and night stands. Molly wanted to protest. This lack of personal security meant that no person or possession was safe from the prying of the Security Force. The inability of locking her living quarters door at night made her skin crawl. Anyone, even other citizens, could enter her living space and…

"Is there a problem?" Louer said as he watched Molly from his side of the desk.

Molly wanted to scream. She wanted to reach across the counter top and slap Louer repeatedly. Instead, she said, through gritting teeth, "I've got a bad headache just now."

"Must be a bad one," Louer shook his head in bewilderment, "shoot, by the way you were grinding your teeth and the way your hands are shaking. Hey, you need to go to a clinic, or something?"

"Um, no," Molly gave her head a shake and wiped the palms of her hands on her pants. She looked down at the upturned and worried faces of her children and suddenly felt like crying. Her emotions crashed over her like a tidal wave, inescapable and powerful. Now, she was wiping tears from her eyes as she attempted to read the list of rules.

Maybe concentrating on the list will get me under control. At first, the words were just that, words. They had no meaning; they were just things to look at. Eventually, and with incredible mental effort, Molly formed the words into meanings, the meanings formed concepts and eventually the emotional tidal wave was returning to the ocean.

The remaining rules on the list were more or less just like those for any public living quarters, mainly concentrating on housekeeping and curfew hours for adults and children. Eventually Molly finished the list of rules and signed her assignment form. Before giving the sheet to Louer, she asked him a question. "What is the Quarantine Compound?"

"It's like a hospital where we send all the folks who have the Influenza." Louer answered, without looking at her face. Louer seemed disturbed by the question. It was as if he had no desire to discuss the topic. Louer placed her assignment sheet in a filing cabinet, directed Molly toward the side door of the lobby and then toward her room.

Molly led Aaron and Jenny outside the lobby and up a flight of stairs to a second story landing. A quick walk down the landing found them entering a door labeled #228. There were two beds inside the main area of the room, the sheets and bedspread folded into neat piles near the foot of each mattress. The carpets in the room were stained with various discolorations, yet had the look of being clean of any debris. Near the entry door were three plastic one-gallon milk bottles with the room number written on two sides. The list of apartment rules stated that each morning someone from the room was to go to the lobby to have the jugs filled with water. This would be their personal ration of water for use while in the room that day: three gallons of water. It didn't seem like much, this three-gallon ration, but Molly and her children would learn soon enough that they would only be in their apartment for eight hours or less each day. The remainder of their day would be spent at their workplace where there was ample water supplied regularly, but at the housing units water was rationed to three gallons per day. The occupants could use the water for drinking, cleaning, personal hygiene, or whatever they wanted: but only three gallons per family, per day. Molly was to discover later that the SFers, who lived in the larger hotel Housing Units, had shower and toilet privileges twice each day.

Aaron quickly explored the bathroom, only to discover that there was no water to the shower, sink or toilet. On the floor next to the toilet was a roll of plastic bags, a roll of duct tape and a roll of toilet paper. "How do we go to the bathroom?" Aaron asked.

"Well, honey," Molly said as she bent down to the floor by the toilet and pulled a plastic bag from the roll. "We place a plastic bag in the toilet, just like this. And then we take a few pieces of tape, like this, and this and this. Then, we tape the bag to the rim of the toilet, like this and this and this. Okay, now we put the seat down. Now, we just keep pooping and peeing into the bag until it gets about half full."

"Then what do we do?" Jenny had her nose scrunched up in disgust.

"Well, the rules sheet says that we take the bag off the toilet and carry it out to the manhole behind the motel, I mean, Housing Unit, and dump it into the hole. I guess it leads to the sewer system and the rains will wash it away."

"I miss our house," Jenny said as she began to cry and bury her head into Molly's chest.

"I know, honey. I know."

Louer directed Molly to drop off her plastic trash bag of personal belongings inside her family room, walk her children to the Youth Facility and then return to the Service Center for her job assignment. The Youth Facility turned out to be a former athletic club tucked away behind the family Housing Units. The athletic club was now a sweatshop of sorts. Currently, the Enclave utilized the Youth Facility as an area for the sorting and folding of fabric products. As Molly stepped inside the main entrance of the Youth Facility, she saw no less than two hundred children involved in various work related activities involving several tons of clothing piled into as many as fifty large piles. The children of the Enclave worked in menial manual labor tasks. As per Council edict, everyone worked if he or she wanted to eat. As she surveyed the flurry of activity around her, it dawned on Molly that she saw no children under the age of five or six. Later, she was to discover that this lack of children under the age of six years was due entirely to the Influenza. Only about one in twenty children under the age of six had survived.

A pair of SFers approached Molly. The SFers added the names of Aaron and Jennifer Niebrugge to a large dry erase board mounted on the wall near the Youth Facility entrance. They then gave Molly a few moments to say good-bye and eventually led the two children toward another adult in the center of the room. This adult began directing the children toward their work assignments. Once the children were out of eyesight, Molly left the building as fast as her shaking legs could move her. Once out the door of the Youth Facility, Molly bent over and vomited into a planter next to the building. As Molly wiped her mouth and face with the sleeve of her blouse, she fought off the feelings of doubt about her choice of bringing her children to the Crossroads Enclave. On one side of the issue were starvation and the constant threat of torture and death by the crazies on the outside. On the other side of the issue was the loss of individuality based upon the brainwashing of those in charge, whose mantra was that everything was *for the common survival*. This is what made Molly sick: choosing between two evils. She wondered whether survival was so important. She contemplated if it would have been better if the deadly Influenza everyone kept telling her about had taken her and her children.

A collection of Security Force guards confronted Molly when she arrived at the back doors of the Service Center. These guards had been lounging on a row of empty pallets along the shaded side of the back wall. She immediately noticed something unusual about this group: all these SFers were carrying guns. The guns made Molly shiver. Since she had left the Indoctrination Center earlier that morning and had traipsed across most of the Enclave, she had not seen one weapon. Now she was eyeing a dozen weapons in one place. One of the guards, a teenager with hair so blonde it was nearly pure white, slung her rifle over her shoulder, walked away from the group of fellow SFers and asked Molly for her work detail form. The name above her left breast pocket said, PRICE. Molly realized that she knew this girl; she had babysat Molly's children several times before the Collapse.

"Wendy?" Molly asked timidly as if to verify her thoughts. The blonde girl in the ugly brown Security Force shirt looked into Molly's face with intense concentration.

"Do we know each other?" Price asked.

"Yes," Molly found herself smiling for the first time all day. "You babysat my two children, Aaron and Jenny, a couple of times last spring."

"Oh yeah," Wendy Price smiled and nodded, "You were off at some kind of college thing or something like that."

"Yes, I was working on my master's degree."

"That seems like a long time ago," Wendy Price spoke pensively, staring through Molly to a spot behind her that no one could see. Security Force guard Price shook her head as if to erase the thoughts in her mind and handed the work detail form back to Molly. "That was a different world. You are to report to your supervisor inside the Service Center, a man named Tom Craven. Go inside these doors, around to the left and continue walking down the back corridor. His office door is labeled with his name. If you get lost, just ask anybody where to find Tom Craven." With that, Price turned her back on Molly and returned to the other SFers in the shade.

That was a different world. The words stunned Molly just as much as the anti-social reaction of the young Wendy Price. In that different world, Wendy would have asked how Aaron and Jenny were, and how things were going. *That was a different world.* Wendy wouldn't want to know how Molly's children were now; for all she knew they could be dead and it would lead to an awkward situation if she asked. As for how things were going, everything had gone south since the Collapse and the best one could hope for was not to starve or be harmed. Forbidden to fraternize with anyone outside of the Security Force, Wendy had already violated her responsibilities by the simple act of acknowledging Molly. All these thoughts circled inside Molly's mind as she walked into the back entrance of the Service Center for the first of many times.

It was reasonable for Wendy to behave this way, she thought, *but I just can't seem to accept it.*

The first time Molly entered the Service Center she was stunned to see the changes made to the overall structure of the floor space since it had been a Wal-Mart store. Gone were the wide aisles with the spit-polished tiled floors. Gone were the produce and frozen food sections with their automatic environmental control systems. Gone were the open areas dotted with racks of clothing. In their place were stacked ugly industrial shelving units that nearly reached the ceilings. Molly wondered where the materials had come from to build these shelving units and where the old displays and shelving had gone. The new shelving aisles were close together and constructed so high as to block the lighting from the fixtures of the old drop ceiling. Molly watched as two citizens pushed a rolling stepladder into place down one aisle. It took them three attempts to move it into position. Once in place, one of the workers climbed to the top landing and yelled to another aisle for help. Within a minute, a fire-bucket chain of humans formed and passed boxes down the rolling ladder to a pushcart stationed below. Molly stood by this organized manual labor brigade until they had the cart loaded. Then she approached one of the workers and asked them where she could locate Tom Craven. The person she had asked, a woman with graying hair and stooped shoulders, didn't look at Molly. Instead, she began walking away and said over her shoulder, "Follow me. It's better if I just show ya."

The woman with the stooped shoulders silently led Molly into the furthest corner of the giant Service Center warehouse through a maze of shelving units. It became apparent to Molly that the woman leading her had been correct in her assertion that it was better to follow her instead of attempting to give directions. It was only a two-minute journey yet, within the first minute, Molly became disoriented. She had no idea in what area of the building she might be. Molly took a chance and asked her guide why the aisles had been set up in such a confusing manner. "Cuts down on theft," was the only answer she received.

The guide led Molly to a hallway with office doors lining one side. The guide's pointed finger then directed Molly into one of the offices. There she met Tom Craven, a thin man with salt-and-pepper hair. He was sitting on a bar stool, bent over a drafting table covered with scattered folders and papers. Much to Molly's relief, Tom Craven did not wear the ugly brown SF shirt. Molly stood just inside the doorway and waited for Tom to acknowledge her presence. After thirty seconds, she cleared her throat and Tom looked up from his desk.

"Yeah?" Tom asked in a blunt manner.

"I'm here on a work assignment," Molly said as she handed Tom her work assignment form.

"Oh," Tom said as he scanned the paper that he took from her. "You must have kids."

"Yes, I do," Molly said hesitantly, as if wanting to ask Tom how he knew such a thing.

"Parents of small kids. They always send me parents," Tom complained. "Well, can you lift fifty pounds?"

"Yes," Molly said.

"Good," Tom reached into a file cabinet, pulled out a hand drawn map and tossed it on the drafter's table. Next, he retrieved a blank sheet of paper, pulled a pencil from a coffee cup on a nearby bookshelf, put the paper on a clipboard and gave all it to Molly. "Take this pencil and paper and copy this map. It's a map of the Enclave with all the places you'll need to know about in order to work as a runner."

"A runner?" Molly asked as she took the clipboard and pencil.

"Yeah, a runner." Tom returned to studying the paper work on his desk. Without looking up, he continued, "You'll be delivering food and supplies to the various kitchens around the Enclave. There's a chair out in the hallway. Make sure you give me back the clipboard and my map. I made that map myself and it's the only one."

For the next twenty minutes, Molly sat in an old folding chair in the hallway of the Service Center office area and copied the strange map that Tom had given her. All of the locations were labeled with numbers and not names or words. When she thought she was finished, she accidentally dropped the map to the floor and discovered a series of handwritten codes and ciphers on the back of the map. Each number had a name next to it. Glancing back at the map she had just drawn, it dawned on her that it might be useless without the codes to go with it. She flipped her map over and copied the codes on the backside. Once that was accomplished, she returned to Tom's office and handed him his map, pencil and clipboard.

"Let me see your map," Tom glared at Molly with squinted eyes and held out his hand. After glancing over her map, Tom flipped it over and viewed the backside. His face softened. "You ever been in the military?"

"No," Molly answered softly.

"Hmmm…good attention to detail, made me wonder. So," Tom looked Molly in the eyes for the first time and asked, "Can you tell me why I assigned the numbers to each building instead of their Enclave names?"

"I suppose it's because numbers are easier to write on paper than names or acronyms. Probably a lot less error with numbers, too."

"Okay," Tom said folding his arms as he continued to stare at Molly. "Good guess. And you're right. Now, can you tell me the significance of each number?"

Molly studied the map for a few agitated seconds. Tom was testing her. Because of her post-graduate education experience, she was accustomed to this type of pressure. Suddenly, it dawned on her what the numbers meant. "These are the old street address numbers."

"Exactly," Tom said without enthusiasm as he reached for a pad of yellow post-it notes and began writing on it. "The work assignment form says that your name is Molly Niebrugge. Okay. Good. I want you here at five A.M. I'm going to make you a runner manager."

"Five A.M.?" Molly asked in astonishment, "What about my…"

"Kids? That's what this note is. Give this post-it to the attendants at the Youth Center. You no longer have to drop your kids off at that rattrap. You'll bring them here. The work's lighter and the food's better. And you'll be closer to them most of the day."

"Well, thank you," Molly stammered. After such an emotionally down day, it was overwhelming for her to see such kindness.

"You'll earn it, I guarantee you," Tom shook off the gratitude as if he didn't like it. "Now, take your map and spend the rest of the day inspecting all the delivery buildings. Put in a wake-up call with the SFer at your Housing Unit and see me here at five a.m."

"They do wake-up calls?"

"In the family units, yes. Now, see if you can find your way out of here without getting too lost." With that, Tom returned his attention to the paperwork on his desk.

For the next two weeks, Tom Craven put Molly Niebrugge through a crash course on how to manage the delivery of food to every kitchen in every eating hall for the entire Enclave. Every morning at 4:30 A.M. the SF night guard at Housing Unit #4 would knock on the door to room #228, then enter with a verbal wake-up call. Every morning, Molly would rouse her children from bed, get them dressed and herd them to breakfast at the Service Center. The typical Enclave breakfast consisted of leftovers from the dinner the night before. The food was edible but was always cold and had that shriveled look to it. Every morning after breakfast, Jenny and Aaron shuffled off to the children's work area of the Service Center to perform manual labor tasks, and Molly would report to Tom Craven's office.

For the first fifteen minutes of their workday, Tom would ask Molly to report on her experiences of the day before and explain to her the solutions to any problems she encountered. It was this first fifteen minutes of interaction that separated Molly from the fifty other runners under Tom's leadership. After that daily one-on-one time, Tom treated Molly just like the other runners. With their morning meeting completed, Molly would leave Tom's office and join the other runners as they milled about just outside the Service Center office hallway, waiting for the morning muster. Tom would come out to the muster area five minutes later carrying a cardboard box filled with clipboards. Roll call by team name came during the morning muster. Each runner belonged to a team of ten people that, for the most part, remained intact day in and day out. Tom tried to keep the teams intact unless there were personal issues that couldn't be resolved between the team members. Each team had a team leader held responsible for the performance of the entire group. To make the roll call as short as possible, Tom called out the team name and the team leader responded for their entire group. After the morning roll call was completed, Tom would pass along any Enclave related news or job related information. Tom would then begin unloading the cardboard box of clipboards by pulling one out of the box, calling out the team name and sending those runners out on their assigned distribution routes. Unlike the other runners, Molly was with a different crew each day.

Each morning, Molly would report to Tom what she had witnessed the day before. Initially, it seemed to her that Tom only wanted to hear her report on current problematic issues. Every time she made a suggestion for a change, Tom would brush off her idea and tell her not to worry about it. This reaction from Tom disappointed Molly, for she wanted to prove to him that she was worth the investment he was making in her. After a week of rejection, however, Molly quit making suggestions and stuck to reporting the problems. Then, Tom began asking her what she thought a solution to each problem might be. Molly was reluctant to answer when he first started this new communication approach, so she spoke cautiously in reply. Tom would listen to her reply and then implement the change. Every time Tom asked what Molly thought would be a good solution to a current work related problem and she answered cautiously, Tom would implement the change immediately. From this exercise, Molly learned how to approach Tom with food distribution changes. Eventually Tom had Molly stand in front of the runners one morning and then announced that Molly was now second in command in the food distribution department.

It created quite a stir when Tom Craven, the food distribution manager of the Crossroads Enclave, announced that Molly Niebrugge, a relative newcomer to the department, was now the runner manager. Several of the team leaders, who considered themselves the best choice for the job, became disgruntled and began to spread rumors that Molly had slept with Tom to get the position. The rumor came back to Molly a week later. One of the runners, who had befriended Molly, told her that several of the runners had propagated the rumor and were plotting some political maneuver to oust Molly from her position. Molly took the situation to Tom at the next morning meeting between the two. Tom asked her what she thought a solution for that problem might be. Molly answered cautiously. Tom gave her permission to act on her solution. That same morning, Molly stood before the runners and openly talked about the rumor. Tom stood three paces behind Molly, silently watching the entire ensemble. She asked for a show of raised hands if anyone believed it to be true. Not one hand raised in response.

"Good," Molly whispered just loud enough for everyone to hear. "Now, let's see a show of hands for anyone who started this rumor or spread the rumor." Molly waited for ten seconds. Molly waited for thirty seconds. She stood before her accusers and, with a neutral facial expression, looked at every person until making full eye contact; this took a full five minutes. In that entire time, no one spoke and no one moved. The silence was deafening. Molly then began writing on her clipboard and handed the clipboard to Tom.

"I'm going to read off a list of names here," Tom announced, as he held up Molly's clipboard. "When your name is read, I want you to walk over to the left, by that stack of two-by-fours over there." Tom began reading a list of twenty names from Molly's clipboard. After he was done and the twenty people stood off to the side, Tom announced that those twenty people would no longer be working in food distribution. Instead, they transferred to a yet undetermined department. A collective gasp sucked through the runner ranks as it became apparent the twenty people cut from the Service Center runner detail were the very people responsible for starting and spreading the rumor. In addition, these same people had collectively planned an act of sabotage against Molly. Tom understood this and considered them rebels to his cause.

Tom Craven then waved to a group of SFers that had congregated near the rear of the muster area. All eyes turned toward the SFers as they formed a semi-circle around the twenty rebels and escorted them out of the Service Center. So smoothly portrayed was this series of events that it left the remaining runners under the impression that Tom and Molly had been planning it days in advance. A new form of respect for the food delivery head and his assistant developed among the workers in the

Service Center. The coup had a negative effect, though, in that it created another problem: a shortage of runners. This meant that Molly had to return to the ranks of a runner until replacements filtered in from the Enclave population. Because of this new set of circumstances Molly would make the acquaintance of two individuals. The lives of whom she would help redirect from a perceived slavery to a certain death.

Two weeks after dismantling the attempted coup, Molly was carrying a load of flour into the kitchen entry of Housing Unit #6 when she heard a loud crashing noise from within. She carefully put the bag of flour on the floor and proceeded to where she thought the noise had come from. Entering the same storage room that she had been stocking with flour, Molly found two men in the process of helping a third person trapped under a collapsed shelving unit and about two hundred pounds of foodstuffs. At first, it was difficult to discern the identity of the trapped person for he or she was completely covered with baking soda. The trapped person was screaming in loud bursts of curse words for the two men to get the fallen shelving unit off his or her legs. The two men, also covered in baking soda from head-to-toe, were experiencing difficulty in releasing the victim from the trap because of the weight of the debris involved. Molly came up behind the two men and suggested they push the shelving unit framing up while she dragged the victim out by the arms. The victim was freed within seconds but a new problem had developed. One of the men had his shirt collar caught on the jagged metal of the shelving unit. Molly saw that the man's strength was wavering so she jumped to his aid and began tearing his shirt free of the metal snag. In the process of freeing the man, Molly slipped on the baking soda-covered floor and cut the palm of her left hand on the metal snag. With blood pouring from one hand, Molly stepped back two paces and coached the two men to drop the entire framework on the count of three. The men did as instructed and the remainder of the shelving unit came crashing to the cement floor, filling the room with a haze of baking soda.

The four people involved made a hasty retreat to the kitchen, amidst fits of coughing and spitting. Oddly enough, the person originally trapped under the collapsed shelving walked away without a scratch. A few people entered the hallway from the kitchen and began asking questions about what had happened. The woman that had the shelving unit collapse on her explained that she had climbed upon the shelves to retrieve something from the top tier, when the whole thing gave way on top of her. Some more people from the kitchen made their way to the hallway, one of them a supervisor, and demanded an explanation. Molly decided that she had no need to be involved in the discussion and began to leave the building. The man whom Molly had freed from the metal snag stepped in front of Molly and said, "Man alive, Ma'am, you cut your hand!"

"Yeah," Molly winced, as she attempted unsuccessfully to stop the bleeding with her good hand. The man took a rag from his back pocket, shook the baking soda out of it and gave it to Molly. After she folded the rag onto her wound, Molly looked from her hand to the man and asked, "Do I know you? Have we met before?"

"Well, shoot yeah," the man exclaimed, "Don't you remember me, Molly? We worked together at the first place."

"The first place?" Molly asked, not understanding what the man meant.

"Yeah, the first place they had us at. Where they made us learn all about this Crossroads place. You and I dug holes in the dirt."

"Dale?" Molly asked.

"Yeah," Dale replied with a nod.

"I didn't recognize you all covered in powder like you are." She remembered Dale from the Indoctrination Center. He was slow, mentally, but a good worker and loyal to those who treated him with any amount of respect. An idea crossed Molly's mind. She whispered to Dale to follow her and she led him out of the kitchen area away from the crowd of kitchen workers descending upon the scene of the accident. Once they were out of earshot of the other workers, Molly asked Dale, "Where do they have you working right now?"

"Here in this kitchen. I'm a mixer."

"A mixer?" Molly asked, once again lost on Dale's meaning.

"Yeah, the cooks put stuff in the big pots and I mix it up with a big stick."

Molly nodded and then asked, "How would you like to come to work for me over at the Service Center?"

"Sure," Dale said directly and turned to leave.

"Uh, Dale, wait a minute. Help me move the rest of these bags of flour into the hallway. Then, I think I need to get some medical help with this hand."

"Sure," Dale said as he stopped and turned back to Molly. "That would be good." Dale stood ten feet from Molly, limbs akimbo, his entire body transmitting every physical nuance that he had no idea what his next action should be.

"Okay, look," she said as she approached Dale, took him by an elbow and led him to a pair of shopping carts on the pavement near the kitchen door. "See these bags of flour in these carts?"

Dale nodded.

"Okay, put these in the hallway just outside the storeroom, you know, the room with the broken shelf?"

Dale nodded.

"Once all the bags of flour are in the hallway, return these two shopping carts to the Service Center in the back. Tell them that Molly sent you. Wait for me at the back doors of the Service Center. You got that?"

"Put the flour in the hallway. Put the carts at the back of the Service Center. And, um..."

"Wait for me there."

"Wait for you there."

"Good, Dale, I'll see you in about an hour," Molly spoke over her shoulder as she walked away.

Serendipity has its own schedule, as evidenced in the moments that followed Molly's departure from Dale. Her immediate concern was to seek treatment for the jagged cut on her left hand. At the Enclave Indoctrination, the SF Officers explained that there was a first aid station located on the west side of the Enclave, somewhere close to where she currently was. Molly tried to recall the exact location. The throbbing from her left hand hindered her memory. Something in her brain told her that the first-aide station was inside one of two former fast food restaurants near the southwest Enclave entrance, but she wasn't sure which one it was. Had she chosen the farthest building, she would have walked right into the first aid station. Serendipity, as well as the painful throbbing of her hand, made Molly choose the nearer of the two possibilities and, as a circumstantial byproduct, a chance meeting with a woman named Stephenie.

CHAPTER SIX

The Crossroads Enclave:
The Indoctrination

"My name is Molly Niebrugge," the woman spoke just as she had been ordered to, "and this is my son Aaron and my daughter Jenny."

"Good," a man replied curtly. He sat in the brown lounge chair near the apartment door. He was young, approximately twenty years old, and wore a stiff brown shirt with the letters SF stenciled above the right pocket and the name KREKE stenciled in large block-style letters above the left pocket. "Everyone say hello to Molly."

A few scattered "Hello, Molly's" echoed through the small apartment living room. The young man squinted and looked at every occupant in the room, obviously disappointed in their responses. He peered down to a piece of paper attached to a clipboard that lay on his lap. The room remained silent as he made a check mark on the paper. Holding his disappointed facial expression, he scanned the room and spoke, "I understand, it's early in the morning and you all are hungry. But I expect better responses from this point on. Understand? I don't want to go starting rumors, but the delivery of your breakfast might depend on your responses."

"What?" one of the men in the room said, in disbelief.

"Okay, look," Kreke said as he stood abruptly from his chair and made his way to the apartment door, "I'm going next door to grab a cup of coffee. When I get back, I hope your attitudes have changed." Before anyone could respond, Kreke left the apartment and shut the door behind him.

The occupants in the room remained silent, but their body languages spoke volumes of anger, fear, frustration and weariness. Molly, who had remained standing in the center of the living room with her two children as previously ordered, slowly lowered herself to a seated position on the floor. Her children followed suit and found comfortable positions on her lap. Molly's actions gave everyone else the opportunity to concentrate on something other than the confusion racing through their minds. Eventually, all eyes turned to a man that stood silently near the apartment door. He, like Kreke, was young and wore a stiff brown shirt with the SF stencil above the right pocket. Unlike Kreke, this young man held a machine gun in his hand and had the name PROBST stenciled above his left shirt pocket. Probst shifted his gun from two hands to one hand and used the free hand to push the lace curtain on the living room window slowly aside. He made a show of peering out the crack in the curtain and then turned to face his prisoners.

"Folks," he said in a desperate voice just above a whisper, "look, some of you folks are locals, right?"

A few people in the room nodded their heads.

"Well then, you probably knew at least someone from my family, and you know we're good people. Right?"

More of the prisoners nodded their heads.

"Well, look," Probst said after briefly peering through the curtain again, "you gotta believe me when I say that this is no game. There's some bad karma going on outside the Crossroads Enclave, right? We're trying to provide a safe place here, keep the bad guys out, you know? So do what you think you gotta do, but I tell you, play the game. Do what you're told to do and you'll get along fine. I had to go through the same stupid crap you're all about to go through. It's better on the other side. Believe me. Just play the game, okay?"

Molly closed her eyes and tried not to scream. She knew exactly what was happening in that apartment living room. She also knew what was going to happen next. She had been studying psychology as a postgraduate student just prior to the lights going out, or what the Enclave referred to as *The Collapse*. It came as no surprise to Molly to hear the others in the room speak up just after Probst finished his speech.

"But we're being treated as criminals," a woman of fifty spoke first.

"Aren't we all Americans?" another demanded.

"Man," said a woman who possibly weighed more than the couch she sat upon, "this is almost like boot camp in the Marines."

Molly still had her eyes closed as she sat on the floor and hugged her children a little tighter. *Next*, she thought, *we'll hear the sympathetic confirmation followed by the threat of death.*

"Well," the young Probst began speaking with a solemn look on his face, "I don't know what Marine boot camp is like, and yes, we are Americans, and true, it may feel like you are being treated as a criminal." Probst was a good actor. He took a deep breath, slowly exhaled through pressed lips and shook his head as if in deep thought. "Don't I know how *that* feels." He took a moment more of silence before raising his eyes to his captives and continuing in an encouraging tone of voice. "But we *have* to put folks through this indoctrination. It's for the good of everybody. I've seen what happens when we don't indoctrinate. And for God's sake, don't make Kreke angry. He's a dangerous man, I mean, I once saw him grab this guy and…" Probst paused, closed his eyes, shook his head and then continued. "…forget it. Just do as he says. Play the game, get your food and things will be better."

Perfect, Molly thought, *he's had practice with this role. What did the police call it? The "Good Cop, Bad Cop Routine". I bet he and Kreke flipped a coin to see who got to carry the clipboard.*

As if by the fate of perfect timing, Kreke entered the apartment and slowly walked toward his lounge chair. He had a cup of steaming coffee in one hand and a piece of buttered bread balanced upon his clipboard in the other hand. Kreke made certain his motions were timed so that every person in the room had to either see or smell the food he brought in with him. To Molly, it seemed as though even the motions Kreke made when he sat in his lounge chair were choreographed. He took a bite from the buttered bread, placed the remains on the arm of his lounge chair and then used his empty hand to brush the crumbs from the surface of his clipboard.

"Okay," Kreke began in the same blunt manner he had originally started with five minutes before. "Molly, um, Niebrugge, will you stand up again?"

Molly stood and urged her children to stand with her. A war raged and her mind was the battleground. She wanted to protest. She wanted to deny the petty monsters in the SF shirts their brainwashing victory. She wanted to tell everyone in the room that they were about to become slaves to a life of fear and would eventually participate in heinous acts against their own friends.

"Good," Kreke said once more as if reciting rehearsed lines in an amateur drama, "Now, everybody say hello to Molly." This time everyone welcomed Molly Niebrugge with voices full of fear. Kreke took a noisy sip from his coffee, smacked his lips and went back into his routine. "Good. Now, Molly, tell us why you are here."

Molly began to perspire. She looked down at her children who were clinging to her side, silently looking at the piece of bread on the arm of Kreke's big brown chair. She decided to play the game and play it well, for now. Her children were hungry and she was too weary to fight.

"Well, we were making it okay just after the lights went out. At first, it was just my husband Mike, our two kids and me out at our farm just north of Effingham. After a few days, we had friends come in and stay with us because we had a good rabbit farm and we could feed about ten people. Then, the hunters came. They tied Mike up and..." Molly began to tremble at the memory. She hated what the hunters had done to her husband and their friends. She hated what the men had done to her. Most of all, she hated that she was expressing her personal feelings in the presence of the young beasts with the SF labels on their chests. Her story would not have been in the spotlight of this SF charade, had she not told it to an SF interrogator the day before. She wished she could take that moment back. Now they were forcing her to use her tragedy for their own benefit. The room was silent. For many in the room this was the first time they would hear about the "hunters," and their imaginations were running wild with fearful possibilities of what these horrible people had done. Kreke gave Molly a moment to compose herself before he interrupted the silence. "What do you mean by 'the hunters,' Molly?"

"Men that show up with dogs. They always have dogs and the dogs are well fed."

"Well fed on what?" Kreke asked the question that everyone else had on their minds.

"Humans. The hunters feed the dogs the remains of the people they kill," Molly could no longer contain her anguish. Instead of crying, which was what her soul was begging for, she hugged her children, her shoulders slumped and Molly said, "It's a horrible thing to watch."

"Probst!" Kreke barked, as he turned his head to look at his fellow Security Force comrade, "How long have you been with the Crossroads Enclave?"

"Um, about a month," the young Probst stammered perfectly, as if he, too, was afraid of Kreke.

"In all that time have you ever heard of any human in the Enclave being hunted or of any human being fed to the dogs?"

"No," Probst replied in a more confident manner.

"Good," Kreke then turned his gaze back to Molly. "Molly, you can sit down now." Molly returned to the floor, with her two children following her lead. "Is there anyone in this room, beside Molly, that has lost a family member in the last three months? If so, could you please stand up?" Every person in the living room of that apartment stood, with the exception of Molly. Kreke peered intently at every person before continuing. "I see. Everyone has lost someone. This is a tragedy. If this person you lost would still be alive had they been given proper medical attention, I want you to sit down." One person sat down, the rest remained standing. "Would this person still be alive if they had proper nutrition and clean drinking water?" Kreke leaned forward a little. One more person sat down. "Would this person be alive if they had the protection of a security group?" Kreke leaned forward from his lounge chair far enough to be no longer seated in it. The remainder of the apartment occupants sat down. "This is very unfortunate. Since the Collapse, the Crossroads Enclave has had medicine, medical professionals, proper nutrition, clean drinking water and a trained group of security officers."

Kreke pushed his body back into his lounge chair, made a few scribbling motions on his clipboard and then closed his eyes with a sigh. Without opening his eyes, Kreke took a sip of his coffee and asked, "Does anyone in this room want to leave this Enclave?" No one moved a muscle. Kreke opened his eyes and continued. "If you want to leave the Crossroads Enclave today, right now, just stand up and walk out the door to the landing. I'll have a couple of my Security Force guards escort you to the barricade of your choice, and you can leave."

"You can't do that!" Probst nearly yelled at Kreke, as he took a step toward him.

"Why not?" Kreke demanded as he turned to Probst.

"It's against Council policy, that's why not. They'll have your butt in a sling for it," Probst had lowered his voice to a near whisper and seemed frightened by the very idea Kreke was expressing.

"I know that," Kreke barked back in a whisper of his own. "But, what's the point of forcing people to stay in a safe place if they don't want to?"

"I, uh, you, uh…" Probst was doing an excellent performance of acting confused. Molly closed her eyes again and held tightly to her children. She knew that no one would take Kreke's offer to leave and no one did. The performance of these two young men was nearly impeccable.

Beginning on the day the razor wire enclosure went up around the perimeter of the Indoctrination Center, this is how the Security Force officers introduced every new arrival to the Crossroads Enclave. At the very moment Kreke and Probst were performing their propaganda magic in one room, twenty other Security Force magicians in ten other rooms within the Indoctrination Center were playing out another ten performances. The script for each performance was identical, having been written by members of the Council and memorized by the eager young SF Indoctrination volunteers. Day after day, more people arrived at the Enclave, and, day after day, each person afforded that one and only opportunity to leave. Day after day, no one took the offer to leave. What brought them to the Enclave varied with each individual? For some it was medical needs. For others it was a lack of food. For a growing number it was for the security that the Enclave offered. The small towns and farm countries surrounding the Enclave had become a breeding ground for feudal lords and clan-like nomadic groups seemingly bent on violence and destruction. This fear of the outside world led the pilgrims to the Enclave; the fear of the armed Security Forces kept them inside.

As each new arrival came to one of the five Enclave entrances, called *checkpoints*, each faced separation into one of two groups: the *sick* and the *well*. As soon as possible, the *sick* were transported to the Quarantine Compound. The *well* remained at the checkpoint until it turned dark outside, when armed SF guards escorted them to a detention hooch just inside the razor wire perimeter of the Indoctrination Center. The detention hooch was nothing more than a pre-existing series of steel carports draped in black plastic tarps, located in the former apartment complex parking lot. Once in the detention hooch, the arrivals ate a small portion of cold soup from a giant pot. An SF staffer, who would record such information as the arrival's name, age, date of birth, would interview each new arrival and a list of anyone they knew had died since the Collapse. All personal effects would be taken from the new arrivals and placed into tagged plastic bags. These bags would be stored in a nearby shed for, in the scripted words of the SFer in charge at the time, *"their safe return to you at a later date"*. Then, all arrivals were methodically searched for hidden weapons. Any protests were silenced with the explanation that *"It's for your safety and the safety of all the children,"* followed by the threat of immediate expulsion from the Enclave if compliance wasn't instantaneous. When this threat came from a young man or woman with a stiff brown SF shirt and a weapon on his or her person, it was 99.9% effective in quelling further debate by the new arrival.

The SF staff would then escort the new arrivals in groups of ten to the apartment unit assigned to them. The SF escort assigned a bed to each new arrival and told them to get some sleep. The SF escort would inform the arrivals that they would be just outside the apartment door all night and expected not to be disturbed, unless it was a life or death situation. In a military fashion, the SF escort would remain awake all night outside the apartment door, weapon in hand, until relieved by the assigned propaganda magicians in the morning. The people inside that apartment were now members of a *cell group* and would remain in the cell group until released from the Indoctrination Center. That is, if they lived through it, which most did.

The new arrivals were offered the one and only false chance to leave the Enclave that first morning, then they were fed, given an opportunity for a two-minute gender-sensitive shower in a community shower stall and were then led back to their apartment room. One of the SF staffers would then give a two-hour history lecture on how the Crossroads Enclave came into being. As Molly sat through the history lecture, she pondered how much of what she heard was truth and how much was propaganda. It became obvious to her that three distinct classes of people lived inside the Enclave: the Council as the ruling class, the Security Force as the enforcers of the Council's wishes and the remaining people as Citizens. She knew from her studies at the university that the greater control a ruling class had, the more they rewrote the history of their deeds. Atrocities would be glossed over to become *victories* and *justifiable actions* or would be erased from memory altogether. The citizens would learn and repeat the key words and tricky phrases often enough to replace logic and sound reasoning. The ruling class would solve only a fraction of the problems caused by the initial crisis, proclaiming loudly of their accomplishments in the name of the citizens, all the while creating position security for themselves. The ruling class would neatly squelch any faction within the citizen class that presented a simple solution to any of the remaining social, political or physical problems. In the typical Politically Correct fascist vein, the word *squelched* was synonymous with the word *eliminated*. It was imperative for the ruling class to maintain the status quo for the citizens, and that this status quo always included some form of struggle for the citizens to face. It was more advantageous for the ruling class if this struggle emanated from a source external to their jurisdiction. The way in which the Council used the Influenza to their advantage was a perfect example of this source-manipulation.

From the first signs of an epidemic, the Council spread the word that the Influenza was *"Brought into the Enclave with the recent wave of immigrants from outside our borders."* The reality was that the Influenza took its roots from within the Enclave. Before the razor wire borders were intact around the entire Enclave, it was possible for immigrants to leave on a regular basis. Thousands came, saw the militant conditions inside and then left. With this initial outflow of people, the Influenza spread outward from the Enclave as people departed for other destinations. The Influenza had its source in the initial over-crowding at the Crossroads Enclave, yet, the Council was the first and only voice allowed to speak on the subject. With just the right amount of politically correct spin, it became common sense among the Enclave citizens, even to those dying, that the Influenza was an *invader* from outside their commune. The Influenza was an enemy from the outside, the scapegoat. It was a near perfect distraction to keep the citizen's minds off their current oppression. The Influenza was a reason to justify the use of extreme authoritarian behavior on the part of the Council and their lackeys, the Security Force.

Molly Niebrugge was willing to tolerate this militant treatment from the authorities in the Crossroad Enclave because she believed it was the only viable method of survival for her children. Drawing from her education, Molly knew that things would get worse for her as an occupant of the Enclave before they got better. As each day went by, she was astounded at how correct she had been in her assessment of the future. The Indoctrination phase for the immigrants didn't end with the propaganda magicians or the two-hour history lesson. There were lists of lectures. There were lectures on Enclave behavior, rules, regulations, and punishments. There were lectures on Enclave citizen responsibilities and general personal hygiene. There were lectures on rank recognition among the Security Force personnel and lectures on how to join this *elite* force after indoctrination. The SFers of Molly's cell group conducted every lecture in the living room of the same apartment where Molly, her children, and the remainder of her cell group slept. The lecturers alternated between various members of the Security Force, but the attendees were always the same ten people who lived together. Even the children were required to sit quietly and attentively through these lectures. Each day for the first week at the Crossroads Enclave, the immigrants could expect to attend eight hours of lectures segmented into two-hour slots of time.

Between the lectures, the cell groups ate quick meals together and attended work details. The tasks performed by the immigrants during these work details always took place within the confines of the Indoctrination Center and were manual labor intensive. The work detail format was a classic model of authoritarian control. The SFers separated the members of all cell groups into three work detail groups: Children, women and men. This one act, the act of isolating a parent from a child, a husband from his wife and men from women, was one of the most important functions performed by the SF guards at the Compound. The work detail was a method of *forced separation*. Forced separation was an exceedingly important tool for the Council, to instill into the inductee's minds that its authority was all-powerful. The Council wanted each citizen to know that its authority was stronger than the authority of a parent over their own child, stronger than the bonds of marriage and that they had the ability to prevent opposite sex interaction. During these work details, Molly found herself separated from her children for the first time since the Collapse.

For the first several work details, she spent most of her time worrying about her children's welfare in her absence. Unfortunately, each time they were reunited after the work detail, her children filled her ears with happy, excited stories. They told her of how the SF guards had taken them to a large tent in the corner of the Compound where they met with children from the other cell groups. They informed their mother that the SFers gave all the children a variety of tasks to perform for the first half of the work detail and the opportunity to play during the second half. Their tasks were always simple and often fun. Playtime consisted of organized activities ranging from art projects to games of physical skill. A group of strict but happy SF guards supervised every moment. Molly's children looked forward to their work details. This didn't lessen Molly's concern for her children's welfare at all. She understood, with frightening clarity, what the Security Force was doing. They were systematically teaching her children to trust the authority of the Security Force and the Council above the authority of their mother. At least this is what Molly thought. The reality of her circumstances could be altogether different, and she hoped it would be.

The work detail for the adults in the Indoctrination Center was a much different experience than it was for the children. Separated by gender, the adults performed exhausting tasks of manual labor. They dug latrine pits, they moved latrines and they buried the old latrine pits. They dug trenches and fence postholes. They hauled dirt, gravel and sand from one area to another. They carried large quantities of materials in their hands and on their backs and shoulders. Hands blistered, backs ached and exhaustion reigned among the adult new arrivals in the Indoctrination Center. A group of strict and unhappy SF guards supervised every moment. The one thing the SFers on guard for the work details seemed to despise the most was the "slacker". Officially, a slacker was any member of a cell group that didn't perform the bare minimum work load during a work detail. Unofficially, a slacker was anyone that the SF guards had a grudge against or just plain didn't like. It was common for the Security Force guards to remove work detail slackers from a cell group. These slackers had a tendency to disappear. An effective brainwashing tool, the adults looked forward to the lectures as much as the children looked forward to their work details.

Each immigrant lived for three week at the Indoctrination Center. For three weeks, they attended lectures and work details. For that entire time, they wore the same set of clothes. Every three days, when allowed a three-minute shower, the immigrants washed their clothes while they wore them. For three weeks, the immigrants ate minimum food rations and allowed no more than five hours of sleep each night. Every day at least one SFer told the immigrants that life was better in the Enclave than it was in the Indoctrination Center. As per indoctrination schedule, one night during that three-week indoctrination, each cell group woke up at two in the morning and mustered at a parking lot area. Then they marched to a place near the exit gate of the Indoctrination Center and told to look across Ford Avenue to the Wal-Mart parking lot. They saw lights, electric lights lit at the gas station and people filling vehicles with gasoline from the pumps. This forced viewing was supposed to support the idea that life in the Enclave functioned at a level of comfort above what they were now experiencing inside the Indoctrination Center.

For three weeks, the immigrants stole glances over the razor wire fence on the south side of the Compound toward the Crossroads Enclave and wondered if it was true. Rarely would anyone from the Enclave, other than the SF guards, venture near the Indoctrination Center. This gave the immigrants the impression that Security Force members in stiff brown shirts populated the entire Enclave. The immigrant, once reassigned to the Enclave when the three weeks were up, would discover that just the opposite was true.

The day came when The Security Force guard released Molly and her children from the Indoctrination Center and assigned them a new life in the Enclave. A smiling SF guard returned Molly's personal effects to her, minus *"A few minor items"* that, the guard informed her, "Were more important for the Enclave to have than you." These minor items included anything made of metal, sewn material, printed material, edible matter or anything that could conceivably be used as a weapon. That left Molly with a torn picture of her husband Mike. Molly felt like crying but couldn't get a single tear to fall.

CHAPTER SEVEN

The Crossroads Enclave: The Influenza

After making an incredible effort to sit up and look out her bedroom window, Tammy Doty felt as if she was going to die. Every muscle and joint in her body ached, especially her neck. It hurt Tammy to turn her head in any direction. No position was entirely comfortable. Sitting was painful. Standing was worse than sitting. Lying down on a bed was the least painful position, but the relief was marginal at best. Sleep arrived in short spurts and, when it did, it came with nightmares and pain. The symptoms of her ailment had begun three days before. It started as a few simple blisters on her neck, chest and upper back. The next day muscle chills, stuffed sinuses and an irritating cough accompanied the blisters. The day after that she had a full fever, bronchitis and a motion-sensitive headache. On this day, as Tammy peered through her bedroom window to a world of gloom and rain outside, the extreme thought crossed her mind that it might be better if she *did* die.

Such a thought, under normal conditions, would have filled Tammy with an inner revulsion strong enough to make her body shudder. However, these were not normal times. She was sick, and she didn't have a clue where her husband was. *Jim,* she thought, *where are you? I need your help. I can't do this alone.* Her thoughts, interrupted by a spasm of coughs that gave her a blinding headache, knocked her to the floor. Just as the coughing fit ended and her eyesight returned, Tammy heard a voice calling out from the other side of her bedroom door.

Danny, I forgot about Danny.

Crawling across the carpeted bedroom floor, Tammy reached for the doorknob and struggled to turn it. No matter how much concentration she poured into the act of turning the knob of her bedroom door, it wouldn't rotate. She had to let go of the knob several times and wait a few moments before trying it again. Her arm kept aching with exhausted. A thought crossed her mind and she called out to the door, "Danny, let go of the doorknob, honey." Immediately, she heard a thump on the other side of the door. This time she reached for the doorknob and turned it without difficulty. Pulling the door toward her, Tammy peered around it to see the motionless body of her five-year-old son leaning in an awkward position against the hallway wall.

"Danny, baby," Tammy whispered as she crawled toward the child, "talk to me, baby." Danny responded with a hoarse series of coughs that brought tears to his eyes as his now frightened mother pulled him close to her. He felt cold to the touch. *He was hot yesterday, or was that the day before?*

How long Tammy sat in the hallway holding her son was a mystery to her. Since she had come down with the flu, time had lost its meaning. Danny's coughing spasm ended, and his body went limp in her arms.

Still breathing, good. Wish I knew what to do now. I don't feel like doing anything…except dying…why doesn't that bother me?

She might have sat in the hallway holding her son and thinking dark thoughts for most of the day, had it not been for a knock at the front door. The noise of the knocking was loud, and it echoed through the living room and down the hall.

Maybe it's Jim?

Tammy laid her son as gently as she could on the hallway floor before crawling on her hands and knees through the living room toward the front door. The effort it took to travel that distance had exhausted Tammy. The pain in her body was severe enough to cause her to black out. She slumped to the floor a mere four feet from her objective.

Moments later Tammy recovered from the blackout, but couldn't remember why she was lying on the floor of her living room. Once again, there was a knocking at the front door. This time, Tammy was closer to the source of the knocking and it gave her a blinding headache. She cried out in agony, holding her ears and pressing her forehead against the carpeted floor. The front door opened a crack, and the frightened face of a man popped through the crack to stare at the moaning body of a woman lying prone on the floor inside.

"Missuss Doty?" The man asked in an uncertain voice. "Is that you on the floor?" Tammy Doty drew her body into a sitting position to face the voice. She couldn't see, even though her eyes were open. The noise from the man pounding on the door had caused her such pain that her eyesight went gray with imperceptibility.

"Yeah, it's me." She said toward the general direction of where she thought the man's voice came from. Slowly, her eyesight began to return and she cocked her head, hoping it would help her get a clearer view. This motion caused her neck to spasm pain and her body to shudder as Tammy drew in a quick deep breath.

"Are you all right, Missuss Doty?" The man asked in a voice that changed from uncertain to frightened. Yet, he remained at the door. His childhood training had taught him that it was *good* behavior to help those in need, but that same training had also taught him that it was *not good* to enter a person's house without permission. It was obvious that he knew Tammy Doty and that she needed help. Nevertheless, she had yet to invite him in. Therefore, the man remained at the door in a state of indecision so severe that he felt like crying.

Finally, Tammy Doty recovered from her pain enough to ask, "Is that you Jim?"

This question seemed to frighten the man at the door even further. He withdrew his head from the doorway and walked in nervous circles on the front porch of the Doty house.

"What do I do? What do I do?" he repeated to himself as his pacing sped up and his gesticulations became erratic. What was worse was that it was cold outside that day. The wind was kicking up quite a storm as it blew the rain at a 45-degree angle. The man was cold and wet and wanted nothing more than to get inside the house. Yet, Tammy hadn't invited him in, so he remained outside.

"Is that you, Jim?" Tammy's voice croaked from inside the house. "Jim, help me. The kids are sick, I'm sick…"

"Can I come inside your house, Missus Doty?" The man on the front porch called through the front doorway; the wind had blown the door open and rain threatened to enter the house.

"Please, come in and help me," Tammy managed to say in a voice just louder than the wind. It took all the energy she could gather to do so, and the price she paid was a coughing fit that racked her body long after the man on the front porch had entered her house and shut the door against the wind and rain. The man stood patiently next to Tammy, who had coiled her body into a fetal position and was lying on her right side with her back to him.

"You got the flu, Missus Doty," the man said, as he stood helplessly two paces away from the woman on the floor. "Mom and Pop got it too. I had to take them to town to get help. Man alive, you gotta get to town, Missus Doty. They got medicine there."

Tammy Doty lay on her side, motionless except for the occasional full-body shivering that accompanied the war ravaging her body. Her eyes were clamped shut in obvious pain. Her breathing was raspy and erratic. When the man repositioned himself before her, she opened her eyes and was able to see who he was. "Dale?" She said in almost a whisper, "Are you hungry? I've got some food down in the basement."

Now Dale was more confused than before. It was impolite to refuse hospitality. Yet, simultaneously, he knew Tammy needed medical help. What he didn't understand was that Tammy was wavering in and out of conscious thought. The Influenza had begun to affect her thinking. Dale's mind twisted into knots. This twisting would have gotten the better of him, had it not been for a coughing sound down the hallway.

"Hello?" Dale stood as he called out. "Who's there?"

No answer came, other than the persistent coughing noise. Dale walked down the hallway to discover a little boy lying on the floor. The boy was shivering but not coughing. The coughing noise was coming from one of the bedrooms off the hallway. Dale entered the bedroom to see a baby in a crib. Dale knew a lot about babies; he had helped raise a few in his own household as a teenager. He reached down for the baby; obviously, a girl based upon the color of its pajamas, and held her to his chest. She was drenched with perspiration. What little hair she had on her head matted flat in a pattern of disarray. The baby girl smelled as if she needed a diaper change. Dale laid her down in the crib and returned to the living room.

"The baby's diaper needs changed," he said in the typical Midwestern way, as he bent down with his face toward Tammy's face. "It's okay if I change it?"

"Yeah, sure…" Tammy had her eyes shut this time and seemed to be half-asleep.

Dale returned to the baby's bedroom and proceeded to survey the room for the proper items to complete his task. Disposable diapers had ceased to be available months before this day. The Collapse had forced the survivors of newborn children to get resourceful. The Doty baby was wearing the remnants of what might have been a gray sweatshirt, held in place by pieces of duct tape. Dale located a pile of clean diapers near the crib and a few pieces of pre-cut duct tape stuck to the edge of a nearby chest of drawers. He also discovered a pitcher of water with a stack of rags next to it and knew this was for cleaning the child before applying the new diaper. The entire diaper changing operation that Tammy had developed for her own use made complete sense to Dale, so once all the components were in place, he set about removing the old diaper. What he saw when he pulled the old diaper off sent shock waves up and down his spine. Dale had changed hundreds of diapers in his life, but had never seen anything like this before. He put a new diaper on the baby girl, who continued to cough and cry throughout the entire event. He carried the dirty diaper out to the living room to show Tammy. No matter what Dale said or how close he placed the soiled diaper to her face, she refused to awake from her slumber. Dale stood upright, swore loudly and then threw the diaper out the front door.

> Damn that Influenza. You never knew whom it was going to take. A family of six is infected. Five of them get sick, five die.

No rhyme no, reason. It always started the same with those nasty little blisters on your neck. This didn't look like any simple case of acne, either. Then you had about five days. It took five days to live through the Influenza or die from it. That judgment was made about the fourth day. If your digestive system started passing black stool, it was over for you. I lost both my sons to that…

Theodore Newgent
An excerpt from his personal journal, May, 2010

The baby in the room down the hallway was severely sick and Dale understood this. He also understood that the baby's mother was in no condition to take care of her own child. Therefore, Dale determined that he was now responsible for the care of the baby girl. *But, what do I do?* The town and the medicine for the flu were over ten miles away. Dale knew from recent experiences that there was no way to get the medicine to the baby. Instead, he'd have to get the baby to the medicine.

"Think, dummy," Dale muttered to himself. He began to pace back and forth between the open front door and the body of Tammy Doty curled up on the living room floor. "They can't walk. They can't walk. You can't carry 'em. Think." Dale began to pound his right thigh with a clenched fist as he continued to pace. The front door blew open, and the wind pushed raindrops into the house. The baby in the bedroom down the hall began to cough again. Dale could take no more. He ran through the front door and across the yard of the Doty residence. He had no plan except to get away from the house. Before he reached the driveway, Dale slipped on a slick patch of mud and fell forward onto the rain-soaked grass. Cursing, Dale began to raise himself up from the ground when he noticed the side door of the Doty garage ajar. An obscure thought crossed his mind and he spoke it aloud, "Better shut that garage door, or Daddy's gonna be angry."

Driven by a fear that only he could understand, Dale carefully walked to the side door of the garage and attempted to shut it. There was something in the path of the door that prevented it from fully closing.

Dale opened the door to see that a motorcycle had fallen over and its handlebars caught in the hinge of the door. Climbing over the fallen motorcycle and into the garage, Dale found himself enveloped in darkness. In order to get the motorcycle erect, he would have to open the main garage door to allow enough light in to see. Dale felt his way to the main garage door and attempted to lift it. It wouldn't budge.

"Must be electric," he said, "gotta find the button." Hand over hand, Dale felt his way around the inside perimeter of the garage until he found the push button for the electric garage door opener. After pressing it multiple times with no results, it dawned on Dale for at least the hundredth time since the lights went out that there was no electricity.

"Dummy, the rope-thing needs pulled," he thought aloud, "just like at home, gotta find the rope thing and pull it down." This meant he'd have to find his way toward the center of the garage. Slowly inching away from the garage wall with his hands stretched out before him, Dale's bare hands contacted a large smooth object. Dale wasn't certain if he was in the center of the garage yet but, just in case he was, he waved his hands in the air in an attempt to grasp the clutch release rope. Coming up empty handed, Dale fell against the large smooth object. Whatever the object was, it was too heavy for Dale to push out of his way, so he began to skirt around it. After groping through the darkness and nearly falling over unseen objects three times, Dale located the clutch release for the automatic door opener and pulled it down. Finding his way to the main garage door once again, he used all his strength and lifted up the door in one clean-and-jerk motion until it slammed itself into a locked position onto the operating motor clutch inside the garage.

When the dim light of the stormy sky flooded into the garage, Dale, for the first time, realized that the large smooth object he had been battling while in the dark was in reality a minivan. This realization made Dale laugh and clap his hands. He hadn't gone into the garage to find a car. Dale had originally begun the task of opening the big garage door to provide enough light to pick up the motorcycle and then shut all the garage doors. However, there it was: a minivan. *Isn't that funny?* All thought of the motorcycle had vanished. He tried to open the front passenger door; it opened, and a light came on inside from the minivan's overhead lamp. A light inside Dale's head went on. *This car is a way to get Mrs. Doty and her children to town.* He could carry them from the house to the garage to the minivan and then drive it into town. It was a simple task and one that Dale thought he could accomplish. He set to it without hesitation. One by one, he carried the failing bodies of the Doty family from their house to the minivan in the garage. The only problem Dale had in the initial process was figuring out how to place the baby in the car seat. It was as if there was a piece missing, so the baby just couldn't be strapped in correctly. Dale did the best he could with the baby in the car seat and wrapped a blanket around her.

With every member of the Doty family loaded in the minivan, now Dale had to reckon how to start it. *The keys, I need the keys,* he thought. After a frantic search of the house and several fruitless queries to an incoherent Tammy Doty, Dale found the keys in the ignition of the minivan. He tried to start the vehicle. It would crank but would not start. Dale heard his father's voice inside his head, *Battery needs checked, Dummy.* Dale returned the key to the neutral spot on the ignition block and peered into the dashboard indicators to read the battery voltage. It read near 11. That was a good enough voltage. *Gas needs checked.* Dale looked at the gas gauge. It was on empty.

Under normal circumstances, when presented with a new set of challenges, Dale immediately went into panic mode and chose to flee his situation. He had done this earlier at the Doty house when he attempted to run away and slipped on the muddy lawn. However, this time, with this new challenge of having no fuel for the Doty minivan, something happened inside his brain that flipped just the right switch. Dale fell back on an old memory instead of running away from his current circumstances.

By no stretch of any imagination could Dale Koester ever be considered bright or intelligent. He had been born with a mental capacity that peaked out at that of an eight-year-old boy. His parents, although average in the intelligence department, had chosen a lifestyle that dipped into the dysfunctional echelon. Dale's parents set the consumption of alcohol as a priority far above that of child rearing. Although never physically violent when drinking, his parents were nonetheless verbally abusive to each other and to their children. After procreating four more children of average ability, Dale's father had found it easier to dump his fathering responsibilities upon his oldest son and explain away Dale's mental condition with a simple, "Dale's just a stupid kid." Imagine this coming from a garbage collector who lived with his family in a run-down trailer on a plot of farmland five miles from town. The plot of land was an abandoned farm that he had inherited from his own father. After the fifth child was born into the Koester family, Dale's mother departed without so much as a "Good-bye" and left Dale to absorb the mother role as well. With such an upbringing, Dale found it difficult to cope with the outside world. As he reached the teen years, his peers shunned him, at best, and tortured him, at worst. Even his own siblings turned on him and took advantage of his lack of intelligence when it was to their benefit. School became an academic impossibility by the time tenth grade rolled around, so Dale simply dropped out. As if to hold his oldest son hostage in the role as the caregiver in the Koester clan, Dale's father restricted Dale from learning several important tasks. Dale was allowed to cook, clean and baby-sit. Dale was not allowed to hunt or drive a vehicle. His younger siblings did not have to observe these same restrictions; they only applied to Dale. While Dale spent his teen years raising children, the children grew up and outgrew the need for their older brother.

One would think that Dale would become fed-up with this treatment and demand his rights, even with his mental deficiency. Rebellion had often been on his mind as a teenager, and it would have taken physical form if not for the pre-emptive threat his father had droned into Dale's mind from early childhood.

"If ya ever think of doin' yer own thing," his father had told him, "why, I'll just hafta send ya off to one of them mental institutions where they'll have their way with ya every day." His father would then spare no detail in telling the young Dale what he meant by "have their way with ya." This fearful mental image frightened Dale, so he never openly rebelled. Secretly, though, he had *done his own thing* in ways his father never knew about.

At age ten, before his peers had begun to discriminate against him, Dale had made a few friends at school who allowed him to go on midnight hunting excursions with them. On those pre-planned hunting trips, Dale would ensure his father's supply of beer kept coming until he passed out. He would sneak out of the house, find his hidden hand-me-down rifle that a friend had loaned him and join his companions at the specified meeting place. These clandestine hunting excursions occurred within a two-year period. That hunting era ended when his hunting companions told him not to join them any further. They did this not because of his lack of mental capacity or because it *wasn't cool to hang out with the retard*; they shunned Dale because he just could not keep quiet enough to hunt. Dale could never quite figure out when or how to be silent.

In the two years of these hunting trips, Dale had learned more than just how to hunt. He had learned how to drive a motorized vehicle. Moreover, not only had he learned how to drive a motorized vehicle, he had learned how to siphon gas from a variety of sources. This is why Dale Koester didn't panic when the gas gauge read *Empty* on the Doty minivan. He had faced this very situation at the end of a clandestine hunting trip with his pre-adolescent friends, over ten years ago. For some reason unknown even to himself, Dale Koester remembered step-by-step how he and his childhood friends had dealt with the situation. Without hesitation, Dale removed the keys from the car ignition, pocketed them and began searching for a gas can. The gas can was easy to find, but what could he use to fill it?

> There hadn't been gasoline available in any quantity since…well, since one could remember. Most survivors didn't know what day of the week it was, let alone what day of the month or even the month itself. Sure, at the time of the Collapse there was refined gasoline stored in thousands of tanks all over the country. Most of the gas was stored above ground and was destroyed by human greed. I've heard many stories of how tons of the petrol became horrific fireballs and engulfed miles of city blocks as American civilization showed its true mettle. The remainder of the refined gasoline was stored under the ground in smaller quantities. But who

could get to it? Most underground gasoline tank pumps at the time of the Collapse were electric. Folks came out of the woodwork with all kinds of the hand-operated pumps, but these pumps didn't have the oomph to get the fuel out of the underground tanks. For a few weeks after the Collapse, them that had the ingenuity to get the fuel out of the underground tanks, and the firepower to protect their ingenuity, well, these became the ruling class. For a while.

Theodore Newgent,
An excerpt from his personal journal, May, 2010

Dale began to search the entire dimly lit garage for any source of gasoline that he could use. Twenty minutes of rummaging produced an eclectic collection of possible fuel sources for the Doty minivan. He found two containers of questionable liquids: some smelled more like turpentine than petrol. These might do if nothing else was found. Dale inventoried one nearly empty gallon gasoline can, half a tank of gasoline from a lawn mower and the contents of the motorcycle gas tank. It wasn't much more than two gallons of combustible liquids, and not the perfect combination for the minivan's engine, but the only performance Dale was concerned about was getting the Doty family into town. It took nearly an hour for Dale to transfer all the fuels from their respective containers into the minivan's fuel tank. He then climbed into the driver's seat and turned the ignition key to the auxiliary position to allow the fuel pump to fill the gas lines to the carburetor. The gas gauge now hovered just above the empty mark. Dale said a quick prayer and turned the ignition. The engine turned, nagged, coughed and, under great protest, roared to life at nearly twice its normal idle speed. It took a few seconds for the electronic brain of the vehicle to adjust to the fuel mixture and settle down to an unsteady idling. Dale felt like crying. It was in this brief moment of relief, after succeeding in the seemingly impossible, that he realized he had not heard a single noise from the occupants of the minivan for quite some time. Even the baby hadn't coughed in the last ten minutes. Dale shut the driver's side door, put the vehicle into drive and pulled out of the Doty garage as fast as the complaining engine would allow.

They heard him coming before they saw him. Two young men were hunkered inside makeshift hooch, trying to keep out of the pouring rain, when the raucous noise of the Doty minivan interrupted a conversation they had been having. Their shelter wasn't much more than a few two-by-fours nailed together and draped with pilfered clear plastic sheets. Grabbing their rifles and exiting the hooch through a slit in one of its plastic walls, the men walked through the rain until they stood in the middle of the old Highway 33. Behind them was the former city of Effingham, now known as the Crossroads Enclave. In front of them was a garish barricade composed of five abandoned vehicles. On the other side of the barricade Highway 33 dipped down into a small valley before it raced up the other side and disappeared over a hill.

Abandoned vehicles of every type lined both sides of the highway as far as the eye could see. These two young men were on watch as security guards at the northernmost checkpoint. Their job was to control any vehicular traffic coming into the Crossroads Enclave. The rifles they held were not just for show. Just like every other survivor of the Collapse, they were hungry, tired, scared and being such, would shoot first and ask questions later if threatened.

"What the heck you think it is?" The taller of the men asked the other as they stood behind the barricade and peered through the rain to the hill on the other side of the valley.

"Sounds like a diesel to me."

"Naw," the taller one said, as he spat on the ground and wiped his chin with his rain jacket sleeve. "That ain't no diesel. Sounds just like that one we had earlier today, you know, the retard in the old pickup?"

"Can't be. Council put out the word that they ain't lettin' anyone out anymore. Like Hotel California, y'know, you check in but never leave. They wouldn't let that retard out of town."

"That guy? He's a local. He knows everybody and everybody knows him, at least the Council knows him. I guess they let him do what he wants. Hey, look," the taller man pointed toward the highway on the opposite hillside, "there it is. Looks like a minivan."

"Spitting out a ton of oil too," his companion added.

Dale, behind the wheel of the Doty minivan, had the accelerator pushed to the floorboards in order to crest the first hill as he drove toward town. He wasn't used to driving this particular vehicle, let alone a vehicle coughing a black cloud of exhaust from its tailpipe. Most of the land in this region is flat, and the car was able to maintain a top speed of forty-five miles per hour. Then he had to negotiate that first hill. The Doty minivan barely made it to the crest. The engine began to race out of control, so Dale eased up a little on the accelerator as the car began to gain speed coming down the small valley. The second hill would be much more difficult to climb because the grade was greater. Dale knew that he had to get the vehicle up to at least fifty miles an hour before the highway began to ascend again, but he didn't want to trash the engine before he got to the edge of town. With much concentration and perfect timing, Dale willed the Doty minivan up the second hill with just enough momentum to reach the barricade where the two men stood. Dale rolled down his window, stuck his head out and yelled through the wind and rain at the two men.

"Got some sick people here. Gotta get them to the medicine."

"Is that you again?" The smaller of the guards complained back at Dale. "Where did you get that piece of crap minivan? Turn around and go back where you came from."

"I got some sick people that need to get to medicine," Dale reiterated, as if he hadn't heard what the guard had said.

An awkward pause ensued between the two parties on opposite sides of the barricade. The Security Force guards were not to let any vehicles into town. All vehicles were abandoned along the side of the highway without blocking the two inner lanes, and the occupants were to walk to the barricade for an interrogation by the guards. Earlier that day, the same two men had given Dale vehicular access into town when he brought his own parents there. He had fueled his father's pickup truck in the same manner, as he had the Doty minivan, and in like manner had driven it, sputtering and coughing black fumes, to this very barricade. The guards knew that the elderly couple in the pickup truck could not walk to the checkpoint; they looked near death. One of the guards had conferred over a handheld radio with his superiors in town and gained permission for one Dale Koester to drive the truck to the Crossroads Enclave Quarantine Compound. The Quarantine Compound, once a Baptist church building and parking lot, was now a medical facility. The Security Force guards directed Dale to the Quarantine Compound and allowed him to pass. A handful of guards, who kept their distance, admitted his parents into the Quarantine Compound. The guards, all wielding machine guns, opened the Medical Clinic front door and ordered four citizens inside the Clinic to haul Dale's parents inside. The moment after the Clinic door shut the SF guards turned their attention to Dale. His pickup was confiscated and removed by one guard while another guard ordered Dale to check into the Indoctrination Center for Enclave Indoctrination. Dale nodded and, as ordered, began walking in the general direction of the Indoctrination Center, a former apartment complex. Somewhere between the Quarantine Compound and the Indoctrination Center, he forgot what the SFers ordered him to do. Instead of reporting for Enclave Indoctrination, Dale found himself wandering through the copse of trees near the north checkpoint on a personal quest to bring more sick people into town.

Ten hours later, Dale Koester found himself at the same north check point of Highway 33 with another vehicle load of sick people and facing the same two guards. "Ah, let's just let him in," the taller guard said, as he leaned his rifle against the nearest barricade vehicle and made his way to the driver's side door of the foremost barricade vehicle.

"Yeah," the second guard said as he followed the lead of his comrade, "might as well."

The two guards pushed the foremost barricade vehicle to the side of the highway, creating a gap in the barricade just large enough for the Doty car to pass through. Dale smiled and waved as he drove the noisy vehicle past the guards and toward the Quarantine Compound. Just as before, weary Quarantine Compound workers admitted the occupants of the Doty minivan, and Security Force guards confronted Dale. On this occasion, the SFers were armed. Word had gotten out to the Security Forces that a man had entered the Enclave *twice* that day. This was in direct violation of Enclave policy. If admitted into the Crossroads

Enclave, you were not allowed to leave. Dale Koester, a man of limited intelligence, had simply vanished and shown up again.

Less than two months after the Collapse, when the Influenza began to sweep through Southern Illinois, it did so with such speed that it became nearly impossible to control its spread. The Council put up a razor wire barricade around their Medical Clinic and converted it into the *Quarantine Compound*. Dale Koester arrived with the Doty family the day before the Council enacted this new edict.

The Security Force guards herded the infected immigrants into the Quarantine Compound to separate them from the uninfected. When Security Force personnel began dying from the Influenza it became clear that more extreme measures were needed. The Council passed a new edict to incarcerate anyone physically exposed to an infected person. Mere association with an infected person gained the unfortunate victim a tour inside the razor wire of the Quarantine Compound. Thousands of Enclave citizens died in a relatively short period, including several Council members. The Security Force lost over 50% of its personnel. Workers within the Quarantine Compound hauled the bodies of the dead across the open parking lot behind the Compound building in wheelbarrows. The corpses were dumped into one of three mass graves. Five of every six people forced into the Quarantine Compound died. Death at the hands of the Influenza was so certain that the Council began forcing any known rabble-rouser or political opponent into the Quarantine Compound. Within the first week of installing the razor wire perimeter, the initial medical staff on hand at the Enclave Clinic had died and the name of the place changed to the Quarantine Compound. The dying were caring for the near dead. What little medicine was available had no effect on the Influenza.

Oh, you've got a problem? Take a pill. You don't like your boss? Take a pill. You've done a crappy job of parenting and your kid is acting out? Give him a pill. For two generations now we Americans have been doing this horrible injustice to ourselves. And the whole fiasco isn't isolated to our psyche. No, those same two generations have overdosed on antibiotics as well. The germs are getting smarter and our bodies dumber. Mark my words, one day in the near future the nation will pay for this liberal behavior in a most unfortunate way.

Theodore Newgent
Areyoulistening.com August 2000

By the time Dale Koester had delivered the Doty family to the Crossroads Enclave clinic in early September, 2009, the effects of the Influenza had yet to reach its peak. A month later, the Enclave Death toll would drop from hundreds to less than fifty per day. The Enclave Council realized that further deaths could be averted through systematic quarantine of every new arrival or newly reported case of the Influenza and that no longer would the Security Force allow infected people to enter the Enclave. This policy change had taken place just after Dale had arrived the first time that day. The two Security Force guards at the north Highway 33 barricade had no knowledge of this policy change when they let Dale through the second time. Unfortunately for Dale, the Security Force guards at the Quarantine Compound were well aware of the new policy change and they weren't so nice to him.

The Council decreed that all non-infected new arrivals to the Enclave must be temporarily housed in a collection of apartment buildings they dubbed the *Indoctrination Center*. Before the Collapse, these buildings had been part of an apartment complex located near the current Highway 33 northernmost checkpoint. Because of their location near the Security Force Headquarters (an abandoned electric utility building) and the Service Center (the former Wal-Mart store), these apartments were occupied by members of the Security Force and their families. As the Influenza reduced the membership of the Security Force, and most Security Force personnel were relocated to the larger hotels on the south side of the Enclave, vacancies in the apartment complex remained. The Council decided to use these empty apartments as an Indoctrination Center. The remaining Security Force members relocated to other quarters.

Dale had made fools out of the Security Force guards. The guards brutally beat Dale after admitting the Doty family into the Quarantine Compound. The Security Force guards would have beaten Dale to death, except that an all points bulletin blurted out from a handheld radio one of the guards carried. The word was that all new immigrants needed to report to the old Security Force apartments for Indoctrination. Despite the fact that Dale had been in direct contact with known Influenza victims, the Council did not enforce the edict on sending him inside the Quarantine Compound. Instead, he was manhandled and dumped at the newly established Indoctrination Center. The SFer there cleaned him up a bit, fed him and ordered Dale into one of the second story apartment units. His instructions were to stay in the apartment until morning. An armed Security guard stood just outside the door. Dale didn't mind. It was dark, it was raining, and he was tired. In addition, he was not hit or kicked while inside the apartment. He crawled onto an empty bed and fell asleep almost immediately.

For the next two days, Dale and a small group of non-infected new arrivals erected a razor wire barrier around the perimeter of the Indoctrination Center buildings. Armed Security Force guards oversaw the entire operation until its completion. From that day forward, all indoctrinations into the Enclave would be conducted in a prison-like manner. Dale Koester was the first inmate.

CHAPTER EIGHT

The Crossroads Enclave:
The MP3 Recording

It had been a rough day for Stephenie Plasters. In the course of one twelve-hour shift at the Crossroads Enclave Quarantine Compound, thirty people under her direct care had died. Each one of the deceased had suffered from the same disease, now commonly referred to as the *Influenza*. There didn't seem to be an end to the Influenza epidemic either. Every day, armed Security Force guards directed the infected to the Quarantine Compound in increasing numbers.

When she was assigned as a nurse at the Quarantine Compound in early August, the facility was called the Medical Center and was a place where injured or sick citizens came to get well. Now it was the place where the infected came to die.

So severe was the initial spread of this Influenza that all medical personnel found inside the Crossroads Enclave were assigned to the Medical Clinic at gunpoint. A week later, when the Council elevated the status of the Influenza from epidemic to endemic, armed Security Force guards surrounded the grounds around the Medical Clinic building and parking lot. These guards allowed only the infected to pass inside and allowed no one out. That same day, forced laborers staked a ring of razor wire to the asphalt parking lot surrounding the Medical Clinic. There was only one entrance to the Clinic, an old metal gate hastily concreted into place on the southeast corner of the razor wire enclosure. Starting that day, no one crossed the Clinic perimeter once he or she came in. Even the few that survived the initial weeks of the Influenza, by Council edict, remained inside the perimeter. The Medical Clinic thus became the Quarantine Compound.

As the death count rose, the guards delivered a backhoe into the compound and ordered the inmates to dig a mass grave outside the buildings. An initial cry of protest arose from those still inside the compound. A mass grave was too Holocaust-like for these former Americans. Machine gun fire from several Security Force guards silenced the protests. After the gun smoke cleared, one of the inmates, waving a white flag, climbed upon the backhoe and began digging a giant trench through the parking lot concrete to the soil below. Once the trench was large enough, every available person in the compound began lugging the corpses in wheelbarrows from the building and tossed them awkwardly into the mass grave. How frightening it must have been for the living participants of this burial ritual to know that soon their body would be wheel barrowed from the Compound building to the grave. This initial dumping process took twelve hours. The Quarantine Compound had become a death camp.

The Security Force guards mercilessly gunned down in cold blood those attempting escape and then ordered the living captives to drag the murdered bodies into the mass grave. Because the death rate inside the Compound was extremely high, eventually there was no one left from the original medical staff who knew the story of how the Quarantine Compound or the Crossroads Enclave came into being. Stephenie, who had been at the Crossroads Medical Clinic a mere two days, had the misfortune of being inside the perimeter the moment the Council quarantined the building and surrounding parking lot. Within a week, almost every single person made a captive by the quarantine had died from the Influenza. Stephenie became ill with the flu and spent three days in a world of delirium before slowly recovering to the point where she could think clearly again. The young man named Matthew, with whom she had been traveling the day the SF guards drove them at gunpoint to the Quarantine Compound, had also survived his bout with the Influenza. It was after they recovered enough to walk again that they discovered they were the sole survivors from the original quarantined group. Because she was a nurse and had survived, Stephenie became the spokesperson for the inside captives.

Every night, Stephenie arrived at the front gate and took in a load of supplies for the Quarantine Compound. Every night, she would receive orders from one of the Security Force guards as to what actions the Clinic was to take regarding the survivors. Each night, a long line of men, women, and children, suspected of exposure to the Influenza, marched at gunpoint into the compound. Each night, Stephenie managed the exodus into the Clinic building. One of the most aggravating parts of this entire management episode for Stephenie was that she had no idea who the armed Security Force guards were, or from whom they took orders. The Security Force guards patrolling the outside perimeter filtered Communication between those inside and those outside the Quarantine Compound. Stephenie was the only person on the inside allowed to communicate with the Security Force guards.

Eventually, some of the Quarantine Compound guards caught the Influenza. Ironically, they were marched at gunpoint to the confines of the compound to die with their former captives. It was through one of these former guards that Stephenie discovered the truth about her current environment. The guard's name was Jacob Shelton. She had met him once before. In fact, he was one of six Security Force guards that had taken Matthew and her captive near the former Effingham city boundary two months before. Stephenie and Matthew, whom she had met a mere twenty-four hours before, were attempting to sneak into Effingham under the cover of darkness. The two travelers were silently walking parallel to Highway 40 just west of town when they found themselves surrounded by soldiers. Night vision goggles obscured all the guard's faces, so it was impossible for Stephenie to know whom she was dealing with. She wasn't certain, but some of the soldiers might have been women. The soldiers began yelling for Matthew and Stephenie to take off their backpacks and lie down on the pavement of the highway. The soldiers violently interrogated the two travelers with kicks from booted feet and raps from gun butts. The soldiers wanted to know where they were going, where they had been and who they were. Before the interrogation became too violent, Stephenie managed to blurt out that she was a nurse. Immediately, the yelling and physical abuse ceased and one of the guards ordered two other soldiers to inspect the backpacks of their captives. When a plethora of first aid supplies strew across the highway from the pockets of one backpack, the soldier in charge ordered Stephenie to pick up her medical supplies from the pavement and put them all into her backpack.

While Stephenie was obeying her orders at gunpoint, the soldier in charge began to interrogate Matthew. Two of the soldiers lifted Matthew from the pavement and held him in place while their leader began slapping Matthew across his face. No matter what answer he gave them, it wasn't what they were looking for. Stephenie immediately jumped up and attempted to stop the soldiers but was thrown to the ground. As she charged toward the soldiers once again, she screamed out, "Leave him alone, he's my assistant!"

"What?" the lead soldier spun and glared at her through his night vision goggles.

"I said," Stephenie gasped though gritted teeth, "I'm a nurse and he's my medical assistant."

Upon hearing that the young man they were beating had experience with the medical profession, the leader of the soldiers immediately ordered the interrogation ceased. As with Stephenie, a gunpoint encouraged Matthew to replace his scattered belongings into his backpack. After the captives completed their tasks, the soldiers ordered them to don their backpacks and then marched them across a field on the north side of the highway and up a small hillside. The captives were led through an opening in a razor wire fence where two more soldiers silently waited. These soldiers did not have night vision goggles, though they held tightly to a pair of automatic weapons. One of these unmasked soldiers was Jacob Shelton.

"Everything cool up here, Shelton?" The leading soldier asked as he removed his night vision goggles. A pattern began to form in Stephenie's mind as she looked into the uncovered faces of the soldiers. They were all young; even their leader was young.

"Yeah, no problem, Hand" Shelton replied.

"Hand? Hand? Hey, Shelton, what's your problem?" The lead soldier barked at Jacob, as he got close enough to spit into his face as he yelled.

"The name is Mette, got it?" The spitting soldier pointed repeatedly to a place on his left upper chest as he continued. "Call me by my name, or I'll have your butt in a sling."

"Okay, okay," Shelton backed away a step, "I get it. I get it."

"Good, now stay here and guard these two," Mette growled at Shelton, then turned to the remainder of the soldiers and said, "The rest of you come over here, we've got a situation."

As Mette and the other soldiers retreated to an area behind some indistinguishable object twenty paces away, Shelton ordered Matthew and Stephenie to remove their backpacks and then sit on them. A few seconds after this, Shelton walked in a small circle around his prisoners and crouched down into a position behind them, facing the spot where the other soldiers had disappeared.

"Man, we saw you guys coming up the road about ten minutes before your capture." Jacob Shelton spoke quietly, as he kept his gaze focused in the direction where the other soldiers were. Stephenie glanced in the same direction but could see nothing distinguishable. It was too dark a night to see more than a few yards. Shelton continued, "Why are you two traveling at night?"

"It's safer that way," Matthew blurted out with a sarcastic tone, "nobody sees you, so they don't kill you."

"Yeah, Hand, there's a lot of that going around, huh?" Shelton lowered his eyes to the ground and shook his head in disgust.

Suddenly, Matthew spoke like a little child at a toy store, "Were those infrared goggles those other guys were wearing?"

This sudden shift of mood made Shelton tense up again and his eyes darted around suspiciously. "Yeah, night vision goggles. That's how we saw you coming."

"Cool," Matthew said in a dreamlike way and then seemed to snap out of it and become serious again, "but how do you keep the batteries charged without electricity? Are they, like, solar powered or something?"

"Oh, we've got electricity," Shelton assured his captives.

"You have what?" Stephenie nearly yelled.

"Shhhhhh!" Shelton warned Stephenie, "I'm not supposed to be talking to you. You gotta be quiet."

"Sorry, okay," Stephenie said just above a whisper.

"Yeah, the Crossroads Enclave has electricity. And water. That's what this place is," Jacob Shelton explained while pointing to the area the other soldiers had disappeared. "The Council hauled a couple of portable generators up here to power the old pump station from the lake and water treatment plant. It gets pumped about four miles from here to the Enclave."

"The Enclave?" both Stephenie and Matthew asked simultaneously.

"Yeah, oh, sure, you guys don't know about that yet, do you? Well, we've got us a safe zone with electricity and water and a hospital and an army and all that…"

"An army?" Stephenie was now leaning forward and speaking intensely. "Do you know Morgan Plasters?"

"Can't say as I do." Shelton looked at Stephenie suspiciously, "Should I know this Morgan, what did you say, Plasters?"

"Yeah, Morgan Plasters, he's my brother. He was in Effingham the day the lights went out. He was in the National Guard. The last time I talked to him, he was trying to round up other National Guard members to secure a safe spot in town."

"Uh, shoot, Hand," Shelton stood up and began looking around nervously in all directions. "I'm not supposed to talk about that stuff, you know?"

"About what stuff?" Stephenie yelled this time. At that moment, footsteps where heard approaching from the direction where Mette and the other soldiers had disappeared in the darkness.

"Keep your mouth shut, Hand!" Shelton yelled at the prisoners. Shelton, shaken by something Stephenie said, and by the fact that Mette was approaching, blurted his last statement for the effect of acting like a soldier, not because he meant it.

"Hey, Shelton, we might just make an officer out of you yet," Mette said approvingly as he approached the prisoners. "Okay, you two are in luck tonight. Normally, we'd take your belongings and make you walk to the Enclave. But because you are medical types, you get to keep your stuff, and you get to ride in a vehicle."

Quite suddenly, the roar of a combustion engine came to life from the darkness where the soldiers had disappeared. Along with the noise came two headlights from the unseen vehicle. Two of the soldiers were moving around the area of this vehicle, as if busying themselves with some important task. The headlights lit up the immediate area enough that it rendered worthless the soldiers' night vision goggles. As the soldiers began removing their goggles, Stephenie noticed two things immediately. Every soldier wore the same style of long-sleeved brown shirt. The second thing she noticed was that the soldiers were guarding a pump station at the top of the hill. Next to the pump station was a shed that housed a gas-powered generator. One of the soldiers began adjusting the generator and both it and the pumps came to life with a mechanical humming. In the glow of the headlights, it became obvious that the soldiers were part of some organized army, for they all wore the same brown shirts. Stephenie noticed the *SF* stenciled on every soldier's uniform. She wondered what it meant and wanted to ask one of the soldiers but never an opportunity to do so.

Mette told his prisoners to keep their mouths shut, told them to stand up and then led Stephenie and Matthew to the source of the headlights. It was a recent model Jeep altered with an extensive roll bar structure and a machine gun mount. It reminded Stephenie of the vehicles she had seen on the news, the kind of vehicle belonging to some crazy rebel army from some civil-war-torn, third world country. One of the soldiers sat in the driver's seat of the Jeep and talked on a hand-held radio; another soldier stood in the back of the Jeep with his hands gripping the mounted machine gun. Mette ordered the two travelers to toss their backpacks into the bed of the Jeep and climb aboard. As the Jeep drove through the opening in the razor wire and away from the pump station toward the former city of Effingham, the last thing Stephenie remembered was the look on the face of young Jacob Shelton. He was scared. In the brief time she had spent in the presence of this young man, she had seen him yelled at, berated at gunpoint, threatened and none of it had seemed to affect him. The moment she asked about her brother Morgan, it shook young Jacob Shelton to his core.

The soldiers immediately drove Matthew and Stephenie to the Crossroads Enclave. Both prisoners were awed and frightened by the sights and sounds of this entry into the Enclave. Hordes of people lined up at gated entry points waiting to get inside the Enclave. A force of twenty armed guards, with automatic rifles and angry expressions, stood on either side of the gate in two lines just inside the perimeter. A ripple of panic spread through the throngs outside the gates as people began yelling, pushing and fighting. There was gunfire, and then there were screams. Armed soldiers waved the Jeep with the two prisoners through the checkpoint amid more gunfire and chaos.

Once they were inside the razor wire perimeter, both prisoners noticed the chaos subsided to an ethereal calm, as if everything inside was in perfect order. There were lights, electric lights, lit in various areas around the streets. The streets were empty but for vehicles manned by young men and women wearing the brown shirts. Matthew noticed that there were lights in some of the buildings, including the hotels to the east of the entry gate. Armed soldiers were everywhere. Yet, there were also people inside the Enclave who did not wear the uniform of the soldier. These *civilians* were all very busy performing one task or another. The Jeep drove too fast for Stephenie to understand the purpose of the civilians that night, but half of them seemed to be involved in clean-up efforts and the rest in unloading large coils of razor wire from the beds of several military trucks. Soldiers with radios and automatic weapons were monitoring all activities.

The Jeep sped down Keller Drive and made a right turn onto Ford Street. As they drove by the Wal-Mart store, Stephenie noticed a flurry of activity at the gas station. Civilian men and women fueled a variety of sport utility vehicles on the west side of the gas station. Each utility vehicle pulled a portable fuel tank on a trailer. At the east side of the gas station, civilian workers had draped hoses from semi- tractor-trailers Fuel tankers to the underground tank filling fittings. More soldiers guarded this operation than any other in the Enclave. It dawned on Stephenie that the Enclave had isolated its own portion of the electrical grid and was powering it with portable generators. The sport utility vehicles delivered the fuel inside the tanks to these portable generators.

The Jeep turned off Ford Street and up to the entry gate of what appeared to be a church building. There was a central building surrounded by a concrete parking lot. On the outskirts of the parking lot walked armed guards. It was apparent these guards were a picket perimeter for the church building. Stephenie noticed immediately that each soldier had some a breathing mask on his or her face. As the Jeep came to a stop at the front of the church building, the driver jumped from the cab of the truck and ordered Matthew and Stephenie to grab their backpacks and enter the building. Several masked and armed soldiers opened the entry doors and began yelling at Morgan and Stephenie to hurry inside the front door. The armed guards shut and locked the doors behind them.

Since that night, forced laborers installed the razor wire and one single gate around the Medical Clinic perimeter. The locks were removed from the outside of the Clinic doors. A backhoe arrived one evening and, after the brown shirts used automatic gunfire across the razor wire to quell a riot inside the Medical Clinic, the first mass grave was excavated in the former New Hope Church parking lot. New Hope Church, briefly renamed the *Crossroads Enclave Medical Clinic*, now became the *Quarantine Compound.*

Stephenie kept track of the passage of time using her day planner to mark the days. She and Matthew entered the Quarantine Compound as junior medical professionals, became sick and had somehow survived. Whoever was in charge of the Enclave had decided to cease sending medical professionals to the compound soon thereafter. The Influenza seemed to kill doctors and nurses at a rate that was greater than the death rate for the general populace. Each night seemed to be the same; an endless line of humans forced by armed and masked soldiers into the compound and an endless procession of corpses filled the mass grave.

When it became apparent that all the original medical staff had died from the Influenza, and only Stephenie and Matthew had survived, those in charge of the Crossroads Enclave chose Stephenie as the spokesman for the Compound. Stephenie decided manage the Compound at night and have Matthew manage the daytime. The *powers that be* accepted this arrangement because it meant that Stephenie would always be available at night.

All communication to the outside world traveled between Stephenie and the soldier in charge of the Quarantine Compound gate when the newest arrivals came each night. This lead soldier would use a bullhorn to call to Stephenie from his position outside the razor wire perimeter. Stephenie would exit the Compound building, walk to a designated spot near the gate and wait for the lead soldier to approach. The lead soldier always stood at a spot twenty feet from the razor wire and spoke without the bullhorn. Each night Stephenie and the lead soldier would communicate statistical information on the compound prisoners, such as how many had died, how many were dying and how many might survive. Stephenie would then relate requests for food and water for the survivors and the lead soldier would make notes on a clipboard. Then the two would part, with Stephenie returning to the Compound building and the lead soldier away from the entry gate. Soldiers in gas masks opened the perimeter gate and a line of new arrivals would enter. The first of the new arrivals would carry in the supplies of food and water requested by Stephenie from her conversation with the lead soldier the night before. The moment the arrivals entered the gate of the compound, they were no longer *new arrivals*. Now they were prisoners. The prisoners always came at night.

Each new prisoner would enter the gates of the Quarantine Compound stripped of all belongings other than the clothes he or she wore. Each group passed through the gate accompanied by a list of their names. Documentation was handled on the *inside* by Stephenie and Matthew, and on the *outside* by the soldiers guarding the compound. Initially, the new prisoners crossing the gate were people with obvious symptoms of the Influenza. As the Influenza began to spread like wildfire through the Enclave, the *powers that be* decided to quarantine anyone who "Might have been exposed" to the Influenza. As these *exposed* people began to arrive at the Quarantine Compound, it became apparent that many of them were victims of a political purging process. The one common denominator among these victims was that they had a strong Christian leaning. Many of them laughed at the irony that the very building they would die in had been a source of life for them before the Collapse: the Quarantine Compound had previously been a Baptist church. It was a political purging of the most brilliant kind. It was from these political victims that Stephenie and Matthew learned who was calling the shots at the Crossroads Enclave. Calling themselves The Council, a small group of opportunists had somehow seized power of the Enclave just after the lights went out. This Council used the Security Force as their enforcers. Although it couldn't be proven that the Council had any direct involvement, a long line of their political opponents had vanished or died in a very short period of time.

"The Council," a dying political foe once said with the saddest of irony, "may not have been good at true civic progress, but was great at killing their critics."

> You know how complacent we've become? A recent poll conducted on the Internet revealed that we Americans *expect* our government leaders to be crooked. We expect them to abuse the authority, the power, that we give them. Has this nation always been corrupt? Probably. Have 'We The People' ever done anything about it? On the rare occasion, yes. But we tend to pick the most ridiculous lines in the sand, don't we? In my time we forced one President from office because he got caught spying on his opponents. Twenty years later we've got a President with a long list of questionable dead bodies in his political wake, and we re-elect him? Re-elect him? Are we that stupid? Yes, we are a stupid nation. We have abused power and call it politics. We have allowed two percent of the population to tell the remaining ninety-eight percent how to speak and how to act. Political Correctness, my clavicle! It's censorship. It's a purging of my unalienable rights. One day in the future the final purging will begin and no one will be able to stop it.

Those two percent will have secured the power base and begin taking-out the Conservatives as if it was a turkey shoot. And it won't just be their rights this time, it will be their lives.

Theodore Newgent
areyoulistening.com May 2001

When the purging had begun, all documentation of arrivals ceased to exist outside the razor wire. This did not stop Stephenie and Matthew from keeping track of the names and deaths of each prisoner in their own record keeping effort. After being in charge of the compound for one month, Stephenie told the Security Force guard at the gate that she needed to dig a new mass grave. Like the previous mass grave, the prisoners dug the new grave under the pavement of the parking lot. Each bucketful of asphalt and dirt from the new mass grave was delivered by the backhoe operator to cover the top of the first mass grave. This new grave was twice the size of the original.

For almost two months, Stephenie and Matthew had lived without the hope of release from the compound. The embarrassing reality was that they didn't have a clue who was in charge of making the decisions at the Enclave. They had heard whispered rumors from some of the prisoners about something called a *Council* that made the political decisions, and that the soldiers, to whom they gave the name *SFers*, were carrying out the orders of that Council. Rumors had arisen that the Enclave was in the process of being surrounded by barbed wire and razor wire to keep people from leaving. Other rumors began to surface that the Crossroads Enclave had an incredible cache of food stored inside the Wal-Mart store, which had been renamed *The Service Center*. Several prisoners talked about being part of a food collection process that had begun to raid smaller enclaves outside the Crossroads Enclave in war-like confrontations. However, not one of these prisoners could tell Stephenie how the Crossroads Enclave had come into being or what fate had befallen her brother Morgan. That is, until Hammer came to die at the Quarantine Compound.

Near the end of September 2009, the Influenza seemed to have peaked and was on a rapid downturn. Stephenie and Matthew had worked on opposite sides of each day, in horrible circumstances, for two months. Each had witnessed the deaths of more than two thousand people. The survival rate at the Quarantine Compound measured out to be one in every twelve. The survivors transferred from the compound to some other location in the Enclave, a location unknown to Stephenie or Matthew. On one of the last nights of September, the compound soldiers opened the gates and admitted a line of fourteen new prisoners. One of these prisoners was a Security Force soldier himself. Stephenie had known him only as *Hammer*. He had been one of the soldiers responsible for transporting new arrivals to the Quarantine Compound.

Hammer was first in line as the fourteen arrivals stepped through the compound gate and became prisoners. He had all the classic symptoms of the Influenza and, from what Stephenie could see, had approximately two days before knowing if he would live or die. Neither Stephenie nor Hammer spoke as she opened the door of the compound building and led the new prisoners inside. After the last prisoner had stepped through the door, Stephenie began lecturing them, using words without feeling, as to what to expect from their imprisonment. What once was the main sanctuary room of a Baptist church became *the three-day room*. The floors were nearly covered with beds and bedding material in straight rows of forty. At this point of the Influenza epidemic most of the beds were empty. The ones that had a body on them filled the new prisoners with a sense of dread because of the constant moaning emanating from each person. Even with all the windows open, the stench of the dying in the three-day room was appalling. Each new prisoner was assigned a bed and told that they each had three days. After three days, they would either start dying or start recovering. Stephenie told them that no pain medication was available and that it wouldn't do anyone any good. Stephenie was intentionally blunt in her lecture because she felt that she had to be.

After Stephenie recovered from her own bout with the Influenza and had been put in charge of the compound, she initially had attempted to coddle the new prisoners. She had tried to ease their suffering with false hope. All this coddling had accomplished was to put unrealistic pressure upon her to come up with a solution to the inevitable death that awaited each person. After two weeks of watching the expression in the eyes of her dying patients turn from hope to bitter disappointment, Stephenie decided not to coddle them any further. She became emotionally detached. She spoke bluntly in her communications. Being blunt kept her from feeling liable for the fate of the eleven out of twelve that would die in the next five days. Being blunt kept her from feeling at all.

Matthew was no better in his bedside manner. In fact, he had become slightly sadistic about the entire situation. When a prisoner began to exhibit the one symptom that guaranteed death, the black stool defecation, he would order a couple of prisoners who could still walk to carry the dying prisoner outside the building. The living laid the dying prisoner near the mass grave and left them to die. News of Matthew's behavior reached Stephenie and she did no more than shrug her shoulders. She trusted that Matthew was doing the things that kept him from going insane. Because they had split the shifts at the compound, they rarely had time to talk to each other. However, when they did talk, the question of their release from the prison always came up in conversation. When a person survived the Influenza and recovered enough to walk on his own, the soldiers would normally order the release of that prisoner from the compound. Stephenie and Matthew had seen hundreds of survivors leave, but for reasons unknown to themselves, they were not allowed to leave. Stephenie had made several "leaving the Quarantine Compound" requests to the lead soldier at the gate over a three-week period. Eventually the soldiers told her not to make any further such requests. With no hope of release and such horrible work conditions on a daily basis, Matthew's dumping dying bodies outside the compound building seemed like a miniscule complaint.

After Stephenie had given her blunt indoctrination to the new prisoners, Hammer approached her and asked if he could speak with her in private. This was a common request with dying SFers. They always wanted preferential treatment. They always demanded their own room in which to die. They didn't want to die among the non-Security Force prisoners. They always requested these things after asking for a private conversation with Stephenie. She always gave them their private conversation, heard their requests and then told them to get back to their assigned bed and shut up. This conversation with Hammer was different. Once alone with Stephenie in a back office room, Hammer unzipped his pants and let them fall to the floor. Several thoughts raced through Stephenie's mind when he did this. First, she thought he was going to attempt to rape her. Then she saw the bruise-like blemishes on his legs, an unusual symptom of the Influenza: she thought he might ask her for some preferential pain medication. Then Hammer removed his boxer underwear to reveal a neoprene, blue belt device that had been duct taped to the base of his inguinal region. With one swift, painful jerk, Hammer pulled the device from his body. After releasing a small scream at having pulled his own body hair from his skin in the process, Hammer took a few seconds to recover his voice before holding out the blue device for Stephenie.

"Take it," Hammer gasped his words out, "I'm sorry but this was the only place we could think of hiding this thing. They strip you down to your underwear before they put you in here."

"Um, what is this?" Stephenie stammered as she cautiously grasped the object with the thumb and index finger of her right hand, obviously not wanting to touch it at all. As fast as she could she tossed the device onto a nearby desk.

"It's an MP3 player," Hammer said, as he took a well-needed seat on an office chair. Awkwardly, but successfully, he pulled up his shorts and pant. He gazed at Stephenie through crazed bloodshot eyes. She knew that Hammer was young, maybe twenty years old, yet at this moment, he looked old, probably older than his own father did. "I owed Shelton a favor. This morning the spots on my neck showed up. Shelton found out that they were going to send me here, to the Quarantine Compound, so this afternoon, he snuck this player to me and I taped it to my…"

"Yeah, I get the picture," Stephenie interrupted, "But who is Shelton?"

"You don't know him?"

"I don't know. Maybe."

"Well he sure as heck knew about you and the other guy here, uh, Matthew." Hammer slowly arose from his chair and began trudging his way to the office door. Just before passing through the office door and back into the three-day room, Hammer paused and said, "You know, you're a legend on the outside."

"What?" Stephenie said with no hidden surprise.

"Yeah," Hammer winced. He was so sick that it hurt him to speak. "I didn't know your name until Shelton told me this morning. Before that, we all called you Florence Nightingale: the nurse who took in the dead at the dead of night. Yeah, you're a legend." Hammer turned slowly and left the office room. Hammer died three days later.

Stephenie Plasters stood in an office room of the former New Hope Church and stared at the blue MP3 player on a nearby desk. After a few moments of indecision, she closed the office door and then sat in a chair behind the desk. She picked up the MP3 player and began removing the hair-laden duct tape from its cover. A small set of headphones fell out of a hidden compartment on the player. After unrolling the headphone wires, she plugged them into the appropriate socket and located the PLAY button. She inserted an earpiece to her ear and heard a male voice speak the words, "Before listening to anymore of this message, Stephenie, go get Matthew, the guy you came into the Enclave with. He needs to hear this message, too. I think I have something important to tell you both. And, I may have found a way for you two to get out of the Enclave."

Stephenie dropped the MP3 player onto the desktop, which in turn yanked the earphone piece from her ear. Frantically, Stephenie retrieved the player and pressed the STOP button. Without further hesitation, she left the office room, found Matthew and woke him up.

Matthew, who had been sleeping in his personal hide-away spot down in one of the basement rooms of the building, was *more than just a little upset* when he noticed that it was still dark outside as Stephenie dragged him upstairs and down the hallway to an empty office. He was used to having Stephenie wake him each morning for his shift, but he was not accustomed to it being so early, let alone being dragged.

"What's going on, Steph?" He demanded groggily as she pushed him into the office room and shut the door behind her. "And why'd you wake me up so early? What time is it anyway?"

"Look, Matthew, sit down for a moment," She said, as she pointed to an empty chair next to the desk.

"This better be important, I'm in a crappy mood." Then Matthew eyed the MP3 player on the desktop and his entire mood shifted gear to wide-awake wonder. "Hey, what's this thing? Looks like an MP3 player."

"Yeah, a new prisoner snuck it in tonight," Stephenie brought a second chair near Matthew and sat on the edge of the chair as close as she could to him. She grabbed the MP3 player and placed it on the desk between them, then handed one of the earphone inserts to Matthew and motioned for him to follow her lead by inserting it into his ear.

"What do you mean; snuck it in?" Matthew asked as he inserted the earphone into his ear. "How did they get it inside the compound?"

"He had it duct taped to his crotch," Stephenie said absently, as she focused on finding the PLAY button on the MP3 player again.

"His what?" Matthew jerked the headphone from his ear.

"Oh come on!" Stephenie hissed at Matthew. "We've been bathing in death for weeks now and suddenly you're afraid of…a man's groin?"

Her logic was impeccable and Matthew struggled internally to counter it. Stephenie had been through enough shared circumstances in the last eight weeks with her young lover to understand that it was time to back off and give Matthew a few seconds of silence to sort out his thoughts. She had learned that he wasn't the fastest thinker. No, Matthew was more of a daydreamer than anything else. She knew that what she had just said to him had tied his brain into mental knots and it would take a few moments of silence for him to realize that she was right, and his behavior was foolish. Then, all would be well. She sat back in her chair, put her hands in her lap and waited for Matthew to come out of his dream-like world. Twenty seconds later, he gave his head a shake and blinked his eyes rapidly.

"Okay," Matthew said as he re-inserted the earphone, "you're right. What the heck was I thinking? So, um, what's this MP3 thing all about?"

"I'm not sure," Stephenie leaned toward Matthew again and pressed the PLAY button. "Just listen for a moment."

They sat silently, leaning forward, their heads nearly touching, as they heard the following words emanating from their individual earphones: "Before listening to anymore of this message, Stephenie, go get Matthew, the guy you came into the Enclave with. He needs to hear this message too. I think I've got something important to tell you both. And I may have found a way for you two to get out of the Enclave."

"Wait!" Matthew yelled, and then covered his mouth in embarrassment. He then lowered his voice to an excited whisper, "I know who this guy is, the guy who's talking. Put it on PAUSE."

"I don't know how to put it on PAUSE," Stephenie frantically attempted to find the right button on the MP3 player.

"Here, here," Matthew took the player and found the correct button to press. When he got the results he was searching for, he looked into Stephenie's face and said, "It's the guy who talked to us that night on the hill. The SFer who got so scared when you mentioned your brother."

"Shelton!" Stephenie said, with closed eyes and a look of recognition on her face.

"Yeah, that's the guy. Is he here?"

"No, a friend of his, another SFer, brought the player in for him."

"No kidding," Matthew stared off into space for a few seconds and then began working his fingers on the MP3 player. "We better listen to this all the way through. No interruptions, okay?"

Stephenie had just recently grasped this aspect of Matthew's personality. When a story was to be told, Matthew wanted the teller to have complete reign over the telling, no interruptions; *ask your questions after the storyteller felt he was finished.* Initially, Stephenie felt offended by this guideline. She felt like Matthew was attempting to control conversation. Eventually, she discovered that when she submitted to this form of communication, it took less time, made more sense and solved more problems. What irked Stephenie at *this* moment was that Matthew acted as if she had never before adjusted to this communication mode. It was as if he hadn't noticed how much she had changed, how she didn't interrupt anymore. She could have made a snide comment at this point, but bit her lip instead and simply nodded. Matthew pressed the PLAY button and both listened intently.

"Okay, I don't know how long the batteries on this thing will last, so I'll try and make it quick. Three important things. Number one is that the Council knows who you are, Stephenie. That's my fault, Hand. After you were sent to Quarantine, I told my superiors who you are and why you came here. I thought I'd get advanced in the Security Force faster if I did this. I was brainwashed, and I'm sorry, really, I am so sorry. My superiors spread the word up the chain to the Council. The Council still remembers your brother and that's why they won't let you out of the quarantine. The word I got from a friend who works inside the Council's offices is that they were hoping you'd die in there. When you didn't, they decided to leave you in there. They wanted to use you until not needed anymore. Then, they're gonna have you eliminated somehow."

"Oh, man," Matthew whispered. Stephenie closed her eyes and exhaled deeply. The monologue continued.

"Second thing: I can get you out of the Enclave. I've set it up for you and your friend, um, Matthew. This morning I got the word that you two are still alive, so here it goes. You've noticed that the Influenza has taken a downward spiral. There aren't as many people coming into the Quarantine Compound anymore. The Council has taken credit for the decrease in the epidemic, pointing to the fact that they've sealed up the Enclave and have isolated the sick. The fact of the matter is that the virus has run its course. That's all. Now, the word I got is that as soon as the infection rate drops to zero, they are sending an assassin inside the compound to kill you two. But hold on because I've created a plan of my own.

"The Council has set up an entire medical professional network outside the Quarantine. There are doctors and nurses all over the Enclave who work out of small clinics located in six different areas inside the razor wire. Two days before they send in their assassin, the Council is going to have a medical team visit the Quarantine Compound. They are there for two reasons. One reason is to ensure the epidemic is indeed over, and the second reason is to ensure you and Matthew are still inside. This medical group has no idea about the assassination plans. They will leave the compound with the promise that in two days the Quarantine Compound will become a free hospital. Okay, I've set up two people to take your place. They're coming with the medical contingent, dressed as nurses. You'll know what I mean by dressed as nurses when they arrive. They will instruct you on what to do to get out of the quarantine compound. Just trust me on this one. Just trust the fake nurses and do what they tell you."

There was a pause in the monologue. Matthew looked at Stephenie and noticed that she'd gone pale and was staring blankly at the floor. He reached out, touched one of her hands and was thankful that she squeezed his fingers as a gesture of recognition. The monologue continued.

"Okay, once you get out you need to get medical supplies. It's your ticket to the outside; I mean, outside of the Enclave. Hand, I gotta tell ya, it's a crazy world outside the Enclave. But, if you're a nurse or a doctor, you seem to have immunity to the violence out there. The reports I've heard tell me that medical people are treated like gods. You can't stay here inside the razor wire. The SFers will find you and you'll be dead. So, once you get out of the Quarantine Compound you need to go to one of the medical supply rooms and get medical supplies. You'll have your backpacks with you, so use these for the supplies. The easiest ones to pilfer are on opposite sides of the Enclave. Stephenie, you go to the old Taco Bell building. There's a back door I have labeled with a small pink dot on the bottom left corner. The door to that medical storage area is never locked because it's the main supply to the clinics on that side of the Enclave. Once inside this storage area, work fast. Nurses go in and out of that place many times each day. Now, Matthew, you go to the south of the Quarantine Compound. Walk across the old Menards parking lot to the back door of the old Ryan's Restaurant. This time I've labeled the door with a blue dot on the lower left corner. The key for this medical storage area is hanging from a wire on the piping of the natural gas meter, just to the right of the door. Once again, when you're inside the storage area you gotta work fast, Hand. Both of you now, once you load up on everything you think you'll need to look like a medical professional outside the Enclave, get your butts over to the old Mexican restaurant on the northwest side. Folks will see you as you walk around the Enclave, but they won't bother you. You'll look like medical people with the costumes you'll be given at the quarantine compound by my people. Once you get your supplies and meet at the Mexican restaurant, take off the costumes and shove them into the dumpster behind the restaurant. Oh, but keep the ball cap. Stuff it into a pocket or something. Always have it on hand. Everyone on the outside knows that a medical person wears the white ball cap with a red cross. Once you get outside the razor wire of the Enclave, wear that ball cap at all times. You understand, Hand?"

Once again, there was a pause from the MP3 player. Stephenie looked at Matthew for the first time and mouthed the word, "Hand," which made Matthew smile.

"Sorry about that. Got a low battery light. Recording on one of these things just eats the juice. Had to find some recharged cells. Took me a couple of hours to pull it off. Anyway, once you're at the Mexican restaurant, head up the hill and into the woods to the west. You need to do this in daylight. At night it's too dark to see. Once you're in the trees, go north. There's a road up there and a couple hundred yards of trees that haven't been set up with razor wire yet. I was put on a detail last week up there. The Enclave has used up all the razor wire it had on hand. The Council has ordered the outer perimeter razor wire of the Quarantine Compound, where you're at now, removed and used up at the north road area. It won't be there yet when you slip through the woods. I should know. I'm in charge of the tree clearing crew. But, I won't be there when you escape. Nope. I'll be about two hours ahead of you. I'm outta here, too. Which brings me back to the important things. One, you're marked for death soon. Two, I've provided for your escape. Three, I know what happened to your brother Morgan. Take a short break, Stephenie. Get a drink of water or walk around a bit, because it's not good news."

"Can you pause this?" Stephenie asked Matthew.

"Yeah, no problem," Matthew paused the MP3 player and watched as Stephenie stood and walked to a window. Pushing apart the horizontal blinds of the window, she peered through the glass to the darkness outside. The window fogged from her exhaled breath, blurring the view through the pane, but it didn't seem to register to Stephenie. She wasn't looking at anything in particular. For all Matthew knew, she wasn't seeing anything at all. After taking in the information that Shelton had left on the MP3 player, Matthew's own head was spinning in an attempt to understand all that he had heard. He couldn't imagine what was happening in the mind of Stephenie. It was obvious that her brother was dead. Wasn't it?

"You thirsty?" Matthew asked meekly.

"No." Stephenie replied a few seconds later.

"I can get some bottled water and bring it back here."

"Yeah, that would be good."

"Good," Matthew said as he stood from his chair and made for the office door. "I'm sorry, Steph."

"Yeah, me too."

Five minutes later, Matthew returned with a plastic sack full of items that he immediately withdrew and set upon the desktop. Included in this stash were two bottles of water, a handful of stale Snickers bars and some pills. Stephenie turned her gaze from the window to the items on the desk.

"What's all that for?" Stephenie asked, as if she didn't care what the answer was.

"Well," Matthew replied, as he sat in his chair and began removing the cap from a bottle of water, "I brought you the candy so you'd have something in your stomach when you take the pills with the water."

"What kind of pills are they?" Stephenie now seemed a little more interested than before.

"They're Skelaxin."

"What the heck is that?"

"It's a muscle relaxer." Matthew began to wonder if he was doing the right thing by stringing Stephenie along with this off-the-subject conversation.

"What do you need a muscle relaxer for?"

"It's not for me, Steph. It's for you. I want you to eat a couple of candy bars and take one or two of these muscle relaxers."

"Why?" Stephenie stepped from the window to stand in front of Matthew. She was chewing on the bend of her left hand thumb knuckle, a habit that told Matthew she was in mental turmoil.

"Because, you will need to sleep after you listen to this next part, I think." Matthew was now looking up into Stephenie's face, wondering if she'd understand his intentions. "And we've got no pain killers or sleeping pills. Just these muscle relaxers."

Stephenie sat in the chair opposite from Matthew and surveyed the items on the desktop. It dawned on her once again, as it had so many times in the last two months, that Matthew, despite his spaced-out disposition, was the best thing that had happened to her since the lights went out. He was trying his best to tell her that he loved her, that he cared for her and that he was willing to take a few rejections in order to get his message across. With a sigh, she opened the wrapper on a candy bar and began eating it. She did not feel like eating at the moment but knew it was the right thing to do. The two lovers force-fed themselves in preparation for the bad news they knew was coming. They ate in silence until all the candy bars consumed and almost all the water drunk. Stephenie put a pill in her mouth and swallowed it with a swig of bottled water. She looked at Matthew and said plainly, "Okay, let's get this over with."

"Okay," the voice of Jacob Shelton sounded through the earphones of the MP3 player, "I've taken a few chances and asked a few too many questions and finally got what I was looking for. There was this old woman that had lived in Effingham all her life. I guess she had a house somewhere to live in, but I grew up here and never knew where it was. This old woman, who goes by the name of Donna, was always seen walking around different parts of the town carrying plastic shopping bags with junk in them. Kinda like a homeless person might do, you know Hand? Anyway, one day she's out on one of her walks over by Menards, and she sees a couple of big trucks pull up in the parking lot at the front entrance to the store. These were military trucks with the canvas top and all that. Well, about twenty soldiers jump out of the trucks and run into the store. A couple more soldiers start unloading a bunch of stuff from one of the trucks and begin setting up barricades in front of the store entrances. People begin streaming out of the store in a panic. Then, Donna asks one of the departing customers what's up and is told that a bomb had been planted in the store and the National Guard was sent to get everyone out."

"Donna decided she wants nothing to do with a bomb threat, so she makes her way over to the Wal-Mart store, only to discover that there's a been a bomb threat there, too. It's a Wednesday, about noontime, so there aren't a whole lot of folks at the Wal-Mart store, but there are enough to attract the attention of a local police officer who happened to be driving by in her squad car. She pulls up to the front of the store and starts asking questions. Donna was standing nearby and overheard one of the soldiers tell the police officer that someone called in a bomb threat at both the Wal-Mart and Menards stores. A branch of the Homeland Security agency had deciphered the threat, and orders for evasive action passed through military channels to the local National Guard. The police officer played right into the scenario and relayed this info to the local police dispatch, as well as calling for back up to these locations. Just as the last of the Wal-Mart employees ran from the store, the cops show up, and soon bullhorns are blaring and they order everyone away from the premises of both stores. Donna heeds the warning and finds refuge under a tree across the street at one of the hotels. Ten minutes later, five more military trucks pulled up and about twenty more Guards began unloading coils of razor wire. The old lady sits under the tree and watches as forty National Guard soldiers encircle both the Wal-Mart and Menards stores in a large oval of razor wire. Crowds of onlookers had begun to gather at places near the barricades, and the police kept ordering them to move away. A news station helicopter shows up and begins its film footage fly-bys."

"That's when the lights go out. Most of the folks who were milling about the big show at the Wal-Mart didn't notice it at first. Then cars started having fender benders over on Keller Drive. Traffic started getting jammed up and horns started honking. People began coming out of every building in the area. Donna, still sitting under the tree, overheard some folks coming out of the hotel talking about a loss of electricity. A couple of police squad cars tore out of the Wal-Mart parking lot toward Keller Drive, only to be forced to an abrupt stop half a block later. The entire Keller Drive, Highway 33 and the Interstate intersection was in complete gridlock within ten minutes of the lights going out."

"Some of the hotel guest on-lookers began to drift from the Wal-Mart parking lot toward Keller Drive to see what was happening there. According to Donna, at this time nobody involved, whether the National Guards, the police or the spectators, seemed to be concerned about the situation. I guess most of the folks in that area of town at that time of day were locals, and the locals were accustomed to the odd inconveniences of small town life. You know, the electricity going out in one part of town, the gridlock caused by an auto accident. Even the supposed bomb threat at the two busiest stores in town didn't seem to faze these folks. People began trying to use their cell phones. No cell phone could get a dial tone. Donna said that people began frantically asking each other if their cell phones worked. Panic began spreading through the crowds of people outside the razor wire fence. Of all the things to set off a full-fledged panic attack…cell phones."

"I guess it began to dawn on people that something huge had come down. Like moths to the light, frantic humans began searching for any form of electronic sound. People ran to their parked cars, or to any of the cars stuck in traffic to seek the electronic voice of the radio stations. I was out at my uncle's farm, working on his combine at the time, so we had no idea all this was happening. There were two local radio stations on the air then; I guess they had back-up generators and could send out a weak signal to the local area without need of a translator. Donna said that she had approached a car stuck in the gridlock on the street. The driver rolled down her windows and let a small group of people listen to her radio. Reports were coming in from various locations in town, from people who had motorcycles and could maneuver around any roadway gridlock, or from folks with CB radios in their vehicles. The reports pointed to the fact that the entire Effingham County seemed to be without electricity. The DJ said that none of the landline phone systems were working, but no one was certain whether this was because of an overload to the phone system or not. So, the radio stations asked their listening audience to not use their telephones."

"Within an hour of the lights going out, several police squad cars had managed to force their way back to the Wal-Mart parking lot and positioned their cars in a line parallel to the southern entrance to the building. In unison, the squad car officers approached the razor wire barrier at the front of the Wal-Mart store, and one officer began calling over a megaphone for the commander of the National Guard to come out of the building and speak with them. Donna decided to stroll near these police officers. When she got within twenty feet of the megaphone, the remainder of the officers at the front of the Wal-Mart store ordered her to stand back a ways. This drew the attention of several onlookers from the hotel crowd and soon hundreds of people were crossing the Wal-Mart parking lot toward the police officers. Two of the officers ran to their squad cars and began pulling out plastic stanchions and rolls of barrier tape in hopes of erecting a barricade between them and the coming crowds. With much effort, a hundred-foot police line that ran parallel to the National Guard razor wire was created using plastic tape, stanchions and squad cars. In ten minutes a stand-off began that had all the potential to become a full-blown riot."

"In the parking lot, you had hundreds of frightened people pushing toward the Wal-Mart store. Holding them back, a handful of peace officers frantically attempting to enforce their frail plastic tape barricade. Near the razor wire, you had one police officer blaring out requests for a conference with the National Guard, who hid inside the store building. Just as the crowd in the parking lot was about to push over the police barricade and rush the razor wire surrounding the Wal-Mart store, forty National Guardsmen armed with full battle gear came running out of the building in two lines, one line from each entrance door. The lines of Guardsmen spread out in two directions to surround the Wal-Mart and Menards stores until there was a Guardsman every hundred yards inside the razor wire perimeter. This movement of Guardsmen temporarily lulled the crowd outside the police barricade. Donna said the people in the crowd acted as if they were watching a parade. Then, something happened that made the crowd go completely silent. One final Guardsman exited the Wal-Mart store and walked directly to the police officer with the megaphone. This Guardsman was unarmed. For a few tense minutes, the policeman and the Guardsman stood a few feet from each other, a razor wire barricade between them, and talked in low tones."

"The police officer with the megaphone then jogged over to a squad car, opened the passenger door and sat in the passenger seat. Donna was right there, pressed up against the locked driver's side door of the squad car. She saw the police officer start messing with the squad car's computer and communications module. She noticed that his hands were shaking. After a few minutes, the police officer got out of the squad car and began scanning the crowd, as if looking for someone in particular. I guess the crowd was still quiet at this point, because the police officer with the megaphone called to someone in the crowd and asked if that person had his Harley with him. When the person answered 'Yes,' the police officer ordered the crowd to part, so the Harley rider could cross the police line. Donna overheard the police officer ask the Harley rider to drive as fast as he could to his dad's place and see what his dad's HAM radio had to say about what was going on around the state. The Harley rider complied and disappeared into the crowd."

"The megaphone was hefted again by the police officer, but this time it was directed at the crowd in the parking lot. The police officer informed the crowd that the bomb threat was still in effect. He asked the crowd to disperse. No one moved an inch. Someone from the crowd yelled out, asking what the situation was with the lack of electricity everywhere. The officer said the electricity outage was indeed a countywide situation. He stated that all normal communications systems were down, but that he had sent someone to a known HAM radio operator with a back-up generator, in order to get more information. The police officer began ordering the crowd to disperse, to go back to their hotels, to go back to their cars and go home. Few, if any, moved. Repeatedly, the police officer requested the crowd to disperse from the Wal-Mart parking lot. The crowd began to murmur among themselves. The Guardsman called the policeman back to the razor wire and spoke a few words to him with his hands cupped over his mouth. The megaphone turned toward the parking lot again, this time informing the crowd that all water systems were down. He then reminded people that it was a hot day and that they needed to drink lots of water. He then suggested that everyone should seek out every possible source of water, including the hotels across the street."

"For some strange reason, this manipulation seemed to work. People in the crowd, which now numbered over a thousand, began pushing and shoving to get away from Wal-Mart and toward a source of water. The handful of police officers between the police tape and the razor wire collectively breathed a heavy sigh. Some were so shaken by the situation that they immediately shrank to the pavement and began muttering to themselves. Only a handful of the crowd seemed not to care about the water...wait, I just got a low battery light. Lemme get some charged cells. Be right back."

"You need a break?" Matthew asked Stephenie.

"No, how about you?"

"No, I'm okay."

"Okay, I'm back. The old lady had a couple of bottles of water in one of the plastic shopping bags that she always carried around. I guess she was so used to walking all over the place that she always had water with her. Anyway, Donna moved around one of the squad cars and got a good look at the National Guardsman in charge. She saw the name *Plasters* on his shirt. She overheard part of the conversation between Plasters and the police officer with the megaphone. The thing she remembers most is the police officer with the megaphone asking Plasters how he knew this whole thing was going to happen to Effingham in the first place. Plasters, she told me, then told the police officer that it wasn't just Effingham. The entire country was without power."

"Right about this time a horde of people are quickly walking from the hotels to Wal-Mart. Leading them are the folks who would eventually become the Council of the Crossroads Enclave. Half of these crowd leaders I had never heard of before the lights went out. But Donna, the old lady, knew each of them. She said that she was a political buff; she liked to follow the local political scene. She said that she read the local newspaper every day and attended as many local political and government meetings as she could. She knew every single one of the leaders of the Crossroads Revolution, which is what they now call it. Of the original seven Council members, you had two teachers from the local high school, a doctor, a lawyer, a nurse, a soccer mom and an unemployed factory worker. These three men and four women were acting as hosts for a local political party convention at one of the hotels when the lights went out. When the people from Wal-Mart began invading the hotels to horde their water supplies, word spread quickly to the hosts about what was going on across the street. Always looking at ways to sway the masses, the politicians quickly organized a march back to the Wal-Mart store to face down the police and National Guard. The marchers approached the police line and stopped just short of the police barricade. The local politicians requested that the crowd keep ten feet away from the police barrier tape and, like magic, the crowd obeyed. In fact, Donna said the folks in the front row facing the police locked arms to form a human chain. One of the politicians, a high school teacher, began grabbing high school kids she knew from the crowd and making them form the human chain. Nobody was going to trample a kid, you know, Hand? The politicians walked up and down the line of the human chain and kept urging the crowd to remain calm. Then, one of the politicians, Marion Hoelstetter, the nurse, took the initiative to approach the officer with the bullhorn. Unlike the conferences between the policeman and Plasters, Marion spoke in a raised voice that was loud enough for the crowd to hear. She asked the police officer if there was indeed a true bomb threat. The officer replied in a hushed tone. The crowd clamored to hear his response. Marion shrugged her shoulders and motioned toward the crowd, as if giving the floor to the police officer to respond directly to them. The policeman used the megaphone in an attempt to both deflect the question and ignore Marion. He began asking the crowd to disperse. The crowd began to push against the human fence of linked arms at the front."

"I guess the gridlock on Keller Drive had begun to affect the traffic on the Interstate to the point where no one was able to move for miles in either direction. Folks were abandoning their cars along the Interstate in droves and pouring across the fences in all directions. Many of them made it to the Wal-Mart area, and soon hordes of frightened civilians surrounded the entire razor wire perimeter. Everyone wanted to know what was going on. Only one person really knew, and he wasn't talking. He just stood near the razor wire fence in front of the Wal-Mart store and watched the crowds pushing against the human barrier in fits and starts. The human chain gave way in one place, and a few people fell to the ground. At that moment, Marion Hoelstetter pulled the bullhorn from the police officer's hand and immediately began ordering the crowd to calm down. Other politicians merged upon the point where the human chain had broken and began to restore order. Marion made a point of helping one of the fallen victims, as she continued to demand that the crowd calm down. Once she saw who it was she helped, Marion decided to use this person for her own advantage. The fallen person was Donna. Marion began berating the crowd for pushing an elderly person to the ground. Donna told me that she wasn't hurt; it was no big deal and she felt embarrassed for being used in such a way."

"The politicians escorted the old lady to one side of the human chain and ordered the people in that area to let her out. The human chain opened and closed just long enough for Donna to go through and become one with the crowd again. Instead of staying in the throng, Donna worked her way out of it and toward the northern fringe. Just as she reached an empty part of the parking lot, the old lady told me she heard a strange noise coming from the north side of the Wal-Mart buildings. When she rounded the corner of the building, she saw a large military vehicle pushing cars off Raney Avenue, as a snowplow would push snow. This vehicle, a mix between a tank and a truck, had a large metal device attached to the front that looked designed for just this purpose. Behind the giant car-plowing truck was a caravan of no less than ten eighteen-wheelers. The convoy looked like it was heading for the razor wire perimeter where Raney Avenue ran between the Wal-Mart and Menards stores. Several National Guardsmen had begun to converge on this spot and began pulling a hole in the razor wire perimeter, as if expecting the convoy to enter the compound. A good portion of the crowd in front of Wal-Mart began running at full speed toward the oncoming convoy. Before the car-plowing truck could reach the gap in the perimeter, a hundred people had stormed toward the opening. The Guardsmen closed the gap in the razor wire before anyone could get in. This was what your brother had been waiting for, a convoy of trucks. A uniformed National Guardsman drove every eighteen-wheeler. His plan had failed, and now a horde of screaming people surrounded the eighteen-wheelers. Men and women began attempting to open the backs of the trailers. One of the trailers was forced open and pandemonium broke out when it was discovered to be full of bottled water."

"Like magic, Marion Hoelstetter appeared on the scene with her bullhorn, this time from the top of the lead eighteen-wheeler. She urged the crowd to surround the trucks, but not to damage them or the contents inside. She promised that the goods inside the convoy would be evenly distributed to everyone in an orderly fashion if everyone would let her and the Council negotiate with the police and the National Guard. This was the first time the word 'Council' was used to describe the men and women who would form and lead the Crossroads Enclave. Once again, the crowd seemed to obey Marion in a way that they wouldn't obey the police."

"Once the convoy of trucks was secure, Marion returned to the police area in front of the Wal-Mart store. With the bullhorn in her hand, she walked through the police barricade, ignoring the main officer, and headed straight to where your brother was standing. The police just stood there, I mean, what could they do? They were outnumbered a thousand to one at this point, and Marion had the upper hand on all counts. A discussion was held between Marion and your brother. No one knows what was said, but after five minutes, the crowd that remained at the front of the Wal-Mart store began to get restless. Marion saw this and began blaring on the bullhorn that everyone needed to keep calm. She returned to talking with your brother through the razor wire for another minute or so. Then, she turned to the police officer and ordered him to come up with another bullhorn from one of the squad cars. The police officer did as he was told. Marion then gave the second bullhorn to another Council member, Donna said it was Frank Penrose, the unemployed factory worker, and instructed him to pass a message along to the people guarding the trucks on the north side of the Wal-Mart store."

"Simultaneously Frank Penrose and Marion Hoelstetter began relaying the same message to their portion of the crowds. The basics of the message was that it was rumored there was no bomb threat, it was rumored that the entire county was without electricity and would remain so for quite some time. Both Frank and Marion emphasized that these were still unconfirmed rumors, but now was the time to act in an orderly manner. The crowd went completely silent with the exception of the crying from frightened children and babies tended by their parents. Right then the Harley rider came back, pulled his bike up to the fringe of the crowd at the front of the Wal-Mart store, dismounted and began shoving his way to the front of the crowd. When he got to the front, the human chain blocked him. Marion saw that the police officer had made his way to the Harley rider and she intercepted the two just as the Harley rider forced his way through the human chain. After a brief private interrogation of the Harley rider and the police officer, Marion called another person from the Council to her side and gave him a message to pass to Frank Penrose."

"Once again, Frank and Marion began passing the same message to the crowd. Both began their orations by claiming that the following news had been relayed to the Council, you know, Hand, giving the Council all the credit. This new information was that a HAM radio operator in the local area had used his emergency generator to power up his equipment and communicate with other HAM operators like himself. In doing so, the HAM operator had collected the following information: The entire country was without electricity. St. Louis, Chicago and Indianapolis had become war zones of gang rampage and looting. Los Angeles, New York, Dallas, you name it, every major city was in chaos. The HAM operators had given a name to the catastrophe: The Collapse."

"Several people in the crowd fainted. A lot of people began to cry and some started screaming. One man near Marion began yelling at the National Guard. He claimed the Guard had lied to them about the bomb threat and that they should give the Wal-Mart and Menards back to the people. The crowd on Marion's side of the compound began to grow restless, and it didn't look good for the Council, and especially not for the Guard."

"Via the bullhorns, a call was put out for any able-bodied teenagers, both male and female, who were not responsible for the care of small children, to assemble at the north side near the trucks. These teenagers would immediately unload the semi in order to distribute bottled water to everyone. Well, everything went smooth on this water distribution thing as hundreds of teenagers came out of the two crowds, as directed by the remainder of the Council, and began unloading the semi. It was just the ticket to get the people occupied with something other than the bad news. Meanwhile, Marion had another conference with your brother and brokered a compromise. She will let the trucks into the Wal-Mart compound, if he allows her teen squads to unload them into the store building. Your brother agrees, and both sides arrange things with their followers. Marion and Frank use the teenagers to form a human chain portal around the trucks as your brother orders his guards to make an opening in the razor wire. Just as the trucks begin rolling into the Wal-

Mart compound, all order breaks into chaos. Donna said that a woman squeezed through the human chain and began running toward the gap in the razor wire. A National Guard soldier inside the compound, a woman soldier, saw the invader coming and ran to intercept her with a football-like tackle. At the moment the two women made physical contact, a gunshot rang out and another Guardsman inside the compound went down. It's not clear what happened next, because most folks hit the pavement at the sound of the gunshot. Others began running to aid the woman who was wrestling with the Guard. No one knows for certain, but I guess people from the crowd had previously begun arming themselves the moment the lights went out. We figure most of these guns came from their vehicles. A flurry of gunshots came from various locations outside the compound, each shot aimed at the members of the National Guard."

"Marion, who had been standing at the entrance to the compound, ran to where the two women were fighting and got them to stop. I mean, bullets are flying all over the place, aimed at the Guard soldiers, and Marion puts herself in the way. She then got on the bullhorn and began ordering the teenagers of the human chain to help her form a human wall at the entrance to the compound. I wasn't there, so I can't tell you what drove these kids, but before you knew it, a hundred young people had run to join Marion. They just stood there and formed a human shield. Some of them ran inside the compound and began aiding the National Guard soldiers. No kidding, two or three kids would run over to a soldier, form a human shield around them and escort them to the shelter of the human wall at the compound entrance. Meanwhile, some kids in the crowd attempted to stop the shooters. People were screaming and attempting to get away from the trucks. Fights began to break out and people were trampled. The gunfire ceased after the final Guard was behind the human shield and the last shooter had been subdued. Marion ordered all confiscated weapons collected and brought into the Wal-Mart compound. Marion told the crowd on her side of the store that a firefight between the Guards and some shooters on the west side had taken place. A group of men in the crowd had coordinated this attack, and it was believed that both firefights were related, because they happened simultaneously at two separate locations. Every police officer on the east side had been killed. Several of the east side Guards had made it to the Wal-Mart entrance to escape the attack. Most Guardsmen lay dead or wounded on the pavement."

"Both crowds had seemingly run for the hills when the gunfire broke out. By the time the gunfire was over, only the dead or injured remained. That is, except for all the teenagers. I guess we young folks are too stupid to avoid danger. I've talked to several young men and women who were there at the time and they all told me how scared they were, but also what a rush it was. Especially since someone was giving them the opportunity to do something that mattered. You know, frying burgers at the hamburger joint was about all we local teenagers were allowed to do before the day Marion got on the bullhorn and gave us an important job. Because the crowd had thinned out, Marion ordered the surviving Guards escorted inside the Wal-Mart. Once the Guards were safe, the trucks were moved inside the razor wire perimeter. About two hundred teenagers entered the compound to unload the trucks, and the razor wire perimeter was sealed again. Okay, this is where the old lady's story ends. Donna witnessed all of what I've talked about so far. The rest of this is information I snooped around and got from other people since I joined the Security Force."

"Wait, batteries are low again. Be back. I'm back. Stephenie, your brother wasn't killed in the east side firefight. He managed to zigzag his way to one of the entrances of Wal-Mart. Remember, he was unarmed; he didn't even have a Kevlar suit on or nothing like that. When Marion brought the surviving Guards into the store, she put one of her fellow council members in charge of unloading the trucks on the north side loading docks. She handpicked a small group of teenage boys to help her with the National Guard members. I guess the Guards all had little closed circuit radio transmitters as part of their battle gear, because Marion had one of the Guards contact the rest of the soldiers and told them to regroup inside the Menards store. Your brother came over the radio and wanted to know who was giving this order. When the word was passed that it was Marion, your brother agreed to meet and gave his men the okay. By the time all the able-bodied Guards met Marion and her boys in the Menards store, they numbered only 20. Marion had them gather in the lawn furniture area to take a load off their feet. She left most of her boys with the Guards and took the remainder of the boys with her to another part of the store for a private meeting with your brother. Your brother was shaking, I was told. Marion asked him to explain himself. Your brother told Marion that he knew the whole Collapse thing was going to happen, but had no way of preventing it. Instead, he chose to isolate and secure a part of Effingham that would be useful after the Collapse. His plans to secure the area and take control had failed. He had wanted to set up a base and use the police to restore order. He had arranged a bomb threat at the IGA across town simultaneous to the Wal-Mart and Menards threats. The idea was to draw the majority of police to the Wal-Mart store, while a handful of soldiers pilfered the IGA supplies into semi-trucks. The food from the IGA was taken to supplement the Wal-Mart compound. The problem was that about ten squad cars showed up at the IGA, and only three came to Wal-Mart. The swarm of police at the IGA delayed the pilfering and transfer operation. That was why the trucks showed up so late to Wal-Mart. He confessed that his intention was to put the police between his Guards and the crowds, so that once the IGA food was inside the Wal-Mart compound, the Guard would give the control of the compound over to the police. But, he hadn't planned on Marion and her group to upset the plan so rapidly."

"Marion treated him kindly. She told him that the throng outside considered the National Guard the enemy. They couldn't stay. Order had to be restored and no order could be held if the Guard was part of it. She said that she had a plan to get the Guard outside the Wal-Mart perimeter, but it would only work if each Guard member laid down his or her weapons, changed into civilian clothes and left the compound that very night. Your brother agreed, but wanted his soldiers to choose for themselves what to do. When the Guards heard of their options, they unanimously agreed to lay down their weapons and leave the compound. The Guards found the clothing section of the Menards store and changed out of their uniforms. She had her boys collect the disposed uniforms and all weapons onto flat carts and push the carts to the lumber yard."

"Marion sent two of the escorts to the north side of Wal-Mart, where the trucks were unloading, to deliver a message to the Council members there. These Council members then got on the bullhorn and began drawing people on the outside to the west side parking lot with promises of food and water in the near future. More bullhorns were found in the Wal-Mart store, and soon nearly a hundred teenagers inside the razor wire were patrolling the perimeter, announcing that food and water would soon be distributed on the east side of the Wal-Mart, near the store entrances. Then Marion sent a couple of her boys out to the Menards lumberyard to find an empty eighteen-wheeler or truck of any kind to use as the Guard's get-away vehicle. Only one truck was available, and it was full of items that had arrived that day but were not unloaded. Marion, her boys and the Guards unloaded the trailer. It was full of work clothes. Apparently, this truck was full of brown long-sleeved and short-sleeved shirts, work shirts, and was making stops at several Menards stores that day to deliver them. Marion got an idea when she saw these shirts and created the Security Force uniform right then and there. She ordered all her boys to put on one of these brown shirts. Once the truck was unloaded, all but two of the Guards went inside the trailer and sat down on the floor. One of the remaining two guards hopped into the semi and drove it to the lumberyard exit gate on the west side. When it was determined that the west side was clear of people, the semi driver plowed right across the razor wire on the west side of the Menards perimeter and into the parking lot. The semi came to a stop, the driver opened the trailer door and the former Guards dispersed in all directions, seemingly unseen by anyone. The last remaining Guard inside the Menards store was your brother."

"Marion had told Morgan that she wanted him to help her address the crowd and assure them that the Wal-Mart and Menards stores were now in civilian hands, and the soldiers had been dispersed. She then promised him, in the hearing of several brown-shirt clad escorts, after he addressed the crowd, she would make an escape for him, as well. He never left the Menards store. Stephenie, I talked to one of the witnesses, a guy I later served under in the Security Force. He said that as the semi full of former National Guard soldiers was pulling out from the lumber yard, Marion Hoelstetter hefted a handgun from one of the confiscated weapon carts and shot your brother four times. Marion, the one nicknamed Massacre

Marion, killed your brother in cold blood right there in front of about ten teenage boys."

"Stop it, stop the player," Stephenie said, as she yanked the earphone from her ear and abruptly stood from her chair. She swore several times, each word building on the next in volume, until she was nearly screaming. She walked angrily to the office room window and tore the horizontal blinds from their wall supports. The blinds cartwheeled across the office and slammed into the wall ten feet from where Matthew sat. Matthew remained still and silent, watching his lover grieve for the first time since he had met her. He wondered if tears would come from her eyes. No tears fell from Stephenie's eyes. She became silent and faced the windowpane, with her hands on either side of the window, elbows bent by her sides and her breath fogging the glass. She stayed in this position for five minutes before she spoke. "I bet that evil woman is behind it all. You know, our imprisonment here?"

"Probably," Matthew was so tense at this point that his voice broke.

"Yeah," Stephenie replied more to herself than Matthew, "Shelton screwed us by naming names. And then he must have put his life on the line to find out this stuff. That's why he's got to leave, too. He can't stay here. It must be like 1984 out there. Only, it's Big Sister watching them this time."

"We can't stay, either, you know that, right?" Matthew found his voice.

"You know," Stephenie turned to face Matthew with an expression full of zealous but controlled rage, "I want to kill her. I want to find that witch, hunt her down and drive a stake through her heart." Stephenie cut her words short and simply stared at Matthew, as if waiting for his approval.

Matthew said nothing but continued to look into her eyes.

"Yeah, you're probably right," she said as she returned to gazing at the fogged windowpane. "I couldn't get near her. Besides, someone else will eventually do the honors for me. Yeah, when the signal comes, when those medical folks show up, Matthew, let's get out of this place. Let's go play nurse somewhere else."

A few moments of silence flooded the office room before Matthew spoke in a near whisper. "Do you want to hear any more of this?" he asked, holding up the MP3 player.

"Nah. I've heard all that I think I need to know. You can listen to the rest of it if you want. If anything important comes up, just let me know later. The muscle relaxers aren't doing a thing for me. I won't be able to sleep. I'm so ticked right now that I don't want to be around the zombies in the three-day room."

"I can take over for you now, if you want." Matthew offered.

"Would you?"

"Sure. Go do what you've got to do, I'll be okay."

"Thanks," Stephenie said as she left the window and reached for the office doorknob.

"You really love me, don't you?"

"Yeah," Matthew said with a blank expression.

"Yeah," Stephenie said as she left the room.

CHAPTER NINE

A Dead Man's Vehicle

A lone figure crept through the underbrush as quietly as he could manage while still keeping the pickup truck in his view. This was difficult for the young man. His immediate surroundings were shadowed by the blackness of night and a sheet of fog which had arisen after the rain from the previous day. Yet, if he was to investigate the pickup truck that sat silently beneath the overhanging branches of a large tree, he had better act now. The darkness of this August night was slowly giving way to twilight of a morning sun and a day that promised another wave of humidity. The man wondered to himself if any of the plants that he was traipsing through might be poison ivy and, as a result, his skin began to itch in the most frustrating involuntary manner. He even developed an itching sensation on his back, which was irritating because of the constant pressure applied by the backpack that he carried.

For hours, he had been walking in the darkness, hoping to remain invisible. Being seen could be bad. He had been witness to the carnage of those who had been seen. In a single four-day stretch, he had escaped his own death at the hands of another human no less than twelve times. He had witnessed the violent murders of more than eighty people. Each of these homicidal episodes had occurred while the sun was high, which is why he had developed the practice of traveling at night and finding a hiding place to sleep during the day. Each of the violent episodes had occurred in well-traveled areas, which is why he chose to journey alone on the blue highways and isolated farming roads as much as possible. This routine of walking the back roads at night had the desired effect of making the man invisible to all but the nocturnal animal eyes. He hadn't seen another human in twenty days.

Despite his overwhelming fear of contact with his fellow man, after three days of self-imposed isolation, a seed of desire for human interaction had developed at the core of his being. By the tenth day, the seed had begun to grow roots and a stem. On this night, three weeks since he'd had a conversation of any kind with another human, the desire had come to full bloom. This is why he decided to investigate the idle pickup truck under the tree: he was lonely.

For most of the night, he had been hiking on a series of back farm roads that ran parallel to Highway 40. Eventually, he ran out of back road just west of Altamont. A cloak of fog had enveloped everything and limited his night vision to twenty feet. Given no choice but to return to the highway itself, the young man found himself hopping a barbed wire fence and noisily rustling his way through some underbrush. On the other side of the underbrush, a path that seemed to lead in the direction of the highway opened up before him. It was difficult to gain any sense of direction, though, with the blinding effects of the fog. Within fifty paces, it became apparent to the young man that he was walking through an arboretum. Through the fog, a large log structure came into view. Although his curiosity partially drew him toward this structure, his reasoning told him to give a wide berth to anything that had a remote possibility of housing a human. He skirted around the exterior of this structure, across an overgrown field of grass and onto a paved road. It was while walking the centerline of this road that he noticed an unnatural silhouette a short distance to his left. By force of habit, he immediately crouched down in the overgrowth nearest the roadway and patiently waited for any signs of movement from the immediate area. The dawning day gave no more audible clues than the occasional call from some hidden bird or the buzzing drone of a latent cicada. Minutes later, he tightened the straps on his backpack and began the slow process of approaching the object, monitoring every footstep to ensure the least amount of noise. When he was within fifty feet of the object, it became apparent that it was a small pickup truck. His heart raced, not from physical exertion but rather from the contradicting thoughts that warred in his mind. Half of his self wanted to find the vehicle abandoned; the other half hoped that it wasn't.

The question of the pickup truck's occupancy was even further aggravated when he came within ten feet of the vehicle and noticed a film of dewdrops on the windshield and windows. *Was the dew on the outside of the glass or on the inside?* There was only one sure way to find out, so he carefully approached the truck, stuck out his finger and attempted to draw a line on the driver's side window. A shiver ran through his body when the results were negative: the dew was on the inside of the truck's cab. This meant condensation from the lungs of a mammal, most likely a human. The young man crouched down once again in a state of fear and indecision. Within seconds, he began participating in a habit that had developed rapidly in his life over the last two days. The young man began to talk aloud to himself.

"Matthew, what are you gonna do?"

"I don't know. I've got that flashlight. I could shine it on the window to see if I can see inside."

"Bad idea. Remember, you took the batteries out of it to keep them from running down. They're in the back pocket of your pack and the flashlight is in your front pocket."

"Crap, you're right. I'd make way too much noise getting to that stuff. I could walk back a couple of yards and take my pack off…"

"Yeah, but what good is a flashlight going to do against a dew-soaked pane of glass?"

There was a shuffling noise from within the cab of the truck. Matthew attempted to crouch lower to the ground, and in the process, lost his balance. Tilting unwittingly toward the pickup, his forehead fell square against the driver's side door with a thud. The internal shuffling inside the cab became a frantic bouncing followed by the squeaking of a hand rubbing against the moist surface of the window. Matthew spun his body around until his backpack pressed against the rear side panel of the pickup's bed in a failed attempt to hide. He wished that he had never started this pickup truck investigation.

"Who's there?" A female voice called out from within the cab. The tone of this voice was a mixture of anger and anxiety.

Matthew held his breath and began considering the idea of fleeing, when the driver's side door violently pushed open. With a cat-like motion, a human figure slid deftly feet-first from the cab bench seat and onto the ground. Before Matthew could respond to this new set of circumstances, he heard a click. A hand-held spotlight immediately blinded him.

"What do you want?" The female voice behind the glaring beam demanded.

Matthew squinted and attempted to use his hands to shield his eyes from the spotlight's violating energy. He couldn't have looked more helpless or vulnerable if his life depended upon it. For all he knew, his life *did* depend upon it.

"I just," Matthew stammered, trying not to reveal the fear he now felt surging through his heart. "I just wanted to see if there was anyone in the truck, you know?"

"No," the woman declared, "I don't know. I don't know what you're talking about at all. Now if you've got nothing else to say, why don't you just shove off."

"To heck with it," the young man said, as he turned his back to the woman and let his backpack slide off his shoulders to the ground, spilling several plastic bottles from the backpack's opening. He then pointed to the back of his head and replied, "I'm so sick of this crap. Just go ahead and shoot me and get it over with. You can have my stuff. I don't care anymore."

This defeatist act was so absurd that the woman began to laugh. At first, her laughter was no more than the restrained nasal hissing of a stifled snicker. Within seconds, it became a nearly hysterical thunder. The beam of the spotlight began to bounce in erratic motions with each exhaled snort from the woman, casting odd shadows on the nearby underbrush. When the laughter died down to mere unstable breathing, the spotlight shut off with a click, and the new darkness enveloped the two humans. The woman sat on the cab's bench seat with her legs extended outside of the truck, as she slowly recovered from her fit of laughter with a series of sniffles and a few wiped-away tears. She was unaware that it would be the last time she would laugh.

Matthew remained in his gangland death-sentence pose, knees on the ground, feet curled under his butt, his arms akimbo and his back muscles erect.

"What's your name?" the woman asked, when it became apparent that the young man before her had not moved an inch.

"What does it matter?" He replied pessimistically.

"Oh, geez," the woman complained. "Look, my name is Stephenie. Okay? And, I haven't got a gun. So turn around and tell me your name."

When Matthew shifted his body and looked into Stephenie's face, he noticed that it was bathed in a dim light. It dawned on Matthew that he was seeing electric light emanating from within the truck's cab. "Um, my name is Matthew," he said distantly, as if it wasn't important. It was obvious to Stephenie that something else held his attention as he slowly crawled toward her. "You mean to tell me that this truck still has juice?"

"Enough to power this monster," Stephenie said, as she held up the spotlight by its spiraled power cord and swung it in front of her. "Whoever owned this truck had it hardwired into the dashboard. He must have used it for hunting or something."

"You mean, it isn't yours? Have you tried starting it up?"

"No, it's not mine. I stumbled upon it an hour ago and decided it would be a good spot to sleep." Stephenie was now feeling defensive because of Matthew's constant line of questions, plus the fact that he was crowding her over to the passenger side of the cab. "And, no, I haven't tried to turn it over."

"The keys are in the ignition," Matthew said, with an enthusiasm that Stephenie wasn't expecting.

After all, wasn't this the same man who, less than two minutes ago, was so downtrodden that he was volunteering to be executed?

"Mind if I give her a try?" Matthew said, in reference to the truck, as he reached for the keys and forced her to scoot further toward the passenger seat.

"Go ahead," Stephenie sighed in exasperation, then immediately said with confidence, "I don't think the owner will mind."

Matthew was not lost to the tone change of Stephenie's last statement and he gave her a questioning look. He was tempted to ask her what she meant by what she had said, but his curiosity as to whether the truck would start took priority for the moment. With a turn of the key, the truck's engine began to crank and, after a small chugging noise, came to life with a constant mechanical hum.

"Yeah," Matthew closed his eyes and leaned his forehead against the steering wheel. When he opened his eyes a few seconds later he announced, "Half a tank of gas. Half a tank. Will that get us to Effingham?" Before Stephenie could reply to Matthew's question, he jerked his head to face her and asked, "What did you mean when you said the owner of this truck won't mind if we start it?"

"He's dead." Stephenie said plainly.

"How do you know that?"

"I found his body earlier when I got here," Stephenie turned away from Matthew to stare at the dew-laden passenger window. She raised her hand to her mouth and began chewing on her left hand thumb knuckle. "It's about fifty yards away from here. Looks like a suicide. Gun was still in his hand."

"Yeah," Matthew said heavily, as he stared blankly at the dashboard lights. "I've seen a lot of that lately."

The truck's engine idled along as a comforting background noise for its two occupants, who, for the moment, needed to remain silent. Matthew waded out of his thought-place a few seconds sooner than Stephenie and found himself staring at her intently in the dim light of the cab's ceiling light. She had short brunette hair that was dirty and matted down in places. Her fingernails and hands were etched with thin lines of grime. The pants she wore were greased and darkened by wood fire ashes. The shape of her breasts was undefined, in a masculine way, from the multiple layers of shirts she wore. Being this close to her, and in a confined space, made him wonder if the stale odor he smelled was emanating from his body or hers. *I'm in love*, he thought to himself.

Stephenie broke out of her thought-place with a snap and spoke abruptly, not noticing his constant gaze. "What makes you think I'm going to Effingham?"

"What?" Matthew shook his head as if coming out of a dream.

"You asked if this truck had enough gas to get us to Effingham. How did you know I was going to Effingham?"

"I, I've got this map. I've been following it for a while now. It looks like the next town on the highway is Effingham. I just assumed you were going there," Matthew shrugged his shoulders and continued, "God knows you don't want to go toward St. Louis. I barely made it out of there alive a couple of weeks ago. I'd hate to be there now."

"Wait," Stephenie turned her shoulder toward the young man and leaned a few inches closer. "Were you in St. Louis when the lights went out?"

"At the stadium," Matthew shook his head, as if in disbelief of what he was about to say. "I was out on the field as part of the grounds crew. We were prepping the infield for the Cards game that night. We thought the electricians were doing some kind of maintenance on the power system. Took us a couple of hours to figure out the lights were out everywhere. How about you? Where were you?"

"About two miles away from the stadium," Stephenie spoke rapidly, as if attempting to get the words out of the way before saying something more important. She waved her hands in front of Matthew's face to prevent him from saying anything further and continued, "Wait, wait, how did you get into Illinois?"

"Like anyone else," Matthew's entire body shivered.

"I don't believe it," Stephenie replied. "I had a good two-hour jump on you. I got to the other side of the bridge about an hour before all of the freaking East St. Louis bangers came rushing over toward the city. I've talked to two people that had watched what happened on the bridges from a distance. How in the world did you make it over that bridge?"

"Blood," Matthew said as if it pained him to do so.

"Blood?" Stephenie replied as if Matthew was insane.

"When the word got to us at the stadium that the whole city was in the dark, I found myself a lookout spot up in the third deck and got a good idea of what was going on in the city. I figured my only way to survive was to get across the Interstate bridge. The first dead body I came across was lying in a pool of blood. I stripped down to my skivvies, you know, like the bangers got to me already and took all my stuff. Then, I painted the side of my head and neck in blood and played dead about a hundred times. Every time I came across a pool of new blood, I smeared it on me. Every time I saw or heard someone coming, I laid down and acted dead. When I felt like I was alone again, I got up and ran. It must have taken me about two hours to get across that bridge."

"Oh, man…" Stephenie simply stared at Matthew with a look of awe on her face.

"Yeah," Matthew whispered. "Not much of a man, am I?"

"Just the opposite," Stephenie whispered in reply.

With that comment from Stephenie, Matthew returned her gaze with a confused expression. *She has to be six or seven years older than me*, he thought. Two months ago, that would be a barrier to any consideration of their having anything more than a casual conversation. She would have been *too old* for him. Things had changed since August, and now she was looking at him, looking at his face. It was at that moment that he saw some new expression in her eyes. True, he was young, only completing 20 full years on the planet, and with such a lack of experience that many common things about people seemed quite new to him. The message spoken through Stephenie's eyes was of an unfamiliar language. He wasn't certain whether she was expressing dizziness, insanity or the urge to defecate. For the moment, Matthew chose to believe she was insane. It felt to him like she was reading his mind.

"Matthew," Stephenie began, in a deeper tone of voice that bordered on sensual, "It takes a real man to survive this long without killing people to do it."

Matthew laughed to himself and looked at the truck's dashboard lights again.

"What's so funny?" Stephenie asked, this time back to her normal, defensive tone of voice.

"For a moment there," Matthew said shyly, "I thought we were seconds away from making love."

"Me too," was her reply.

The older model pickup truck slowly made its way east on Highway 40 in the early dawn. The morning's light had cast an eerie yellow hue on the highway, which limited visibility to forty feet at best. On several occasions, the truck slowed to a near stop in order to maneuver around other abandoned vehicles left at precarious positions on the pavement. God only knew how many times the original owner of the pickup had driven this very same stretch of highway before the lights went out. God only knew why the owner decided to pull his vehicle over at an isolated stretch of pavement and end his life. These thoughts were running through the minds of the current passengers of the pickup as they navigated through the highway carnage. With such thoughts, under such circumstances as the total collapse of an accustomed civilization, the nagging idea of committing suicide was always present. Like a bad memory that one expends mental energy on in order to push it back from where it came, the thought of suicide was a daily visitor to all of the sane survivors of the great Collapse.

Stephenie sat in the passenger seat with her backpack crammed between her legs and Matthew's pack leaning up against her left side, so he could operate the stick shift. She had never learned how to use a stick shift and, up to this point in her life, it hadn't made much of a difference. The thought crossed her mind to observe how Matthew operated the vehicle so maybe she could learn how to operate a manual transmission, but it was seemingly too complicated. Instead, she concentrated on the road ahead and tried not to think of the former owner of the truck.

"You said we were pretty close to Effingham, right?" Matthew asked, as he stared intently through the windshield to the road ahead.

"Yes, it's only about ten miles from where we got this truck."

"Feels like we've already gone fifty miles," Matthew said, as he bent his neck to read the odometer. "Nope, only five miles. Must be the fog. Seems like it's taking forever."

"Where are all the people?" Stephenie asked as she peered out her window.

"What people?"

"There are a couple of little towns along the highway between Altamont and Effingham," Stephenie explained, "and a whole bunch of houses and farms. But, since I skirted around Altamont last night, I haven't seen a soul. I mean, this truck is making a heck of a racket, so don't you think we'd attract some attention? Don't you think people would come out and see what's up with the only vehicle on the road?"

"Yeah, come to think of it, it is weird. Maybe they all hit the road for Altamont or Effingham awhile back. And, have you noticed all the vehicles in the last mile or two?"

"Uh, I wasn't going to say anything about it," Stephenie said as she began chewing on the bend in the knuckle of her left hand thumb, "but, yeah, I noticed. Every car has at least one dead body in it."

"Good," Matthew said plainly.

"Good?" Stephenie asked abruptly.

"Yeah, it's good that you noticed it too, you know, all the dead bodies in the other cars. I thought I was hallucinating. I was afraid to mention it because I thought you'd think I was going crazy, which really shouldn't be one of your top priority worries, I mean, considering your other concerns—"

"Look out!" Stephenie screamed and pushed the steering wheel from Matthew's hands as far left as it would go.

A large object came out of the looming fog and appeared to be heading straight for the small pickup truck. Stephenie's rapid action had caused the pickup to veer far enough to the left-hand side of the highway to avoid the large object. Matthew watched helplessly as the pickup truck slid sideways across some form of liquid sheen on the asphalt surface. Although they were traveling at a mere thirty-five miles per hour when the large object came into view, it was enough velocity to catapult the pickup over a small drainage ditch and into a field of corn, where it came to a stop. A few seconds later, Matthew turned to Stephenie and asked, "Are you okay?"

"I think so. I think so. Geez, that was a close one."

"Shoot," Matthew exclaimed in a frustrated tone, "the engine died. Let me get it going again so we can get outta here."

"Yeah, good idea." Stephenie said, as she attempted to look through the back window of the pickup cab. "What in the heck is that smell?"

"I don't know," Matthew said absently as he turned the ignition key and waited for the engine to turn over. After a few false starts, the engine came alive, and Matthew attempted to back the truck through the path it had cut into the cornfield. For five minutes, all Matthew could achieve was a rocking motion, as he speed-shifted the manual transmission from reverse to forward repeatedly. The soil of the cornfield, saturated by the rain from the night before, created mud in all directions. The truck did not have the power or the tires to get out of the muddy rut it created. Stephenie managed to push open the passenger side door against the tight rows of corn stalks enough to see the surface of the soil. Immediately, a stinging odor swept into the cab of the truck, and Stephenie slammed the door shut.

"Ammonia!" Stephenie cried out between gasps for air.

"What?" Matthew, overwhelmed by the rancid smell, pulled his shirt collar over his mouth in an attempt to filter out the violent odor.

"Here," Stephenie reached for a water bottle from Matthew's backpack and poured it over the front of his shirt. After performing the same act on her own shirt and pulling it over her mouth and nose, she wiped her tearing eyes and said, "We've got to get out of here. But, the ground is polluted in watered-down ammonia. We've got to cover up our feet."

"With what?" The wet shirt material and the mucous running at will from his nostrils muddled Matthew's voice.

"With these. Thank God I saved these stupid things," Stephenie said as she unzipped a side pocket from her backpack and extracted a wad of plastic shopping bags bound together by rubber bands. A moment later, the cab of the pickup filled with the frantic noise of shoes shoved into plastic bags and the snapping of rubber bands to hold them in place. With this done, Stephenie looked out the windshield and said, "The wind is coming from my side. That means we should go out my side and go into the wind. Ready?"

"Let's get outta here, my eyes are burning," Matthew spoke in staccato tones of fear and pain.

As part of her former employment, prior to the Collapse, Stephenie attended multiple training sessions on the topic of ammonia handling, storage and transfer. It was part of her job to learn the safety rules for this chemical, even though her job description never led her anywhere near ammonia. Fortunately, Stephenie was one of those idealists who reckoned if paid to sit through the safety lectures, she might as well pay attention.

She and Matthew forced a path through the muddied corn field and trekked upwind from the ammonia source enough to breathe safely once again. The two travelers stood in the middle of Highway 40, four miles west of Effingham and gazed at the large object that had almost killed them. It was an overturned tanker truck. It had been heading west on the highway when it had obviously been involved in an accident with another vehicle. The truck's skid marks told the story of how the entire rig had slid sideways for over fifty yards, before it went into a roll and the tanks split open. The tank had held several tons of anhydrous ammonia.

"That's why everyone died in their cars," Stephenie shook her head as she stood next to her motionless companion.

"I don't get it," Matthew said honestly. "I mean the stuff was bad, but we made it out okay. How come they didn't?"

"We made it out because this accident happened a couple of days ago, maybe a couple of weeks ago. Then, it rained last night. Water has a way of neutralizing ammonia. But when this semi cracked up, the ammonia turned to vapor and the wind sent it west. I bet that no one for a half mile had any chance. Maybe a couple of miles. It's bad stuff."

"So, how come you know all about this ammonia stuff?" Matthew said, as he tilted his head and looked doubtfully at Stephenie.

"I had a job that required me to know about it."

"What job was that?"

"I'm an electrical engineer. I worked for the company that caused…" Stephenie paused, looked at the pavement and sadly said, "…forget it. I don't do that work anymore."

"Uh-huh," Matthew said as he pivoted on his feet to look toward the fog-shaded sun behind them, "by what you've got in your backpack I'd say you are a nurse or doctor or something like that."

Stephenie turned her back to the wreckage and began walking to the east, toward Effingham. Matthew followed suit and was soon keeping pace with her along a weed path on one side of the highway. For a few minutes, the two travelers walked in silence as the morning fog began to burn away to a humid haze that seemed welcome compared to their recent experience with the ammonia vapor. Finding a deep enough puddle of water in a drainage ditch, Stephenie slowly waded into the water until it covered the plastic bags on her shoes. When satisfied that the ammonia residue rinsed off from the plastic bags, Stephenie removed them from her shoes and tossed the bags into a nearby soybean field. Matthew repeated the procedure for himself and joined his now silent companion as she waited a few paces away.

"Before the lights went out," Stephenie began speaking as they walked, "I couldn't stand the sight of blood. I couldn't stand getting a shot at the doctor's office. But the day after the lights went out, I was faced with the choice of becoming a nurse or becoming a killer. I chose to be a nurse. I had no idea what I was doing, you know? Yeah, I had first aid and CPR classes for work, but nothing like what I've been faking my way through in the last couple of weeks."

"You mean, you're acting like a nurse in order to survive." Matthew said this as a statement, not a question.

"Pretty selfish, huh?"

"What do you mean by that?"

"Do you have any idea what it's like to have people think you can save their lives because you walk around wearing this?" Stephenie retrieved a white ball cap from her back pocket and pulled it down on her head. There was a glaring red cross sewn on the front of the ball cap. "I stole this off a dead Red Cross worker in East St. Louis, about an hour after I became an EMT."

"An EMT?" Matthew asked, "Like one of those folks that shows up at accidents and whatnot?"

"Yeah, like that."

"How did you become an EMT?"

"It's a long story," Stephenie replied as they continued to walk along the highway. "The Collapse caused a lot of changes in my life."

"The Collapse?" Matthew asked.

"That's the name for this whole fiasco. Some HAM radio operator out of Montana coined the phrase."

"Oh," Matthew said, with a look of confusion on his face.

"Anyway, I put this Red Cross ball cap on my head and suddenly I've got hundreds of sick and dying people crying out for me to save them. Do you know what it's like to let people die because they put their faith in you to save them and you don't know what you're doing, so they die when a real nurse could have saved them?"

"Do you know what it's like to act like you are dead, when twenty feet away a gang of hoods are slitting the throat of some guy who just happened to be in the wrong place at the wrong time?"

"But I'm..." Stephenie stopped walking to face Matthew, clenching her fists as a reaction to finding no words to explain her feelings.

"Tired?" Matthew asked.

"As tired as I can be."

"Me too. In more ways than one. The sun is coming up. Maybe we should find a place to sleep for the day and go into town tonight?"

"Yeah," Stephenie sighed and looked toward the hazy rising sun. "It's going to be humid today. If we can't find an abandoned building, we might have to sleep in the trees. You got any netting?"

"Netting?" Matthew asked with a puzzled expression.

"For blocking out the mosquitoes. I've got a roll of netting that I've been using to keep from being bitten to death when I sleep."

"No, I don't have any of that. I've been putting socks on my hands and a ski mask on my face. Seems to be working okay, I guess."

"Well, let's get off the highway," Stephenie said as she pointed toward the east, "Maybe we can find a place to crash out over there."

"Yeah," Matthew said wearily, as he turned and began walking east.

It took an hour for the two companions to find a place to sleep for the day. After investigating several abandoned structures as possible places of refuge, they stumbled upon a tree house in a copse of trees near the weathered remains of an abandoned barn. The tree house hid from cursory view by the overgrown branches of the trees surrounding it. If Matthew had not seen the series of ladder-like two-by-fours nailed horizontally to the trunk of the tree, the tree house would have gone unnoticed. Like a monument to a bygone era, the tree house seemed to be a relic from forty years before; its usefulness outgrown and its existence forgotten. Most of the floor and walls were rotting and in need of replacement, several of the ladder rungs had broken and one of the major support limbs had died several years before. Despite the disrepair of the tree house, the two travelers were able to ascend the tree trunk and find refuge inside the dilapidated structure. Under Stephenie's careful leadership, Matthew rigged a tent of mosquito netting to the walls of the tree house, and sleep finally came to the travelers.

Matthew awoke to a constant beeping noise and a subsequent rustling of the mosquito netting as Stephenie attempted to silence the alarm emanating from her wristwatch. After struggling for several seconds and saying just as many curse words, she finally got the wristwatch to cease beeping.

"Sorry about that," she said to a bleary-eyed Matthew, who was now slowly attempting to sit upright and untangle himself from the mosquito netting around his head. "Picture an electrical engineer who can't seem to figure out how to turn off the alarm on her watch. I've played with the thing a dozen times, but can't seem to get it to work properly."

"What time is it?" Matthew asked, as he rubbed his eyes.

"Five-o-five. It always goes off at five-o-five. I've been awake for a while. I slept pretty good, how about you?"

"Had bad dreams all night, uh, day. I kept waking up wondering where the heck I was. Hey, what's that you've got there?" Matthew pointed to a small black book Stephenie had propped on her lap.

"A day planner. My brother gave it to me last Christmas, just after I got a new job."

"A lot of good it does now," Matthew said with sagging shoulders and a moping tone of voice.

"You don't think so?" Stephenie asked.

"Well, duh. Are you working that job now?"

"What day is it?"

"What?"

"What day is it? Mr. Just-Shoot-Me."

Matthew grinned and shook his head, "I don't know what day it is. I don't know if it matters, does it?"

"It matters to me," Stephenie slowly became pensive, staring at the little black book as if watching a TV screen. "I always know what day it is because of this book."

"So?"

"So what?"

"So what's the date today?" Matthew asked, with a tinge of irritation in his voice.

"You sure are grumpy when you get up, aren't you?"

"Are you gonna tell me what day it is, or not?"

"I thought you didn't think it mattered."

Matthew moaned and flung his body back to a sleeping position. There he lay vigorously rubbing his eyes and temples for several seconds before quipping, "No wonder the divorce rate in this country was so high."

"Oh great, typical male answer to everything, blame it on a woman."

"Look," Matthew said, as he leaned up on one elbow to face the now upset woman with the little black book. "Consider for a moment our current circumstances, okay? The world has gone to crap. There are dead people everywhere you look. God only knows what we'll find when we get around the next corner. You've seen it, I've seen it, and there doesn't seem to be an end to the self-destruction in this part of the world. So, please, put your emotions into perspective for a single moment, and answer my stupid question."

"You sound just like my brother," Stephenie said defensively.

"Sounds like a smart man."

"He is," she said softly, as a concerned look swept across her face. Her reaction was blunt. She had gone from defensive to depressed in a matter of a second. Matthew thought for a moment, and then slapped himself on his forehead.

"Oh, no kidding, I think I get it now. Of course!" Matthew sat up again and gently touched Stephenie's shoulder. Matthew had a tendency to shift his mental gears so rapidly it startled most people, Stephenie included. In one breath he was sarcastic, and on the next breath he was sympathetic.

"Is he why you're heading to Effingham? You're trying to find your brother, right?"

"Yes, I hope to hook up with him there," Stephenie spoke in almost a whisper. She returned to staring at the little black book in her lap, as if by doing so, it would speak to her.

"Is there something wrong? I mean, you don't sound so positive about seeing him," Matthew asked.

"The last time I talked to him, just before the lights went out, my brother Morgan was planning to take military control of a specific area of Effingham. He was an officer in the National Guard there and was about to enforce martial law with a small group of Guardsmen."

"Wait, how did you talk to him after the lights went out?" Matthew removed his hand from her shoulder and sat upright. "The few civil people I've talked to since the lights went out told me that the cell phones went out immediately, and the landlines were so screwed-up that no one could use them. How did you know your brother was doing this military thing?"

"We talked about it just before the lights went out."

Matthew's eyebrows shot up to his hairline as his mouth fell open. For several seconds, he simply stared at the woman under the mosquito netting as if she were a god. All the drowsiness from his recent fitful slumber had vanished. His mind was racing with so many questions that he wasn't certain which one to ask first. Eventually, he settled for what he felt was the most pertinent question.

"Are you telling me that you and your brother knew the lights were going to go out?"

"Yes," Stephenie seemed hesitant to continue.

"And you know why it all happened?"

"Yes."

"Huh," was all Matthew could gather to say.

On several occasions in the last month, she had tried to express this foreknowledge to people with whom she had come in contact. Not one of them seemed to be interested in what had caused their nation's greatest disaster. In fact, on each occasion, the listener had acted sarcastically indifferent. One listener had even gone so far as to push her to the ground and began kicking her; blaming Stephenie for the catastrophe. Such reactions had made it clear to Stephenie that no one wanted to know what she knew. Once again, she had taken a chance, this time with the young man who shared her mosquito netting. Matthew pulled his backpack toward his torso as if to don it and make a rapid exit. She waited for the barrage of bitter words, but they didn't come. Instead, he rummaged through a side pocket and pulled out a power bar, wrapped in a sealed aluminum wrapper, and offered it to Stephenie.

"You hungry?" He asked, the silver object still held out for her to take.

"Um, kinda," she spoke hesitantly, as she took the power bar from his hand. It seemed that Matthew was unsettled by what he had just heard, but was acting peculiarly. *Why would someone suggest food at a time like this?*

As if to answer her unspoken question, Matthew turned his gaze upon Stephenie and said, "Well, I figured we won't hit the road until it gets dark, what, about four hours from now? And you've got a lot of talking to do from now until then. I don't know how you can walk around, knowing what you know about this whole fiasco and not be babbling continuously to anyone in earshot about it. It'd drive me nuts. I couldn't hold it in."

"I've tried," Stephenie admitted, as she exhaled a breath laden with pent-up fear.

"I'm an idiot, Stephenie, and I'm sorry for acting like an ass. You can tell me anything about what you know. Please, tell me about it, that's one heck of a load to carry."

"August 3rd," Stephenie said quickly, as a tear began to fall from her right eye.

"August 3rd?"

"Today is August 3rd. It's a Monday."

Four hours later, the two travelers climbed down from the tree house and began the final trek across the farmland to the town of Effingham. In that four-hour period, a catharsis had taken place in the heart of Stephenie Plasters, as the young man named Matthew allowed her to unload every detail of the burden she had been carrying all those weeks since the Collapse. In allowing her to do so, Matthew became the first person that she could trust since the disaster started.

CHAPTER TEN

The Sabotage Device

It had been a crazy day. The shipment of memory chips that were supposed to arrive last Friday and now it was Tuesday afternoon and the chips still hadn't been delivered. These memory chips were needed as parts for security system transmitters. Morgan had hired three extra part-time workers just for this production run. For the last two workdays, he had to figure out how to keep them busy until the memory chips showed up. As if that wasn't bad enough, the office computer network caught a nasty virus and he had to spend three hours weeding the bug from every hard drive in the system. Add to this the constant stream of phone calls that kept interrupting his day. First, the engineering firm that wanted certain specifications e-mailed to them on the newest design changes; then the loan officer that wanted six faxed documents signed and faxed back before noon; followed by the Industrial Park rental officer that wanted to know when Morgan was going to send last month's rent check. Now his sister decided to drop in for a visit.

"Mr. Plasters," the male voice of his admin assistant spoke on his office speaker phone, "Your sister is here. She says it's important."

"Send her in," Morgan shook his head in disbelief and muttered, "It *better* be important. I don't have the time or the patience for anything else today."

Morgan walked around to the other side of his desk and arranged two chairs. Expecting only his sister, he moved one chair to the far wall of his office and positioned the other at a welcoming angle at the *visitor* side of his desk. Then, Morgan straightened his shirt, pants and belt and then opened his office door. The moment the door was open, a young woman carrying a large cardboard box walked straight in without so much as a "How are you?", pushed the *visitor* chair aside and plopped the box down on Morgan's desk top.

"Stephenie, what the heck is this?" Morgan asked, now trying to skirt around his sister and take his place behind the desk.

"We need to talk, alone," Stephenie spoke anxiously as she turned around and closed the office door. She returned to Morgan's desk and began opening the lid on the cardboard box. "Did I tell you that my company had developed a new transmitter?"

"Yeah," Morgan sat in his chair, folded his hands in his lap and tried to look patient as his sister continued.

"Well, we got permission from the Grid Masters two weeks ago to perform a rapid-fire refit on all the old units. Since then, I've been out in the field helping the road crews pull Generation One and install Generation Two."

"They sent you out with the road crews?" This information had captured Morgan's interest, so he leaned forward and put his hands on the desktop. "I thought you said you were hired to do quality assurance on the individual components, not go out and install the final product like some lower level hourly worker?"

"Yeah, yeah," Stephenie stopped opening the cardboard box and began waving her hands in front of her, as if to stop Morgan from talking. "That's what I'm saying. This retrofit is such a big deal that they've got every able-bodied engineer, admin assistant, computer geek and techno-monkey on the company payroll, flying and driving all over the country to install the final product in the field. Its nuts, I tell you. I mean, Carl Larkin calls this all-hands meeting two Mondays ago and tells us that all one thousand units have to be installed and verified operational by Wednesday, which is tomorrow."

"Wait a minute," Morgan leaned forward in his chair until his abdomen was pressing against the edge of his desk, "They want to replace one thousand transmitters in two weeks?"

"Yeah, it's insane. AGS flew a couple of electricians and me from St. Louis up to Minneapolis. From there, we hooked up with a bunch of techies from the local electric utility. A shipment of the Gen-Two units was already there, waiting for us. The locals take us out to a transformer sub-station and our electricians show everyone how to do the retrofit. We then split up, using pre-marked maps and began driving around in the locals' utility trucks. After we'd get the Gen-Two unit installed, we'd call into the AGS dispatch for feedback verification. Once we got verification, it's back into the truck again to the next transformer station on the map."

"Well, then, if you're supposed to have all these new units installed by tomorrow, what are you doing here?"

"Yeah, yeah," Stephenie was now clenching her eyes shut and rubbing her temples. "After three days, we had a certain section of the grid completed up north, so AGS rented a car for me in Madison, Wisconsin. I drove it to Urbana and hooked up with some techs from Nileren. On Sunday, the locals gave me a utility truck and ten units to retrofit. This morning, I'm on my last unit at a sub-station out in the cornfields about twenty miles from here, when I dropped the stupid thing off the tailgate of the truck."

Morgan stood from his chair and walked around his desk to look inside the cardboard box that Stephenie had brought. She held down the box flaps as Morgan reached inside the box and pulled out a device that was about the same size and shape as a PC tower. Unlike a home computer, this device was surrounded by a metal casing with expensive weatherproof features. One corner of the device had the telltale signs of a healthy impact with an unforgiving surface. It was obvious to anyone that the device had been dropped.

"Let me guess," Morgan smiled, as his set the device on an open space of his desktop, "this is the baby that got dropped?"

"I was in a rush, it was my final unit, and well, I guess I'm just tired, you know?" Stephenie plopped herself down in the *visitor* chair, a good two paces away from Morgan's desk.

"So, why did you bring it to me?" Morgan asked, as he inspected the outside of the device.

"It doesn't work."

"Then take it back to wherever the spare units are and get a new one." Morgan felt it was a reasonable thought.

"I can't."

"Why not?"

"I'd lose my job," Stephenie spoke with utter resignation. It came out as a whine.

"Okay, okay, how long have you worked for…"

"AGS, American Grid Security," Stephenie said sarcastically.

"Right," Morgan continued, "How long have you worked for AGS?"

"Almost two years."

"Do you like working for AGP?"

"AGS," Stephenie snapped back at Morgan, as she clenched her eyes shut once again, "It's AGS. And yes, up until the last two weeks, I liked working for AGS."

"Did you get a raise in the last year?"

"Well, yeah, everyone got a raise last year."

"Why would they fire you?"

"Carl Larkin himself said so two weeks ago."

"Okay, let me get a clear picture on this," Morgan sat down behind his desk and looked at his sister. "Carl Larkin, the CEO of AGS, told you personally that if you break one of these units he'd have you fired?"

"No, he told the *entire company* that if anyone broke one of the Gen-Twos, they'd be fired."

"Huh," Morgan said, as his eyes returned to the metal-clad device on his desktop. "How do you know this unit doesn't work? Did you install it and call in verification with Nileren?"

"No, no," Stephenie said emphatically. "That would have raised red flags everywhere. After I'd done about ten of these units, I figured out a way to jumper the things parallel with the old units without having to pull the old units. You know, just a simple operations check. Well, after I dropped this one, I jumpered it and didn't get the same indications as I had on the others."

"What indications?" Morgan asked.

"I didn't get the whirring noise," Stephenie answered, trying not to sound stupid.

"Whirring noise?" Morgan asked with a cruel smile on his face.

"When you jumper it, the green power light comes on, the reboot LED blinks and there's supposed to be a whirring noise from the fan inside the unit. I didn't get the whirring noise."

"Gotta have a whirring noise, for sure," Morgan jested.

"I'm freaking serious here, Morgan," Stephenie said angrily, "I brought it here to see if you could fix it for me at your shop, so I can get my butt back in the field and install it."

Morgan leaned back in his chair and looked at the ceiling. His day had been no walk in the park either, you know. He felt as if his sister was being slightly irrational. If it had been anyone else, he would have given her the old, "Come back in a week" line.

"What makes you think I can fix this thing?" Morgan returned his gaze to his sister.

"Well, you're an electronics company and this is an electronic device. And, you've had all that electronics experience in the Army" Stephenie added, to bolster her point.

"Steph," Morgan shook his head in disbelief, "I was an explosives expert, okay? I blew stuff up. I didn't design the explosives, I just learned how to set up the devices and blow things up. My company is not so much of an electronic device-engineering firm as it is a home-security system retailer. We don't design or manufacture the parts. We take other company's parts, and throw them together as a system, then sell it to John and Jane America."

"I know, I know," Stephenie waved her hands in defeat. "But, can you at least take a look at it? Look, I'm going back home to Edwardsville right now. I haven't been home for almost two weeks. I'll be back in Effingham tomorrow morning early. If you can fix it, go ahead and fix it. If not, well, then I guess I'll take my chances in getting fired."

"Okay, Steph," Morgan grinned and shook his head. "I'll take a look at it. See what I can find out."

"Thanks," Stephenie stood and looked around Morgan's office. "You haven't changed a thing in this office since the last time I was here."

"You're funny," Morgan stood and gave his sister a hug.

"Thanks," Steph returned the hug and said, as she broke away and walked toward his office door, "I'll see you tomorrow morgan, Morgan."

"I hate when you say that," Morgan laughed as he watched his sister leave his office.

Two hours later, Stephenie was unlocking the mailbox for her townhouse in Edwardsville. The mailbox, packed with magazines and envelopes that had been crammed inside the small space, included an official USPS notice declaring that the remainder of the mail which would not fit into the box was *on hold* at the local postal office until further notice. Stephenie swore under her breath. As she walked from the community postbox area toward the front door of her townhouse, Stephenie wondered if anything important in the way of bills might be included in that hostage bundle of mail. She stuffed what mail she had received into the purse she was carrying and made a mental note to remember to pick up the on-hold mail the next time she had a chance. She didn't know it at the time, but she would never get the *on-hold* mail at the local post office.

Once inside her townhouse, Stephenie dropped her purse on the floor and began stripping her clothes off as she headed straight for the upstairs bathroom, leaving a trail of clothes behind her. A long hot shower was her first priority. Before she could get all the way to the bathroom, she took notice of the phone answering machine that sat on a small table just outside her bedroom door. Her eyes caught a blinking "1."

"Two weeks gone," she said to herself, "and only one message. I need to get a life." Curiosity got the best of her and the shower idea was temporarily set aside. Stephenie pressed the message button on the answering machine. As she stood stooped over the small table, clad only in her bra and underpants a familiar and urgent, voice blared from the answering machine. It was her brother Morgan.

"Steph, call me on my cell phone, immediately, no matter what time it is. Okay? I'm serious. Call me now. The number is 217-555-5790. That's 217-555-5790. Hurry."

An odd feeling began to sink into Stephenie's stomach. It was like that sudden drop on a roller coaster. She picked up the hand receiver of the answering machine and played back her brother's message, to get the number he had left on her machine. After two rings, a click followed by a garbled, "Hello?"

"Morgan?"

"Steph?"

"I can't hear you very well," Stephenie replied.

"Daggonit, batteries low. I'll call your house, bye." Seconds later, her phone rang, and she pressed the answer button on the handset.

"Steph," Morgan began speaking as soon as she got the receiver to her ear, "Did you have *anything* to do with the quality assurance on these Gen Twos?"

"Yes. In fact, that's why AGS hired me. I was in on the ground floor for the Gen-Twos."

"Well, then, what the heck are you guys up to?" Morgan sounded scared.

"What are you talking about?" Stephenie said defensively.

"Okay, how about this," Morgan said a little calmer, "Did you inspect each and every unit before it got shipped?"

"Yes," Stephenie replied, trying not to sound guilty of something she feared she had done wrong but was unaware. "I inspected each of the Gen-Twos three months ago. It took me two weeks to QA all thousand units."

"And you didn't notice anything unusual about the two battery packs?"

"One battery pack," Stephenie corrected her brother. "Each Gen-Two has one battery pack."

"What did that one battery pack look like?"

"It looked like a plastic-coated carton of Haagen-Dazs ice cream. Um, yellow in color."

"You mean the battery pack was colored blue, right?"

"No, yellow. We had yellow battery packs installed on the Gen-Two."

"Oh, great. Was there any space left inside the casing of each unit?"

"Look," Stephenie said with a tone of impatience in her voice, "What's this all about? Did you…"

"Answer the freakin' question," Morgan interrupted her, "was there any available space inside the Gen-Two casing?"

"Yes," Stephenie thought for a moment. "There was enough space inside those things for another battery."

Morgan swore.

"You gonna tell me what this is all about?" Stephenie said after a pause of silence had passed.

"There's something else in the Gen-Two, Steph," Morgan sighed, "and it ain't a battery."

"What is it?"

"Explosives," Morgan said evenly.

"What?" Now it was Stephenie's turn to curse.

"I swear to God, Steph, there's a soft-wrap canister of plastic explosives in this thing."

"Are you sure?" Stephenie asked in disbelief.

Morgan swore again. "Come on, Steph, I know a freakin' explosive when I see it. This stuff looks a lot like what we used in Iraq. What I want to know is what it's doing in a transducer unit."

"I don't know what to say," Stephenie said after a pause.

"Do you have any drawings for these things?" Morgan asked.

"Not here at my house. They're all at work in St. Louis. We weren't allowed to leave the building with any drawings of any kind."

"Can you get to them?" Morgan asked. "Can you get to a set of drawings for these Gen-Twos?"

"Yeah, I can go to town and get to my office. I've got a set inside my desk drawer."

"Can you do that right now?"

"Um, sure, I suppose so," Stephenie paused to look at her watch. It read six p.m. "I've got an access security card. I can get in."

"Good," Morgan said. "Go there now. Like, right away."

"Um," Stephenie stammered. The last three minutes had been too much of an information overload on her brain. Morgan realized this. He had a one-hour advantage over her. From the moment he opened up the Gen-Two and saw the explosives inside, he had an hour to mull it over in his mind while waiting for Stephenie to call back.

"Look, I know this is all of a sudden for you," Morgan began to explain, in a much softer tone, "But there's one more thing in this Gen-Two that I haven't told you about. Once you get a set of drawings in front of you, call my cell phone. Have you got my cell phone number written down?"

"Uh, no," Stephenie began search the small desk drawer for a pen.

"Find a pen and write it on your hand, okay?"

"Sure, got one, go ahead."

As Morgan recited his cell phone number, Stephenie wrote it in ink on the back of her left hand. It would be the last phone number she would ever call.

It took Stephenie just over an hour to make it to her office at the AGS headquarters in downtown St. Louis. She would have been twenty minutes earlier, had it not been for a period of post-vehicular accident gridlock on the interstate. Once inside the Costar Building, home of the four floors of AGS headquarters, Stephenie began to get the feeling that she was about to do something illegal and dangerous. Even after waving hello to the night shift security guard seated behind a Plexiglas encased surveillance camera booth, she felt as if she was about to get busted.

"What are you thinking?" She spoke aloud as she stepped into a vacant elevator. "I mean, what are you doing wrong? You've done this a dozen times in the last two years. You've come into work after hours because you've got some extra work to do. Yeah, no big deal. People at AGS do it all the time. In fact, I wouldn't be surprised if a dozen folks are up there right now doing last minute stuff on the retrofit. But, just in case..."

Stephenie pressed the elevator button for the eighth floor, four floors below her destination. She knew of a set of emergency exit stairs that the techno-geeks in the AGS Information Technology department had bypassed from the fire control system. Only a handful of employees knew about the bypass and used these stairs as a quick route between the seventh and twelfth floors. Stephenie had successfully used these stairs twice when she had been late for work. She figured on this night, under these circumstances, it would be better to enter the twelfth floor from the fire escape stairs rather than the front elevator entrance. She did not want anybody to see her. Clutching her purse with both hands so it wouldn't make any noise, she exited the elevator on the eighth floor and quietly made her way down the main corridor toward the emergency stairs.

What Stephenie was not prepared for when she entered the twelfth floor, the security wing of the AGS engineering division, was the total absence of human beings. No one was there. It was like walking into a ghost town as she made her way through the sea of drafting tables to her cubicle on the far side of the floor. She pulled her purse to her chest and hugged it for security. Every single computer monitor was black. It was normal procedure on the security wing for personnel to log off their computers when they left each day. But, even in the log-off condition, an AGS-approved screen saver would click on after ten minutes. None of the computers had its screen savers rolling. It was as if the computers and monitors were without power. Only a third of the lights on the security floor were illuminated; that meant the emergency lighting system had been activated.

Stephenie made it to her cubicle, fished a key from her purse and unlocked her personal drawing drawer. She pulled out several large flat sheets of paper, placed them on her desk and flipped a switch on her desk lamp. The lamp didn't come on. *No electricity?* she asked herself as she bent to peer down the side of her desk to check her power bar. The power bar was plugged into the wall but the red power light on the power bar was unlit. *No electricity.* It was then she remembered the flashlight. She rifled through her purse and eventually withdrew a small day planner. Inside the metal rings of the day planner she kept a Maglite. With a two-handed twist, the Maglite came on and shed a small circle of light on the drawings. Stephenie began reaching for her desk phone when she stopped short and stared at the face of the phone. A single red light glowed from one of the twenty phone stations.

It struck Stephenie as odd that the phones still had power, but the remainder of the floor did not. Using the Maglite, she traced the two lines from the back of the phone to an junction box on the far wall of her cubicle. Both the power to the phone and the communications line were hardwired into a circuit that was separate from those for the computers and electrical outlets. Returning to the desk phone with the Maglite, Stephenie leaned forward to peer at which station showed communications activity. *Odd*, she thought, *it's one of the two stations on the phone without a station label. I never noticed that before.* Shaking off the curiosity of where the in-use phone might be located, Stephenie returned to her original task. She decided not to use the company desk phone. It might give away the fact that someone was on the twelfth floor. Instead, she used the company cell phone in her purse to call her brother. She had to hold the Maglite in her mouth while she read Morgan's cell phone number off the back of her left hand and dialed her own cell phone with her right hand. After two rings, she got a clear, "Hello, Steph."

"You sound better this time," she said absently as she attempted to focus in on the drawing covering her desk.

"I charged the batteries," Morgan replied calmly. Then urgency kicked in. "You've got some drawings?"

"Yeah, it might take me awhile to find what you're looking for because we've got emergency lights for the entire floor and no outlet electricity."

"What?" Morgan asked, as if he hadn't heard her at all.

"I said we don't have electricity on the twelfth floor."

"Is anyone there?"

"It's the weirdest thing, Morgan. There isn't anyone here. Nobody."

"We've got to work fast. Now look, on the right side of this Gen-Two unit there's a wire terminal block with spaces for, um, twenty connections."

"Right," Stephenie said, "Only sixteen are used, the rest are empty."

"Nope, not on this unit," Matthew said, "I've got three more wires. Terminals fifteen, sixteen and seventeen. Fifteen and sixteen go to some kind of relay."

"Okay, wait, you're saying that there are wires on terminals fifteen and sixteen?"

"Yeah, and they go to a relay."

"Hold on a minute," Stephenie perused the drawing with the Maglite in her right hand, as she held the cell phone to her ear with the left hand. "I don't see anything on my drawings for those two terminals."

"Okay," Morgan said slowly as if preoccupied with something else. "The wires on terminals six and seven, where do those go on your drawing?"

"To the signal dampening unit. It's like an inductor. Smoothes out any spikes before the feedback is sent to the satellite transmitter."

"Okay, Steph," Morgan said officially, "There's a thing in this unit that wires six and seven go to, but it's no inductor. It looks more like an LED box of some kind. But, it's installed backwards."

"Yeah, there's an LED readout box, but it's attached to the face of the keyboard inside."

"Yeah, I see that thing, but there's a smaller one all by itself." Morgan then took a deep breath and exhaled before going on. "Okay, I'm going to use a screwdriver to pull the second LED from its mount on the casing. I wanted to wait until everyone had left work for the day before I did this." Morgan paused a few seconds. She heard a grunt from his end of the cell phone.

"Wait, Morgan," Stephenie tried to remain calm, "Don't do it. It might be a trigger for the explosives."

"Too late," Morgan said, "I've got it free. It's an LED readout, just like I thought."

"What's it say?" Steph asked, as she awkwardly twisted the Maglite to the off position.

"It's a counter, Steph, and the numbers are…decreasing."

"Oh, no," Stephenie froze at the implications. Her brother was staring into the face of an explosive timer.

"Okay, um, Steph," Morgan said, as if he was thinking too hard to speak, "Do you have a good source of the current time?"

"Let me check," Stephenie stepped away from her desk and eyed a nearby wall clock. "Yes, I do. It's an atomic clock. Battery powered, satellite and all that."

"Good," Morgan said, "get a pen and a paper, okay, and when I say the word 'mark', write down the exact time at that moment. Okay?"

"Sure, I'm standing by the clock."

"Okay…mark."

"Got it."

"What was the exact time?" Morgan asked.

"Seven thirty-four and fifty six seconds."

"Okay," Morgan said, as if satisfied by whatever he was doing on his end of things. "Give me a minute with my calculator, okay; I think I can figure out when this timer is set to go off."

"Oh, great," Stephenie said sarcastically, as she crept back to her desk. She could hear her brother set his cell phone down, and the background sounds of his fingers tapping away on his computer. She heard a distinguishable but distant "Huh?" come over the cell phone receiver pressed against her ear. Then, more typing, followed by the sounds of shuffled papers. Eventually, Morgan came back on the phone and sounded uncertain from the very first word.

"I've crunched the numbers twice, and both come out the same, but it doesn't make sense," he offered.

"Well, when does the timer get to zero?" Stephenie asked.

"Wednesday. At twelve-thirty-four in the afternoon. Wednesday, twelve-thirty four and fifty six seconds," Morgan sounded confused.

"Wait," Stephenie said as she re-twisted the Maglite and shone it on her wall calendar. "You're talking this Wednesday, right? Like tomorrow Wednesday?"

"Well, yeah."

"Oh, no!" Stephenie slapped her hand across her mouth. She had forgotten the Maglite was in that hand and received a fat lip for her forgetfulness.

"What is it?" Morgan seemed urgent in his need to know.

"It's all in order," Stephenie said, through the pain emanating from her lower lip, "When you spread the numbers out. It comes to one, two, three, four, five, six, seven, eight and nine. All the single digits."

"What are you talking about?" Morgan demanded.

"The date and exact time," Stephenie explained, "Twelve thirty-four and fifty-six seconds on the seventh month, eighth day, in the year nine. It comes out one through nine."

"You're kidding me." This time it was Morgan who yelled. "Do you know the exact locations of all these Gen-Two retrofits? Like, do you have a big-picture map of every retrofit?"

"Yes, I have the drawings right here in front of me, give me a minute to pull them out." Stephenie set her company cell phone down on her chair, put the Maglite into her mouth and began shuffling the large drawings on her desk. Finding the correct map for what Morgan was requesting, Stephenie retrieved her cell phone and told Morgan that she was ready.

"Good, um, do you see a pattern?" Morgan asked.

"A pattern?" Stephenie asked frantically.

"Yeah, yeah, a pattern. When we did demolition in Iraq, we did it for a specific purpose. The idea was to impede travel to a certain area or to impede communication to a certain area. Our demolition points were based on the most efficient way of doing this impeding. You know? Why blow up six bridges when all you need to blow is five? What I'm asking is, do you see a pattern to the placement of these thousand Gen-Twos?"

"Okay, hold on a minute." Stephenie used the snub antenna of her cell phone as a pointer to trace out the connecting points of the United States electrical grid. Within one minute, it became apparent that a pattern did exist in the placing of the Gen-Two retrofits.

"Morgan, you're right, there is a pattern."

"Well, what is it?"

"If my knowledge of the grid is correct, if every single one of these Gen-Twos is set to explode at the same time, the entire U. S. grid will go down."

"Wait, I thought the powers-that-be had set up the grid with sufficient back-up lines to cover a blackout. You know, bring back a blackout area in one hour."

"Morgan, they did," Stephenie explained, with a heavy sigh, "But, every one of these Gen-Twos is placed in such a way to render the backup lines inoperable, too. You see, each one of these Gen-Twos is attached to a high-power transformer. The Gen-Ones and Gen-Twos get their power from the electromagnetic field that surrounds the transformer when power goes through it. It wouldn't take much to damage these transformers. I mean, one smack with a pickaxe to the right spot could destroy the entire unit. So, unless we can disable the explosives, by this time tomorrow, the entire grid will be down."

"I can't believe this." Morgan said, "Can any of the grid be recovered? I mean, after the detonations."

"I looked for that. No, Morgan, no recovery until new transformers can be reinstalled."

"And how long would that take?"

"My guess would be about a week for each transformer if it was only one unit. But, man, this is bad. We're slated to see a thousand of these substations go down simultaneously. There's no way to recover, maybe ever."

For a few seconds that seemed to stretch for an eternity, neither Morgan nor his sister spoke. Across the hundred-mile expanse of telephone lines that separated them, one could still hear their breathing seesawing through their receivers. The thoughts racing through their individual brains were creating enough energy to light a small city. Raised in the same household, the brother and sister under such extreme circumstances reacted in the same fashion. They took the time to let all the information sink into their brains and be sorted. Almost instantaneously, they spoke the same word: "Why?"

Why would a company such as AGS, who had so much money at stake, destroy the very system that had made it so rich? Why would an organization, whose product reputation had become synonymous with the word *integrity*, suddenly rebel against the society it helped to bring a wall of security? Who was behind the conspiracy? Was it one person or an entire cadre? The situation boiled down to one question and that was "Why?"

"I don't know, Morgan."

"Neither do I. I suppose it doesn't matter. You know what's going to happen, don't you? Without electricity, this country folds. The chaos will be intense. Picture the first Rodney King verdict happening in every city of over a hundred thousand in population, all at once. We'll internally implode, Steph. It's over. The country is dead."

"Maybe I can stop it, but I'm not sure how." Stephenie offered weakly.

"How can you possibly do anything about it?" Morgan demanded. "You don't have the time to replace all the units in the areas that you worked on, and, even if you did try that, wouldn't someone find out about it?"

"Yeah, you're right. There are so many different entities involved in the retrofit that the moment I pulled a Gen-Two off line, it would raise red flags all over the place. I'd have to find someone here, at the central nervous system of AGS, and try to warn them of the situation. But I don't know who to trust, or how deep the conspiracy goes."

"You're right, Steph," Morgan said, the weariness and worry clear in his voice, "I'm racking my brain on what I can do and who I can trust. I tell you, if we had a week, we might be able to pull-off something. We don't have a week. We have less than twenty-four hours."

"What are you going to do, Morgan?"

"I was thinking of going to the news media, you know, carrying this Gen-Two with me as proof. That wouldn't give us enough time, and I figure the news media would screw it up and cause a nationwide panic. I considered going to the police. But since I got on their bad side earlier this year for that gun shooting incident near my house, they'd never listen to me."

"Oh, that's right," Stephenie cut in, "I forgot all about that. Didn't they harass you for a while, give you random speeding tickets and stuff like that?"

"Yeah, for about two months, until they figured I got the message to keep my mouth shut." Morgan said with a forced laugh. "So, with the police being out of the question, I thought about going up through the channels of the National Guard. But that's a bureaucratic maze. So forget that. Maybe I can use the Guard's channels to the FEMA or Homeland Security agencies. I guess that's all I can do. How about you?"

"I don't know." Stephenie sounded frightened. "This is all hitting me so fast."

"I don't think we can stop it, Steph." Morgan offered in a sympathetic tone.

"I know. Is your passport up to date?" She asked.

"Oh, man," Morgan let out a deep breath, "no, how about you?"

"No. We can't even catch a flight out of the country. We're stuck, bro."

"This is insane."

"I know it is. I'm scared, Morgan, really scared."

"Well, whatever you do, Steph, since Mom and Dad are dead, why don't you come out here to Effingham. We can face this together."

"Yeah, that sounds like a good idea. Where will you be?"

"The armory," Morgan said, "On the corner of Temple and Henrietta. You know where I'm talking about?"

"Yes, I know where that is. Will you have this same phone number, the one for your cell phone?"

"Yes. Now, get out of that building and get your butt over here, you hear me?" Morgan put out his best effort at playing the older brother role.

"Okay, I love you, Morgan."

"Love you too, sis, bye."

"Bye," Stephenie said sadly and pressed the END button on her company cell phone.

After folding her drawings up and tucking them inside her blouse, Stephenie scanned her cubicle for anything else she might need to take with her and began tossing these items inside her large purse. It's odd what a person decides to salvage in such a situation. Her entire world was about to come to an end and Stephenie was oddly concerned with such items as a stapler, a calculator, a handful of writing pens and roll of cellophane tape in a desktop dispenser. After throwing these items in her purse, she spied a set of photographs on her desktop. They were framed in a cheap metal device with a hinge between the two frames. Smiling back at her from one frame was her mother and father in a photograph taken three months before they died in a car crash. The other frame contained a picture of her brother Morgan. He was dressed in Army issue combat fatigues. He was kneeling on one knee, an automatic weapon gripped tightly with both of his hands and his face revealed both friendliness and bravery. In a rush of quick movements, out from her purse went the office supplies, and in went the framed photographs.

Just as she was turning to leave her cubicle and the Costar building, Stephenie caught a glimpse of movement from her desk telephone. The red light on the phone's face went out. Startled, she turned back to the phone and stared at the two unlabeled phone line indicators. Seconds later, both unlabeled lights went on like a pair of evil triangular eyes staring back at her. Stephenie jumped back a step, as if shocked by static electricity. This meant that there was more than one person communicating from the four floors occupied by AGS. Despite her fears, the curiosity of these unknown phone stations got the best of Stephenie, and she decided to investigate their whereabouts.

In her last two years of employment, she had spent time on each floor of the Costar building occupied by AGS. She knew most of the layouts for each floor, and in that vein of thought, was aware that she didn't know the purpose of several of the offices on each floor. The unknown phone stations, she assumed, must generate from one of these mystery offices. Starting with the floor she was on, Stephenie began to silently approach each office door and gently place her ear against it. After a few attempts at this elementary form of eavesdropping, Stephenie began to wonder if she was accomplishing anything substantial beyond warming up her earlobes. Each door sounded the same. All she heard for her efforts was a constant humming noise, which could have been structural vibrations from the building's air conditioning systems or the auxiliary machines three floors above her. The thought crossed her mind to find and utilize a glass vessel. She ruled this idea out when she noticed that her hands were involuntarily shaking. Dropping a glass object at this point would be a disaster.

With the entire twelfth floor covered to the best of her knowledge, Stephenie used the emergency stairs to investigate the eleventh floor. Once again, the floor was deserted, had its lights dimmed and all visible computer monitors were black. Thirty minutes later, Stephenie exited the eleventh floor to investigate the tenth floor, having failed to hear anything from any of the closed doors. The tenth floor was just as fruitless as the eleventh. Finally, on the ninth floor, Stephenie found more than she expected.

The ninth floor was the administrative office area for AGS. It had an entryway with a large desk usually manned by a receptionist or two. On either side behind the receptionist's desk were floor to ceiling one-way glass walls and doors that separated the entryway from the two main office hallways. A person inside the entryway could not see into the hallway, but a person in the hallway area could see into the entry area. This was the advantage Stephenie had in her dumb-luck favor. Like the previous three levels, the ninth floor was dimly lit. In odd contrast to her side of the situation, the entryway well lit. Stephenie could peer into the entryway without being seen.

On the hallway side of the one-way glass partition was a series of permanent cubicles normally used by admin assistants to the top administrators. While slowly maneuvering her way through the rows of cubicles of the ninth floor, Stephenie happened to glance toward the entryway and noticed a human figure sitting at the receptionist's desk on the other side of the glass doors. With as much stealth as she could summon, she moved closer to the glass doors to get a better view. Two men occupied the receptionist's desk. She recognized neither of the men. They were dressed in expensive looking suits, had black, short hair and had dark complexions.

Just as Stephenie was contemplating relocating to a better vantage point near the reception desk, a door to one of the offices, a mere ten paces from where she crouched, opened, and a human figure draped in red light exited the office. Stephenie darted for the nearest cubicle as the person turned to shut the door. Stephenie waited until the figure had passed by her hiding place before poking her head out to get a better look. The figure turned out to be a man, once again wearing an expensive suit, who was making his way across the cubicle area toward the men's restroom. Stephenie stared at the door the man had exited.

Red light, like a dark room, she thought to herself, *or like a submarine movie when its battle stations time.*

Moving to a different cubicle that was closer to the mystery office door, she hid under a desk and waited. A minute later, the man returned to the mystery office and opened the door. Just as the man was entering the door, Stephenie leaned out from under the desk to capture a glance inside the office. Everything was dimly lit by varying hues of red light that emanated from special fixtures hidden somewhere inside the ceiling. Inside the office was one other man. Dressed as impeccably as the first man, this second man sat at a small table with a phone on its surface.

The door to the mystery office shut, but Stephenie could still hear muffled chatter on the other side. She waited one minute before crawling out from under the desk and approaching the door. Placing her left ear to the door, the first thing Stephenie heard was her own heartbeat. It dawned on her, for the first time, just how frightened she was. Pulling away from the door one step, she took a moment to inventory her reasons for the risks she was taking. Once again, it all boiled down to the one question, "Why?" She had to know the "Why?"

Why was her company sabotaging the electric grid? Why was her company destroying her country? These questions were the catalyst that Stephenie needed to take a step forward, and this time, plant her right ear on the door surface. Initially, she heard the same background humming that she had heard on every other office door that evening. Just when she was contemplating giving up on her eavesdropping quest, Stephenie heard a distinct ring from inside the office. One of the men inside picked up a phone and answered with a simple phrase, "American Grid Security". There was a pause of silence in the office, followed by the same man's voice saying, "Very well, please tell me what sector and substation?" Followed by, "Yes ma'am, we've got it marked off our list, and if you have any problems with that unit, please call this same number. Have a nice day."

Stephenie heard the man return the receiver to the phone cradle and then the squeal of chair wheels. The thought of running away raced through her mind. Was the man heading for the door? Then she heard another man's voice speak in a language with which she wasn't familiar. It wasn't Spanish or German. She knew some of those languages. Then the first man spoke in the same language. A conversation between the two ensued for about ten seconds when a third voice came into the conversation. This new voice spoke in English and sounded as if transmitted over an intercom.

"Rashid, how many do we have left?"

"Fifty-two," was the reply from one of the men in the office.

"Good, how often is the phone ringing now?"

"Once every ten minutes, sir."

"I'll need one of you to give the security guards a quick break."

"Very well, sir. I'll do it right now."

This time, the sound of the squealing chair wheels sent Stephenie darting away from the door as fast as her legs could move. The door opened almost immediately. Stephenie had taken ten running steps away from the door before she heard a man begin shouting in an odd language. As she turned the corner on a row of cubicles, she heard the sound of footfalls on the carpeted floor behind her. Crashing through the emergency escape door, she spun spastically in an attempt to redirect her body toward the downstairs direction. Fortunately, the emergency stairwell had lighting; otherwise, she would have careened off a handrail and fallen at least one hundred feet to the bottom of the stair shaft. Time became a blur for Stephenie as she ran and hopped down the stairs. There seemed to be no sound other than her heartbeat and the footsteps of her pursuer. All her sight reduced to the spinning handrails that seemed to have no end. Eventually, her lungs began to sing with pain and her leg muscles joined in the chorus. Just after passing the emergency entry door for the fourth floor, she noticed a change in the stair structure one flight below. There seemed to be an exterior exit door. With her eyes and mind focused on using that exit, Stephenie did not notice the sharp report of a mechanical device from up above her, nor did she notice the stinging that had begun to throb from her upper back. What she did notice was that the exit landing seemed to be blurring and the exit door felt like marshmallow as she crashed through it. A dull metal bar, like a handrail kicked her in the stomach and tossed her head-over-heels into the air. Now, there was something large and multi-colored coming at her. She put out her arm to fend it off. Just as she fell asleep, it swallowed her.

The smell was the first thing Stephenie sensed. Nothing in her life up to this point had smelled so horrible. Then, she felt the sensation of movement. Although surrounded in darkness, she could feel her body shaken. Then, she sensed sound. Even though the prevailing sound seemed muffled, it was easy enough to decipher. She heard the roar of a combustion engine. Then, she felt the rolling motion inside her stomach, the screaming headache and the need to vomit. As if by instinct, Stephenie realized she was lying on her back and needed to roll to her stomach in order to keep from throwing up on herself. Before she made any motion of her own, her body vaulted into a sitting position by some unseen force. Light and vision suddenly became the predominant senses as she began to slide headfirst toward a cardboard box full of shredded paper. Just as she fell into the cardboard box, she began to dry heave and all motion seemed to cease.

"Holy cow, lady," a husky male voice came from outside the confines of the cardboard box, "Are you okay?"

Stephenie felt the wave of nausea subside and attempted to extricate herself from the box but found it difficult.

"Hey," the husky voice called out, "Stan, hold up a minute. Help me out."

"What is it?" A new voice asked from some distance away.

"There's a drunken woman inside this one, help me pull her out."

"Aww crap, another one?"

Stephenie felt hands grabbing her clothes and under her armpits as she was dragged out of the cardboard box. Once again, she was able to see her environment and realized two men dragged her from the inside of a dumpster. She attempted to speak, but found that her mouth wasn't functioning. The world spun for a moment in a haze of blurred motion, and, when it stopped, Stephenie found her back propped up against a building and her legs outstretched before her. She watched helplessly as one of the men bent over and began pulling at her clothes. She could read the name sewn on his jumpsuit. His name was Victor.

"Hey, Vic, what the heck you doing?" She heard the second man say.

"I'm trying to get some of this crap off her clothes. Man, she's covered in all kinds of stuff."

"Hey, look," the first man stood a couple paces back and put his gloved hands on his waist. He kept looking to the left and to the right, as if concerned that anyone might see them. "We pulled her out of the dumpster and probably saved her life. Isn't that enough?"

"Come on, Stan," Victor looked over his shoulder at his partner, "Show a little compassion. Ain't you ever had a bad morning?"

"Yeah, but I never spent the night in a trash can. Come on, let's get outta here."

Stephenie got a good look at Stan. He was dressed like Victor in a dirty jumpsuit with his name sewn into the fabric above the left breast pocket. Behind Stan was a city trash truck. The trash truck was running but not moving. Stan and Victor were city garbage collectors. Their truck was parked in an alley behind a large building in St. Louis. Hoisted on the back of the trash truck was the dumpster from which Stan and Victor had pulled Stephenie. It dawned on her that she had come very close to the trash men dumping her into the back of the trash truck. She would then have been compressed by the hydraulic powered gate and most likely suffocated to death.

"Wait a minute," Victor said. Stephenie seemed unable to move her arms as Victor leaned her body forward and pulled at something on her back. Whatever Victor had done, it caused a sharp pain to ripple up and down her back and a muted shriek to come out of her numbed mouth.

"What are you doing to her?" Stan said as Victor returned Stephenie to an upright position against the wall.

"Take a look at what was sticking in her back, I just pulled this out."

Stephenie watched in blurred amazement as Victor turned to Stan and held out an object in his hand for Stan to see. Stephenie had no idea what it was, and neither did Victor, but Stan did.

"A freaking dart? She had a trank dart in her back?" Stan carefully picked the object out of Victor's hand with the thumb and index finger of one hand and adjusted the position of his safety glasses on his nose to get a better view of it.

"What's a trank dart?" Victor asked, as he stood to join his partner.

"A tranquilizer dart. See this part here? You put tranquilizer in there, maybe like a capsule, or something like that. You put the whole thing into a special air gun and shoot it at your target." Stan then shifted his eyes from the dart back to Stephenie. "Um, Vic, last I heard, the only folks around this town that would use one of these were those psychos working for the Mafia out of Chicago."

"You mean," Vic took a step toward the trash truck and began to look up and down the alley. "That this woman had a contract put out on her?"

"Looks that way to me," Stan said as he tossed the dart on the asphalt near Stephenie's legs and began to walk briskly toward his trash truck.

"Yeah, let's get this over with and get out of here," Victor said as he jogged back to the dumpster lift controls at the rear of the trash truck.

Stephenie watched helplessly as the two trash collectors went about their business and disappeared down the alley. Stephenie returned her gaze to the dart on the pavement near her right leg. She began to wonder why the Mafia would want her dead. She began to wonder why she had been in a dumpster. It was light outside but felt cool, so it must have been morning. The alley was deserted and mostly quiet with the exception of the sounds of city traffic somewhere nearby. After a few feeble attempts to raise her arms from her side, Stephenie finally managed to get one hand onto her lap. When she did, she felt a distinct hardness to her abdomen. Within ten minutes, she had unbuttoned her blouse and was extracting a set of folded drawings. The moment she looked at the name on the drawings, American Grid Security, the events of the previous night came back to her. She looked up at the building across the alley from where she sat. It was the Costar Building; the one she worked in and the one she had been attempting to get out of the night before. Stephenie looked once again at the dart on the asphalt. She realized that the man that had chased her down the emergency stairwell had shot her. She had burst through the third floor exit door, hit the handrail across her midsection and fell into a dumpster in the alley thirty feet below.

The trash in the dumpster must have hid me, Stephenie thought, *the shooter must have thought I made it down the stairs outside and ran away. But why was I running?*

Just as she asked herself this, the reason came back to her in a flood of powerful memories that almost made her vomit again. It suddenly became imperative for Stephenie to get out of the alley and to her car. After several attempts to stand, it became apparent that her body hadn't recovered from the tranquilizer enough to do more than crawl a few feet at a time and then take a rest. Several people walked down the alley during this crawling phase. All acted as if they didn't see the filthy woman bent down on her hands and knees. It was during one of the rest times in her crawling that Stephenie noticed a familiar object. This object lie on the ground where the dumpster had been before the trash collectors had moved it. Working vigorously, Stephenie made it across the alley in one exhausting session and pulled her purse from its resting place on the pavement to a spot on her lap. Rifling lamely through the purse, Stephenie pulled out her company cell phone and attempted to dial Morgan's number. The phone wasn't working. The battery had run out.

Anger filled her head and she swore loudly. She heard her own voice echo against the alley walls.

"I can talk now," Stephenie said in amazement, astonished that she had attempted to make a cell phone call a few seconds ago even though she couldn't speak at that moment. Tossing the cell phone aside, Stephenie rummaged through her purse and withdrew her car keys. "At least I can remember where I parked my car." She tossed the keys back into her purse and attempted to stand erect once again.

Fifty minutes later, Stephenie sat upon a guardrail in the Costar Building west parking structure, staring at her reserved parking space. The car was gone. In fact, there were no cars in the AGS reserved area. The night before, when she had arrived to look for the Gen-Two drawings, her car had been the only one in the reserved area. *They took my car, now they know I was up there last night.*

Her legs were exhausted from the quarter mile of staggering she had accomplished on her trek from the alley to the parking garage. Her clothes and hair looked a mess. She smelled of garbage. People ignored her because they thought she was just another homeless derelict roaming the early morning city streets of St. Louis. Without a car, she thought, I might as well be homeless. She rummaged through her purse and found her wallet. It contained two credit cards and fifty-five dollars in cash. She had to get to Effingham but wasn't certain how to do it. Even with over fifty dollars in cash, it would be difficult to persuade a taxi driver to take her anywhere. She looked and smelled too much like a drug freak to be trusted. Just then, a beeping sound came from her arm. Her wristwatch, normally silent of any alarm or sound, had recently received enough of a jostling to set up an hourly tone. While attempting to eliminate the hourly tone function, Stephenie noticed that the time was just past eleven o'clock in the morning. Suddenly, a thought crossed her mind, and she found herself staggering toward the parking structure stairwell to the street below.

Fred Tompkins had come to St. Louis to see the Cardinals play in their new stadium. After spending twenty years accumulating a small fortune as a day trader, Fred found himself traveling across the United States in 2009, making a childhood dream come true. His dream was to spend an entire summer traveling from state to state on a strict time line in order to see at least one baseball game in each of the Major League parks. By July 7th, he had seen games in all but ten ball parks, having spent the 4th of July weekend in Chicago for a Cubs and White Sox game. On the morning of July 8, Fred drove into the city of St. Louis in his brand new Corvette and parked it in the valet entrance lanes of the Adams Mark hotel. For one reason or another, there was no attendant in the valet parking area at that particular time of the morning. For one reason or another, Fred decided to leave his Corvette and find an attendant. For one reason or another, Fred left his keys in the ignition.

Stephenie knew the Adams Mark hotel inside and out, having performed several Public Relations tasks there for AGS over the previous two years. AGS always used the Adams Mark Hotel to wine, dine, and entertain its potential customers because of the hotel's convenient location. She had been responsible for the travel arrangements for several industry dignitaries. This included acting as a chauffer from the airport to the hotel. She had witnessed, on more than one occasion, travelers pull up to the valet parking area of the Adams Mark Hotel, leave their keys in their cars and enter the hotel. She also knew, from personal experience, that the eleven a.m. checkout time was a busy time at the valet parking area. She remembered sitting in a rented luxury car, acting like a chauffer for AGS and wondering, *how easy it would be to steal one of the cars just arriving at the hotel?* This memory prompted the idea for Stephenie Plasters to hide behind one of the valet parking structure pylons on the morning July 8, 2009, and wait for a specific type of traveler to arrive. After forty minutes of patient waiting, Stephenie watched a middle-aged man drive up in a dark blue Corvette, park his car, and enter the hotel without his keys. Two minutes later, Stephenie was cruising at a moderate seventy miles per hour on an eastbound lane of Interstate 64 in that very same dark blue Corvette.

As soon as Stephenie made the crossing of the Mississippi River from Missouri into Illinois, she heard a muted ringing noise emanating from some hidden place inside the Corvette. The first ring made her swerve in her lane just enough to cause the car in the lane next to her to honk its horn. The ringing continued at regular intervals and brought Stephenie to the realization that there was a cell phone inside the car. The onset of this ringing added to the nervous rush of fear she already had pulsing through her veins for having committed, for all she knew, the worst crime of her entire life. It was as if the stolen car she drove was attempting to tattle on her. As an initial response, Stephenie put effort toward ignoring the phone. Stuck in heavy traffic in a dangerous situation, she did not have the time or the ability to search for it. Instead, she gripped the steering wheel, tried to focus all her attention on the lunch hour traffic all around her and let off some steam by yelling at the hidden cell phone to shut up. This yelling had no effect. After an entire minute of the continuous ringing, Stephenie was cursing the owner of the Corvette for not enabling the automated answering service the cell phone company provided. In the midst of her fuming, a thought crossed Stephenie's mind that the cell phone might have a tracking service and the police would be able to pinpoint it and the stolen car. In a split second decision, she looked quickly in all three rearview mirrors and pulled sharply into an available right-hand breakdown lane. Not accustomed to the high performance vehicle she stole, Stephenie lost control of the Corvette and began a series of over-compensating maneuvers. The final maneuver caused her to fishtail the back end of the car into the three-foot concrete guardrail. Eventually, the Corvette came to a stop, but not until after spreading one hundred feet of the breakdown lane with shards of what once was a beautiful car body.

Immediately, Stephenie put the Corvette into Park, left the engine running and began searching for the hidden cell phone. Less than a minute later she found it stuffed in a hidden map pocket on the front of the passenger seat. The cell phone continued to ring, even as Stephenie held it in her trembling hands. She pressed what she thought was the OFF button and the ringing ceased only to be replaced with a tinny metallic sound emanating from the device. Holding the cell phone up to her ear, she heard a man's voice saying, "Hello?"

"Yeah?" Stephenie replied.

"Where's my car, scumbag?" A male voice dripped with acidic hatred.

Stephenie's body jerked in response to the man's voice and she dropped the cell phone onto the floor of the Corvette. She could hear the man screaming in what now sounded like a far-away, garbled voice. This was worse than the constant ringing. Fishing around the floor, Stephenie eventually retrieved the cell phone and put it to her ear. The man was cursing a blue streak about all the horrible things he was going to do to her. Stephenie yelled back at him to shut up.

"Who do you think you are?" He demanded.

"Look, sorry about stealing your car, I just had to get out of town."

The man began seething again, and once again, Stephenie ordered him to shut his mouth.

"Look, man," Stephenie said with all the reserved calm she could muster, "Whatever you do, get out of St. Louis. The crap is about to hit the fan, so get out of town, do you hear me?"

The man began to swear vengeance. This time, Stephenie pressed the correct button and the tinny voice ceased.

Stephenie threw the cell phone on the passenger seat and put the car into drive. Looking over her shoulder and into the rearview mirrors, Stephenie realized that she had parked herself into a bad situation. She had brought the Corvette to a stop on a curved breakdown lane and had no clear view of oncoming traffic for more than fifty yards. Cars were racing by the dark blue Corvette at a rate of one every three seconds. Every so often, a semi rig would drive by just close enough to rock the car in its wake. There seemed no way to pull into traffic. Once again, the cell phone began to ring. Jamming the Corvette into Park again, Stephenie grabbed the cell phone and made a motion to slam it against the steering wheel. However, something printed on the back of her left hand caught her eye. It was a smeared set of numbers she wrote less than twenty-four hours before. It was Morgan's cell phone number. Carefully, Stephenie silenced the cell phone's ringing then dialed the number on the back of her left hand. Holding the cell phone to her ear, she heard an electronic buzzing that indicated her call was going through. After three buzzes, she heard her brother's voice say, "Hello?"

"Morgan?" Stephenie asked.

"Geez-o-Pete, Steph, where the heck are you?"

"In Illinois, I just got out of town." The weight of what she had just said began to sink in and tears ran from her eyes.

"Are you okay?" Morgan sounded shaken, and there was a commotion of distorted noises from his side of the conversation.

"I'm okay, I guess," Stephenie was trembling now, sobbing so much that she could hardly breathe.

"Steph, are you okay?" This time, Morgan was speaking in a demanding tone.

"Yeah, yeah, I'm okay." Stephenie took a deep breath and attempted to quell her crying. "I'm just a little shaken by what I've been through. Look, I gotta get off the phone. It's not safe for me to be talking right now. I'm on my way to Effingham."

"Good," Morgan replied, with just a hint of doubt in his voice. "Look, get here ASAP, come to the Wal-Mart store, you got that?"

"The Wal-Mart store?"

"Right. I couldn't get anywhere with emergency services of any kind or any of the Guard chain of command. So, I took things into my own hands. I'm going to be busy for the next couple of hours, so I won't be able to talk on this phone with you. You got that?"

"Morgan, what are you doing?" Stephenie asked in a concerned voice. She knew her brother had a brazen tendency to act on the most illogical ideas. Once, when he was fourteen, he thought he could wire the entire house with hidden surveillance cameras and watch the goings on of his household from his bedroom closet. In the process of installing wires, he drilled through an electrical conduit inside a wall and nearly set the house on fire.

"Look, Steph," Morgan said with a nervous laugh, "This isn't like the hidden camera thing, okay? You and I both know the world is coming to an end. I've decided to, um, take care of my little corner of it."

"What are you doing, Morgan?" Stephenie demanded in an angry tone.

"Okay, Stephenie. I'm taking control of the Wal-Mart and Menards stores here in Effingham. I'm using my military position to secure the best place in the area to control by martial law and eventually restore order to this area of town. It's the largest single store of food, water and shelter in the entire region. It's also the largest store of electrical generators and building materials. I'm temporarily using my Guards to take it over until a new order can be established after the lights go out."

There was a moment of silence on the line, with the exception of the background sounds emanating off and on from both ends of the connection. Eventually, Morgan spoke first.

"You still there?"

"Yeah, still here. It sounds like you've got a better plan than I have."

"Look, Steph, I gotta get back to stuff here, okay?"

"Yeah, okay. Um, Morgan?"

"Yeah?"

"I love you."

"Me too, sis. See ya when you get here and—"

Stephenie pulled the cell phone from her ear and looked at the LED display window's face plate. Amid the various function symbols on the LED, dead center was the word, "Searching…"

Stephenie looked at her wristwatch. It read 12:36. She felt as if all the oxygen had been sucked from the atmosphere.

Cars were still whizzing past the dark blue Corvette parked along the right hand breakdown lane, as the driver of the car attempted to pull out into traffic. Despite her turn signal, the traffic kept coming at speeds greater than seventy miles per hour, and no one would let her join them. This forced Stephenie to cruise at low speed in the breakdown lane, hoping a gap would open up. Knowing what she knew about the oncoming chaos, and lacking the ability to get out of the breakdown lane, caused Stephenie to break into a fit of screams and curses with each passing car. For nearly a quarter mile, she drove a pitiful twenty miles per hour in the narrow gap between the hurtling vehicles and the concrete barricade, until it dawned on her that she was the only vehicle in motion. Her rage had blinded her to the fact that a total gridlock had occurred on the eastbound Interstate 64 and, because she was in the breakdown lane, she had the only open lane. Soon, other vehicles began to enter the breakdown lane until it too came to a standstill. Stephenie had had enough. She opened the driver's side door of the Corvette, stepped onto the pavement and climbed up on top of the car until she was standing on the hood of the cab. What she saw was something out of a Los Angeles gridlock nightmare. Thousands of vehicles, as far as the eye could see, stood still. Not only on Interstate 64, but also on 70 as well as every on-ramp, every off-ramp, and every service street connected to the Interstates.

"It's already happening," Stephenie said wistfully to herself. "I can't believe it's happening so fast."

The drastic sounds of a nearby vehicular collision broke Stephenie out of her dreamlike state, just in time for her to catch a glance at a furniture delivery truck smashing into a small sedan six vehicles behind hers. The initial impact of the collision caused by the delivery truck led to a domino effect of fender benders that was heading right toward the Corvette. Stephenie's feet were knocked out from under her and she landed, lower back first, on the hood of her car. Once the Corvette stopped shaking, Stephenie rolled to her knees, jumped back on the pavement by the open driver's side door, retrieved her purse and began jogging carefully through the gridlocked lanes of the interstate. After traversing one hundred yards through the rows of idling vehicles, it became apparent to her that the greatest danger in her journey was not from the motor vehicles themselves. Rather, Stephenie's biggest threat came from the people inside the non-moving vehicles. Car doors began swinging open, without a moment's notice and with great regularity as the drivers began to exit their cars for a better look at the cause of all the gridlock. As Stephenie ran eastbound toward the on ramp of Interstate 70, she was nearly blind-sided several times by car doors opening directly in her path. In one instance, she collided with the owner of a minivan and knocked the driver backwards into her vehicle.

"Sorry about that," Stephenie said in a hasty manner as she closed the door just enough to squeeze between it and the vehicle in the next lane.

"A lot of good that does." The minivan driver yelled at Stephenie's back.

After a mile of dodging doors and smelling the noxious carbons of idling engines, Stephenie made it past the heart of the 64/70 interchange and had to take a break. Sitting on an overpass structure guardrail and breathing heavily, she heard a man's voice nearby say, "This is quite a mess we got here, isn't it?"

Stephenie glanced at the source of the voice and watched as a well-dressed middle-aged man approached her. He was carrying two bottles of water. He took a swig from an open bottle. The other still had its white plastic cap in place. Never before had Stephenie felt so thirsty.

"Can I get a drink of water from you?" She asked, for the first time feeling the damage she had done to her voice in all her recent screaming fits.

"Yeah, sure," the man said as he eyed Stephenie suspiciously, yet handed the bottled water to her from a socially acceptable distance. As Stephenie wrestled eagerly with the bottle cap and took her first drink, it dawned on her just how frightening she must appear to this upper-class man.

"Yeah, after about five minutes of sitting in a non-moving car," the man began talking and pointed to the gridlock below, "I decided to pull it over in the breakdown lane and come up here to have a look-see. Criminies, have you ever seen such a thing? Looks like a bunch of accidents happened all at once."

"It's gonna get worse," Stephenie spoke with a raspy voice after consuming half the bottle of water in one gulp.

"What's that?" the water bearer asked.

"This is just the beginning. Look at eastbound 70. See how clear it is?"

"Well, yeah, that is weird, isn't it?"

"It's because the lights are out." Stephenie continued as she pointed toward all the exit ramps. "There's no electricity anywhere. The traffic jams began at the exit ramps because the lights went out. The jams spread up into the Interstates as a result. Soon, the only folks moving will be the ones that were by the 64 and 70 interchange before the jams got bad. They're only going as far as the next big traffic jam, or until they run out of gas."

"Hey, you're right," the businessman said as he covered his eyes with one hand to block the sun and stared at the street traffic on both sides of the interchange. "By God, there *are* no traffic lights. In fact, the only lights anywhere are the headlights on the cars."

"Where were you going?" Stephenie asked abruptly.

"Me? Um, well, I was going to Indianapolis."

"Are you from around here?" Stephenie asked.

"Well, yes," the man eyed Stephenie suspiciously once again. "I live just outside of St. Louis on the west side.

"Bummer," was Stephenie's reply.

"Why's that?" The man asked with a cautious, forced smile on his face.

"Look, there's not going to be any electricity anywhere you go." Stephenie looked the man in the eyes and spoke sincerely. "The lights are out for a long time, if not for good. Every major city is going to become a war zone. The only hope you have for yourself is to get out to the farm country as soon as you can."

"What are you talking about?" The man said incredulously, as he waved his hand briskly at the chaotic scene around him. "This is just a fluke, a blackout of some sort. No big deal. The authorities will get it all sorted out in a day or two, and we'll all be back to normal."

"Uh-uh," Stephenie said, as she placed the white plastic cap back on her bottled water and placed the bottle into her purse. "I know what I'm talking about. Every major electrical power substation in this country has been destroyed by bombs that my former employer installed. Believe me. The world as you know it has ended."

"You're nuts," the businessman shook his head and began walking away from what he thought was a vagrant bag lady without all her oars in the water.

"Trust me, don't go into the city."

"Right," the man chuckled to himself, as he disappeared from view.

"Thanks for the water," Stephenie said silently to no one.

If you had asked the hundred most knowledgeable or most experienced political scientists or sociologists on July 7th, 2009, how rapidly our so-called civilization would decline without electricity, you would have been given the wrong answers ninety-nine percent of the time. The experts would have told you that social order would remain mostly status quo for about a week or two before fragmenting into clans and civil wars. Well, social order in the former United States disintegrated within the first day. The question is WHY? The answer is because we had few values left. We had exploited the poor and called it The Lottery. We had rewarded laziness and called it Welfare. We had killed our unborn and called it

Choice. We had shot abortionists and called it Justifiable. We coveted our neighbor's possessions and called it Ambition. We polluted the air with profanity and pornography and called it Freedom Of Expression. We ridiculed the time-honored values of our forefathers and called it Enlightenment. That's WHY.

Theodore Newgent
An excerpt from his personal journal, July 2010

It was Stephenie's goal to get to the city of Effingham as soon as she could, in what ever way that she could. Being forced to travel by foot so soon after the lights went out had put a definite dent in her plans. After leaving the 64/70 interchange, she hoped to hitch a ride with someone else or confiscate another vehicle as she had done before. However, within twenty minutes, she was surrounded by a flood of humanity in turmoil. To set foot on an Interstate freeway near a large city in a national disaster was one thing. To set foot in East St. Louis on the Illinois side during that same disaster was another thing altogether. It was a very bad thing.

Fifty years before, after the Shelton Gang had been de-clawed and eliminated, the area known as East St. Louis was a relatively safe place to live. After the turbulence of the 60's race riots and multiple demographic changes, East St. Louis became a haven for the lowest rungs on the criminal element ladder. When the lights went out on July 8, 2009, the chaos in East St. Louis started as a trickle. Electrical blackouts are historically predecessors to full scale looting in most overpopulated areas. Immediately, the gangs and petty thieves of East St. Louis came out of the woodwork to loot their own turf. When it dawned on the looters that the blackout went beyond their side of the Mississippi River to St. Louis in Missouri, they took to the interstate and any other possible crossing to take-on the biggest city in the area.

In order for the looters to get to St. Louis in Missouri, they had to do so on foot, just as Stephenie had been doing, but in the opposite direction. Within a relatively short period after the lights went out, thousands of violent raiders swept upon the Interstates on foot. Nothing was sacred in their wake. Vehicles were destroyed, people were beaten, people were raped, and people were murdered, all for no good reason.

Fortunately for Stephenie, she had abandoned her path along Interstate 70 for a parallel side road with less congestion. If she had remained on the interstate, she would have faced a horrible experience in the last minutes of her life. The horde of raiders passed within a quarter mile of where she walked. She had traveled no more than a mile on the side road when she came upon the remains of a gruesome traffic accident. Unlike every pile-up she had seen that afternoon, and there had been hundreds of them, this one had an ambulance on the scene.

Stephenie had steered clear of every one of those accident scenes. This one, for an unknown reason, seemed to call her name, to draw her. Maybe it was the fact that it was the first time all afternoon that she had seen any form of civic response: there was an ambulance at this accident. Maybe it was because she was thirsty and had consumed all the water the businessman had given her. Whatever the reason, Stephenie felt pulled to the accident.

"Hey you, lady," yelled a short woman in an official-looking uniform. The uniformed woman bent over, so her head was just a little lower than her behind. She was in this awkward position, because she had both hands on the fiberglass handles of a stretcher. On the stretcher was a small black child, about ten years old, who wore a bloodied sling on his arm. The child was gritting his teeth and writhing in pain. "Grab the end of this thing, will ya?"

"I, uh, just wanted to get some, uh, water," Stephenie was stammering because of the insanity all around her. It looked as though a dozen vehicles had been totaled in this particular accident. Like every other accident scene she had observed that day, miles of cars were idled in gridlock in all directions. Unlike the other accident scenes, this scene had two divided groups of accident victims facing off against each other, just off to one side of a busy intersection. The melee between the two sides was unfolding in the parking lot of a corner gas station about one hundred feet from the ambulance. It reminded Stephenie of an absurd rendition from a scene in the Broadway musical, West Side Story. Both sides were accusing the other of causing the accident. The verbal clamor of both sides was deafening and the gesticulations and body language of the participants had all the motions of a primitive tribal war dance. In the midst of all this stupidity were three EMTs: two men who were carting a stretcher into the back of the ambulance and the short woman that was talking to Stephenie.

"Okay, you'll get your water, just help me get this kid away from the brawl," the woman EMT impatiently replied.

Concerned by the cacophony of the vehicular tribesmen at the gas station, Stephenie pushed her purse strap up on her shoulder and bent down to help the EMT. As they hefted the stretcher, Stephenie saw the name *Candace* on EMT's jacket. Stephenie noticed that Candace, who was walking backwards while carrying her side of the stretcher, was leading her away from the ambulance.

"Aren't we taking him to the ambulance?" Stephenie asked between labored breaths.

"We've got too many injured people inside that thing already," Candace spoke out of the side of her mouth because she had her head turned sideways to see behind her. "This kid isn't hurt as bad as the others. We'll have to put him over here on the sidewalk and wait for the ambulance to return. That is, if it can get out of this mess."

Stephenie felt a wave of relief when they reached the sidewalk and set the stretcher down. Before she could ask for her water again, Candace stood upright and began walking toward the ambulance.

"Hey," Stephenie yelled, clutching her purse, "Where you going?"

"I gotta get some meds for the kid. Just stay here with him, okay?"

"Um, not a good idea to leave me like this," Stephenie said as she rubbed her left forearm with the index finger of her right hand. Candace turned around, saw Stephenie's odd signal and gave her a strange look. Then, as if a light had gone on in her head, she looked over at the angry people near the accident scene and realized what Stephenie was trying to say.

"Yeah, you're right. Here, take this," Candace took off her ball cap and tossed it to Stephenie. "I guess it wouldn't be too cool for them to see a white street person bent over a battered black kid. Put the cap on and you should be all right until I get back."

"Thanks," Stephenie said gratefully, as Candace trotted back to the ambulance. The boy on the stretcher had begun to cry out in agony and attempted to sit up. Stephenie bent down on her knees and got her first good look at the child since she arrived on the scene. Blood was pouring out of the sling that held his arm. A revulsion came over Stephenie so strong that she almost went into shock. She would have had it not been for a sudden shift in the momentum at the gas station. Several people were walking rapidly toward Stephenie. The man in the lead of this angry-looking pack began yelling at Stephenie.

"What are you doin' to my kid?"

"You leave that child alone!" another person of the pack yelled.

Before Stephenie had time to stand up, the leader of the pack shoved her to the ground and stood over her as if he was going to beat her to a pulp. From out of nowhere, Candace pushed herself into the pack and began shoving the spectators away from Stephenie. Even though this woman was at least a foot shorter than most of the men that she was pushing around, not one of them fought back.

"Leave her alone, I said," Candace pushed the angry father away from Stephenie, "She's my assistant. Can't you see she's got a red cross on her ball cap?"

"I, uh, didn't see it," the angry father stammered, as if ashamed of himself, as he turned his gaze to an open spot on the sidewalk.

"Now, just give us some space so we can take care of the boy, Okay?" It was an order, not a request. Stephenie was stunned when the entire formerly hostile mob began to walk back to the rumble that continued to ebb and flow on the gas station parking lot.

Candace un-shouldered a backpack she had been carrying and tossed it to the ground next to where Stephenie had been pushed. With the motions of a well-trained professional, the EMT began unzipping various pockets on the backpack and extracting medical supplies.

"Stupid animals," Candace spat, in reference to the retreating horde, "They didn't give a crap about this kid at all. I've been here for almost an hour and none of those pigs have given me one ounce of help, even for their own kid. Can you imagine that?"

"Why'd they let you push them around?" Stephenie asked, as she crawled on her hands and knees toward the child on the stretcher.

"I can't figure it out myself." Candace gave an ironic laugh and tossed a roll of gauze bandages at Stephenie. "See if you can take the plastic bag off that gauze for me, okay? I'm gonna do something illegal here, and I want you to be busy with something else so you don't see me do it."

"Sure," Stephenie said, but kept her eyes on what the EMT was doing. Candace noticed this but didn't seem to care. She turned a small bottle of liquid upside down and injected a hypodermic needle into the rubber stopper at the mouth of the bottle. Just like in the movies Stephenie had seen, the EMT removed the needle, gave it a few flicks with a finger, a small compression to eject some of the liquid inside and then attempted to hold down the good arm of the writhing child. The child was in too much pain to understand what he was supposed to do. Stephenie jumped into what looked like a three-person wrestling match to help Candace inject the child. Once the process was completed, the EMT tossed the syringe into a small sharps container and wiped the sweat from her forehead with the back of her sleeved forearm.

"Thanks, uh," Candace said.

"Stephenie."

"Yeah, Stephenie. I needed the help. I'm out of my league here. I can't get ahold of the dispatch to the hospital. I'm not supposed to dose people with the painkillers until I get physician permission over the radio. Problem is, we've got a real garbled connection on the emergency band. We can't understand a thing they're saying and I don't think they can understand us."

"The emergency systems are overloaded," Stephenie said, as she gazed at the bleeding child on the stretcher. The boy had already begun to show signs of the medication taking effect.

"Hey, we've had blackouts on the East side more than once and never lost communication. Something must be wrong with our transmitter unit."

"It's not just East St. Louis," Stephenie picked at a weed growing from a crack in the sidewalk and tossed it on the concrete by her feet. "It's everywhere."

"What do you mean by 'everywhere'?" Candace asked absentmindedly, as she began to prepare a splint for the boy on the stretcher.

"Everywhere," Stephenie sighed and looked into Candace's eyes, "as in the entire country. The entire grid was knocked out about four hours ago. And, it isn't coming back on any time soon."

Candace stopped what she was doing and stared at Stephenie, as if the homeless woman in front of her had just told her that she was Jesus the Christ. Before Candace could reply, she heard her name called from a man sitting inside the ambulance. She turned to see another EMT waving her over to the open passenger door.

"Stay right here," Candace said in a serious tone, "and don't do anything to the kid. I'll be right back."

"Uh-uh," Stephenie said, as she stood to follow Candace to the ambulance. "I'm coming with you."

"To heck with it," Candace shrugged violently and allowed Stephenie to follow her.

When Candace and Stephenie arrived at the passenger door of the ambulance, they joined the two other EMTs who were listening intently to the receiver of the emergency radio unit inside the cab. A conversation blurted-out on the Emergency Broadcast channel between several entities of unknown origin. The conversation was an argument of sorts.

"You are violating federal emergency communications codes by using this frequency; please use a different frequency immediately," came a female voice over the receiver.

"Federal?" A boisterous male voice responded. "Federal doesn't exist anymore, sweetheart. I got the news thirty minutes ago from another HAM radio operator in DC that the city is being ransacked."

"Please identify yourself," Spoke an official-sounding male voice.

"Identify myself?" The boisterous voice replied. "I've been identifying myself for decades now and few listened. Okay, for the deaf of this world, my name is Theodore Newgent. I'm transmitting from my compound in the former state of Montana. And, I'm trying to let you yahoos know that the whole damn grid is down. It's gone. It ain't coming—"

"Cease using this emergency channel immediately," blurted a new male voice, this one more powerful in signal than the others did. This new signal had the strength to walk over the others.

"—and just like I said back in ninety-five, we got too dependent upon our mass consumption of electricity. Now we—"

"I order you to cease using this channel!"

"—don't you get it? It's a collapse. Less than a hundred years ago we had the Great Depression, now we've got the Collapse. It's over man. And the crap has just begun to hit the…"

"Newgent, Newgent, come in Newgent," came a new signal caller.

"Yeah, Newgent here," the boisterous voice replied.

"Its K-Sammy-niner-five-, ah you know who."

"Sammy, what's the news from Chicago?" Newgent asked.

"It's burning, the whole place is burning. Same thing in LA and down in Florida. No one's got juice except for some of us HAMs."

"*Now* are you listening, Mrs. Federal Emergency Code?" The Montana HAM operator named Newgent said, in a spiteful manner. "There is no electricity. The United States is gone. I'm trying to do you a favor by shattering your illusions, before it's too late for you to survive. For anyone who is listening, get away from populated areas as fast as you can. Things are going to get worse. Ah, to heck with it. Theodore Newgent over and out."

The radio receiver remained silent for a few seconds. Then Candace picked up a microphone from the dashboard and called in a series of code words. A frantic voice replied, "Unit six, report your status."

Candace's hands were shaking as she pressed the microphone button and replied, "Unit six has seven injured, three critical."

"Unit six, what's your twenty?"

"Um, three miles east of the 64/70 junction."

A pause ensued for what seemed like an eternity. The silence broken by the following words spoken in a frightened tone of voice. "Unit six, I'm sorry. You'll have to hang tight where you are."

"Dispatch, say again." Candace yelled into the microphone.

"Unit six, do not attempt to transfer patients. All hospitals are overloaded. Do what you can where you are until further notice."

"Until further notice?" Candace screamed into the microphone, "Can't I transfer to Mercy General, or even to Jefferson?"

"Negative, unit six. Sorry. There just isn't any way for you to get to any emergency room now. Every ambulance that has tried is stuck in gridlock. I think the man from Montana is right."

Candace held the transmitter microphone before her and stared at it, as if it disgusted her. Then she turned her eyes to Stephenie and stood staring at her for a few seconds. The microphone fell from Candace's hand and swung aimlessly in a pendulum motion just above the pavement under the ambulance. No one seemed to notice the microphone. Just as Stephenie began to realize that the EMTs were experiencing the same cultural shock that she had experienced the day before, Candace lunged at her and pushed her to the ground.

"You!" Candace seethed as she randomly hit and kicked Stephenie. "You knew about this, didn't you? You were a part of it, weren't you?"

"Candace," one of the EMTs inside the cab of the ambulance called to her, as he jumped out to protect Stephenie. He was a tall broad-shouldered young man with the name *James* on his EMT jacket. James embraced Candace in a strong, but gentle, way and pushed her back two steps. "Cool it," he said to Candace, "Now, what are you talking about?"

"She knew there was no hope; she knew there was nothing left, she knew all about it, she knew…" Candace's words drifted until she simply stood silent and pointed at Stephenie, who cowered on the ground. The EMTs watched Stephenie carefully as she raised herself to her feet, and picked up the EMT ball cap. When Candace pushed her to the ground the ball cap had been knocked off her head. Cautiously, she looked at each of them, and in turn, saw looks of fear.

"Is what Candace said true?" James the EMT asked.

"In a way, yes."

"How?" James asked, still clutching a now dormant and listless Candace.

"The company I worked for had replaced their electric grid monitoring devices with explosives that all went off at the same time and took the entire grid with it," Stephenie explained and then looked up to meet faces of anger. "I found out about it yesterday and tried to stop it.

I was caught, kind of, and drugged with a dart gun. I tried, you know, I really tried to stop it…" Stephenie's words trailed off into a whisper, as a pathetic look crossed over her face. She was attempting not to cry, but was failing, as her lips began to quiver, and she covered her face.

The three EMTs stood still and silent for a few moments, as the accident scene mob behind them continued with their feuding. James let go of Candace and took a step toward Stephenie.

"Why?" James asked Stephenie, "Why would they do that?"

"I don't know," was all Stephenie could manage to say between her sobs.

"It doesn't matter why," Candace burst forth and pushed at Stephenie again. This time James and the third EMT jumped in to keep Candace away from Stephenie as Candace raged on. "The *why* isn't important. The *why* isn't going to get these victims to the hospital. The *why* isn't going to protect us."

"Candace, calm down," James said, as he successfully maneuvered Candace away from attacking Stephenie.

"Calm down?" Candace screamed, as she backed away from the ambulance a few steps. "Didn't you hear what that guy on the radio said? It's over. We're doomed. We might as well just kill ourselves. I can't even get to my apartment, I can't even go home. What am I going to do, I…"

Stephenie and the two male EMTs stood stunned as they watch Candace turn and run away from the accident scene, shrieking. James lost his footing, fell against the ambulance and slid to his butt. The other EMT, an older man with slightly graying hair, turned his back to Stephenie and stared at the mob of people at the gas station a mere hundred feet away.

"What do we do now?" The older EMT said over his shoulder.

"I'm going to Effingham," Stephenie said.

"Effingham?" the older EMT said blankly, without looking back. "Well, you better take the medical gear that Candace left behind."

"The medical gear?" Stephenie asked, as she walked around to face the older EMT. When she got near enough, she could see that he had tear tracks running down his cheeks.

"Yeah, that backpack that she left over by that kid on the stretcher. Take that backpack with you."

"Won't you need it?" Stephenie asked the man and this time saw his name badge on his jacket. "Frank, won't you need that gear?"

"I got my own," he said as he wiped his eyes. "Woman, ever since I got this job I noticed that no matter what was going down around me, no one bothered me so long as I looked like I was doing a medical job. Even the meanest S.O.B. would make sure I wasn't hassled. You got that? So, take the medical gear and go. Good luck."

"What about the boy on the stretcher?" Stephenie asked, as she walked in that direction. Frank followed Stephenie to where the boy with the broken arm lay and looked down at him. He was still bleeding through his sling but, instead of writhing as he had been before, he was now staring skyward with glazed eyes and a slight smile on his face.

"Candace drug him?" Frank asked. Stephenie nodded in the affirmative. Frank reached into his jacket pocket and pulled out a long-shanked tweezers. With the tweezers in hand, he bent down and pulled away part of the boy's sling. Stephenie winced and turned away.

"The boy ain't gonna make it, M'am." Frank said sadly and turned back toward the ambulance. "Just take the gear and good luck."

Stephenie watched as Frank the EMT reached into the back of the ambulance and extracted two backpacks similar to the one that sat on the ground near her feet. She saw Frank take a long look at the accident victims that she assumed were in the back of the ambulance, shake his head and walk toward James, who remained crumpled in a crying heap next to the front of the ambulance. Frank coaxed James to his feet and led him slowly away from the accident scene. Suddenly, the sound of gunshots added to the melee at the gas station. People were ducking for cover, others were running and screaming and still others were attempting to tackle the shooters. Stephenie's first reaction was to sprawl to the pavement. In doing so, she came face to face with two things. The first thing was the death of the boy on the stretcher. His body shook violently and then became very still. His chest had stopped heaving. Stephenie turned her head away from the boy and saw the medical backpack that Candace had left on the pavement near the stretcher.

Several items removed from the backpack by Candace were lined up in a systematic order on the pavement. Stephenie had no idea what these items were.

As the insanity at the gas station parking lot continued and more gunshots fired, she decided to take Frank's advice. Crawling on her belly to the backpack, Stephenie began to gather all the unpacked items and stuff them into any available pocket. Then she rolled her purse into as tight a bundle as she could and stuffed it into the main compartment of the backpack. Once done with this, Stephenie noticed that the gunfire from the gas station had dwindled down to a fraction of its former intensity. Using the backpack as a shield, she propped her head and shoulders up on her elbows just enough to scope her environment. The gas station parking lot was empty, with the exception of a few bodies that lay prone on the asphalt. Both sides of the feud had retreated behind the tangled vehicles and seemed to be content to stay where they were. Taking a deep breath and a deeper chance, Stephenie stood, hefted the backpack to one shoulder and walked toward the ambulance.

She arrived at the back door of the ambulance, seemingly unnoticed by anyone. Inside were a gurney and several stretchers. Each device supported the body of a dead person. At least, they looked dead to Stephenie. After a few seconds of nervous inspection, Stephenie found what she had been looking for: an insulated hard plastic box strapped near the back doors. Unlatching the lid of this box, she revealed a cache of drinking water bottles. A gunshot rang out, was immediately answered by another and then all was silent again. Hastily, Stephenie began stuffing all available space in the medical backpack with bottles of drinking water, until she could fit no more. Having done this, she put both arms through the backpack straps, made some minor strap adjustments and then turned toward the accident scene. She knew she had to cross through the accident scene to get to where she wanted to go. It was time to put what Frank had said about acting like a medical professional to the test.

A surreal feeling flowed over Stephenie as she walked through the maze of gridlocked vehicles. Some of the cars still had their engines idling; others were silent. No one hiding inside or outside the vehicles made any attempt to stop her. Certainly, they saw her. Nothing was more conspicuous than a white woman in this part of town. Once they saw the ball cap on her head and the insignia on the backpack, they turned their gaze back to their immediate concern of not being shot. Two city blocks later, Stephenie was clear of the traffic jam. Once again, she walked the side road parallel to the eastbound lane of Interstate 70, toward Effingham.

CHAPTER ELEVEN

Launching Gen-Two

The tension inside the conference room was heavy enough to make the participants inside fearful of breathing too loudly. Carl Larkin sat motionless in his oversized leather chair at the far end of a long dark oak table and prayed silently that the heaviness inside the room would lift. His protégé, Janet Deering, was uncharacteristically stumbling through her presentation. Janet stood to the side of a large video screen using a laser pointer to highlight specific words and graphs that appeared on the screen. Carl had personally spent the last four years grooming Janet for this day. He and Janet had worked ceaselessly on this very presentation for the last two weeks, cutting and adding words, fine-tuning every gesture and tone of voice. The targeted audience was not buying into the message, and Carl wasn't the only one to notice this.

Seated to his right hand side at the long end of the table were the representatives of the eleven most powerful power generation coalitions in the nation. Carl had a gift for reading the body language of such powerful men and didn't like what he was reading. None of the representatives seemed to be hearing what they wanted to hear. Janet had noticed this innuendo within the first minute of her ten-minute presentation and was desperately attempting to find the mark, to locate the one piece of information that would spark the listener's interest. She wasn't finding it, even as she neared the last minute of her professionally executed presentation.

They've been here for thirty minutes, Carl thought to himself, *thirty minutes of the best hype we could come up with, and they aren't buying.* He shifted his position in his chair ever so slightly as Janet was preparing to wrap up her presentation and pass the baton to Carl. *What is it that they are looking for?*

"Thank you for your time," Janet said, with a much practiced pitch, "and now, I'd like to turn the floor over to our Chief Executive Officer, Carl Larkin." There was no applause at this point in the meeting. None was expected. These powerful men and women were gathered in this tastefully decorated conference room at an incredible expense to both sides of the particular issue at hand. On one side of the issue was Carl Larkin and his company, American Grid Security, risking every spare dime of capital they had squeezed from their *small but respected* company in what seemed to be a last ditch effort to become *large and respected.* On the other side of the issue were the powerful, but volatile, power brokers who were suspiciously considering whether the products and services of AGS would be the solution that they had been seeking for decades to smooth out their volatility. Significant profits or losses were at stake for both parties involved.

"Ladies and gentlemen," Carl Larkin spoke without moving from his chair. Janet Deering, who had yet to reach her own chair after leaving the front of the conference room, felt a jolt of surprise spring up and down her spine. This was not how they had practiced the presentation wrap-up. She tried to glance inauspiciously at the other three AGS administrators that sat next to her. Each had his eyebrows raised in wonder. Carl continued speaking from the relaxed confines of his leather chair. "I want to thank you, all of you, for coming to our offices today. I realize that what it cost in direct and indirect expenses for you all to be here today would equal the gross national product of several emerging countries." This comment elicited some shuffling of feet and a few laughs. Carl propped himself up and stood from his chair as he continued to speak. "With that said, let me waste your time no further with words you don't need to hear."

Carl Larkin, dressed in a modest, but appropriate, three-piece suit, bent down and reached under the table by his chair. Without taking his eyes off the assembled men and women, Carl hefted a metal cased box with both hands and set it upon the table. This box was about the size of a modern home computer tower and was painted haze grey, which gave it a boring industrial appearance. Once the box was up on the tabletop, Carl gently placed his right hand upon it and moved his left hand to the small of his back. With a slow, but intentional, tilt of his head, Carl now was in perfect imitation of the hired model that AGS had used in its now-famous advertising campaign they had run for the very product under his hand. This irony was not lost to the assemblage, for they were well aware of the advertisement that had flooded the trade periodicals two years before, and smiles broke out around the table.

"Two years ago," Carl spoke without a smile, as he maintained his pose, "AGS offered this product at a cost of ten thousand dollars per unit, including a two-year service agreement. We called it the EX-1. In the first year of production, AGS sold over seven hundred of these units to the companies and subsidiaries that you represent. We made seven-hundred thousand dollars in sales from you. We also made another forty million in data retrieval contracts with our internet website. The industry watchdogs rated our products and services within a one-percent margin of perfection. What I'm getting at is that the EX-1 was very kind to AGS."

This comment brought more than a few laughs from the power broker representatives. Carl broke his pose with the EX-1 and bent once again to retrieve another box-like device from under the table. This, too, he set upon the table surface next to the EX-1.

"This, ladies and gentlemen," Carl Larkin said, as he presented the new box with his palms up and fingers pointing toward the device, "is the reason you are all here today. We have decided to call it the Gen-Two, Generation Two of the data retrieval transmitters. You've heard two presentations today on the precise differences between the EX-1 and the Gen-Two. You've been told how much projected revenue and grid security your organizations should gain from upgrading to the Gen-Two. What we haven't talked about is the bottom line."

This last phrase produced the desired effect for which Carl had been waiting. Each person in the room, including his own people, raised his or her eyebrows and bent over to look at the prospectus that Carl gave to each person at the start of the meeting. The bottom line, the short term and long term costs as prospective clients of AGS for their Gen-Two proposal, had already been spelled out in definite terms on page one of the prospectus.

"We at AGS have a product; you and your companies have a need for this product," Carl Larkin strolled leisurely around the table until he stood between it and the large video screen. He was now facing every one of the power brokers. "AGS is in this for the long term. The long term." Carl Larkin smiled, and it wasn't just because he knew that he had the rapt attention of every person in the room. No, it was something else, something ironic in the last two phrases that only he understood. "If indeed you replace the nine-hundred or more EX-1 units with the Gen-Two retrofit, my company, AGS, will sell them to you for three thousand dollars apiece, enough to cover our manufacturing and installation costs."

This announcement caused a shift of body position from every broker at the table and a gasp from all four of the AGS representatives. Carl did not look at his protégés. Instead, he stood with his hands behind his back and reveled in the reactions from the power brokers, as he seemingly gave away the farm. Eventually, all eyes were upon Carl once again and the room was silent enough to hear the hum of the street fourteen stories below. Carl stood in place but began to speak as if there was nothing he would enjoy more.

"You must understand something. AGS, my company, stands to profit more than two hundred million in the next ten years. That's profit, and it doesn't depend on how much you pay for each unit. It depends upon the nearly instantaneous information updates at our website and the ten thousand contracts we have pre-approved for access to this data."

There was clamorous shuffling papers as people around the table began searching the prospectus for the information Carl Larkin had just given them. Carl glanced at Janet Deering, who stared back at him with a dumbfounded look on her face. She reflected disappointment as she silently mouthed the word, "Why?" toward Carl.

"Did you say *ten thousand* contracts have been approved and paid for?" One of the power brokers asked.

Carl stepped forward, in front of the broker who had asked the question and put both of his hands on the table. He leaned forward close enough to smell her perfume, looked into her eyes and said, "*Over* ten thousand."

"I can't imagine for one instant," she replied, as everyone around the table stared at them and listened closely, "why you would make up such a story, if it is a lie, or why you would reveal such information, if it is the truth."

"Janet?" Carl said loudly enough for everyone to hear, yet didn't take his eyes off the woman in front of him.

"It's, um, it's true," Janet Deering replied, as if it hurt her to do so.

"Very well," the power broker returned her gaze to Carl. "What insanity drove you to tell us information that we could quite possibly use against you to bring our costs down further?"

"Because," Carl spoke to the broker's eyes. The woman stared straight back at him, as if in a battle of wills where the first one to blink loses. A wicked smile came across Carl's face as he nearly whispered, "Without your agreement, my contracts are worthless and my company folds. Without my company, all the EX-1 units are pulled, and the grid goes back to the pre-2000 age of bickering, black-outs and deregulation derailments."

"I see," the woman said, as she blinked and withdrew her gaze from the eyes of Carl Larkin.

Carl Larkin stood erect, removed the smile from his face and began slowly walking toward one of the conference room exit doors. As he passed by Janet Deering and the three other AGS representatives, he motioned for them to follow him. Janet busied herself in collecting her belongings, as did the other three, while Carl held an exit door open. None of the brokers at the table watched Carl. He stood behind them and allowed his staff to exit the room before he shut the exit door, stood with his back to it and said, "It would seem as though I have made myself temporarily indispensable. Certainly, someone else will come along soon enough and create a better, cheaper product than the Gen-Two. However, I know certain things to be true. I have collected and read your data. You, and the companies that you represent, do not have the time to wait for this to happen. In addition, neither do I. I'll expect your decision before you leave this building today. The telephone in the center of the table is how you contact me. Pick it up, and press the only button with a label; it goes directly to my office. Thank you for your time." With that said, Carl Larkin exited the conference room and left the power brokers alone to decide his and their fate.

Desperate eyes from fallen faces followed Carl Larkin as he passed the open office doors along the broad corridor leading to his office. Staff members had worked tirelessly over the last two years, only to watch their leader seemingly toss caution to the wind at the eleventh hour and risk the entire project. Each staff member now stood aimlessly in the doorway of their individual office and watched Carl stroll by as if he were the grand marshal of a local parade. Carl met their woeful stares with a confident, almost condescending smile and a simple phrase, "Fear not, God is with me." This didn't seem to help the listeners, as their shoulders slumped further.

Carl reached for his office door knob and stole a glance at the reflective surface on the large nameplate adhered to the face of the door. Four years before, when he started AGS and chose this room as his office, the nameplate was the first *improvement* Carl had made for his fledgling company. It was a large, oval-shaped brass plate with his name in small black letters at the bottom, with an embossed company logo taking up the majority of the surface. No one had suspected the real use of this nameplate. The polished brass surface could function as a mirror. Carl had used it on more than one hundred occasions over the last four years, to catch a glimpse of his staff members' body language behind his back. This day, as he pretended to unlock his office door, Carl Larkin watched as each staff member retreated, in defeated manner, from their positions in each doorway, to the interior of their offices. Carl chuckled and shook his head.

Once inside his office, Carl Larkin shut and locked his door. It was a modest office for belonging to the CEO of a successful company in a town of success stories. His desk and chairs were more practical than pricey. His bookshelves and wall decorations could be found for sale on the floors of any Wal-Mart store. The laptop he used on a daily basis was a middle-of-the-road edition from two years before. The view from his windows was nothing noteworthy; it faced the south side of St. Louis, with no view of the arch or the stadiums. The only extravagant thing inside Carl Larkin's office was the entertainment center on the west wall that housed twelve television monitors.

Inside and outside of AGS, Carl Larkin was known as an avid sports fan. Often people had seen Carl inside his office with a remote control in his hand, flipping the volume off and on for the various monitors, each monitor revealing a different sporting event. Rumors told a story that from the moment he rented the entire ninth floor of the Costar Building to house his company, the first thing Carl installed was the nameplate on his office door and the second was the satellite connections to all twelve monitors. If there was a sports pool to bet on within the Costar Building, Carl not only knew about it but also had a bet or two on it. The joke behind Carl's back was that he was married to AGS but had an ongoing affair with ESPN.

Carl Larkin had caught wind of this joke and it filled him with deep satisfaction. As he crossed the open floor of his modest office on this particular day and eyed the twelve television screens on the west wall, an even greater satisfaction began to well up in his heart. He moved behind his desk and slowly sat down into his chair. Reaching into a small refrigerator that sat on the floor next to his desk, Carl pulled out a bottle of beer and shut the refrigerator door. This was when his eyes caught the photographs on the bookshelf behind the refrigerator. Each photo framed in the same kind of inexpensive gold metal frame; each frame sat upright on the same shelf of the bookcase. Each photo had the same three people in it: Carl, his adoptive mother and his adoptive father. Carl twisted the cap off his beer, stared at the far left photograph, and began to participate in a ritual he had started over the last year of his life.

The left-hand photo, taken a year ago, almost to the day, caught Carl's eye. One of his parents' friends from their church had taken it at the

Sending party the night before his parents had gone off to Israel on a Christian missionary trip. The photographer took a bad picture, yet it was a meaningful one none-the-less: his father hugging Carl on his left side, his mother hugging him on his right side, both parents looking back at the camera with gleams of pride for their son; a smile on the face of Carl, yet a look of sorrow in Carl's eyes. Three days later, a suicide bomber ended the lives of Michael and Theresa Larkin as they traveled on a bus from Tel Aviv to Jerusalem. Closing his eyes, Carl spoke quietly, "May God have mercy on their souls."

Opening his eyes, Carl took a swig from the beer bottle and looked at the second photo from the left. Once again, his adoptive parents flanked Carl. This time, they stood outside the door to his office at AGS, on the ninth floor of the Costar Building. Once again, the light of pride shown in the eyes of his parents as they pointed to the small black letters of their son's name on the shining brass nameplate of the door. Once again, Carl was smiling back at the camera. Yet, this time, the look in his eyes reflected an excitement, as if he was hiding a secret. The photograph had been taken four years ago, a month after he had started AGS. Carl closed his eyes and said, "May God have mercy on their souls, they were good people."

Opening his eyes again, Carl took a sip from the bottle of beer and peered at the third photograph from the left. Carl was twenty-one years old in this picture and draped in the cap and gown of his graduation from MIT. The diploma in his hand was a prop, given to him by one of his friends at the ceremony, to hold for family photographs. His real diploma came in the mail two weeks later and now hung on the wall of his office. Carl pulled his eyes away from the third picture long enough to see his name on that diploma, hung on the back of an empty shelf, two levels up from the photographs.

"Electrical Engineer," Carl said to himself, with an ironic laugh, "Yes, an Engineer of one form or another." His gaze fell back on the third photo. His parents were so proud of him that day. They drove all the way from their home in an Indianapolis suburb to see him graduate. He could just see the write-up on the local website: *Local missionary's son does well with his full-ride scholarship*. The words *genius* and *brilliant* came to mind as he looked at the third photo. Carl closed his eyes and spoke in a whisper, "May God have mercy on *my* soul."

It took some time for Carl to open his eyes and look at the fourth and final photograph on the bookshelf. This photo reminded Carl Larkin of his real name, a name he had abandoned twenty years before, on the very day the picture was taken. Carl opened his eyes and stared at the inanimate object, as a small tremble rumbled through his entire body. As part of the ritual, he had to face this picture. The ritual kept him focused, kept him balanced and reminded him of what his purpose in life was. The most difficult part of the ritual was looking at this fourth photograph. He was twelve years old and had been in the United States for less than ten minutes when the camera caught the image. Once again, surrounded by Michael and Theresa Larkin, their eyes gleaming to match the hope they had for the young man that stood between them. It was amazing to Carl how much he had changed. His skin looked darker in that photograph. His eyes seemed darker than they did now. The young lad in the fourth picture had a look in his eyes of violence and fear that matched the expression on his face. Suspended above the three people in the photograph was a homemade sign that read, "Welcome to the United States, Carl."

Before he could finish the ritual with a short prayer, the phone on his desk buzzed and shook Carl from his trance-like state. Based upon the particular light on the phone's faceplate, Carl knew it was the call from the men and women inside the conference room. He placed the open bottle of beer on the bookshelf in front of the fourth picture. Carl Larkin held the phone receiver to an ear. He heard the words, "The coalition has decided unanimously to accept your offer. You will have complete licensing and approval for retrofit in ten business days."

"Very well," Carl said plainly, "I will have my staff send your offices the itinerary of retrofit activities." He replaced the phone receiver in its cradle.

Carl Larkin grabbed a remote control device from his desktop and began turning on several of the satellite system monitors on the west wall of his office. Images from a variety of sporting channels flashed upon these screens: a soccer game from Europe on one set, a sports talk show on another, a baseball game on yet another.

"Good," Carl said aloud, and pressed two buttons on his desk phone.

"Yes, Mr. Larkin," came a female voice over his speakerphone.

"Janet, could you gather the staff and have them meet in my office?"

"Yes, Mr. Larkin," Janet Deering replied with a nervous break in her voice, "Right away."

Carl pressed a button on his phone, stood from his chair and walked across his office to unlock his door. Returning to his chair, Carl pressed a button on the remote control and a sudden blare of crowd noise came from hidden speakers in the dropped ceiling of his office. In a matter of thirty seconds, his office door opened and his staff members filed in to the raucous sounds of the European soccer game. Carl sat behind his desk with the remote control poised in one hand, his body facing the monitors on the west wall. He acted as if he hadn't noticed that his four-member staff had entered his office. Carl stared at the west wall until he heard the door to his office shut, whereupon he muted the audio from the soccer game and swiveled his chair to face the four staff members. They stood in a line before his desk, facing the man that had personally interviewed them, hired them and had groomed them to excel in specific areas of his company. No one spoke as Carl spent a few seconds to look each of his staff members in the eyes. Reflected in their faces was a mixture of dread and hope. Just at the point where the silence in the room became too much for even Carl to bear, he spoke these words, "Gen-Two is a done deal. Retrofit goes on line in two weeks."

Janet Deering nearly collapsed as she exhaled deeply and put her palms upon Carl's desktop to keep from falling. The others had similar initial reactions. Carl stood from his chair and offered a handshake and congratulations to each member of his staff, starting with Janet and working down the line. Immediately, a compressed jubilation replaced the heavy sense of despair inside the office.

"Everyone, call it a day and come back in to work tomorrow morning, two hours later than normal," Carl said after the last handshake. "We'll discuss the final details of the retrofit tomorrow at ten in the conference room. You've all done well."

"Thank you, Mr. Larkin," Janet said, as she struggled to regain a normal breathing pattern. The others echoed her words as they left Carl's office and shut the door.

Two minutes passed before Carl crossed his office and locked his door. With a few pressed buttons of the remote control, every satellite monitor went black. Carl then returned to his chair and removed his beer from its perch on the bookcase photograph shelf. He wondered if any of his staff had seen the beer. *Probably not*, he thought to himself, *they were too busy with other concerns.* Carl took a sip from the bottle of beer and shrugged his shoulders. This ritual of drinking a beer and perusing the photographs had been a recent quirk in his life, and it was a quirk that he had made every effort to keep hidden from all but God. Carl had decided that God didn't care if he had an occasional beer. The others, no, they should not know about it. Where he was going once the plan was in its final stages had strict laws forbidding the consumption of alcohol.

Carl leaned his head back and drained the last of the beer from the bottle. In doing so, his eye caught a glimpse of the fourth framed photograph. The empty beer bottle went back into the small refrigerator to join the other empties Carl hid in it. He bent over to lift the fourth picture from the shelf. With the motions of experienced fingers, Carl carefully took the frame apart and began separating the photograph and glass plate from the cardboard backing. Hidden behind the fourth photograph was a faded picture, taken many years before by a street vendor in a market area of the West Bank. Looking back at Carl were the furious eyes of a young Palestinian man with a bandana wrapped around his head. The young man wore a stern look on his face. The young man was Carl's older brother, Saeed.

"The plan is working, Saeed," Carl spoke to the image of his brother. "And, soon I will be home again." *Home*, he thought to himself, *will I really ever have a home?*

CHAPTER TWELVE

Launching the EX-1

The memory of his brother's death haunted Hassan Al-Sarraj even to this day, as he sat on the ninth floor in an office building in a land far, far away from that place. His family had ridden a bus to the West Bank to visit an uncle. Hassan was ten years old. He remembered the smells of the market and the flurry of activity all around him. He remembered his mother warning him to stay close to her as they made their way through a river of people. He remembered the street vendor taking his older brother's picture with a Polaroid camera and his mother complaining over the cost. Saeed looked at the photo and smiled with satisfaction. Hassan could still hear his brother's voice as he bent down to his ear, "Keep this to remember me by." Saeed shoved the photograph into Hassan's hand and turned to leave. Hassan remembered his mother pulling him along as she ran after his older brother, yelling at him to come back, that he was going the wrong way. Hassan remembered people screaming and running toward him and his mother. Hassan remembered his brother standing in an open area where two streets connected. Hassan remembered his brother's hands wrestling with his shirt buttons as an Israeli soldier shot him through the head.

"They murdered you," Carl Larkin said, with a tinge of anger in his voice. He reached down to the door of his small refrigerator and opened it. Three full bottles of beer stood to one side amid just as many empties. The temptation to drink a second beer came into Carl's mind like an itch he couldn't scratch. *No, there is still work to do today,* he thought to himself. Knowing it would be a mistake to drink two beers in one sitting, Carl gently shut the refrigerator door and returned to staring at the picture of his deceased brother.

Watching his brother shot down in the streets of the West Bank had filled Hassan with anger, with the need to seek vengeance. Behind his mother's back, Hassan sought out and enlisted himself into the most radical Hezbollah cell in the West Bank. He had been in *training* for less than a month when an elder brought him before a council of clerics for testing. The cleric council discovered that Hassan was a genius. Immediately, two of the clerics kidnapped Hassan from his Hezbollah cell group, as well as his family. The kidnappers deposited Hassan in a special orphanage in Jerusalem. Every child at that orphanage had the same story. The old men in the council had kidnapped them and imprisoned them at the orphanage. Hassan had tried to explain to his captors, fellow Palestinians, that Allah had chosen him to kill as many Israeli soldiers as he could, in vengeance for the death of his brother. His captives explained to Hassan that Allah had a much greater calling for his life than the lives of a few harmless Israeli soldiers.

"A few harmless soldiers," Carl Larkin spoke these words while in the dream-like state of remembrance.

At the orphanage, the clerics drilled the children inmates daily on how to talk, how to walk and how to act. The clerics trained the children to weed-out typical Arabic catch phrases like, "How evil the Israelis and Americans were" and replace these with strenuous lessons on speaking perfect American English. They were taught to say the word "God" instead of Allah. They were taught some basic principles of the Judeo-Christian ethic and trained to act as if these were true and righteous principles. The clerics made personal hygiene a priority in ways that Hassan had never heard of. He learned to take a shower every day, to comb his hair a certain way, to wear certain styles of clothing. Within one year of his arrival at the orphanage, the clerics deemed Hassan presentable and pushed him through his final stage of preparation. His mentors persuaded him that Allah had a special plan in store for him to destroy the United States of America. In order to do this, he must live within the beast, become like one of the American infidels, and wait.

Wait for what?

Wait for further instructions. The cleric promised Hassan that hidden within the boundaries of the great Satan America was a *Network* of brothers that would one day contact him. These brothers would guide him in his steps toward his great destiny before Allah. Hassan, now Carl, could still smell the breath and hear the words of his mentor, an elderly man that had long since departed this life, as he gave Hassan his final instructions before leaving the Middle East.

"Soon, some very kind people will come to take you to America. They will be your family while you are there. They will give you a new name and you will answer to it. You are to act like an American. You are to learn to talk like an American. You are to go to their churches and pretend to be one of them. You are to be the best citizen of their country. All of this is done on the *outside* of who you are. It is this *outside* appearance that will protect you from great harm. On the inside, though, you will be Hassan Al-Sarraj. On the inside, you will be a soldier for Allah. In time, the Network in America will contact you and will relay what your course of action will be. The important thing to remember, Hassan, is to keep the *inside*, inside and the *outside*, outside. Never tell another soul who you truly are."

Three days later, a cleric took Hassan outside the orphanage compound to a building he had never seen before. This was the building where potential adoptive parents to met the orphanage children. One of the clerics brought Hassan before a man and woman who spoke broken Arabic. The cleric introduced them by their names, Michael and Theresa Larkin. They were pale-skinned Americans who dressed in some strange combination of half-western and half-eastern garb. Hassan remembered how strange their names seemed, as they smiled at him and reached out to shake his hand. Hassan returned their handshake with a smile, as taught by the clerics, as well as a heavily accented, "Glad to meet you." His response made the couple smile to the point of joyful laughter. Hassan looked to the cleric and received an approving nod. He had done the right thing.

Michael and Theresa Larkin were Christian missionaries who, for the last four years of their life, had been traveling throughout Israel as relief aid workers. Wherever there was famine or outbreak of disease, the Larkins went there as soon as they could to bring food, shelter and medicine where needed the most. Sent to Israel and financially backed by a large conservative congregation in America, the Larkins gave aid to all people regardless of race or creed. They were consistent in this principle. For this reason, when the orphanage clerics heard that the Larkins were returning to live in America and were looking to adopt a child to take home with them, the clerics led the Larkins directly to the orphanage to meet Hassan Al-Sarraj. The clerics knew that this was a narrow window of opportunity to get one of their children inside the borders of America and into the proper set of circumstances. The Larkins spent an hour with twelve year-old Hassan inside the meeting building before leaving with the promise to return and take him to America. A month later, they kept their promise. On the plane ride between Tel Aviv and Greece, the Larkins revealed to Hassan his new name: Carl Joseph Larkin.

Despite his genius, Carl Larkin faced difficult obstacles as he assimilated into the American culture. His aptitude for grasping the American English language astounded his grade school teachers. His understanding of mathematical principles went off the charts. Even as he rose in stature among his academic peers, grade school was not kind to Hassan. For two years his peers taunted and teased him. As was typical in any society, the list of reasons for this torment was both shallow and unpreventable. His skin was too dark. He looked like an Arab. He spoke with a funny accent. Even the children within the Christian culture, the ones specifically taught to act differently, gave Carl difficulties. In all that time the *outside* of Carl Larkin reacted like the torment was all water off a duck's back, that it didn't bother him. However, on the *inside,* he stockpiled hatred. On the outside, he acted as if he had *turned the other cheek.* On the inside was an overflowing cup of *an eye for an eye.* Despite the love and encouragement of his adoptive parents, who gave Carl a fortress of shelter from the horde of infidels that surrounded him, Carl Larkin felt completely alone. After two years inside the great Satan of America, no one from the Network had contacted him.

It wasn't until Carl began his first year in High School that one of the Network brothers made a move to communicate. The Larkins, who had eked out a meager living in full time Christian ministry since their return to America, found themselves on the receiving end of a gift from an unknown source. The donor of the gift, who wished to remain anonymous, drop-shipped a series of boxes to the main office of the church building where the Larkins worked. Inside the boxes was a top-of-the-line home computer system. That very day a letter arrived in the mail slot of Michael Larkin. The envelope had no return address and was post-marked from three days prior. The postmark was from Dallas, Texas. There was a single sheet of plain paper inside the envelope with the typed words, "I know of your service to God. Please accept my gift to your family." The letter was not signed. The Larkins sensed the letter and the subsequent gift was an answer to prayer, for their son was constantly talking of his desire to own a PC, a device they could not yet afford.

This home computer system opened up two new worlds to young Carl Larkin: the Internet and E-mail. Through a series of brilliant manipulations within the proper channels, Carl was able to work toward a Bachelors Degree from an accredited college. He did this via an on-line service at the same time that he was putting in his time at high school. One of the wonders of the Internet world for Carl was that no one could see him or hear him talk. No one would know that he was different. Through interaction with other on-line students, Carl had developed friendships with a variety of them from around the country, none of which he had ever met face to face. They did not know him as a fourteen year-old Palestinian with an odd accent. Instead, his college acquaintances knew him by the lies he carefully crafted and thought he was a twenty-year old white male. His small group of on-line friends spent hours each night poring over homework together, e-mailing each other and occasionally meeting in private chat rooms. Eventually, it got to the point where Carl's parents did not see or talk to their adopted son, with the exception of breakfast and dinner meals, and even then, they had to drag him away from his computer. It was during one of his all night college course sessions that Carl heard the symbolic tone from his computer signifying that he had received mail in his E-mail box. The sender's address looked similar to the address of one of his fellow on-line college students, so he opened it up without thinking twice. Written across the page, in what seemed to be a gibberish collection of letters, was a hidden message. It took Carl a second or two to see it but, when he did, it almost made him faint. Written in an American English translation with no spaces between each word, was an Arabic sentence that told him if he understood the message to reply back using the Arabic word for *Network*.

That was over a decade ago. While the memory of that first e-mail, that primitive form of communication from the Network, was still fresh in Carl's mind, he turned his gaze toward the west wall of his office. The twelve monitors stared blankly back at him. *9/11 changed everything*, he thought to himself as he looked at one particular monitor on the wall, *it rendered the Internet too risky to use anymore*. No one who had ever been inside that office had noticed that the one particular monitor was always black. No one knew its real function. Carl glanced at his wristwatch and noted the time. *Thirty minutes and you will call me*, he thought, as he returned his gaze to the one particular monitor.

From the moment of his first American contact with the Network, Carl set upon a new course in life, with all the necessary doors opened and waiting for him to walk through. Every month or so, Carl would receive a coded E-mail from the Network. He never met the sender or asked who it was. At first, he was cautious in his obedience to the requests made in the messages. One of the first orders from the network was as simple as calling a certain telephone number on his parent's phone, waiting for a buzzing tone, and then punching in five numbers from the phone's keypad before hanging up. Other times, the orders were more complicated and required Carl to be in specific public places at specific times doing specific activities. On one of these public occasions, the Network instructed Carl to help his church youth group pass out Christian tracts to people exiting a high school football game. Each time he completed one of these tasks, the Network rewarded Carl's family with money or personal possessions. The lion's share of these rewards came in the form of college scholarships.

Carl Larkin graduated from high school and college at the age of sixteen and then entered the campus of MIT to acquire an Electrical Engineering degree. While at MIT, the Network instructed Carl to focus his studies and projects on the topic of the U.S. electric power grid system. Carl was unclear as to why he was to concentrate on this area of the American infrastructure. Often, he wondered why the Network was leading him in this educational direction, and Carl always came to the same conclusion: The most effective way to destroy Israel was to destroy the United States, and the most efficient way to destroy the United States was to take away their electricity. How could you possibly do such a thing without the involvement of thousands of people?

Even after graduating from MIT at the age of nineteen, Carl had no answers to the question of what the Network had in store for him. With his perfect grades, a diploma and his mensa membership as credentials, Carl Larkin had no problems in landing a job after graduation. Nileren, a large electrical utility in the Chicago area, recruited Carl as a process design engineer, despite the fact that he was only nineteen years old and had no previous experience. In early 2000, Nileren gave Carl the responsibility of running a feasibility study on the use of a new form of communications technology.

A company from Kentucky, Kenstar, had developed a telemetry device that could read the ebb and flow of electrical power through any high voltage power line, and transmit that reading as a signal to local satellite systems. That signal could be further transmitted to a central location where the *raw* data was translated into *readable* data on a computer screen. The most useful function of this device was that power generation entities throughout the United States, like Nileren, could now monitor the outputs of their competitor's power plants with *near real-time* information. In an industry where every second carries a dollar value, this technology had a prime place and an important purpose. This technology would aid the various power generation entities in joining coalitions with each other in order to survive economically. Most importantly to Carl, it was a technology that could be improved now and used later as a weapon.

After performing industry insider research on Nileren's dime, Carl discovered the two feasible improvements of the current Kenstar system that would get his foot in the door as an industry competitor. The first improvement was to move the transducer unit closer to the grid's substation transformers and use the induced field of the primary side of the transformer as a power supply. This would eliminate the need for a telemetry device and the bureaucracy of leasing land space needed for reading induction changes off high voltage power lines. The second improvement was changing the data at the user end from near real-time to real-time. This would mean taking an existing form of technology and improving it a mere 10%.

There was a drawback to Carl's plan: a person couldn't reverse engineer and then alter a piece of technology until he had it in his hands. Therefore, Carl submitted a formal recommendation up Nileren's chain of command that the company invest into this new form of information technology. After a month and a board meeting or two later, a proposal to invest in this new technology was drawn and ratified. As part of the contract that Nileren drew with Kenstar, land and resources owned by Nileren were leased to Kenstar for the installation of over twenty telemetry devices. Since this was his project, Carl performed hands-on inspections of every installation site, side by side with the grounds crew provided by Kenstar. Carl contacted the Network and passed along the pertinent information. Two days later, one of the telemetry devices was stolen from the back of a Kenstar utility vehicle in a hotel parking lot in Elgin, IL. Kenstar contacted the local police immediately, but, due to a perfect theft, the telemetry device was never recovered. Kenstar shipped another telemetry device to the Elgin technicians and installed it in place of the stolen one. The Kenstar near real-time system was fully installed, tested and lauded as a great success by the traders of the Nileren power-broking desks. More importantly to the Network, Carl Larkin had made a name for himself as a successful innovator and moneymaker.

Once the pilfered telemetry device was in the hands of the Network, they contacted Carl and asked him what he wished to do with it. Carl sent back a reply listing the various types of tools and electrical equipment he would need for the job. The Network granted his wishes. The telemetry device would be waiting for him at a predetermined location chosen by the Network. Using his off-work hours and weekends, Carl spent three weeks dissecting and testing each component of the telemetry device. For the first time in his life, Carl came face to face with a person from the Network. An elderly man of Middle Eastern origin met him inside the warehouse the first night. He said his name was Joseph and that he was sent to help Carl in any way that he could. Carl, who had excellent first impression capability with everyone he met, couldn't get a read on the old man that stood before him. Joseph wore tattered, soiled coveralls and well-worn, steel-toed work boots. Joseph's facial expression and body language remained clearly neutral at all times. He reflected neither passivity nor aggression. Carl suggested that the old man hide somewhere near the warehouse entrance to deter intruders. Joseph shook his head in an almost condescending manner as he explained to Carl that he had already taken care of the security of the warehouse. Carl shrugged his shoulders and proceeded with his technical work, completely unaware of the three women and two men who kept watch from various vantage points surrounding the warehouse.

After three weeks of clandestine labor on the part of Carl and Joseph, the telemetry device's inner workings had been de-mystified and catalogued. In reality, the transponder unit from within Kenstar's telemetry device was easily duplicated with parts that were readily available on any number of Internet websites. It was up to Carl Larkin at this point in the project to create a more efficient paradigm of real-time information collection. Kenstar's near real-time system had the telemetry devices taking data from power lines between the various sub-stations of the grid. The current Kenstar device was set on the ground and its transponder aimed at the high voltage power lines. Carl's idea was to move the transponder closer to the intended target: the transformers at the sub-stations.

Throughout the continental United States, there exists a veritable web of high voltage power lines connecting electrical power sources to low voltage electrical power loads. This system of connecting the power generators to the power users is unofficially referred to as *the grid*. Dotting the landscape like some form of ill-shaped, crystalline structure exist the thousands of power generation plants that create, through one form or another, electricity for the grid. Spattered throughout that same landscape are millions upon millions of electrical power users. The manufacturing industry uses the vast majority of this electrical power, followed by the millions of air-conditioned American households. During a given year, the need for electrical power in the United States rises in the spring, peaks in the summer and dwindles in the fall. During any given day, the need for electrical power in the United States rises in the mid-morning, peaks from noon to evening and then dwindles toward night. Day after day, season after season, the grid pulses as if driven by an unseen heart. This pulsing continues uninterrupted, until something within the grid goes wrong.

For instance: a power generation plant in sector *A* trips off the line with some form of long-term mechanical problem. Sector *A* now needs power from another source. The local utilities have contracts with multiple local power plants to make up for the loss and, with a few clicks of a mouse button, a technician in a control room within Sector *A* diverts electrical energy from a back-up portion of the grid. However, dollars are being lost in the process. Over the phone, bargains are struck between corporate entities in far away cities and, within minutes, Sector *A* is receiving electrical power from as far away as Sector *F*, five hundred miles away. Sector *A* is now happy and all but a few technicians and power brokers are completely aware that this entire event has happened. How does electrical power travel five hundred miles?

The electricity that leaves a power generation plant is of too high an amperage to travel great distances. The power lines would have to be huge in order to carry that high of an amperage. It would not be cost effective for anyone to attempt to build an electrical grid with heavy power lines and the monstrous towers necessary to carry that weight. In order for electricity to travel great distances, it must be reduced in amperage and boosted in voltage. High voltage electricity can travel great distances through power lines that are small in comparison to those used for high amperage. The device used to convert electricity from high amperage to high voltage is a *transformer*. Transformers are all around us:

from the small transformers in household appliances to the large transformers of the grid.

The transformers in the grid are probably the most reliable part of the system. Rarely do they fail. If they do, human error or stupidity is the usual cause. The beauty of the grid transformer is that it has no moving parts. Picture two large coils of wire within the same giant metal containment, physically separated by a gap filled with oil. The oil dissipates the heat generated by the transformer as electricity passes through the two coils. The larger transformers are equipped with exterior fans to aid the oil in removing the heat. That is all a transformer needs in order to function.

The grid is arranged in a way that even if one or two of the transformers fail, other power can be transferred to the affected area with back-up sources. In worst-case scenarios, a temporary blackout of electrical power would ensue until the utility in the affected area put the back-up source into service.

What if the back-up source transformer failed? What if enough main line transformers and back-up transformers in the grid failed at once?

In the three months it took Carl to modify his transponder unit to suit his intentions, he had spent nearly every spare, non-sleeping moment with Joseph in the small warehouse in Elgin, Illinois. After all that time together, Carl knew no more about the old man than he did at their first meeting. Joseph was a closed book as far as personality and character went. He would have been an excellent poker player, if he indeed played poker. Carl asked Joseph about this one Saturday morning, as the two busied themselves in removing test leads from one of the transponder prototypes.

"Do you play poker, Joseph?"

Joseph simply shrugged and continued working. This just about summed up the conversational connection between the two men.

When the transponder prototypes passed all their benchmark tests in the warehouse, Carl submitted a plan to the Network. His idea was to create a front company for his prototype product and market it as a transformer safety device, not as a real-time monitoring transponder. The Network assured Carl Larkin that what he wished would be done and sent him a data testing permission letter from a fantasy company in St. Louis, Missouri.

Carl then pushed a proposition up Nileren's chain of command to install a *transformer efficiency-testing device* on one of their transformers. This proposition was, simply put, a lie. Carl had convinced his supervisors that, because of an unprecedented recent string of transformer failures within the industry, such a test device could prevent transformer failure. In the wake of his successful implementation of the Kenstar units, the Nileren powers-that-be basically gave Carl Larkin a blank check to do whatever he wanted with his transformer efficiency testing device. Carl selected a transformer substation to test the device on and within two business days an installation plan approved by Nileren engineers. The FCC approved the appropriate broadband licenses and several communication entities were brought onboard the project. Carl Larkin brought one of his prototype units to the specific substation on the approved day led a three-man Nileren crew in the installation of this device. The technicians connected the prototype to a back-up transformer for the main transformer in that sector of the grid.

Once Carl was certain the prototype device had been installed correctly, he drove to the local Nileren control center to meet three other Nileren engineers. Carl had worked with each of these engineers previously at different phases of the Kenstar project, but never before had he seen all three in the same place, at the same time. As he approached them in the parking lot of the control center that morning, he couldn't help but think these three engineers had stepped out of Alice's looking glass. The physical representation of these engineers almost made Carl laugh the first time they stood next to each other. From left to right was an extremely tall skinny man, an average height but extremely obese man and finally, a short and rail-thin woman. Putting his first reactions in neutral, Carl cordially shook their hands and asked them to follow him into the control center. After performing the appropriate introductions to the control center staff, Carl led the three engineers toward an unused computer terminal, tucked away in an isolated area of the control room.

Engineers normally used this computer terminal as a mock-grid testing station for logic system changes prior to putting them into effect on the real grid. The other computer terminals in the control room were manned by full time Nileren operators, whose job it was to maintain the integrity of this sector of the grid. On one wall of the control room was a giant map of the local grid sector. This map contained LED readouts and indication lights, which could give any operator in the room a *big-picture* glance of what was happening with their portion of the grid at any given moment.

From out of his briefcase, Carl extracted a single DVD and inserted it into the engineer's station computer. Seconds later, as the other engineers watched with anticipation, the computer monitor went black and then filled with a simple, one-line diagram of the grid in the affected prototype-testing sector.

The DVD player inside the computer began to hum as various parts of the one-line diagram began to acquire rectangular fields with tiny boxes next to diagram components. Seconds later, every tiny box in every field contained a numerical value. Some of the values changed, others remained the same. One of the engineers standing behind Carl leaned back and glanced at the giant *big picture* wall map. He noted aloud that the numbers on Carl's drawing matched the precise values of the megawatt values currently on the wall map. One of the number box fields, the field for the prototype device, had nothing but unchanging zeros in each number box.

"The program written for this testing device utilizes the Kenstar software. That's why you see the exact numbers coming off their telemetry devices," Carl explained, as he pushed his chair back and stood up. "The testing device on the transformer, called an EX-1, sends SCADA signals just like the Kenstar units. Now, all we need to do is get one of our operators over here to shut the appropriate breakers, and we'll see what comes up."

Carl held a short discussion between one of the control room operators and he concerning the next step in the transformer testing procedure. Carl returned to the engineers crowding around the mock-grid computer monitor and sat down in his chair. Nodding to the operator, Carl watched his monitor as the operator took the appropriate actions to put the back-up transformer online. Suddenly the number boxes on Carl's monitor filled up with numerical values.

"What are these numbers?" One of the Nileren engineers, the man with the weight problem, asked Carl. The man seemed self-conscious when around Carl and was constantly attempting to tuck in the loose shirttails that kept pulling out of his expansive and over-stretched waistline.

"In order, from top to bottom," Carl said as he pointed to the number field boxes, "transformer oil temperature, oil pressure, oil reservoir level and relative efficiency."

"Relative efficiency?" Another engineer, this one the woman, asked in disbelief.

"Yes," Carl turned to face her, "the EX-1 test unit takes an induced reading from the secondary side and converts it to a digital value. This value is inserted into a logic block and the software spits out a comparative value based upon the input to the primary side. All of this is done inside the EX-1."

"What kind of feedback timing are we talking here?" The obese engineer asked, as he leaned back to glance at the big-picture wall map.

"I'm not certain," Carl lied, "but, I can retrieve the numbers from the historical hard drive and decipher the graphs back at our office."

"I'd like to see that data," the forty-ish woman said, with an aggressive tone in her voice.

"By the way, what company did you say this EX-1 device belonged to?"

Carl reached into his briefcase and pulled out an official-looking form with a logo on the letterhead made up of the letters *AGS*. He laid the letter on the desktop to his left, so the other engineers could see it. In simple terms, the letter gave Carl Larkin and Nileren the permission to install and test their prototype unit at the transformer of their choosing, for the duration of one month.

"AGS?" The obese engineer said, as he attempted to tuck in the front of his shirt again.

"American Grid Security," Carl said plainly. "Out of St. Louis."

"I've never heard of them," the woman replied, unimpressed.

"Well, from what we've just seen," the tall, skinny engineer said with a smile, "we will be hearing about them. I'm impressed."

"Well, I'd like to see the raw data on this from the historical drive before I make any recommendations," the woman said as she stood with arms folded in a defensive position.

"Me too," the obese man said.

"It'll be in your inboxes tomorrow morning," Carl replied, as he manipulated several mouse-click buttons on the face of the one-line drawing. He inserted a second DVD and burned several files of data onto it before ejecting it and dropping it into his briefcase.

"Anything else?"

The three engineers shook their heads.

"Okay, I suppose we should go now and let these operators get the situation back to normal."

The day that Carl ran his prototype test on the EX-1, AGS did not exist as a company. If one of the engineers were quick enough to memorize and call the telephone number on the phony AGS letterhead, he would talk to a woman who claimed to be the administrative assistant for the fledgling company, AGS. She would take a message and promise that someone would get back to them. In reality, this woman was answering the phone in her St. Louis apartment. She was part of the Network.

After Carl Larkin returned to the warehouse the day of the prototype test and downloaded the historical data onto his personal laptop computer, AGS ceased to be phony. According to the database program on his laptop, the EX-1 sent *real-time* data, four seconds faster than the data from the Kenstar unit and four times the amount of parameters monitored. Unknown to anyone but Carl and the Network, this data also included the megawatts delivered on the secondary side of the transformer. Carl then manipulated the data from the historical files to eliminate the information he did not want the other engineers to see. He then burned copies of the doctored information, along with a glowing synopsis of his own, onto three DVDs. The following morning, administration assistants at three separate locations delivered DVDs into the inboxes of the three engineers who had witnessed the prototype testing.

Carl then E-mailed a report to his contact in the Network, explaining what had happened in the prototype test and what he thought should happen next. The Network's reply was immediate. What started as a front business operating from the apartment of a Network operative soon evolved into a real company. Over the next year, patents on the EX-1 were applied for, legitimate small business grants secured, office spaces leased and production facilities acquired. In the summer of 2001, Carl Larkin handed in his resignation to his superiors at Nileren and began the process of selecting his administrative staff at American Grid Securities. He leased a five-office slot on the ninth floor of the Costar Building in St. Louis and purchased five sets of the same desks, chairs, phones, lamps, and computers. Carl hired his first four employees and started grooming them to believe they were on the ground floor of a soon-to-be large enterprise. The initial plan was to start production of the EX-1 in the spring of 2002. Every part of the plan seemed to be heading full speed into fruition.

Then came 9/11.

On September 11th, 2001, Carl Larkin called his four staff members on their office phones and instructed them to bring their chairs with them into his office. He turned on his cable monitor and had them watch in abject horror as the second plane flew into the Trade Center. No one could watch the footage of such carnage without some kind of extreme reaction inside his heart, unless he was insane. Carl observed the members of his staff as each one of them came close to going into shock over what they were witnessing on the various cable channels. Carl was affected in a similar way, but for different reasons. The attacks had *terrorist* written all over them from the very beginning. But which group? And how would this affect his plan with the Network? He sent his staff home early that day and informed them to take the next day off from work. They left that Monday in September of 2001 and never set foot on the 9th floor of the Costar building again.

The moment his staff left his office, Carl sent an E-mail to his contact in the Network. He received a reply the following day with instructions to close down his current operation. He was to use the *small business grant* funds as personal cash until further notice. The Network instructed Carl to dismiss his employees with a decent severance and use the excuse that his financial backers went down with the Trade Center. His contact instructed him to cease all production plans, break the lease with the company that owned the production warehouse and take an extended leave of absence from his office for an undetermined period. He was not to E-mail the Network ever again. Lastly, the Network ordered Carl to download all EX-1 information onto a secure memory storage device and then destroy his personal laptop computer. Carl complied with every detail of his instructions.

After three months of spending most of his time at his rented apartment just on the outskirts of the Hill district of St. Louis, Carl felt like he was going insane. Never before had he felt so *watched* by the infidels in the country where he grew up. It didn't matter where he went, in the small towns or the big cities; his Arab features were given a suspicious eye.

Carl drove to Indianapolis to visit with his parents and, once again, found a refuge of acceptance. Unfortunately, he couldn't stay with them long. The plan made it impossible for Carl to get personally involved with other people, even his parents. Once again Carl Larkin found himself alone and lonely.

One night in December of 2001, Carl heard a knock on his St. Louis apartment door. When he spied through the eyehole, he saw a person he knew. It was Joseph. Joseph stepped into Carl's apartment the very moment the door was open, pushed Carl back and shut the door behind him in one rapid motion. Joseph was dressed much the same as he had been the last time Carl had seen him, over a year before. However, this time everything he wore was new: new shoes, new overalls and a new winter work jacket.

"Do you still have access to your office?" Joseph asked with an expressionless face.

"Yes, I have a security card to the building and a key to my office door," Carl answered directly. He knew that there would be no small talk with Joseph, and he knew by Joseph's question that they would be leaving his apartment immediately.

"Very well. Get that card and that key, and come with me." Joseph stood, motionless, two paces inside the apartment and waited for Carl to join him. After retrieving his office key, building security card and donning a warm jacket, Carl followed Joseph out of the apartment complex and across the street to a waiting utility van. In large letters across the flat white surface of the driver's side of the van was painted, *RTS Satellite*. Carl was instructed to enter the van from the back passenger side door. Once inside the van, Carl found himself flanked by two other men of Arab descent. Joseph entered the van, sat in the front passenger seat and spoke the Arabic word for "Go." Fifteen silent minutes later, four of the five passengers left the RTS van on the second level of the Costar parking lot. Each person carried a large toolbox. Carl Larkin was one of these four men. In their trek from the parking lot to the ninth floor, they saw no one other than the night guard on the first floor. He was easily drawn away from his post by the forcing open of an emergency exit door on the backside of the third floor landing. This alarm was caused by the fifth person from the RTS van.

Upon gaining access to Carl's office, Joseph and his two companions set to work ripping apart the entire west wall of the room. Carl sat at his office desk and watched silently. No one spoke. It was as if Joseph and his two workers already knew every step of the strange procedure they were following. After gutting the wall, the three silent workers began rewiring electrical and communications outlets from preexisting cable runs inside the defaced wall. Once the work had reached a certain point of demolition and reconstruction, Joseph motioned for the other two workers to leave. Meanwhile, Joseph began uncoiling a roll of special cable and cut it into specific lengths. These cables were spliced to connectors and inserted into a signal splitter device. The splitter device was mounted inside the wall. The two RTS workers returned a half hour later, pushing a large cart toward Carl's office door. The cart was loaded with television monitors. Three times, the cart made the journey from the RTS van to Carl's office, until all twelve monitors and a large entertainment-shelving unit cluttered the floor. Four hours later, at two in the morning, the workmen had erected the entertainment center and all twelve screens. All packing materials and flattened boxes were loaded onto the large cart and hauled back to the van by the two workmen.

Joseph remained in the office with Carl. From his toolbox, Joseph withdrew two items. The first item was a laptop computer, which he placed upon Carl's desk. The second item was a remote control, which he handed to Carl. After five hours of silence, Joseph finally spoke.

"This device will operate eleven of the twelve monitors." Joseph instructed, "Eleven of the monitors are connected to the satellite dish at the top of this building. Eleven of the monitors can be programmed to any channel available through the dish. We suggest you program each monitor to a specific station and keep it on that station for the duration of your stay in this office. Instructions for choosing the stations are in the book on your desk. The twelfth monitor is not a monitor at all."

"I noticed when you put it in place, it seemed much heavier," Carl added.

"Exactly." Joseph pointed a bony index finger at the monitor in question, "Its insides have been replaced with a highly sensitive signal scrambler. This is how you shall communicate with the Network from this point on, through the remote connection in your laptop. The laptop gets its signal from the scrambler."

"I see," Carl said, as he flipped open the top of the laptop computer and examined the keyboard. "Is there a program on this laptop I'll need to boot up, in order to communicate?"

"One day soon, you will receive a phone call on your cell phone. It will sound like a telemarketer. The telemarketer will quote you a special price on a product they are offering and an expiration date for this offer. Take note of the price. It will tell you what time the Network will contact you. Take note of the expiration date. It will be the date the Network will contact you. Kindly decline the offer of the telemarketer, and make sure that you are sitting at this desk on the correct date and precise time. Ensure that at all eleven monitors are on, with different channels on each. Ensure that you are alone and that your laptop is on. The scrambler will do all the rest."

"Very well, I understand," Carl said with a nod of his head.

Joseph took a weary breath and exhaled it slowly as he inspected Carl Larkin's office. Seemingly satisfied with what he was saw, Joseph turned to leave.

"Joseph," Carl stood from his desk chair and pointed to the monitors that now covered the west wall of his office. "Why so many monitors?"

"Hassan Al-Sarraj," Joseph referred to Carl by his birth name and noticed a visible tension come upon the younger man's face, "What you have discovered in the EX-1 has become the most important project of the Network. All other Network projects have been systematically put on hold. We will now communicate with you again in the most secure manner available. The signals to the eleven other monitors mask our signal to your laptop. We take the outputs from your monitors and feed them back through the scrambler. No one will be able to trace it or unscramble it because we are using eleven masking signals instead of the normal three." With that, Joseph hefted his toolbox and left Carl's office.

That day, after Carl returned to his apartment to get some sleep, he was awakened by a telemarketing phone call. The next day, Carl was in his Costar Building office, alone, with all eleven monitors tuned in to different channels. He turned on his laptop and waited. At the exact time given by the telemarketer phone call, Carl's laptop screen came to life and was filled top to bottom with a streaming video player screen. Carl watched in amazement as the face of an elderly gentleman appeared on his screen and began talking to him. It was Joseph.

"I see that you have succeeded in the business at hand," Joseph spoke with the same expressionless face he always wore. "And you can see me?"

"Yes, I can," Carl said as plainly as he could. He wasn't certain if he was allowed to use names in this form of communication. Suddenly, it dawned on Carl that Joseph had been his Network mentor from the very first E-mail, nearly ten years before. A stupefied look came across Carl's face as Joseph continued talking.

"Good, now put the following information into your memory," Joseph's eyes looked down to something in his hands, as if reading off a list. As Joseph spoke, he crossed items off the list. When Joseph finished, he gave the paper to the two hands of an unseen person to his left who, by the background sounds, put the paper into a shredder immediately. Carl, a genius with the capability to retain incredible amounts of verbal information with one hundred percent accuracy, needed no paper.

Three months later, the ninth floor of the Costar Building was once again a beehive of AGS activity. Carl Larkin had followed his Network instructions to perfection and rejuvenated his dormant company. He hired Janet Deering as his protégé. Fresh out of Washington University after earning a six-year straight-shot Masters in Business Administration,

267

Janet was like putty in Carl's hands. Similar was the relationship with the three other administrators he hired. Carl Larkin had chosen each because not one of them had ever worked full time for a company before. Each had gone into college as freshmen and, six years later, left college with master's degree. Carl was looking for this specific background criteria. After working with Carl for one year, all four would tell their families and friends that Carl Larkin was a good boss and a creative engineer with a couple patents. They said he only had one quirk: he spent too much time watching sports shows on cable. Beyond these characteristics, no one knew much about him, which is exactly as Carl wanted it.

According to the Network, the first plan of action was to develop a marketing strategy for the EX-1. What better way was there to do this than with four newly hired, overeager and overpaid administrators? Carl informed the administrators that they would be very busy for the next year, so he personally interviewed and hired an administrative assistant for each of them. The first phase of the plan involved pressing the flesh. Carl Larkin's four administrators began making contacts with people in the power generation industry; first by phone, and then in person. The four administrators began flying all over the country to wine, dine and play golf with the power industry's upper crust. None of the administrators seemed to question where the money came from for all this. AGS, after all, had not produced a single unit. To quell any doubts in advance, Carl told them a lie. He told them a patent on another of his inventions had made him a fortune and he was using the incoming profits from that invention to pay for this one.

The second telemarketer phone call and subsequent Network communication from Joseph gave Carl information regarding an upcoming production run on the EX-1. A full-fledged manufacturing facility was secured with Network funds, as well as a crew of highly skilled factory workers that Carl personally interviewed and hired. The original EX-1 production run was for 1000 units. With such small numbers, there was no need for retooling an existing high-tech production facility or creating an entirely new one from scratch. Carl had designed the EX-1 to be assembled by hand from components already in existence. It took the twenty contract worker technicians three months to assemble and bench test all 1000 EX-1 units. There was no rush on EX-1 production. The real money for AGS wouldn't come from the EX-1 itself, but the revenues realized over a two-year period by the Internet contracts for access to the data that the device would provide. With the EX-1 ready for installation, now it was time for the third phase of the plan: get the EX-1 on the grid.

With the blackout of a large portion of the American and Canadian grids in August of 2003, the American public temporarily turned its eyes away from the war against external terrorist organizations and toward the internal security of their electricity source. Various government entities stepped up to the plate and began swinging their bats at the issue. A joint Canadian/U.S. task force formed to tap the root cause of the blackout. Kenstar, the manufacturer of the original near real-time telemetry device, stood to make a huge windfall if the task force put anything in their report about recommending an upgrade of all grid sectors to include a data collection and distribution system. AGS, if it got its foot into the power generation market, stood to profit, as well, from a favorable recommendation by the task force. In November of 2003, the task force came out with its interim report on the *causes* of the August 2003 blackout, but no *recommendations*. This caused a wave of disappointment among the four AGS administrators, but it didn't seem to bother Carl. He encouraged them to keep up the one-on-one public relations work they were doing. From the data these four administrators were gathering and turning in to Carl, it was easy to decipher that his group was slowly narrowing the field down to the top power brokers in the power industry. This is what Carl needed to set the fourth phase into motion: the ear of the people that could, with a slash of a pen, put his EX-1 onto the grid.

The fourth communication from the Network came just before the release of the final report from the joint Canada/U.S. task force on the August 14th, 2003 blackout. Joseph got to the point immediately and asked Carl if his people had narrowed the power broker field down to a persuadable number. Carl answered that they were close, but not on target. Joseph nodded and gave Carl the go ahead to start the fourth phase of the plan.

"We recommend you aim for PJM," Joseph's eyes stared lifelessly back at Carl from his laptop.

"PJM, why not MISO?" Carl asked.

"We have people in MISO. Therefore, we can control, to a certain degree, what occurs in that portion of the grid. Once you get most of PJM under the protection of the EX-1, an incident in MISO will cause a blackout in the regions around PJM. A substantial portion of MISO will go down, but PJM will not be affected. And for good reasons."

"Washington, D.C.," Carl said with an understanding nod.

"Exactly. D.C. will be spared and we well see an instantaneous governmental approval of this miraculous EX-1 device." Joseph ended the conversation at this point and Carl's laptop screen went blank.

The final report on the August 14th, 2003 blackout came out in April of 2004 and, with it, a recommendation to evaluate and adopt better real-time tools for operators and reliability coordinators. The four AGS administrators flew into Baltimore, Maryland and began a four-week, ten-city road trip of business meetings and golf games, in which they basically gave away the EX-1 system to various power utility companies doing business in the PJM region of the grid. Within 12 months, the PJM region was 90% covered by the EX-1 system. In August of 2005, a virus planted by a Network operative caused a blackout in three grid regions surrounding the PJM region. Three weeks later, a government task force would be blame this blackout on *operator error*. The government report stated strongly that because PJM had the real-time technology to protect their region, it was, for the most part, unfazed by the blackout. In fact, the press had a field day with the theory that the PJM region had stopped the spread of the blackout to other regions. Just as Joseph had predicted, the government recommended the EX-1 system installed immediately throughout all regions. Carl Larkin now had a new problem: he had the *problem* of needing to hire 100 more employees and lease three more entire floors of the Costar Building.

With the EX-1 system in place by the end of 2007, AGS had hired an entire law firm just to prevent venture capitalists from buying-out his small company. Like vultures waiting for the right moment, the greedy capitalists drooled for the tastiest, non-public company in the hemisphere. Reports of the AGS profits projected for 2008 were penciled-in at just fewer than forty million dollars. Carl Larkin hired a public relations team to help him with his AGS's image. Unlike any other client this PR firm had ever handled, Carl hired them to keep his name *out* of the public spotlight as much as possible. Janet Deering, they determined, would be the best bet as the AGS spokesperson. Carl agreed, and tried not to smile when he heard this recommendation; he had chosen Janet from the very beginning for this very purpose. Carl wanted Janet in the spotlight, not himself.

The fifth phase of the plan involved hiring engineers fresh out of the university system to design the Generation Two. The Gen-Two, a trade name for the upgrade of the EX-1, had to have marketable features to justify the current client's purchasing it. Carl Larkin had premeditations in mind for this upgrade, but he wanted to toss it out to some fresh, young minds to see what they conjured. In July of 2007, Carl interviewed and hired six electrical engineers to start from the ground level on the Gen-Two. Not one of these new hires knew exactly why he or she was hired until their first day on the job. One of these newly hired engineers was Stephenie Plasters.

The six new engineers were indoctrinated into AGS on the same day, in the same room, as Janet Deering herself gave the lecture on the company's policy regarding the security of the Gen-Two project. She had them each sign a legal document stating they would not divulge any information, of any kind, on the Gen-Two, under the penalty of the loss of employment with AGS, the threat of heavy fines and a five-year tour in the nearest penitentiary. As the young engineers sat around the large boardroom table and got the pre-riot-act lecture from Janet, you could literally hear each of their hearts beating from across the room. After ensuring that the consequences were both real and dire for any breach of AGS security policy, Janet gathered the legal documents together and then left the room. Seconds later, Carl Larkin entered the room, met by looks of awe from each of the six young engineers. To them, he was a legend. It was known from press investigations that Carl was a genius. It was known that Carl was born in the West Bank of Israel and was a Palestinian orphan. It was also known that he was the only son, an adopted son, of Christian missionaries and grew up in the suburbs of Indianapolis. However, the true awe of these young engineers came not from those facts, but from the fact that this man had theorized, created *and* marketed one of the most efficient devices of their time. Carl Larkin looked into their faces as he slowly walked to the side of the boardroom and stood in front of a giant screen. He had met each of them at least two times prior to this day, as part of his hiring process. He knew exactly how to start their relationships with him.

"Anyone want anymore caffeine?" He asked, with a smile, as he pointed to a tray of coffee urns and condiments on the table between himself and them. Every person at the table shared a unanimous decline.

"Well, in the near future you may become addicted to coffee and need twice as much as you consume now, *if* you consume now," Carl spoke seriously, as he pressed the button on a remote control device that he had withdrawn from his pocket. "AGS has a problem and I've hired you six to solve it for me. Solve it for me and there will be huge profits all around. *All* around," Carl emphasized as he swept his hand toward the six onlookers. When he pressed a button on the remote control in his hand, the screen came to life with a photo of the EX-1 sitting on a stage with the perfect circle of a spotlight on it.

"This, as you all know, is the EX-1, rated by the top six energy industry periodicals as the most efficient information gathering and transfer device on the market. You would think that its efficiency shouldn't be a problem, but it is."

The next slide on the screen showed a bar graph representing estimated profits of AGS over the next four years. "Our number crunchers put together this graph six months ago. As you can see, profits look good for the next two years, but experts predict a drop in the third and fourth year. I'm an electrical engineer like you, not a market analyst. Therefore, I asked the accountants why profits would dip in two years. Do you know what they said?" No one dared to answer. Carl was pleased.

"Because of a thing called Inherent Product Value Depreciation, or IPVD. In other words, a thousand folks sign up for a service, let's say, a cell phone. Over a certain period, two hundred of those people will turn in their cell phones and cancel their service. Why? Because they think that they don't need it. Well, the IPVD for the EX-1, according to the accountant's computer generated models, turns out to be two years from now." Carl flipped to another slide; this one showed nothing but a big white question mark on a jet-black screen. "How do you prevent the IPVD dip?"

Carl stood silently for ten seconds, looking at his fledglings. *Now*, he pushed his thoughts across the room toward his newly hired engineers, *this time say something*. One of the engineers raised his hand; it was a young man with long hair and a thick beard. With his other hand, he pushed his plastic rimmed glasses up on the bridge of his nose. *Perfect*, Carl thought.

"Yes, Marty," Carl said without expression.

"Uh, Americans need to feel like every year they get something new, like Christmas," Marty spoke slowly with a deep voice. He almost sounded stupid when he spoke, like someone with a slight retardation. Carl knew just the opposite was true. Marty looked at the other engineers for a second, and then continued speaking to Carl. "That even applies to companies and relatively intelligent people...and grid operators. AGS has to create a second model and make it sound improved. You know, New-and-Improved. It's what Americans expect."

"Exactly." Carl was elated at the young man's response, but tried his best to repress his feelings. "To get the EX-1 on the market two years ago, I basically had to design the system as close to perfect as possible. It had to be a ten percent improvement on the Kenstar system or no one would even look at it."

Carl clicked the remote control again and a new slide came on the screen. This slide was a blueprint drawing of the EX-1 casing. Before the engineers had an opportunity to focus in on this slide, Carl flipped to a new slide with another EX-1 drawing on it. As Carl continued to flip through the slides, he began his final lecture to the engineers.

"These are the drawings of the EX-1. AGS will assign each of you a workstation inside our security area on the twelfth floor and a personal set of these drawings. Your workstations have the latest model computers with the latest edition of CAD programs. Go up to the twelfth floor, talk with Stan Golden, the security chief, and he'll assign you your workstation. The task I have assigned to the six of you is to find a way to alter the EX-1. Make it *New-and-Improved*. You can work individually or in groups, or both; do whatever suits you at each phase of the project.

Remember, on *this* project you get rewarded as a group. On *this* project, AGS will not recognize one individual above another. You have six months to come up with a solid idea. Good luck."

With that last statement, Carl clicked off the images on the screen, pocketed the remote control and left the room. Walking the long corridor from the conference room to his office, Carl had to exert all his will to keep from chuckling. After entering his office and shutting the door, he finally did give in to the feelings surging through his being and let go with a sound that was half exhalation and half laugh. Carl already knew what the six-engineer Gen-Two team would develop. He had intentionally built a fault within the EX-1. He knew they would find this fault and knew exactly what changes the engineers would recommend.

Carl Larkin had placed an oversized battery pack inside the EX-1 that would eventually cause faults with the units. Because of this large battery pack, there would be overheating problems and subsequent maintenance issues with the EX-1 units currently in service on the grid. There would also be reports that the EX-1 had a problem with the ever-occurring grid voltage spikes. These voltage spikes, inherent in any high voltage system, would cause the EX-1 transducers output signal to fluctuate for ten seconds each time a spike occurred. Carl knew the solution would be to install a smaller battery pack and an inductor circuit to flatten the inherent spikes of the alternating current induced into the unit from the transformer. Carl knew the engineers would come to this same conclusion. In five months they did.

What the six engineers didn't know was that after they had made the recommendations, created the testing prototypes and performed all the Quality Assurance tests on the Gen-Two units, the finished products would then be shipped to a warehouse in East St. Louis. In this clandestine warehouse, an elite team of Network technicians would perform several changes on the Gen-Two units. The East St. Louis team would pull the smaller yellow-colored battery packs and install slightly larger blue-colored battery packs. They would replace the spike-dampening inductor units with pre-programmed timing circuits. The spare space inside each unit was filled with an explosives carton prefabricated by the same Network members months before. The timing unit and the explosive pack were wired into the circuit with the battery pack for each unit. The Network crew would reset each timing device to close its associated explosion relay at the same exact second as every other unit. The Gen-Two's were then drop-shipped to their final destinations to await their installation. Installation would only occur after certain entities, the power brokers, approved the process.

The original Network plan was to install the Gen-Two units a month before they exploded. However, the power brokers balked at the need for a retrofit from the EX-1 to the Gen-Two. They saw no need for an upgrade. In fact, several smaller utilities in three regions of the grid had threatened to break their contracts with AGS and remove the EX-1 from their substations because they thought they no longer needed the service. With less than a month left before the pre-programmed timing units reached zero, Carl convinced the power brokers to come to his office and hear his new proposal. They came, but they weren't playing ball. His plan, the Network's plan, almost fell through, until Carl spoken frankly and then threatened to shut down the AGS website, therefore rendering the information from the EX-1 units useless. It would have been a disaster for both sides, but even worse for the power brokers. The power brokers relented.

In late June 2009, there was an intense flurry of activity at AGS, as all employees flew off like bees from a hive in order to get the Gen-Two retrofit completed. All administrators went on long-deserved vacations to resorts in Mexico. All other AGS employees immediately flew around the United States and Canada to help local utilities replace the EX-1 units with Gen-Twos. Carl was supplied with a security staff from a pool of Network members who took control of the four floors of the Costar Building and began disassembling the company, even as every AGS employee completed the retrofit in the field. The Network security force was under strict orders to allow no one to enter any of the four AGS floors. Network security members, who commandeered a small office on the ninth floor of the Costar building, fielded all calls from the AGS retrofit employees in the field. Once every Gen-Two was installed in a specific sector, the Network security told the involved AGS employees to go home and take the next couple of days off from work, with pay. The

Network flunkies told all AGS employees that Carl Larkin did not want to see a single employee anywhere near the Costar Building until Monday, the 13th of July. It was supposed to be his way of saying thank you for working every day for the last three weeks. As each call came in, the Network security members would tally up the results and occasionally report to Carl Larkin, who was with his administrators in Mexico.

On the morning of July 8th, 2009, Carl Larkin would board a plane in Mexico City, bound for a final destination of Saudi Arabia and a new life.

CHAPTER THIRTEEN

The Missionary Newsletter

Cross Roads:

A Christian outreach ministry to all Palestine

Dear Prayer Partners,

Thank you for your ongoing support of our efforts in Israel. We've been very busy in the last several weeks, giving humanitarian and spiritual aid to both sides in the Palestinian and Jewish situation. In that short time span, we have traveled over 2,000 miles and delivered twenty tons of relief supplies. Tomorrow, we will be back on the road again until the end of the month, which is why this newsletter is as short as it is.

Michael and I planned to take four days off from travel while staying in the home of a Palestinian friend located in the West Bank. However, the recent unrest caused by an incident in a market yesterday has made it too dangerous for us to stay. Israeli soldiers in the market place had shot down a young Palestinian man. Michael was standing less than twenty feet from the man when he was shot. The Israeli soldiers claimed that the young man was carrying an explosive device; the Palestinian authorities claimed he was unarmed. The political situation in the West Bank is volatile. Normally, Michael and I would be rushing into the aftermath of such circumstances to help in any way we could to make peace. Unfortunately, Michael witnessed the entire event, and yes, the young man, armed with explosives, was attempting to detonate them when the soldiers shot him. Since Michael is a witness to the event, we cannot remain impartial and must leave the area.

Please continue to pray for us as we impart peace, the Lord's peace, to this troubled corner of the world. We are planning on staying in Israel for yet another year or until God has other plans (like giving us a child, hint, hint).

Until the next letter,
Michael and Theresa Larkin
Michael and Theresa Larkin

PS: Did any of you see of this shooting incident on US television news? We were curious how it was reported if it was indeed covered.

Printed in the United States
62361LVS00004B/1-105